A CONSTELLATION OF ROSES

Also by Miranda Asebedo

The Deepest Roots

A
CONSTELLATION
OF ROSES

miranda asebedo

HARPER TEEN
An Imprint of HarperCollins Publishers

To those brave enough to change the story of their scars

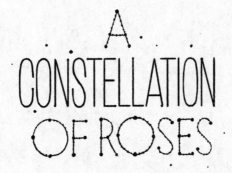

ONE

My HAND SLIPS INTO THE woman's gaping purse like it's my own. Fingers nimble and sure on her wallet, I brush against her as if I am just impatient to get through the crowds of people milling around in the Eastside Mall. It's not hard to do. Everyone here is in a rush to get to the next big sale. That's why I always pick this place. And because it's lightly patrolled by burly security guards who stand idly outside upscale department stores and watch for the wolves among the placid, woolly shoppers.

My touch is only the softest graze against the woman; she doesn't even notice. Before I can inhale a full breath of her expensive perfume, I'm gone, her billfold in hand. I stuff it into my beat-up bag and lose myself in the throngs of people. This is the third wallet tonight, and by the glimpse of the designer insignia, I'm guessing that I can retire for the evening. I only need enough to cover the week at the motel and maybe something to eat a couple times a day. I steal just enough to get by. No more, no less.

I follow the stream of other shoppers as they trickle out of the mall, but when they go to the parking garage to load up their Mercedes and their BMWs, I pull on my hood and walk into the wind. It's barely September, but lately the evenings are cool enough to make me hope I remembered to turn the radiator on low before I left the motel.

One of the security guards making the rounds in the parking lot briefly scrutinizes a girl with a black hoodie and ripped jeans and says something into his walkie-talkie, but I don't worry about him.

You see, I've got a gift.

Once I watched a movie about this little boy who could heal people with his hands. They said he had "a gift from God." I've never seen God, and from the few times I prayed with the pious foster mom whose husband whipped me with a belt when I spilled juice on their new carpet, it became clear to me that if there was a God, he didn't see me, either. But my gift is okay, too, regardless of where it came from. My hands are swift, undetectable. I was born a thief.

I'm sure there are more people out there like me. Some strange twist of DNA giving us gifts like perfect pitch or immortal cells or quick hands or even healing ones. I don't think I was chosen or found worthy. I think I'm just damn lucky. Sometimes for fun I like to watch the security-camera footage at the bodega next to the Happy Host. I wander in the aisles, loading up, barely a shadow on the screen above the register, just someone in a hoodie with her hands firmly in her pockets. No one sees a thing. Ever.

I catch a city bus on the next block, careful not to meet the eyes of the other commuters as we make our way to the west side of town. Sure, most of these people are the unseen—the busboys, the cleaning ladies, the trash collectors. But a few are thieves and pickpockets like me, and they're on their way home, some licking their lips and others licking their wounds. I want to blend in with the unseen. Nothing in my bag but minimum wage and an empty lunch box, not stolen rent money.

Instead I stare at the sturdy shoes of the older couple sitting across from me, their clasped hands resting between them on the vinyl seat. I get my sketchbook from my bag and begin to draw those hands with stolen pencils. Sketching my surroundings is something I've done since I was old enough to notice the shadows moving from the small split in the curtains of whatever motel room I was living in, some desperate admiration for the way dark and light give depth and meaning to everything. I use short, scratchy strokes to show the way the couple's fingers intertwine, nicks on the knuckles where the dry, red skin has split. There's something beautiful about the way her hands look as rough and cracked as his, so you can't tell which hand belongs to which person.

I like the bus because it makes me feel connected to other people, sharing their stories, even if only for a little while. But eventually, I always remember that I am still alone, and I close my sketchbook and watch the street signs for my destination.

I get off at the dark stop two blocks away from the Starlite Motel. Keeping my head down and walking quickly, I ignore the voices and laughter from the doorways and the parking lots I pass. I don't want to buy anything, and I'm not selling, either. As I get closer, I see that the motel sign says NO VACANCY, which means that the ladies who are my neighbors are probably working.

Mom used to work with them sometimes, too, when we lived here. Until she said she was going to get a pack of cigarettes one August afternoon and never came back. That was a little over a year ago, in one of those brief, hopeful lulls when she said she was going to get clean again. I've been a lot of places since she left, but I keep drifting back here. I guess because it's familiar.

When I get to the Starlite, there are a lot of cars in the parking lot. It's Friday, and men do stupid things with their paychecks. I stop at room 7 and, looking over my shoulder, I pull my keys out of my pocket. Once I'm inside, I immediately lock the door behind me and do a quick inspection of the room. I am alone.

Mel, the night manager, has kind of a soft spot for the kids who live here, and that's why he lets me rent a room even though I'm by myself and not eighteen. There aren't many of us at the Starlite. Me, Charly, and the Quinter twins. Charly shares room 11 with her mom, and Janie Quinter, barely older than me, and her twins are one door down in room 12. The twins are little, though, and usually Charly watches them when their mom is working.

Shane used to live here, too.

I dump the wallets out on the queen bed. The coverlet is a faded floral print, and it sort of matches the brown carpet and the yellowed curtains. I thumb through my haul, checking every possible pocket for cash that might be hidden.

I peel out carefully folded, clean bills. That's what I like about rich people. Even their money smells better. There's three hundred seven dollars. Sighing in relief, I clutch the crisp cash to my chest. It's enough to pay for another week at the Starlite and food for a while. Not a bad night at all. I take half the money and cram it into the jar I keep in the toilet tank, careful to screw the lid back on tightly so my stash doesn't get wet. No one ever thinks to look in the toilet tank. They always look under the mattress, in the top drawers of the dresser, the cupboard in the corner. I shove the other half of the money into my pocket to pay the rent.

The stolen billfolds go in the metal trash can I've designated as the burn trash. There's a small outdoor grill behind the Starlite, and I burn everything but money. I'm not stupid. Credit cards, IDs: those are traceable. I only take the cash. Marie leaves the bottle of lighter fluid out there. Who knows what the young, pretty maid burns, but I'm not alone in my activities.

My stomach growls. I check the small clock that hangs above the kitchenette area. Calling it a kitchen is a little extravagant when it's really only a hot plate and a bathroom sink with a dish drainer next to it. I should've stopped at the QuikMart to grab a bite on the way home, but it was late, and I knew I should get back before Mel started playing cards with the old man who lives in room 2. Once they start drinking, it's hard to say if my rent will make it into the till or into the game.

I hesitate by the door. I don't want to go all the way back to the QuikMart, so I do something nice for myself. I order a pizza. Not a cheap one, either. I order one of those deluxe ones from Sal's, the kind that leaks grease through the cardboard so it leaves stains on the coverlet. I can live off one of those for a couple of days.

Then I leave the motel room and lock the door behind me. Hood up, head down, I make my way to the main office. "Trix!

Hey, Trix!" The sound of my name seizes my shoulders and urges me to run before I recognize the voice. Charly.

"Hey," she says, jogging up beside me. "Thought that was you. Rent time, huh? Mom just sent me to pay for next week, too." She holds up the wad of cash so I can see it, the cheap gold rings on her fingers glinting in the lights from the neon NO VACANCY sign.

"Don't flash that around," I hiss, watching the two guys leaning on an Impala in the parking lot. I don't know if they're staying here or waiting for someone, but I don't want to catch their attention by looking like we're two easy marks.

Charly shrugs and stuffs the money in the pocket of her snug jeans. "What's the fun of having money if you can't show it off?" she asks. "Anyway, what are you doing tonight? Can I come over?"

"Aren't you watching the twins?" I ask.

"No, Janie's sick, so she's not working." Charly's a year younger than me, but there's a tightness in her face, a hardness that makes her seem older. I don't know; maybe I look that way to other people, too.

"You can come over if you want," I tell her, knowing there's a fifty-fifty chance she'll blow me off. Anytime a boyfriend texts, she bails on plans with me. But tonight, I could use the company. I haven't spoken to another person in nearly a week. Just me in a crowd, me in my room. Just me, alone. Sometimes drifting can be lonely, and it would be nice to feel that somebody cares I'm here. So I add, knowing it will sweeten the deal, "I've got a pizza coming."

Charly grins, revealing the large gap between her front teeth. "I'm starving."

We both go into the empty motel office, the small bell on the door alerting Mel and Room 2 Old Guy in the back room that we're there. Mel lumbers in and leans on the front desk, a cigarette hanging out of the corner of his mouth.

"I've got the week's rent for room 11," Charly says, holding out the wad of cash.

Mel takes it, making a face at the crumpled bills. "Tell your mama to stop leaving her shit in the only working dryer," he grumbles.

"Yeah?" Charly says, crossing her arms. The motel has a tiny laundry room with two machines that are out of order more than they're working. I just wash my clothes in the sink. "Why don't you fix the other damn dryer, Mel? And since we're bitching, tell Marie to stop stealing my stuff when she comes in to change the sheets."

Mel grins. He likes spunk.

"Room seven," I tell Mel, handing him my money and avoiding the argument altogether.

"Another week?" he asks, as if he's surprised. This will be my second week in a row here. I know I should change motels again, but this one feels safe to me. I guess it's because Mom and I lived here for three years before she left, which makes it the longest time we ever lived anywhere, and the closest thing to a home. The picture I drew with stolen charcoal pencils on the day we moved in is still on the wall, still hidden behind the generic framed picture of a palm tree on a beach that hangs in every room at the Starlite.

"Just one more," I tell him. "Tell Marie I'll pick up clean sheets tomorrow. I can change them myself." Marie's okay, but Charly's right: that girl's got sticky fingers. I would know.

"Sure, kid. You going to be in your room tonight? Check out the free movie channels. Some kind of promo from the cable company."

I shrug. "Yeah. No big plans." Or any in recent months.

Charly and I wish Mel good luck with his card game, and then she leaves me at my door to go down to her room. "Let me grab something to drink," she says. "I'll be back in a few."

I unlock my door and go inside, carefully locking it again behind me. If I know Charly, she'll be bringing back a red plastic cup nearly full of vodka she swiped from her mom, and a few cans of soda to cut it with. The guy who fills the vending machine by the front office has a thing for Charly, and he's always leaving cans of Sprite or Coke by her door like they're bouquets of flowers.

Surprising me given her track record, Charly gets back before the pizza. I know it's her from the way she kicks the door with the toe of her worn-out sneakers because her hands are full. "Open up. It's the police," she bellows, knowing it will terrify all our neighbors. Laughter peals outside the door. Charly never could keep straight-faced during a joke.

I peer at her through a crack in the curtains, just in case, before I open the door. There's a few muffled thuds and then some swearing from the room next door when they realize it's just Charly out there. She whisks inside with her arms full of exactly what I thought she'd have.

When Charly's mixed us drinks with the cheap plastic cups

from the kitchenette, she spills her guts as we lounge on the hard bed, the television turned to a comedy on Mel's free movie channel. She and her mom are on the rocks again, and she has to dump Dante because he's still cheating on her, this time with some rich girl on the East Side. Nothing is good anymore, she says, not like it used to be. She twirls her hair as she talks, sips carefully from her drink before she drops her next words. "Let me come with you next week."

"What do you mean?" I ask her, taking a slug of the drink and wincing at the burn. Charly was a little heavy-handed with the vodka, which doesn't surprise me now that I know she wants something.

"You never stay here long anymore. Not like when your mom was still around. I know you'll leave again. So take me with you." She looks down into her cup. "I want out. I'm tired of living with my mom. I'm tired of the johns hanging around, and babysitting every night, and just *living* in this shitty motel."

"So you're just going to drop out of school and hit the road?" I ask.

"Why not? You haven't gone to school regular since your mom left."

I read once that when you lose an arm or a leg, sometimes you get phantom pain, this ache where there's nothing left to hurt. That's what it felt like, since Mom walked out. I know she felt like she could never forgive herself for all the things that had happened between us, and maybe she could never forgive me, either, but somehow her absence hurts even more than having her here. You can't forgive someone if they never come back to you.

It wasn't that I didn't like school, it was just that I had lost interest in books and tests and tardy slips when Mom left and what small foundation I had crumbled apart. Also, you need a guardian to enroll, and I'd sworn off those about six months ago, after I'd run away from my last group home.

"You going to get a job? Or am I supposed to be your sugar mama in this scenario?" I take another swig of the drink and let the vodka sing in my bones, willing it to drown out that phantom pain.

"I'll find a way," she says. "If Shane was here, he'd help me out. He was going to get us out of here, you know. He promised."

I know she means well when she brings him up. I know she has as much right as I do to say his name. He was my boyfriend for only a year before he went to prison, after all, and Shane had been Charly's brother all her life. But it stings anyway.

I set my cup down on the nightstand and slide off the bed. I go into the bathroom, shut the door, and sit down on the edge of the grimy bathtub. I only need a minute. I haven't talked about Shane or Mom for a long time. It's easier that way.

I hear Charly standing on the other side of the door. "I'm sorry," she says, her voice muffled. "I shouldn't have brought him up. We just haven't talked about him in forever, and I thought you were probably over him by now." There's a soft clink of her rings against the knob, but she doesn't turn it. When you live in a motel with paper-thin walls, you learn to respect boundaries. "It wasn't your fault, you know. Even if you'd been with him, it wouldn't have ended any different." I hear the scrape of her rings as she pulls her hand away.

The truth is, I am over Shane. Or I think I am, anyway. Mostly now I feel guilt when I remember him. My gift would have protected him if we had been together when everything happened. But even Shane didn't really believe me back then. It was luck, he said, when I tried to convince him.

I stand up and flush the toilet like I'm not a coward hiding in a motel bathroom.

There's a knock at the door, three times, quick and insistent.

Charly calls, "Pizza's here!"

"Wait! Look before you open it!" I shout, flinging open the bathroom door.

But it's too late.

Two uniformed police officers are standing outside. "We're looking for Trixie McCabe," the younger, female officer says, her hands on her belt.

"There's no Trixie here," Charly lies easily, starting to close the door. "You have the wrong address."

The other officer, an older man, puts up a hand to stop her from shutting them out. He stares at me where I stand dumbly in the frame of the bathroom door, the toilet still running behind me. He's seen me already, and slamming the door or running isn't going to make any difference now. I hear swearing and slamming, other people in the Starlite getting out before the cops come knocking on their doors, too. The older cop holds out the same photo the foster homes always use when I run away. Long dark hair, light-olive skin, and gray-green eyes that glare angrily into the camera.

"Miss McCabe, we're going to need you to come with us," he says.

TWO

Ms. Troy is as kind as she has ever been, even though there's a ziplock bag of stolen wallets from my burn can sitting between us. We're sitting in a small office in the police station that smells like old coffee. I wonder if the cops found my stash of money in the toilet tank, too. I'd ask, but I don't suppose they'd give it back to me if they had.

"I can see that those other homes didn't work out for you, Trix. But I've been looking for you for six months. Why didn't you call me?" Ms. Troy was fresh out of college when she took my case the first time, back when I was still a kid. Somehow, despite the years she's spent trying to fix a broken system, she still manages to seem young and optimistic.

"Bad signal, I guess." I shrug, like it puzzles me too. Pushing people away is my specialty, even people like Ms. Troy who sincerely want to help. But what she doesn't understand is that I'm tired of being placed with foster families, sick of being a burden to people who either think they can fix my seventeen years of shit or are just waiting for my support check, and I'm definitely not going back to a group home.

"I've talked with the local precinct and a judge. I explained your unique circumstances." She neatly avoids saying *troubled past*, which I've taken offense to before. "Since you have no previous record, they're willing to make a bargain."

"And what's that?" I ask, thinking of my mom and all the bargains she'd made with dealers and johns before she disappeared.

"The judge will drop the charges if you go into the custody of your aunt and agree to stay in school until graduation."

"Is this a joke?" I ask, leaning back in the chair. "I don't have an aunt."

"Your mother maintained since your first stay in foster care that you had no family other than her, but since she hasn't yet returned to claim you, we did some more digging, and it seems that you do have some family on your father's side who are still alive," Ms. Troy says, shifting the papers around on the table. "They were difficult to find since your father is deceased, and they don't reside in the city. But we got in touch, and your aunt agreed to let you live with her. As long as you stay in school and get your diploma," she repeats.

I barely know my father's name other than the McCabe part that's been tacked on to mine. *His name was Connor*, Mom said once. And that was it. Nothing else. No reason for why there was never a visit or a birthday card shoved under the door. We never talked about him, the same way we never mentioned my scars or the Good Year after everything that happened. Communication, you could say, was not our strong suit.

"I don't need to stay with some old lady I don't know. Just let me be on my own. Can't I apply for my emancipation? I'll finish high school on my own if that's the deal."

"The parameters of the agreement with the judge are very clear, Trix. You stay with your aunt and graduate from high school, and no charges will be filed against you for theft. Stray from that, and you'll be prosecuted. As an adult. That means no juvenile detention center. You could go to prison if you're found guilty."

I visited Shane in prison, and that was sufficient to convince me that I didn't want to go there. The walls, the guards, the eyes on you all the time. For someone like me, who thrives on her ability to blend in and drift away at a moment's notice, taking what she wants with whisper-quick hands, prison would be a nightmare of bright-orange visibility.

"Fine," I tell Ms. Troy. "Set it up. Take me to my long-lost aunt." I can do this for a year, I tell myself. And if I can't, well, screw it. I can run away as easily as I have all the times before. I slipped up going back to the Starlite. I won't make that mistake again.

On Saturday, Ms. Troy picks me up from the county child welfare office in her red Toyota Camry. We leave the city, cruise two hours down the interstate, exit onto a highway, and then continue on progressively smaller roads until we're bumping along a dirt lane that's barely a step up from a footpath. "We're almost there," Ms. Troy tells me. "They are so excited to meet you."

"You didn't tell me we were leaving civilization," I reply.

Either side of the dirt road is lined with rusty barbed-wire fences, endless open fields occasionally studded with stunted cedars, and black cows placidly observing our journey. They may be the only beings living out here besides this aunt of mine.

Ms. Troy continues to smile. "There's an adorable town only a mile away. Rocksaw. That's where the school and your aunt's business are located."

I let Ms. Troy babble on as I reach back between my seat and the passenger door and slide my hand into her purse that sits on the floor behind me. She'd given me a pained smile when she put it back there, as if she didn't want to mention that leaving it on the console between us would be a mistake, given my history. She underestimates me. With my eyes still on the road, I slide a bill out of her wallet. And a stick of gum. Then I slip my hand up, take a swift peek at my loot, and stuff the Jackson into the pocket of my hoodie. I never got my stash back from the motel room. I have to build it up again, just in case I need to hit the road sooner than expected. I unwrap the stick of gum slowly and take a hesitant sniff at its lime-green color before I pop it in my mouth.

Soon enough, an old, battered mailbox comes into sight at the end of the road. It reads *1173 McCabe*. We turn left into the driveway, and immediately a huge, rambling farmhouse and a faded red barn fill the horizon. Roses climb the pillars of the open porch that spans the front of the gray house, and thick, thorny vines wrap themselves around nearly everything in the farmyard.

As we drive closer, three figures emerge from the front door to stand on the porch. I suppose a car coming up the driveway is pretty exciting out here. It deserves an audience.

Ms. Troy parks behind an old blue Suburban with rust creeping up along the wheel wells. There's no garage, just a dirt loop in front of the farmhouse. I catch a glimpse of what looks like a fat red chicken pecking in the dirt near the corner of the barn. Then a rooster crows, filling the silence as Ms. Troy and I stare at the three women on the porch. The first is an old woman whose chin barely reaches the railing, at least from this angle. She's stout with silvery gray hair in a messy bun. The other woman is tall and lanky, and her hair is brilliantly red, even in the shadows. The last figure is a teenage girl, and she stands close to the last pillar on the far end of the porch. She's average height with girlish curves shrouded in a loose green dress. Her skin is light brown, and her black, curly hair is a cloud around her face but for one twisted braid that she's pinned up like a headband.

Together, they stare down at me from their house of roses.

I imagine what it would be like to sketch them there, a study on perspective and the human body through the years with the contrast of light and shadow and the blooms around them.

Ms. Troy interrupts my imagined strokes of charcoal on paper. "Looks like they've all come out to greet you."

"I thought I was living with one old lady."

"Mia has custody of you. That's her with the red hair next to your great-aunt, and the girl is Mia's daughter, who, um . . ." She digs in her purse for my case file, nudging aside her open wallet that is twenty dollars lighter than it was when we got in the car. "Yes, her name is Ember. She's a year younger than you. Sweet girl, your aunt says."

I hate to break it to Ms. Troy, but girls who find their position in a house challenged by an interloper are rarely sweet. I bounced around a few foster homes the year Mom lost custody of me when I was ten, and then again after she disappeared, before I decided to strike out on my own. I can tell you that none of them had sweet daughters, foster or no.

"Why didn't you tell me there were other people living here?" I ask Ms. Troy.

"I didn't want to overwhelm you. I know you haven't had much success with foster care in the past. Even though I really thought you'd take to the Willards." She adds that last part wistfully. There were good foster families mixed in with the crappy ones, of course. People who truly wanted to help me. The Willards were a nice young couple with a little boy they'd adopted out of foster care. They were eager and optimistic, and if I hadn't been so hollowed out by the time I reached them, maybe I wouldn't have pissed that chance away.

But I did. So it was group homes after that.

Ms. Troy reaches over and gives me a pat on the shoulder. "But this is your actual family, Trix. It's amazing that we found them. You're getting a second chance with your *real* family. It's so rare to have a story with a happily-ever-after like this."

I don't know what Ms. Troy sees as a happily-ever-after here. Rundown farmhouse. Being forced to go back to school with whatever hicks live this far out from civilization. Not to mention the fact that I'll be staying with relatives of the man who contributed half my DNA but then never came back to say hi or anything.

I answer, "I don't like surprises."

Ms. Troy sighs. But she unbuckles herself and grabs my file, so I know she's serious about leaving me here.

I have no choice but to unbuckle my seat belt, too, and fling open the car door. I get out and slam it shut behind me with more force than necessary and circle back to the trunk, waiting impatiently as Ms. Troy finds the latch to pop it. The air is thick and sweet with the scent of roses. When the trunk opens, I get out the donated backpack handed out to everyone leaving for a new home. It's got my sketchbook that Ms. Troy recovered from my room at the Starlite, a package of clean underwear, a new toothbrush, and a box of tampons. Everything a girl like me needs to survive.

"Good morning!" Ms. Troy says, waving at the women on the porch. "It's so lovely to see you again! Goodness, but your roses are gorgeous. I don't think I've ever seen so many before."

The old woman is descending the stairs with far more speed than I expected from someone her age. She's got to be at least eighty. Maybe a hundred. She takes the hand Ms. Troy offers, but not in a handshake. Instead, the old woman flips Ms. Troy's hand over and examines her palm, running gnarled fingers over it.

Ms. Troy is clearly taken aback, and she shoots a glance up at the other woman on the porch, Mia, who looks to be somewhere in her late thirties. "Don't mind Auntie," Mia says, coming down to join us. "She's just saying hello."

"I can see you've had a difficult road," my newfound great-aunt pronounces, her nose nearly in Ms. Troy's palm as she scrutinizes it. "No roses yet, only thorns. But this seedling's roots are strong, and soon the whole garden will be in bloom."

"I, uh," Ms. Troy mumbles, pulling her hand away.

Oh, good. I'm being left in the care of a bunch of freaks.

"And Trixie," the great-aunt says, coming to me next with open arms. I wonder if she's going to read my palm, too, but instead she claps her withered hands on either side of my face and squeezes, like she's trying to pop my face. "You look like Connor." She glances over her shoulder at Mia. "Doesn't she, Mia?"

Mia's hand is on her chest, her mouth open. "I can't believe it, but she does. Look at those eyes. Connor's eyes." She tears up and sniffs a little. "I'm sorry," she says, her voice quavering. "It's just, my goodness. I can't believe it."

I don't tell them that I look almost identical to my mother. There's a chance looking like my dead father will work out to my advantage.

"I'm so happy that we were able to connect you with Trix since you lost her father in . . . an accident of some kind?" Ms. Troy fumbles through her file on me like she might be able to find the answer.

"His fighter jet crashed in the desert. Boom. Dead," the great-aunt woman says, remarkably unfazed by this spectacular ending.

"I'm so sorry for your loss," Ms. Troy says, because she has enough manners for the both of us. "How tragic. We weren't able to find much information on Mr. McCabe, other than that he was deceased."

"What you hear all depends on who you ask," Mia answers, tossing her hair. She shoots a half smile to the old woman, some gruesome joke that I don't get.

Ms. Troy doesn't seem to know what to say to that, so she turns to me. "You have everything, right? And you have my phone number. Be sure to call if you need anything. Otherwise,

I'll be returning for a home visit in a few weeks, okay?" She puts a hand on my shoulder that's meant to be reassuring. I shrug it off. She's just another in a long line of people who have abandoned me at one time or another. "Could I have a few words with you privately?" Ms. Troy asks Mia, who nods.

They wander over by the fence, talking, and it isn't hard for me to make out the words Ms. Troy is whispering when there's no sounds other than the lowing of cows in the distance. *A history of running. Trust issues. Theft.*

Mia just nods, still smiling, as if Ms. Troy is telling her that I'm a Girl Scout who likes to bake cookies and read to the blind.

When they've finished talking, I stand between Mia and my great-aunt, and we watch as Ms. Troy leaves us in the rose-lined driveway.

The great-aunt swears. "I thought she would never leave," she says to me. "Come on, Trixie. We have work to do. You can call me Auntie, by the way. Everyone does."

"I'm your aunt Mia. But you can call me Mia, or . . . whatever you feel comfortable with," Mia says.

I narrow my eyes, waiting for her to cross an invisible boundary. Something that shows me she's like all the others who have taken me in at one time or another. I don't know this woman, and unless something changes dramatically, I doubt I'll be here long. Mia puts her arm around my shoulders and leads me up the porch steps. I try to shrug her off as we climb them, but she's like superglue. "And this," Mia says when we reach the teenage girl who is half hiding behind one of the rose-covered pillars, "is my daughter, Ember." When Ember peeks out, I notice she has a scattering of freckles on her cheeks, and her eyes are a brilliant green like her mother's. "Ember, meet your cousin, Trixie." Ember gives me a barely fluttering wave.

"It's Trix," I tell them. "Just Trix."

"That's a *little* better," Auntie says with a sigh of relief. "Trixie sounds like a hooker name."

"Auntie," Mia groans. "Please."

"What? *It is*. It's a hooker name."

For once, I'm actually at a loss for words.

"Let's just get you changed, and then we'll head to the shop. I put up a sign saying we'd be late, but I know Mrs. Gunderson said she was worried we wouldn't be open in time for her to pick up the pies for her horseshoe tournament," Mia says. "Her team needs all the Lucky Lime it can get."

Auntie grunts, "Yeah, well, people in hell want ice water. Take your time." She herds me inside the front door, which creaks when she opens it.

The first thing I notice is the smell. It's pies and bread with faint undertones of lemon. Then I adjust to the rest. Everything in the farmhouse is worn. Dusty light falls in from big front windows, whose calico curtains are pulled back like the McCabe women have been watching for me all morning. The front door opens directly into the living room, which has a couple of couches that are covered in mounds of colorful afghans and quilts. The TV looks like it's at least twenty years old, and the dark wood floors are scarred in paths where they must have the highest traffic. There's a massive stone fireplace with a wooden mantel above it, which is covered in small, framed pictures of Ember at various ages. It looks like a damn shrine. I can't help but think about how there are no pictures of me in the world other than the ones I've drawn myself and the one the cops used when they picked me up. Mom had a few, but we'd left them in a hurry one night when she couldn't come up with rent money.

From the entryway, I can see the dining room and the kitchen to the left. The kitchen has old white appliances that look like they might have lived through several wars, and the cupboards are fronted with a glass so ancient it's wavy, revealing dishes and bowls of varying colors and origins. There's a heavy, scarred wooden work table in the middle of the kitchen holding various baking pans and a mixer. The dining room has a table long enough for ten people, and it's littered with novels and magazines and empty teacups. A fat, fluffy orange cat is sprawled across the middle of it, bathing in a pool of sunshine. To my right is a huge staircase, which Mia leads me toward.

Every stair creaks as Mia continues the herding, and soon I find myself in what must be Mia's bedroom, a lavender room that smells of furniture polish and vanilla. Mia continues babbling as we go. "I'm sorry that we have to go to work. I should've just closed the shop for the whole day. I want to hear *everything* about you as soon as you get settled." She beams at me, her eyes still tracing the features she thinks belong to her dead brother. "You would have loved Connor. He was amazing, you know."

She looks at me again, like I'm supposed to agree, but who the hell am I to say? I never knew him. He might have been a real dick.

"We grew up here," Mia continues. "I was six and he was

seven when our parents died in a car accident. So we moved in with Auntie and Uncle Javier." She beams at me, then looks at Ember, who is trailing behind us at a safe distance. "Go find those jeans. The ones we picked up at Rory's Treasures. They're too long for you, but if you haven't hemmed them yet, I bet they'll fit Trix." Without a sound, Ember retreats into the dark hallway, and Mia ducks into a small closet. She sings softly to herself as she sorts through shirts on hangers. Finally she pulls out a faded orange-and-gray henley that says *Rocksaw Tigers* across the front. "Here," she says. "This is perfect. And you won't cry if it gets messy."

I barely manage to catch it as she throws it at my face. "I can wear what I have," I tell her. "I don't need your clothes."

Mia eyes my baggy black hoodie and jeans. Ms. Troy washed them in extra-hot water with lots of detergent, far better than what I was able to pull off in a motel bathroom sink on my own, but they're admittedly stained and torn in places. "Please, honey. People would come into the shop, see you, and turn right back around."

Ember steals quietly back in the room, holding a neatly folded pair of jeans. I notice that she wears a long necklace that hides between the folds of fabric on her loose dress. It's a thin gold chain with an owl with tiny jewels for eyes on the end. Somehow it reminds me of Charly and the rings she wears on every finger. But Charly isn't here, and Ember hands the pair of jeans to her mother, snubbing me already.

"Perfect," Mia says, ignoring the slight and tossing the jeans at me. "We'll let you change." She leaves the room, Ember following and shutting the door as quietly as possible.

There's nothing left to do but go along with them for now. Once I get a better feel for the place, I can figure out my exit strategy. I toe off my sneakers and pull off my loose, ripped jeans. Then I unzip the hoodie and tug it off. The white, stained men's T-shirt beneath reveals my bare arms. I haven't looked at the marks for a while, a constellation of five perfectly round pink scars on the inside of my left forearm. Once Shane traced them with his finger and swore that they looked like the Big Dipper. I don't look at them if I can help it. That's what's so great about hoodies. They hide everything.

I pull on the new jeans—which I can tell are used, but clean and without holes—and then the shirt. The outfit shows off my body in a way I haven't for years. It's safer to be on the streets and alone in motels if you're an indeterminable sex in a baggy hoodie and loose jeans. The henley and tight jeans hug my curves, and the three-quarter-length sleeves reveal three of my round scars.

My skin heats, something twisting ever so slightly in my gut when I see my reflection in the mirror: not a nameless, faceless person on a city street, but a Trix McCabe I haven't seen since the Good Year. Palms sweating, I wipe them on the jeans as I look anxiously around the room until I notice a gold wedding ring among a handful of costume jewelry and tubes of lipstick on the dresser. I swipe it with a swift, even motion despite my nerves and tuck it into the pocket of my jeans. It's best to have insurance. I don't think I'll last long here.

Before I leave Mia's bedroom, I try to tug the left sleeve of the shirt down, but it won't go any farther. Some of my scars will always show, whether I want them to or not.

THREE

EMBER AVOIDS MY GAZE AS we drive into town. Despite the uneven country roads, Auntie uses the visor mirror in the passenger seat to apply red lipstick, smacking her lips when she's through. Mia tells me it's only a mile or so as the crow flies, which feels like a strange way to measure after growing up counting distance in city blocks and bus stops. I hold my hoodie in my lap, still feeling uncomfortable with my bare arms and snug clothing. Ember and I are sitting side by side on the bench seat in Mia's old Suburban, but she is careful not to touch me or look at me. I wonder if she hates me already. I can deal with hate. It's pity I can't stand.

Town is a loose term for the collection of buildings I see as we enter. The sign for Rocksaw says, "Population 5,062." It's picture-book pretty, with big trees that divide the lanes of traffic in the middle of the brick-paved Main Street. The road is lined with raised sidewalks and storefronts that feature hand-lettered signs advertising things like "Fall Lumber Sale," "New

Scarves," "Buy Local, Save Big!"

On the end of the second block sits a small shop with big windows and a door situated exactly on the corner of the building itself. The wooden building is painted burgundy, the windows edged with gold paint that's starting to peel a little. A sign hangs out over the sidewalk, swinging in the breeze. It says, "McCabe Bakery & Tea Shoppe, est. 1919." Red roses with twining green stems and leaves are painted on either side of the words, their colors faded from the sun.

There's a growing cluster of people gathered around the sign in the window that reads, "Delayed Opening Saturday Morning." When Mia parks in front of the business and gets out of the car, the crowd gets louder, their voices carrying through the open door.

"You're finally here!" a woman exclaims, as if we were arriving with some sort of lifesaving medicine in the middle of an epidemic. "We thought maybe something terrible had happened."

Another huffs, "I *told* you their niece was arriving today."

I listen for more about the mysterious niece, but there's nothing. I wonder what story the McCabes told about me and why I'm here.

One of the waiting women seizes Mia in a hug, thanking her for something involving pie, and when Mia manages to extricate herself, she hurries to unlock the front door, ushering in the crowd after. I don't know what I'm supposed to do, but I get out of the car anyway, watching the people.

"Trix!" Auntie shouts as she climbs down from the Suburban. "Come help Ember with the pies."

"Thank God, the pies," a young woman says from the

26

sidewalk. She's wiping her eyes, which are red-rimmed, like she's been crying.

Three more women push into the shop, carrying tote bags with bits of yarn and what might be a half-knitted sock hanging out. It's hard to look away from them as they clamber to get inside.

I circle around to the back of the Suburban, which Ember has opened. Inside are huge metal trays of pies. Some are topped with a sugar-dusted crust, others with crisscrossed strips of pastry that reveal juicy innards, and still more with crowns of meringue. Without so much as a glance at me, Ember grabs one tray, hoists it to her shoulder with practiced ease, and takes it up onto the sidewalk and into the shop. I assume that I'm supposed to grab the other one, so I pick it up, panicking when the pies slide to one side of the tray. Luckily I don't drop any, and I'm able to right it and follow Ember inside.

The inside of the shop is filled with small tables with delicate chairs, though the right wall has a line of four booths, one of which is already filled with the knitting group. The walls are the same burgundy color as the outside of the shop, relieved here and there with old carved moldings in mauve and gold. It would be dark if it weren't for the light spilling in the windows and the brass chandeliers hanging from the pressed-tin ceiling.

The left side of the shop has a big glass case with a rounded top, and Ember is busy filling it with her selection of pies. Mia is arranging a chocolate cake on a pink glass plate, covering it carefully with a clear glass topper. There's a small wooden counter with a register at one end of the case that looks like it must have been with the place since it opened in 1919. Behind the counter is a swinging door, and when Mia ducks back in to grab something else, I catch a glimpse of Auntie at a massive stove, putting on a big iron kettle.

I slide the tray up on top of the glass case, and Ember takes it without making eye contact again, sliding the pies off the tray and placing them gently in the case, as carefully as Charly putting the Quinter twins down for a nap.

I wander back into the kitchen, where Mia meets me. "Perfect! I was just coming out to get you." She tosses an apron to me.

"What is this for?" I ask, unfolding it. It's short and black with front pockets.

"Work, of course. All the McCabe women work in the shop. It's a tradition."

"What's the pay?" I ask as I tie the apron around my waist and dig into one pocket to find a notepad and pen. I've never worked a regular job. Jobs require some sort of stability, like staying in one place for an extended period, which I'm not great at. And when you're working with other people, sooner or later they get all chummy and want to know your life story. Mine's not one I like to share. Besides, why work at all when I can steal?

"Minimum wage. Do your job well and we'll look at giving you a raise in a month," Mia says.

I almost brag that I could wander among the customers out there and have more money in a day than she could pay me in a week. But I don't. There's no point.

"Great," Mia says, as if I'm not staring her down. "Go on out and start taking orders. Tell the customers that we've got the kettles on. Tea will be coming out shortly. Refills are complimentary here, you know. And so are the readings." She lists these things out on her fingers in a matter-of-fact way.

"The readings?" I ask.

"Auntie's readings. She's always giving them out. But we never charge for fortunes. Because if she's wrong, people might want a refund. But usually"—she makes a face that indicates she's not quite sure how to phrase her thoughts—"it's hard to tell exactly what Auntie's readings *mean*."

"So she just spouts off weird shit like she did to my caseworker?"

If Mia has sensitive ears, she doesn't show it. "Fortune-telling isn't a science. It's an art. And sometimes art is messy," she says with a shrug.

"Are you a fortune-teller, too?" I ask.

"Oh, of course not!" Mia says with a laugh and a wave of her hand. "I bake. That's why the bakery part of the business is so popular. Before I moved back, Auntie's muffins were legendary only for their ability to double as hockey pucks." A glance back through the swinging door as Ember enters reveals the dining area is nearly full now.

"They must be good pies."

"Oh, they are. Never-Lonely Lemon is always a hot seller before the holidays start ramping up. And then there's Bracing Blueberry. Cherish Cherry. Lucky Lime. Ardent Apple."

"Excuse me?"

"My pies have a secret ingredient that, well . . . helps out however it's needed."

"You're saying your pies can cure those things? Or make

them happen, or whatever?" I ask. "That's ridiculous."

Mia sighs. "No, honey. You being a McCabe woman and *not* believing me is ridiculous. I bet you've got some special talents of your own, too. It's genetic."

"Well, we both know that's the only thing we have in common. Half my DNA," I mutter, still irritated that I'm supposed to jump right in and join the family business when I only found out the family existed a few days ago.

Mia pretends she didn't hear me and nudges me toward the door. "Now, go take orders. It's not rocket science, and the customers know the procedure. They'll train you as you go."

I leave the kitchen and make my way to the closest table, which is occupied by the young woman with the red eyes and balled-up tissues. She's wearing a lumpy sweatshirt and leggings, her hair twisted into a messy bun. "Bracing Blueberry, please. Tell Mia not just a slice. I need at least two. Actually, just keep them coming. And a cup of chamomile."

I jot down her order, glancing up once to stare at her while she blows her nose loudly into one of the tissues. She looks like she might start crying again at any moment.

"It's my own fault," she tells me, crumpling the used tissue and dropping it onto the table. "Auntie told me storms were on the horizon for me. And she was right. I should have seen the signs. Ben dumped me. Six months! *Six months* we were together!"

I don't know what to say, and crying makes me uncomfortable, so I wander over to the next table as inconspicuously as possible. Two women are sitting there, both middle-aged and

30

sighing over stacks of magazines, flipping through pages and gesturing at articles.

"Never-Lonely Lemon for me," the first woman says. "And the rosehip tea."

"A raspberry muffin," the second woman says. She hesitates before she adds, "And a cup of coffee, if Auntie says it's all right."

"It's a café, right?" I ask. "Don't they make what you want?"

"Oh, no," the muffin woman says, sitting up straighter. "This is a tea shop, and Auntie only makes coffee when she feels like it."

"Got it," I say, jotting it down on my notepad.

"But maybe," the muffin woman says, lowering her voice even though the chatter around us would drown out a helicopter landing, "add a slice of Ardent Apple in a takeout box."

"Yeah, okay," I tell her, making a note. I can't believe these people actually buy into this whole magic-pie gig.

I take the orders of a few more tables before I deliver them back to the kitchen, and then return to take the remaining orders from two more tables and the booths in the back. Aside from the group of women knitting, there's another booth of old farmers, three wearing dusty jeans and cowboy boots and one in overalls, who ask if Mia made any of her banana-nut muffins, and whether or not I think Auntie is in the mood to make coffee today. When I return with the second set of orders, the first are ready to be delivered. Mia is loading up the first tray with blueberry pie and chamomile in a delicate china cup with roses painted on the sides. "I could use some help," I say pointedly to Ember, who is loading tea diffusers with rose petals. "It's kind of busy out there."

Ember's green eyes widen, and she scurries back into what must be a walk-in cooler.

"Oh, this is normal for a Saturday," Mia says as she slices pie. "And you shouldn't pressure Ember into going into the dining room. It's hard for her, you know."

I have no idea what that's supposed to mean, so I shoot back, "That's a lot of tables to wait on all by myself."

"But you're doing great!" Mia cheers, sliding a piece of pie onto a plate. She pushes the tray toward me. "Oh, and if Ella with the Bracing Blueberry starts to perk up, you should tell her I have it on good authority that Morris Walker is back in town, and he's single and looking real good these days."

I don't know Ella or Morris, but I feel like there's some serious favoritism going on here. Was I brought here just to be a waitress? Were they looking for cheap labor? Is Mia trying to remind me that Ember is the real McCabe daughter and I'm merely some girl thrust on them by social services?

The crying woman, who must be Ella, grabs the pie off the tray when I return. "I'm sorry," she apologizes through a mouthful of pie as I set the cup of tea down sloppily. It spills a little, but it doesn't look like Ella's going to complain about anything right now.

"Do you *really* think the pie is going to help?" I ask Ella when she's swallowed a couple of bites with very little chewing.

Ella nods, dabbing at her eyes. "It does. Trust me. I've been coming here since Mia moved to town. Three boyfriends ago. It always works."

"It's just pie, though." I keep waiting for someone to crack a smile, let me know that this is some kind of joke.

Ella shrugs. "Everyone in Rocksaw was a nonbeliever at one point. But Mia converted us. She brings a whole new meaning to the words *comfort food*." She sniffs and looks up at me like she's seeing me for the first time. "Wait, you must be the niece?" she says.

I nod.

"I'll see you Monday, then. Try to forget this ever happened," Ella says, gesturing to her crumpled tissues and red face.

"Um, yeah," I mumble, confused by the strange people in this town.

I move on to the table of two older women with magazines. I'm still a little unnerved by the town's devotion to this supposedly magic pie, but I try to move past that and do my new job. Auntie did deign to make a pot of coffee, and I'm careful not to splash as I set their cups down on the table and barely manage to keep the serving tray from wobbling at the same time. Maybe I'll get tips, right? There must be tips involved here. Anything to help me build up a stash for when it's time to hit the road.

"Oh, it's a coffee day!" the muffin woman exclaims, hand over her heart.

"Auntie and Mia must be happy about your arrival, huh?" the Never-Lonely Lemon woman asks.

"What do you mean?"

"You're the new niece, right? Mia was talking about you last week. Said you were coming to live with them. Something about how your mom was going to be gone on a trip for a while?"

I can feel myself bristling. What the hell did Mia tell these people?

It must show on my face, because the muffin woman continues down a different conversational path. "Well, it's a small town, so you know we're always excited about new faces. And a McCabe? Well, they're *always* interesting people to meet." She raises her eyebrows, like she's waiting for me to tell her that I can make magic bagels.

"Sure," I reply, leaving them to eat and drink and gossip about me and my potential talent in peace. If they only knew what I could do.

I covertly watch Ella eat her Bracing Blueberry. By the second slice, she's stopped sniffling, and another woman her age has joined her and ordered a slice of Never-Lonely Lemon that comes wearing a fluffy crown of gold-tipped meringue. In another hour and another slice apiece, they're both laughing. When Auntie throws me a rag to wipe empty tables, I muse to myself that technically the pie didn't cure anything for Ella, and the only thing I really saw was a friend come cheer her up while she was eating pie.

I look at the pies at the counter and wonder which ones might cure what ails me.

If they work.

Which they probably don't. At least my gift is effective.

It's on my seventh trip back to the kitchen for refills that Mia finally notices the scars on my left arm. She flinches, the same way everyone does when they first see them, like they hurt to look at. I slide the tray onto the counter to load it with more tea, and then, in a practiced habit, I pull my arm back against my side when I've finished, hiding the marks from view.

"Are those——?" Mia begins.

"They're nothing," I reply, keeping them hidden as I pick the tray back up from the counter.

Mia doesn't say any more, but she can't hide the pity in her eyes either.

After I deliver the tea, I go out to the old Suburban and get my black hoodie and put it on so that Mia won't stare anymore. I place a hand over the lump of her wedding ring in my pocket and make a mental note to look for anything else around the house that might be of use to me when I leave.

At lunchtime, Mia covers the dining room for me while I sit in the kitchen at the empty prep table and eat a turkey sandwich. Before I came into the kitchen, I heard her out there gossiping with Ella and her friend about eligible bachelors in Rocksaw. Mia seems to know the name, occupation, and marital status of every man in town.

In my apron are exactly thirteen crumpled dollar bills I made in tips, plus two tens I snagged out of tote bags of yarn and sippy cups. This is abysmal, but I remind myself that with the twenty I took from Ms. Troy this morning, things could be worse.

I amuse myself by drawing an outline of a piece of pie in the dusting of flour on the table. Next to it I draw a cup of tea. Then I check my pay-as-you-go phone, which has no signal. Of course it doesn't. There's no signal out here in the boondocks. The last message I received on my phone was from Charly, and it simply said, *I'm sorry.*

I read the message over again, tracing the words with my flour-coated finger. I'm sorry, too. Sorry I got caught. Sorry I agreed to this stupid deal. Sorry I got carted off and dumped in the middle of nowhere.

I look up from my phone and catch Ember watching me from behind an open wire shelf of baking supplies.

"What do you want?" I snarl.

Her pretty green eyes, just like her mom's, widen, and she dashes back into the walk-in cooler.

"You've got a sharp tongue for a girl who just had a family and a home and a job handed to her," Auntie grunts out, lowering herself down onto a stool next to me. Damn it, that old woman came out of nowhere, but I take a bite of sandwich like she didn't spook me. Auntie pops one of my potato chips in her mouth, crunching loudly.

"I didn't ask for this," I reply, my mouth full of turkey sandwich.

"Really? Well, I heard you did. I heard you *asked* for this over *prison*," she replies, taking another chip. Apparently Auntie is not one to mince words. That's okay, because I'm not either.

I swallow the turkey. "So?"

"So stop being nasty," she replies. "We took you in."

"She doesn't like me," I say with a shrug. "So why should I be nice to her?"

"Ember is shy. Which you would realize if you weren't so full of yourself and your little pity party."

"Pity party?" I reply. "You don't know half of what I've been through, and I've never once, *never*—"

"So it's a *pissy* party," Auntie interrupts. "Well, news flash: Everyone's life is hard. Get over it. Stop taking it out on whoever gets in your way." She nods toward the walk-in cooler. "Go say you're sorry, or I'm docking your pay."

I open my mouth to tell her she can't do that, but I guess technically she *can* do that since she owns this place.

I push myself away from the table, reaching down and grabbing the last bit of sandwich and shoving it in my mouth before Auntie eats it like my chips. Then I stroll over to the walk-in cooler, throwing open the door. Ember is arranging cartons of eggs and sticks of butter on a shelf, and she jumps about a foot when I enter. When she sees it's me, she drops the stick of butter she's holding, and it falls to the floor with a noise like a slap.

"Hey," I say as I approach her, leaning over and picking up the stick of butter. I hold it out for her to take, but she doesn't move. Her owl necklace catches my eye again. "Auntie wants me to tell you I'm sorry. For scaring you or whatever. So I'm sorry."

Ember just stares.

I turn to leave, stick of butter still awkwardly in hand, and Ember squeaks out, "Why?"

I stop, turning back around to face her. "Why what? Why am I apologizing? Because Auntie says she'll dock my pay."

"No," she says, looking down at her shoes. "Why do you hate me? Is it because you heard? Did someone tell you?"

"Tell me what?" I ask, crossing my arms.

"About what I can do." She hazards a glance at me.

"Nobody told me anything about you," I reply. "So what do you do? Auntie tells weird fortunes. Your mom thinks she makes magic pies. Can you fly?"

Ember laughs, and she's so surprised by it that she covers her mouth. "No," she says. "I wish I could."

"Then what can you do?"

"What can *you* do?" she counters. "Mama says all the McCabe women have gifts. We always have. If you tell me what you can do, I'll tell you what I can do." She's so serious when she says it that I realize this might not be fake after all. I know my gift is real. So why couldn't theirs be just as real and powerful as mine? Maybe Mia's pies are real, and Auntie's fortunes are real, and this green-eyed, shy girl who maybe doesn't hate me after all is also real.

So maybe it's another mistake in my long list of mistakes, but I reach past her, like I'm going to set the stick of butter on the shelf, letting my hand brush against her neck, just barely.

When I pull back after setting down the stick of butter on the shelf, I open my hand.

I'm holding her owl necklace, coiled in my palm, the chain still warm from her skin.

FOUR

EMBER'S HANDS IMMEDIATELY FLY TO her neck.

"Oh!" she exclaims shrilly. "How did you? I didn't feel—"

"Yeah, I know."

"That's your gift?" she asks, laughing again. "You can do magic? Like sleight of hand? That's amazing!"

"I can *steal* things," I reply, dropping the necklace into her open palm. "It's not pulling a rabbit out of a hat."

"Wow," she breathes, and there's actual admiration in her voice.

"So I showed you mine. Show me yours."

Ember licks her lips as she puts her necklace back on. "I can read your deepest, darkest secrets—the things that you most want or fear—just by touching your skin with my hand," she whispers.

I immediately take a step back. Running away is a reflex by now. But the idea of someone getting inside my head freaks me out.

Ember nods. "Most people do that."

"So are people afraid of you?" I ask.

"The ones who know are. But mostly, it scares *me*."

"Why would it scare you? That's *power*. Knowing the weakness of anyone you meet."

Ember shrugs. "It's invasive. And personal. And I hate it. People's deepest, darkest secrets aren't always good. So it's best if I just stay away from people," she says, turning back to her sticks of butter as she puts in her earbuds.

I wait to see if she's going to say *especially you*, but she doesn't.

Back in the warm kitchen, I find that Auntie has finished off my chips and left the table. Mia is there instead, and she looks excited to see me, as usual. Even her red hair seems bigger, as if it, too, is thrilled. "Perfect!" she says. "I had a brilliant idea while I was out in the dining room. Ella helped me think of it. You're new to Rocksaw, so you should have a tour of the place. And I have just the perfect outing for you. Jasper's coming by to pick up the deliveries, and you could ride along with him. He's a junior, he's cute, and he's *single*. What better tour guide could there be?"

My heart drops. Why won't they just leave me alone? "I signed on to be a waitress. Not a delivery girl. And I don't need to be set up with some hick from Nowheresville. Just let me do my job, graduate from high school, and be on my way." I don't add that I'll probably be gone in a couple weeks anyway.

Mia's face falls just a bit.

Auntie shuffles into the kitchen behind Mia and silently mouths the words *pissy party*.

"Fine," I grumble, glaring at Auntie and taking off my

apron. "I'll go. But I don't need a boyfriend. I'm here to fulfill my end of the bargain with the judge."

Mia beams, as if I'd said thank you and hugged her rather than grudgingly agreed to go. "How about some lipstick? Reckless Rouge or Madcap Mango?" she asks, pulling out a couple tubes from her apron.

"No."

Mia still grins at me. It's like she's impervious to brush-offs, this flame-haired whirlwind of a woman.

I push through the swinging door of the kitchen, and the guy, Jasper, is standing at the glass case in the dining area, a stack of pink cardboard delivery boxes tied with white string in his hands. "Is this everything?" he asks Mia when she follows behind me. He's got golden-brown skin and golden-brown eyes and longish black hair that falls in big, loose curls over one side of his forehead. He wears a plain white T-shirt with faded jeans and brown, square-toed cowboy boots that look like they've got more than a few miles on them. I refrain from asking him if he left his lasso outside with his horse, though, mostly because he manages to make cowboy look pretty damn good.

"Almost!" Mia crows. She is in her element. I should have known, with those Ardent Apple pies. She's a matchmaker. Or at least a wannabe. "This is my niece, Trix McCabe. She's come to live with us." I notice that she says *live* and not *stay*. Living and staying are two very different things. I remember the wedding ring in my pocket, and I fidget a little under the heat of her smile as she tosses her red hair over one shoulder. Must have been something weird in that turkey sandwich she gave me. "Trix, this is

Jasper Ruiz. He's our part-time delivery boy. And his family pays cash rent for our farmland. You'll probably see his dad and him at the farm soon to harvest the corn."

Jasper smiles at me, and it pulls on a thin white scar that slices through his right eyebrow and hooks down just underneath his eye. "Hi," he says. "I'd shake your hand, but mine are kind of full right now."

"Yeah, I'm good," I tell him, shooting a glance back at Mia. This is so embarrassing, and I'm not sure if he's aware that she's trying to set us up or not, which makes it even more awkward.

"Since Trix is new to town, I thought maybe she could ride along with you," Mia tells him. "Just so she can get a feel for Rocksaw. She's from the city, you know." She makes it sound like I may have difficulty navigating the vast expanse of this village without his expertise. I barely withhold the urge to roll my eyes.

"Sure," Jasper says, giving that charming smile again that makes the scar pull on his eye. That's what it is, I realize. The scar somehow makes him not *too* perfect. I try not to stare at it because I hate it when people do that to mine.

I follow Jasper outside. The weather is a little warm, but I leave my hoodie on anyway.

Jasper leans over the bed of an old black Chevy truck, placing the pies in a wooden crate just behind the cab. I pull on the passenger door, but it doesn't open. From the driver's side, he laughs. "Pull up and *then* out. The door sticks."

I do what he says, and the door opens with a metallic wail. I climb inside. The seat is faded maroon fabric that might have once had stripes, and there's a chain with a heavy gold class ring hanging from the rearview mirror. It smells like old pipe tobacco and dust. The ancient stereo system confirms that this truck existed long before either of us was born.

"Nice ride," I comment.

"Thanks," Jasper says with a grin.

Sarcasm is apparently lost on him.

"We don't have too many deliveries," he says. "So this will be a short tour. But if you want, we can take the long way back from our last stop."

"I'm fine with taking the regular, short way back," I tell him, attempting to buckle my seat belt.

"You've got to put it in at an angle," he tells me, reaching over and guiding my belt into the buckle. "Otherwise it won't latch."

His hands are rough, and I pull back as soon as my seat belt is properly latched.

"You didn't need to do that," I say. "I could've figured it out."

"Sorry," he says. "It's just that most people can't get it on their own. Cleo is a fickle beauty."

"Cleo?" I ask.

"That's the truck's name."

"You named your truck?"

"Sure, everybody names their truck."

"I don't think everybody names their truck."

"Then you haven't known enough *truck people*," he says with a shrug, starting up the engine. It growls to life, sounding like his muffler must be lost on some back road. But he's unfazed by it and cranks up the stereo.

The old Chevy rattles down the brick street, and we drive two blocks before making a left turn, then four more blocks before we're at a little green house with tricycles in the front yard. "Never-Lonely Lemon," Jasper says when he puts the truck in park along the street. "Hank's been deployed for six months now."

I nod, as if this whole scenario makes perfect sense. I sit in the truck and watch Jasper deliver the pie to the front door. A pretty blond woman answers, and two toddlers push at the screen door to get out at Jasper. He says something to both of them and they dart back inside, laughing and shrieking. The woman smiles at Jasper again, and he leaves after taking the cash she offers him.

"She seemed pleased," I remark when he gets in the truck and puts it in drive.

"Yeah. The twins are going through some kind of sleep regression. Suzie says it's been hard on them."

I don't know much about sleep regression, but I'm suddenly reminded of the Quinter twins, and I wonder if Charly is getting ready to babysit them again tonight. I pull my phone back out of my pocket and check for a signal. Still nothing. I groan in frustration.

Jasper glances over. "No signal?" he asks.

I shake my head, shoving my phone back into my pocket.

"You must have NorthStar. There's no signal here if they're your provider. Unless you're on top of Cedar Mountain."

"Excuse me?" I ask, looking around as if we're somewhere other than Rocksaw, Kansas.

Jasper laughs. "Cedar Mountain. It's this huge hill behind the practice field near the high school. The football team runs up and down it for conditioning, and at the beginning of the season the freshmen always puke their guts up there before practice is over."

"Gross."

Jasper shrugs. "I'm just trying to help you out."

The next stop is a small pink cottage with white shutters and a heart-shaped sign in the front yard that says, "Mitzi's Love Shack."

Jasper puts the truck into park and shoots a glance over at me. "It's a honeymoon cottage," he explains.

"There were a couple other things I thought it might be," I reply, crossing my arms.

"Do you want to help?" he asks. "The order is for two Ardent Apples and a Cherish Cherry. Mitzi asked me to get the key under the mat and leave them on the table before the couple gets back from their vineyard tour."

"Sure," I grumble, tugging on the seat belt twice before it releases. I try to open the door, but Jasper is already around the truck, pulling up and out on the door handle with one hand while he balances the pie boxes in the other.

"Sorry," he says, and I shoot him a glare that has him pressing his lips together as he tries not to smile again. He smiles a lot, and I'm trying to figure out what exactly it is that makes him so damn pleased about everything. "It doesn't open from the inside. I forgot to tell you about that. You have to roll the window down and open it from the outside if you're riding shotgun."

"Has anyone told you that Cleo is kind of a death trap?" I ask him, sliding down from the bench seat and shutting the door.

"I thought girls liked dangerous guys," he says. One of his black curls actually falls forward over his left eye, like it's a move he's been practicing in the bathroom mirror.

"Girls like guys who have seat belts that work."

Jasper shrugs. "The bond between a man and his truck is unbreakable. I'll drive Cleo till she goes up in flames."

"That's really noble of you."

"Yeah, I'm pretty great like that." He leads me to the tiny pink cottage, turning and handing me the pies so he can get the spare key. "Mitzi says it's under here . . ." His voice trails off as he leans over to look for the key.

"So, you do this a lot?" I ask.

"Deliver pies or break into people's cottages?"

I think of Shane, and something seizes in my chest. "Deliver pies."

"Yeah. Usually on Saturdays, but sometimes there are some deliveries after school." He finds the key, pulling it out from under the mat with a flourish. "Mostly I work for my dad on the farm."

"Sounds riveting."

"Well, I can see how you might think feeding the world isn't as prestigious a job as waitressing," he parries amicably, "but I make do with what I have." He gives me a smile that doesn't tug at his scar.

I don't even have a good reply ready when Jasper turns away to unlock the door. I stand next to him, interested in gawking at the inside of Mitzi's Love Shack since no one's here right now. I guess after all those motels I've lived in, I'm curious about what a rental looks like here. He swings the door open wide, and there's a heart-shaped hot tub in the middle of the room, bubbling and steaming away. But the most surprising part of the scene is the couple inside the hot tub, who are most definitely not wearing clothes. The woman, her blond hair pinned up on top of her head, sees us first and screams shrilly, and then the balding man looks up from the glass of pink champagne he's pouring and is so surprised by our presence that he nearly drops the glass into the frothing water of the hot tub.

"What in the hell are you doing?" the man shouts, reclaiming his grasp and hurling the flute of champagne at Jasper. Luckily, the man's hands are wet, or he's just got bad aim, and the glass goes far right and crashes against the wall, the contents fizzing as they run to the shards of crystal on the floor.

Jasper is undeterred from completing his mission. "These pies are from Mitzi, and we'll, ah, just leave them here. Nice to meet you!" He takes the pies from me, sets them down on the cottage floor, and slams the door shut.

There's swearing and crashing inside, and Jasper yelps, half laughing, "Hurry! Get in the truck! I think he's coming!" He wrenches open the driver's-side truck door and shoves me in in front of him, so I have to scoot across the bench seat while he climbs in and starts the engine. We're barely in first gear when the man throws open the door of Mitzi's Love Shack, still naked and pink from the hot water, and yells at us, pitching the half-empty bottle of champagne at the back of the truck. It crashes against the tailgate as we peel out.

We make it two blocks, just the silent shaking of my shoulders before I erupt in gasping gulps of laughter that leave me breathless and achy. I don't remember the last time I laughed like this, with tears in my eyes and totally helpless to stop it.

Jasper manages to drive to our next stop and put the truck in park before he looks over at me. "Don't forget. What happens on pie deliveries *stays* on pie deliveries," he says with a face that's struggling to look serious.

"Your secret's safe with me," I reply, wiping my eyes. "I'll never tell anyone that you were chased by a naked man out of Mitzi's Love Shack."

When I remove my hands from my face I see that he's grinning too. That scar pulls at his eye, and that's when I realize that it only does that sometimes when he smiles, not every time. I don't know why, but it seems important.

Scars tell a story, even when we don't want them to.

FIVE

WHEN WE GET HOME FROM the tea shop Saturday evening, Mia leads me up to the attic. "This is your room," Mia says, gesturing around the big room in the eaves of the farmhouse. There's a bed tucked under the right side wall with a small side table made out of an ancient upright wooden banana crate that someone's taken the time to nail shelves into. An antique globe-style lamp with pink roses painted on it sits on top of the crate. The left side has a dresser with a mirror over it and a desk, as well as a hanging rack with some hangers on it. The faint smell of fresh paint hangs in the air. The walls are pale blue, and rag rugs are scattered here and there on the dark wood floor.

"Okay," I reply, shifting my backpack a little higher on my shoulder.

"It used to be Connor's. We tried to freshen it up for you, but we weren't really sure about your tastes."

I look around the room. So, this is Connor's old room.

Connor, my father, slept here. He probably did his homework at that desk. Maybe he had old jeans and ratty socks in that dresser, a pack of cigarettes or a bottle of rum stashed away in the back of the bottom drawer. He's never felt real to me before now. The sheen of resentment toward him is slowly chipping away, mostly being replaced by curiosity about the man I'd never met, who, to hear it from these women, was practically a saint.

I don't answer, so she continues. "I'm sure you'll feel more like chatting when you've settled in. You know I want to hear absolutely everything about you. And I can't wait to tell you all about Connor. Go ahead and rest while I throw something together downstairs. It's my turn to make dinner." She smiles at me. "Pancakes, I think. Connor always loved breakfast for dinner. What about you?"

I shrug. Sometimes I ate dinner. Sometimes I didn't.

"Okay, then. I'll let you settle in."

I listen to her climb back down the creaking stairs. When I hear her shut the door at the bottom of the stairwell, I release a shaky breath.

Breakfast for dinner. I file this information away, the small note more than I have ever known about Connor. I wonder if he would have liked me. If he might have even loved me.

But mostly I wonder why he never knew me.

I look around the attic space. I've never had a bedroom like this, all done up and waiting just for me.

My earliest memories are of being carried out of motel-room beds and laid carefully down in cold bathtubs with a pillow and blanket. Then Mom saying, *Lock the door, Trix, and don't come out till I knock five times. That's how you'll know it's safe.* And then the door of the motel room would open somewhere in the distance, and I would fall back asleep.

I learned to count to five real early.

I walk over to the bed and put my backpack down on it, taking a moment to run a finger down the seams of the square-blocked quilt, the loosely woven afghans folded at the bottom of the bed. At the edge of the room, I have to lean over so I don't bump my head on the ceiling. I unload all my worldly possessions, putting away my package of clean underwear in the dresser. There are already a few things in the drawer, like maybe Ember was here while I was delivering pies, figuring out what they had around the house that might fit me.

Then I look for a good hiding place. In books and movies, there'd be a loose floorboard somewhere in a house this old, but I don't notice anything that looks useful, so I take my tips, the cash I stole from Ms. Troy and the tea-shop customers, and Mia's ring, and wedge them between the banana crate and the wall along the floor. It's not the best hiding place, but I doubt anyone will look there. They'll check the dresser and under the mattress first.

When I've finished that, I take my sketchbook out of my bag. I settle myself on the bed. The mattress squeaks a little, but I sink down into the layers of quilts and afghans and feather pillows, adjusting them until I've made a nest. That's when I open the sketchbook. I've had dozens of them over the years. Some were misplaced, others left behind like the few photographs Mom used to have of us, lost in speedy, dark-of-night flights from eviction or angry dealers. But this one I've managed to keep. I flip through the pages. Some drawings are motel rooms, bus stops, and neon signs. Others are shoes I saw on the bus, or the clasped hands of the older couple that I briefly sketched the night I got picked up again.

A few even have color, from pastels that I lifted from an art store downtown. But my favorites are of the people. I don't have a photo shrine like Ember does downstairs. But this is my own monument. All the people I've loved. All the people I've lost, either because I left or they did. There's one of Charly holding her red plastic cup watching television while the Quinter twins play on the floor of the motel room, so close that their golden curls are touching. And a pastel-smeared one of Mom smoking a cigarette outside the Starlite, in one of those blissful lulls where she swore she was going to get clean and we'd try for another Good Year, smoke twining around her dark hair like shadowy vines. Wendy Yang and me in the back booth of the Jasmine Dragon, the restaurant her parents owned, where we used to study and play and share secrets while Mom was waitressing. Another done in dark charcoal of Shane leaning against the doorway of room 7, as if he's waiting for me to come back. The neon lights glare off his shaved head, the tip of his tattoo: three black-lined feathers, barely visible above the collar of his jacket.

Shane.

I let myself remember, just for a little while. He'd just finished a year in juvie, returning to the Starlite not as a boy who didn't see me, but as a young man who saw everything. Falling in love with Shane was like getting drunk. A terrible first taste—he'd come over to yell at me for having the television on too loud in room 7 while his mom was trying to sleep. But after that, it was a warm tingling that crept up my fingertips and flushed my cheeks when he stopped by later with Coke-and-cherry slushes from the QuikMart and an apology. Then weeks and months passed, and it was giddy, tumbling laughter, the way his lips felt on mine, his hands on my bare skin. The way he traced my constellation of scars, the way he dreamed of a real house of his own and built it room by room with words murmured into my hair. Until one night when I lay safe in the circle of his arms, there was a room in his house for me, and I was lost.

Blackout, falling down, lost in love.

And then came the hangover.

I close the sketchbook.

A knock sounds at the door at the bottom of the attic stairs.

A small creak, as if someone has opened it just a crack. "Trix?" a small voice calls hesitantly. It's Ember. "Supper is ready. Mama made pancakes."

"I'm not hungry," I reply, picking up one of the pillows and hugging it to myself.

"They're chocolate chip," Ember adds, as if this might make some difference.

I don't even bother to answer her. Someday she'll be just a sketch in this book, a distant memory that has no hold on me anymore. Eventually she closes the door.

When I sleep I dream of goodbyes.

I wake up ready to run again.

I check my phone and see it's nearly one in the morning. The house is quiet. I can't do this. I can't stay here. I don't know why I thought I could even try for a little while. It's as if the walls of this attic are closing in on me, and everything feels tight and heavy, like maybe it's hard to breathe in this house full of pies and quilts. It feels like Connor is here, the ghost of him looking at all my drawings over my shoulder, and wondering what kind of daughter I am, this strange girl made of sharp edges and secret sketches. I dig out the money and the ring I hid behind the banana crate. When I go downstairs, I'll snag another twenty from Auntie's purse and hit the road. Maybe I can hitchhike back into the city, drift away like flour dust in the tea shop's kitchen.

I change into my old clothes, zipping my hoodie up like it's armor that will protect me from the darkness and isolation that wait for me outside on my own again. I jam the rest of my belongings into my backpack, and I tiptoe down the stairs, wincing every time one of them creaks. I open the door at the bottom slowly, but a thud and a clatter on the other side makes me nearly pee my pants. I step out into the hallway and see a broken plate and what looks like a glob of yellow mush on the floor.

I look up, and Ember is standing in the hallway, her arms wrapped around herself. She must have been trying to come in as I was trying to sneak out. "I thought maybe you could use some pie," she whispers, reaching up and tugging the earbuds out of her ears.

There's a hitch in my chest, a feeling of surprise that she was coming to show me some small kindness without being asked. "Oh. What kind was it?" I know she sees my backpack, and there's no hiding what I was planning to do.

"I thought you might need some lemon meringue." She doesn't call it Never-Lonely Lemon, maybe because it would make me sound even more pathetic than I am for sneaking away in the night without saying goodbye.

"I have to go," I say, my voice cracking a little. I don't know if it's an apology or not, but I feel like I have to say it. "I can't stay."

"I understand," she says. "I make a lot of people uncomfortable."

"It's not you. It's me."

"Isn't that what they all say?" she asks, her mouth twisting a little like maybe she has a sense of humor when she's not hiding from the world.

"I'm not cut out for this. I need to go back to the city."

"You'd rather be on your own? Living in motels and stealing?"

"What do *you* know about it?" I ask her, my temper flaring. I wonder if she can see the shape of her mother's ring in my pocket.

"The caseworker told Mama you were homeless for the last six months. That you ran away from all the foster homes they put you in before that because you didn't like them. And I know that we're not perfect, but we *are* your family. You might give us a chance before you run off again."

"I can't breathe here," I tell her.

"I know what that feels like. Come on," she says, motioning with her hand. "Come outside with me."

I eye her warily. Outside is where I wanted to go, but not with her.

"I swear I won't touch you. Your secrets are safe." She puts her hands in the pockets of her pajama pants.

I wasn't even thinking about her abilities. I wanted to sneak out without being seen.

"Fine," I mutter.

I follow her down to the first floor, where Auntie is sleeping on the couch in front of the television, which is playing some kind of infomercial. "Don't mind her," Ember says. "She sleeps like the dead." I eye Auntie's purse, sitting wide open on the small end table by the front door. She's got a wad of cash in it wrapped up with a rubber band, and I can practically smell it as we pass by.

We step out on the front porch, letting the door creak shut softly behind us. The night air is cool, the sweet scent of roses heavy on the breeze. Ember sits down on the bottom step of the porch, her slim, bare feet in the grass in front of her. I sit down next to her, dropping my backpack. There's just enough space between us so we don't touch. Heat radiates from her skin, along with the faint scent of coconut. She leans back, putting her elbows on the step behind her. "Now look up," she says with a jerk of her chin toward the sky.

I lean back, too, and at first it's hard to believe how many stars are peering down at us. They're tiny spotlights in the sky shining down on me, and the moon is the largest spotlight of all, glowing brightly with a hazy ring of gold around it. The wind rustles through the roses, which make walls on either side of us where they wind around the stair rails, and without prompting, I drink it all in deeply, breathing in until it fills my lungs and loosens that tightness in my chest.

"Is that better?" Ember asks after a few minutes.

I shrug, because I don't know how to put into words the way the stars and the wind make me feel. So I go back to what I do understand. "I still should probably leave." There's a waver in my voice that I don't recognize.

"Leave if you want," Ember says. "I'm going to go get some pie. If you're here when I get back, you can have some."

She treads lightly up the stairs into the house, and she doesn't look back.

It would be so easy to leave. Just to get up and walk. I'm good at leaving. Good at slipping away. I learned it from my mom. She slipped away from me, after all.

But I don't move. I keep looking at the stars looking down at me. Pulling up my sleeve and tracing the constellation of scars on my arm, I wonder at how we never saw the stars in the city. I never imagined that they would be this bright, and I search for the Big Dipper in the sky, hearing Shane's voice in my head when I do, remembering how he told me that long-ago travelers, as well as escaping slaves, used the stars at night to guide them, that the Big Dipper would point them to the North Star. Recalling how he'd once traced my scars with his fingertip, his touch feather-light, whispering, *They're not scars. They're a map. Where will they lead you?*

The fat orange cat appears at my feet and climbs the stairs, twining between my legs. I push him away, but he takes it as an invitation and rubs against my shoulder, his tail flicking in my face. Without warning, it brings back memories of a nearly forgotten evening.

* * *

"Is that what you want for your birthday?" Mom asks as we stand in front of the pet-shop window. There are white, fluffy kittens with gray-tipped ears and paws nestled together in a wicker basket lined with soft flannel.

"Aren't they cute?" I sigh, pressing my face to the window. My tenth birthday is right around the corner, and sometimes, if Mom is feeling restless, we take a bus across town and walk down Harper Street and look at fancy things through the shop windows. For her birthday, I stole a butter-soft leather handbag after she admired it for weeks on end, lingering glances and fogged breath against the display-window glass.

But a purse isn't like a cat. I know that you need an apartment to have a cat. They won't let us have one in the motel. But that doesn't stop me from wanting one.

"They are beyond cute. I will take all of them, please." Mom laughs, pretending to hold out her hands for the kittens.

I smile. "Maybe two, and then they'd never be lonely." One of the kittens squeezes out of the pile and stretches, its pink tongue peeking out as it yawns. It's warm, so I push up my sleeves, the skin on my arms still smooth and perfect.

Mom is feeling silly. "Let us vow that we shall never have a cat until we can get one like this." She leans forward and checks the barely visible price card tucked next to the basket, her eyes widening. "A registered Persian for five hundred dollars."

My face heats. "I'm sorry," I say. "I didn't know." The kitten notices our presence, and it approaches the window to examine us with its ice-blue eyes.

"Don't say sorry," Mom says. "If you really want one, we'll get one someday."

No, we won't. Five hundred dollars is weeks of rent. It is the distance between the sun and moon. Even if I stole one, we'd never have a place to keep it. You need a real home for that, not a weekly rented motel room. I remain silent, looking at our reflections instead of the kittens now. I cut my own bangs, and they are uneven, but Mom said I look cute. She even cut bangs for herself, so we look alike and I don't feel stupid anymore.

"Hey," Mom says, nudging my shoulder. "Just try it. Like making a wish. Say we'll get one someday. I promise you it will happen."

The kitten presses its tiny pink nose against the glass to say hello. I place my finger on the other side, as if it could feel my touch. I close my eyes because you can't make a wish with your eyes open. Wishes don't want to be seen, Mom told me once. "We'll get one someday," I say. "And we'll live in a big house, and you'll never have to work again."

"You're a good kid," Mom murmurs, putting her arm around my shoulders. "Let's go inside and ask to hold one. We'll need to practice."

Ember returns with two plates of pie, pulling me out of my memory. She hands me one without a word, careful that our fingers don't touch as the plate transfers ownership.

I wonder what will happen if I eat the pie. If I will feel like someone else, someone who doesn't ache inside. Someone who pets kittens and makes wishes with her eyes closed. Someone who doesn't run away.

I take a bite. Lemon. Never-Lonely Lemon.

It's a bright burst of citrus at first, then an empty tang follows, the feeling you get when the door closes as someone walks out. But the fluffy meringue softens it somehow, like someone else holding you back, keeping you from screaming at that closed door. The emptiness fades slowly with each bite.

Ember eats lemon, too. We eat pie together, not speaking, just looking at the stars. The orange cat lies down on my feet like some kind of anchor so that I can't drift away like I want to.

After a while, I feel my flight instinct dulling. "I'm going to bed," I say, glancing up at the sky again. Something about the stars makes me uneasy, and I shift under their gaze. I just want to go back inside and curl up with my sketchbook. I want to look through it until I feel like me again. I don't know which me, the one who wished for kittens or the one who runs away.

"You're staying?" Ember asks, laying down her fork.

"For now," I reply.

SIX

IT'S MORNING WHEN I REALIZE what the stars were telling me last night. All my life I've felt unseen, forgotten. But when I gazed up at the stars, they were looking right back down at me. I never felt so visible in my life, as if the universe was telling me, *There you are, Trix McCabe. Abandoned. Thief. Drifter. We see you now.*

It's both beautiful and frightening to feel like you're being seen, truly, for the first time.

I don't think I like it.

I settle in at the bottom of the attic stairs, the door barely cracked open, to learn the routine of the McCabe women on their day off. From this vantage point, I have a clear view of the staircase that leads to the second floor, and no one can go up or down without me noticing. This attention to detail, to routines, to little quirks, is one of the things that has kept me alive for the last seventeen years.

Auntie, having retired to her bedroom while Ember and I

ate pie last night, rises at seven and goes downstairs wearing a floral robe, her gray hair in two braids down her back. At seven thirty, she goes outside. The rest of the house is silent. They must be sleeping in.

Thinking the coast is clear, I see my opportunity to sneak down to use the only bathroom near the kitchen, treading carefully on the ancient, creaking staircase. I round the corner and tiptoe through the living room and dining room, to the bathroom that hides neatly behind a narrow door between the dining room and kitchen.

I nearly jump out of my skin when I see Mia at the kitchen work table, placidly sipping coffee like she's been waiting there all night for me to have to pee. It's then that I notice the back staircase that leads down to the kitchen. Damn it, I can't believe I missed that.

"Good morning!" Mia chirps, clearly thrilled to have me all to herself.

I nod, still unsettled by how she got down here without me knowing, and dart into the bathroom.

As soon as I come out, Mia accosts me about going thrift shopping for some new clothes.

"I want to stay here," I reply.

"Would you like something to eat? Let me make you breakfast."

"I'm not hungry."

If she's frustrated, Mia doesn't show it. She keeps smiling, and I back away slowly, as if sudden movement might startle her. Her cheerfulness is unnerving. I creep back up to my hiding place to see what else unfolds.

When Auntie comes back inside with eggs from their chickens at eight o'clock, she says something to Mia about Mr. Ruiz coming over to harvest the corn on the fields over by Ruger Creek before she settles herself in front of the television, the sound cranked to a deafeningly high volume.

At exactly nine o'clock, the house phone rings, and Mia answers it before the second ring can wail, hissing at Auntie, "Shhh! Turn the TV down!" So Mia was not just waiting for me, she was waiting for a call.

I lean as far forward as I dare, barely inching open the attic door farther to hear exactly what's being said.

"Hello, Ms. Troy. Yes, I've been waiting for your call. Things are great.

"Uh-huh, we'll enroll her on Monday like we agreed.

"She's all settled in her new room. I thought she'd have more things with her. Clothes and the like.

"Uh-huh.

"Uh-huh.

"No, of course it's not a problem. We'll go shopping today.

"Yes, of course. Yes, I'm aware that shoplifting has been a problem in the past.

"We're so happy to have her.

"Yes, I've got the home visit in my calendar. We'll be glad to see you again.

"Thank you. Thank you so much."

When Mia hangs up the phone, she tells Auntie with a forced cheeriness, "I think that went well. I'm a little nervous about the home visit, but I'm sure things will smooth out by then, right?"

Auntie only grunts in response.

I don't blame her.

By ten o'clock Ember and Mia leave to go shopping, and Auntie is fossilized on the couch for a day of binge-watching made-for-TV movies. I listen absently to the sounds of dramatic montages and commercials for laundry detergent and minivans.

By noon, I'm bored enough that I return upstairs to wander around the attic bedroom, looking for pieces of Connor. I doubt I'll ever know why we never met in real life. Mom's not exactly here to volunteer information, and from what I can gather from Mia, she was as in the dark as I was about our mutual existences up until my social worker found her. But if he was like any of the other men Mom associated with, my guess is he was a loser. Perhaps Mia and Auntie don't know as much about him as they thought. All I unearth in my search for the real Connor is a worn baseball glove underneath the bed with the initials *C.M.* inked into it. I file this information away with everything else I've gathered so far.

Then I sit on the staircase and draw with a plain number-two pencil I found in my new desk. Mostly loose, pale sketches of roses and my feet in the grass. One of a fat orange cat who I have discovered is named Bacon. I wish I had some other pencils, though, and maybe some charcoal, and some pastels. But I make do with what I have—like I always do.

At one o'clock, I scurry down the stairs, pass a napping Auntie, and steal some leftover chocolate-chip pancakes from the refrigerator. On my way back upstairs, I pause and examine the shrine on the mantel, photographs of Ember at every stage of life. Some include Mia. They go back to the day Ember was born, and all the way up to what's clearly a recent selfie they took in front of the roses. As I scan the photographs, I realize that I am looking for Connor's face. I am looking for a picture to add to my small collection of facts about him. Pictures, sketches, even scribbled drawings have always been a way for me to build stories and memories even when something is gone. But then Auntie snorts in her sleep, and I scurry back to the attic steps.

Mia and Ember return around four in the afternoon, giggling together at some private joke. Auntie's been sniffling at some melodramatic scene in one of her movies, but when they get home she claims she's not crying; it's just that those gluten-free muffins Mia made this morning smell so damn bad.

I laugh, and then shut my door before they can hear me.

When everything gets quiet after dinner, which I also rejected attending, I come downstairs to get something to eat on my own. I have that tight feeling in my chest again, and another slice of that Never-Lonely Lemon sounds pretty good right about now. I freeze in the kitchen doorway, though, realizing that Mia and Ember are still in there, whispering and snickering together. Mia is finishing a braid in Ember's freshly washed hair, pinning it up so it makes a crown in front of her cloud of curls. They're both in their pajamas, and if they hadn't seen me, I would've backed right out of there before I interrupted their mother-daughter moment.

But Mia's eyes latch on to my shadow in the doorway, "Trix!" she calls as I attempt to back away. "I'm glad you came down. Are you hungry?"

"No," I lie. I can't stop myself. It's like I say the exact opposite thing she wants to hear just because I can.

"Why don't you let me give you a trim?" Mia asks, undaunted. Ember slides off the tall kitchen stool and gestures for me to take it. There are combs and scissors and hair creams on the kitchen work table. The air smells of coconut.

"I don't need a trim," I say automatically, though even as I do, I remember the bangs that I cut myself. How they'd been crooked, but Mom had loved them anyway. I touch the ends of my hair, dry and brittle. How long has it been since I had a haircut?

"Okay," Mia says, moving to put the stool away.

"Just a trim," I say quickly. "Nothing weird."

Mia presses her lips together, like she's trying not to smile. "Okay," she agrees. "Just a trim."

I climb up on the old stool and let her comb through my hair. She uses a plastic spray bottle to dampen it and continues to brush with a steady rhythm, gentle enough that it makes me close my eyes and enjoy the sensation of someone taking care of me. I listen to the steady snick of the scissors as she trims my long hair.

Ember leaves while Mia is trimming, her footsteps light and brisk. I wonder if she is pissed I interrupted them.

"You know," Mia says quietly, her voice just as gentle as her brushing, "Connor cut his own hair once. It was awful. He had this thick, dark hair, but it stuck out over his ears when it got too long. So one day, when he was about nine, Auntie was gone, and he cut it himself with an old pair of school scissors. You know, the safety ones?" She laughs.

I listen, my shoulders growing tight now that she's interrupted the quiet I was enjoying.

"Anyway, it was a total hack job. He'd gotten nearly down

66

to the scalp in the front but there were these awful wisps in the back. I laughed until I cried when I saw him. So when Auntie got home, she had no choice but to buzz it all off so it would grow back evenly. But you know Auntie, she couldn't let a joke die, and every time his hair got too long, she'd yell, 'Hide the safety scissors!'"

Ember returns at the end of the story, carrying a bright-pink laundry basket loaded with folded clothes and a generic plastic bag with a pair of brown leather boots inside. She sets them on the work table in front of me.

"We found some great deals at the vintage stores," Mia says. "Next time you should come with us so you can try things on. I'm just glad Ember was there to pick things out. She's the one with the eye for fashion." She sets the scissors down on the work table next to the basket. "All done. Give us a turn so we can see how I did."

I can't stop looking at the basket of clothes, freshly washed and folded. Things I never asked for. Just kindness, freely given, like the gentle stroke of a brush on my hair. It makes my throat tight like my shoulders, and I bolt out of the kitchen, abandoning the new clothes and boots before I do something embarrassing like cry.

Later that night when I creep back down the attic stairs to look for the pie I'd forgotten earlier when I had my impromptu haircut, I find the basket of clothes and the pair of boots outside the attic door, waiting for me.

As I step over them, I can hear classic rock playing on the radio downstairs in the kitchen. There, I find Mia rolling out dough for pie crusts, her face smudged with flour and one long red curl hanging down by her cheek. Damn, this woman never sleeps.

I would retreat again, but I haven't eaten since those leftover pancakes, so I press on.

"Hungry?" Mia asks, smiling at me. She doesn't mention that I ran away earlier, or that my haircut, nearly three inches off the ends and some gentle layers, makes me look ten times better than I did when I arrived. For once I don't have the urge to cover it up with a hood. "I just finished a batch of muffins. Apple-cinnamon." She studies my face a moment longer. "Or there's plenty of pie. A slice of lemon, maybe?"

Some obstinate part of me twinges, and even though it's what I really wanted, I ignore the offer of pie and cross to the cooling racks by the sink that hold row after row of enormous, fat, fluffy muffins. "Why are you baking so late?" I ask, my stomach rumbling loud enough that I'm willing to brave another conversation.

She beams again, probably because I actually instigated some kind of conversation. "I usually get up around four and make the muffins and the scones, and then do the pies late morning in the shop kitchen while Auntie watches the dining room. But Auntie's going to take you to school tomorrow morning to get you enrolled because I've got some bakery orders that I can't put off, and I need the industrial-grade oven to finish them. I thought if I got a head start on the muffins and pies tonight, tomorrow would be a little less chaotic." She smiles at me. "Besides, I couldn't sleep, anyway. It's been an exciting couple of days. How about you? What are you still doing up?"

"I was hungry."

"You should've come down when we had supper," Mia says, and though it ought to sound like a scolding, it sounds more like

68

a gentle worry. "Or let me reheat something for you when I cut your hair."

"I was tired at suppertime," I tell her, which is mostly true. I'd napped after she and Ember returned from shopping. It's as if after six months of tossing and turning and checking and recheck-ing lonely motel-room locks, my body finally decided that it's time to catch up on all that missed sleep.

Mia smiles sympathetically. "Sure. Teenagers need a lot of sleep. Connor used to sleep till noon every weekend when he was your age." When she's rolled out the pie dough to a thin, pale circle like a moon, she lays it out on a piece of wax paper, and then puts another sheet of wax paper on top of it.

I lean against the kitchen counter and pick up one of the muffins, blowing on it a little. I've noticed that while the rest of the farmhouse is dusty and covered in piles of various objects, the kitchen is spotless. I wonder if this is a difference in Auntie's and Mia's personalities. The rest of the farmhouse is Auntie's, but the kitchen belongs to Mia.

"Your dad was really great," Mia continues as I take a bite out of the muffin. "Everybody loved him. He was so funny. And he had this laugh that was just infectious. You've probably got his sense of humor." She scoops out another big handful of pie dough from her mixing bowl and molds it into a ball on the work table.

I shrug. I wait for her to tell me something more about him, some story that will bring him closer to me, to the McCabes that I am supposedly a part of. But she does not. She turns her questions back to me.

"How about your mom? Ms. Troy said her name was

Allison. Allison Fiorello?" The way she says Mom's name with that hesitancy reveals a lot to me. She must not know a lot about my mom or my past, other than the warnings Ms. Troy gave her. Mia doesn't look at me when she asks, "Did she have a good sense of humor?" Mia picks up the rolling pin and begins to roll out another crust. She's too casual. It's obvious that she's dying for any bit of information I'll throw her way.

"Yeah, she played this funny prank where she left one day and didn't come back."

Mia glances up at me.

"Funny, huh?"

She stacks her new crust on top of the wax paper from the one before, then layers another sheet of wax paper over it. "I'm sorry."

"You don't have to be. You didn't do it," I reply, finishing off the muffin. I can't say that I think Mom left because she could never believe that I would forgive her. And she could never forgive herself for everything she'd done. I'm still hungry, so I reach for another muffin, figuring Mia will probably feel guilty enough for prying that she won't mention I'm eating what's supposed to be sold in the shop tomorrow.

"But you haven't heard from her or anything?" Mia prods. "Ms. Troy said—"

"Can we not talk about it?" I ask.

Mia grabs another ball of dough from her mixing bowl. "Sure. Of course. We've got all the time in the world to get to know each other, right?"

I take a bite of muffin. Damn, these are good. I can see why the bakery is popular, even for people not looking for magic pie.

"So what would you like to talk about?" she asks.

I inspect the muffin more closely. "What's in these? They're not going to make me fall in love with a cow or anything, are they?"

Mia laughs. "The muffins are safe. So are the scones and the cakes."

"Just the pies are funny?" I ask.

"Just the pies."

"So what do you put in them?"

"When I was little, my grandma had the same gift. And she told me, just think of the flavors. How do they make you feel? Lemon, it's kind of sour, kind of tangy, like that lonesome feeling you get when you feel left out, like everyone's life is moving around you but you're just standing still, alone. And blueberry, well it's got that heavy sweetness that you feel after your heart breaks. It hurts like hell, and it slows you down, but there's still that sweetness of the love you had underneath."

"Yeah, but what do you put *in* them?" I ask. "Are you like the happy feelings dealer of Rocksaw? Am I going to get addicted if I have another piece?"

Mia makes a face like the question stings. "I swear there's nothing in them but a little bit of magic. Nothing that could hurt you. Just regular pie ingredients. There's no fairy dust or anything," she says.

"But you said yesterday at the tea shop that they had a secret ingredient."

"The secret ingredient is being a McCabe. I just put that feeling in them, and a little bit of hope that they might make things better for someone. I suppose I could do it with anything, but I like making pies the best."

I eye the crusts suspiciously. I'd seen that crying woman, Ella, perk up after eating three pieces of Bracing Blueberry, and I'd felt quite a bit better myself after the Never-Lonely Lemon on the front steps with Ember. So I believe that they work. I've just never met anyone else who has such a peculiar gift. And the idea of it being hereditary, some strange gene running down generations of McCabe women who were only fictitious creatures to me before yesterday morning, well, that's pretty damn weird to think about. My family has only ever been me and Mom, so this sudden connection to other women feels strange.

"So are we witches, or what?"

Mia laughs. "Probably somewhere along the line people thought we were. But now we're called *gifted*. Or just a little odd. Even if you're not technically born a McCabe, the women who marry into the family tend to be a little . . . different. Quite a few of them have been from Cottonwood Hollow, a few towns away. They're known for their strange talents. And the even stranger things that seem to happen around them."

"Ella said the town was skeptical until they ate your pies."

Mia gives a small smile, as if I've given her a compliment. "What about you?" she asks. "I bet there's something special about you, some talent you've had since you were born. Auntie tells fortunes. Ember, the poor dear, she can read more of people than she wants to. Your great-great-grandma could tell a lie so good she could make it come true. *She* won the talent lottery, if you ask me."

I pause, unsure whether or not I should tell her. But I've

already told Ember, and I know after what Ms. Troy said when she dropped me off, Mia probably has a pretty good idea that my gift isn't making rainbows and sunshine. "I can steal things," I reply. "Nobody ever catches me, security cameras or sensors, nothing." Maybe I'm a little bit proud of that, too.

Mia's eyebrows rise, and her mouth twitches, like she's somehow conflicted about this information. She picks up her stack of pie crusts and opens the fridge door to place them on top of an already impressive pile of crusts. When she shuts the door, she turns back to me. "You know," she says. "Ms. Troy only told me a little bit about you. I know things were hard, and that you needed to do whatever you could to get by." She reaches out to touch my hand where it rests on the counter. "But I want you to know that nobody blames you for that."

I pull my hand back from hers, something deep inside me bristling at her words. "I don't need your forgiveness for what I've done," I reply. "I don't feel bad for anything." *And not for stealing your ring, either*, I think.

"I didn't mean that you should," Mia begins. "I only meant that—"

"That I may have been a thief, but you'll forgive me and take me in because I didn't know any better before?"

"No, Trix—"

"I'm not sorry for anything I've done. *Anything.*" I pull away from the counter, from her. From the people in this house, this tangled web of McCabe women who think they know who I am.

And most of all, I pull away from memories of Mom and what I did to her.

73

SEVEN

THE NEXT MORNING IS A mess, which doesn't bode well for my first day of school. Mia, having slept through two alarms, is running around the house with one shoe on and carrying the other, barking orders instead of trilling sweet requests. With less than an hour to get ready, we braved the rodeo that was four women trying to use one bathroom. Mia declares no one is allowed to do their hair or makeup in the bathroom. Get in, pee, brush your teeth, shower, and get out in under fifteen minutes. That's the rule. This isn't hard for me, but when Mia makes the announcement, Ember looks like her world might be ending.

But thanks to Mia and Ember's bargain hunting, I do come downstairs in a new (to me) pair of brown boots, jeans, and a light sweater. The sweater is loose, and a pretty wine color that I would never have picked out myself. It's not the armor of my worn black hoodie, but I'm at least not as exposed as I was in the short sleeves on Saturday. When the brunt of the chaos passes, Mia presses a tube of lip gloss into my hand that she swears will never look as good on her or Ember as it will on me. I'm happy to take it, as it seems like she's not mad at me for last night, and the worst of her morning barking is over.

"Wow," Auntie says, coming out of the kitchen to see me standing awkwardly in the living room with my backpack. I emptied out everything from social services, and Mia filled it with school supplies from the Dollar Tree. Only after she was done with it did I covertly add my sketchbook too. "You clean up good," Auntie says. "Who knew there was a girl under all that mess?"

"Auntie," Mia chides, dusting off her hands on her apron. She beams at me. "You looked pretty before the new clothes and haircut, too," she tells me. She casts a look over at her daughter, who's watching with perceptive green eyes. "Ember picked the sweater, and she was right: the color is lovely on you."

Ember is wearing her earbuds again, listening to something on her phone, but it must be low enough that she still hears her mom, because she blushes and flits away into the kitchen.

While we're waiting for Auntie to finish getting ready to go, I look at the pictures on the mantel again. While I search for the face that supposedly resembles my own, I stumble upon one of Ember and a man helping her to ride a bike. Probably her dad. And another of her holding an ice cream cone with a banner behind her that says *County Fair*.

Mia appears behind me. "That's one of my favorites," she says, pointing to the picture of Ember at the fair. "She dripped ice cream all over herself and then we took her to the petting zoo and the goats licked it off."

I nod, unsure of what to say. I don't know much about county fairs or goats.

"Connor loved the county fair. Especially all the fried food. And the fast rides. He said it wasn't a good time unless there was a chance you'd puke."

I try to imagine him, this man who thought it would be fun to puke. My father.

"Do you have some photos you want to put up here?" Mia asks. "Maybe one of you and your mom?"

There's only one picture left of me and my mom, and it's one I drew on the wall of our room at the Starlite not long after we'd moved in there. A secret portrait that would outlast our time there together. I wanted to remind myself that we would never be a perfect family like the Yangs at the Jasmine Dragon. It would only ever be the two of us.

"I don't have any photos," I tell Mia.

Mia makes a sound of disappointment in the back of her throat, like she's kicking herself for having asked.

But there's no time for Mia to feel bad because it's time to leave. After we pile into the car, Auntie drops off Mia and her trays of muffins and pie crusts at the shop, and then we continue on to school. I'm pretty sure we're going to die before we get there, though. Auntie blows through two stop signs and narrowly misses a mail truck before she parks directly in front of the school in a handicap spot, even though we don't have a permit.

"Auntie—" Ember begins.

"Hush," Auntie bellows. "I'm not walking all the way from kingdom come. I'm old. I deserve this spot."

Ember flicks a glance at me.

I shrug. Whether or not Auntie gets a parking ticket is no skin off my nose.

I follow Auntie and Ember through the parking lot. I notice it's filled with old trucks and battered, dusty four-door sedans. There's even an El Camino with a weathered set of antlers secured to the front grill with baling twine. Then we enter the sprawling school. There are wings here and there like they added on over the years with very little concern about matching colors of brick or architectural styles. There are no metal detectors, no guards. It's nothing like the schools I went to in the city.

It's been almost a year since I was in school regularly, but Auntie assures me Ms. Troy had my records transferred to Rocksaw High. One more year, I tell myself. If I could really stick this deal out, it would only be one more year and then I would be out of here.

In the hall in front of the principal's office, Ember stops before a brightly colored flyer about the homecoming dance. Glancing down the corridor, I see about a million more taped to every vertical surface. It must be a big deal here. Ember glances around to see if anyone else is looking before lightly tugging down the flyer and slipping it between her books. When she notices that I'm watching her, she gives a timid wave goodbye before leaving Auntie and me waiting in front of the principal's office.

Next to the principal's door is a big glass case filled with gold and silver trophies, some dating back ten years or more. But it's a picture inside that catches my eye. Golden skin, golden eyes, curly black hair. Jasper, I think at first. But I lean down and see the small plaque attached to the wide frame. *In Loving Memory of Jesse Ruiz. Senior Class President, Honor Council, Varsity Football, Varsity Basketball, Varsity Baseball, Drama Club, Scholars' Bowl.*

My first thought is that maybe he died from all those extra-curricular activities.

Auntie sees me staring at it and makes a *tsk, tsk* sound. "Too bad. Jesse was a nice boy."

"Is that Jasper's brother?" I ask.

Auntie nods, and she opens her mouth to say more, but a man comes out of the office and declares, "Auntie! A pleasure to see you." He shakes her hand, and then reaches for mine. "Miss McCabe, I'm Principal Lopez. So nice to meet you. Trixie, isn't it?"

"Trix," I reply, pulling my hand away from his after he's pumped it a few times. He has a big belly and a handlebar mustache. He smells faintly of pipe tobacco.

"Trixie's such a cute name," he continues as if he hasn't heard me. "You look like your father. Has anyone told you that? I knew him way back in the day. Good man. Shame he was hit by that train."

I look over at Auntie, my mouth hanging open in shock at this new story. Auntie shrugs. So far I've heard two different theories on how Connor died, and none of the McCabes bat an eye. I shouldn't care what the real story is—after all, I don't want everyone knowing mine—but some part of me wants to know the truth about the man everyone in Rocksaw knew but me. The thing is, I'm not ready to ask anyone. Because once I do that, they'll think they can ask me things. *Where do you think your mom is now? How did you get those scars? Exactly where have you been for the last six months?*

The principal ushers us into his office, and a young, dark-haired man who looks like he spends a lot of time lifting weights at the gym joins us. "Ladies, this is Mr. Jindal, our school guidance counselor. He's been looking over your records, Trixie, and it looks like you're just in time to start your junior year."

"No," I spit out, leaning forward in the uncomfortable wooden chair I'm sitting in. Auntie, sitting in a chair next to me, looks over placidly. "I'm a *senior*. This should be my senior year."

Mr. Jindal purses his lips, riffling through the papers he's brought with him. I watch the corded muscles on his forearms move as he shifts. "Miss McCabe, I can see why you might think that, but your records indicate that you didn't complete your junior year. You don't have enough credits to be a senior."

"But I'm seventeen," I argue.

"Well, yes, but that's not how the system works. You need to have enough credits to graduate with a diploma. It's not a matter of age." He gives me a sympathetic smile.

I feel sick, like I could puke up the blueberry muffin I pinched from one of Mia's trays this morning before realizing that everyone in the house was eating them and no one cared.

Mr. Jindal hurries to add, "But your grades were adequate before you stopped attending classes. And it's only September, so while you're a week or so behind the other students, if you work hard, there's no reason you shouldn't catch up and be able to graduate in two years."

"Two years?" I ask again, my voice sounding pitiful, even to me. One year. One year was the plan. The super-optimistic plan where I didn't run away less than a week into my forced vacation

79

in rural America. I didn't bargain on *two* years. What was the deal again? Graduation or prosecution? Or was it stay in school until I'm eighteen? Because at this rate, I'm going to graduate as a nineteen-year-old. I'll practically be a senior citizen. The same age as Auntie.

Auntie absorbs this information before telling me, "You'll get to be in Ember's class."

Mr. Jindal nods, like this is something to look forward to.

I can't even form words.

The principal continues, handing me a stack of papers. "Here's the schedule for our juniors. Now, we're a small school, but you'll see we have a decent variety of electives. Once you choose those, Mr. Jindal will take you to get your books."

I blindly circle a few classes, handing the schedule over to Mr. Jindal. He looks pleased with my choices.

"And then, Auntie, there's the matter of Trixie's enrollment fees."

"Enrollment fees?" Auntie asks, finishing with a couple of creative swear words. "I thought this was a public school."

"Well, yes, ma'am, but there are certain fees for textbook rentals and technology use . . ." His voice drifts off as Auntie sends him a withering glare.

"I thought we were in America! Free education for everyone!"

"Auntie—" the principal begins again.

"I'll make you a deal," Auntie says. "I won't charge your wife for all those Ardent Apple pies she has delivered. For the next month."

The principal blushes, and Mr. Jindal pretends to be engrossed with his biceps. I remember now from the delivery run with Jasper. One big white house had two apple pies delivered on Saturday. That must have been the principal.

"Sounds fine, Auntie," the principal mumbles, standing up and ushering us out of his office. While he's helping Auntie out of her chair and Mr. Jindal goes to a supply room to get the books I'll need, I swipe the fountain pen on the principal's desk, just because I'm irritated. And maybe because I want to prove to myself what I told Mia last night. I don't feel guilty at all for who I am or what I've done. "I'll take care of Trixie's paperwork, and you can be on your way. I'm sure Mia needs your help."

Auntie cackles as the principal leaves us out in the hall. "He got the shit end of the stick on that one. The Ardent Apples are the cheapest. We'll still come out ahead."

When Mr. Jindal returns with my textbooks, Auntie salutes me goodbye with a grunt and half a wave. Mr. Jindal helps me find my locker and store my school supplies. I keep my backpack with my sketchbook inside it with me. He offers to walk me to my first class, but I shake my head, still unable to find words to express how angry I am at the strange twist this day has taken. So he gives me directions to the first classroom and assures me anyone in class would be happy to help me find my second-period class as well. I shrug like it doesn't matter to me either way.

When he finally leaves me alone, I peel off the prescribed route at the first small empty room with the door propped open. The sign next to it says "ISS," which I know from personal experience stands for "in-school suspension." Inside is a small teacher desk and one student desk. But it's the phone on the teacher desk that catches my eye.

I dart inside, pulling the door shut behind me, and grab the phone. I dial Ms. Troy's number. She had me memorize it last year, even though I swore I'd never need to use it.

Ms. Troy picks up on the second ring, and I don't even bother to say hello. "They said *two years*," I hiss. "Two whole years until I'll graduate."

"Trix?" Ms. Troy asks.

"Yes, it's Trix!" I'm practically shouting now, etching out a diamond on the corner of the desk with my stolen fountain pen. "We made a deal. One more year and then I was free. I didn't sign on for two more years of high school and living in this village."

"Trix, we did make a deal. You get your high school degree, or you get prosecuted as an adult."

"But I thought it was only one more year," I complain.

"Sorry, Trix. You barely have enough credits to be a junior. You can't drop out of school for six months and expect to start back as a senior. You weren't even attending regularly when you were in foster care. You should be grateful they've offered to let you catch up."

The stupid thing is, I did think that I'd be a senior. All this time I was focused on my eighteenth birthday, but that wasn't the end goal. The end goal was my diploma. And that's two years away now. Suddenly the idea of me actually sticking this out seems more ludicrous than ever.

"But once I'm eighteen, the state has no more control over me," I counter.

"Once you're eighteen, you don't need a social worker. But that's not going to end your deal. It's a diploma or prosecution for theft, Trix."

I don't ask the question that's sitting in my gut. What if the McCabes won't have me after I'm eighteen? What if they're only in it for the small stipend that comes with my upkeep and then I'm out on my ass?

"Trix," Ms. Troy says, her voice tired. "Don't give up just because it's hard. You're a bright, resourceful young woman. Enjoy this time. Some people say their high school years were the best years of their lives."

I don't know who those people are, but I'd like to punch them right now.

"Fine," I practically growl. "Bye." I hang up before Ms. Troy has a chance to say goodbye back, as if that somehow gives me the upper hand.

Two. More. Years.

I feel my chest tightening again, like metal bands are constricting around my rib cage.

What was I thinking? Even in passing, it's ridiculous, this thought that I could ever live this deal down. I can't do this. I can't stay here two more years in this little town. I etch out a four-letter word next to the diamond I drew.

Then I head straight out the front door. There's no one to stop me.

This is who Trix McCabe really is. Abandoned. Thief. Drifter.

Anything else is just pretending.

Head down, I march toward the parking lot. I don't know

where I'm going, but as long as it's not here, it's fine with me.

Right when I get to the road outside the school, I'm nearly run over. I leap back as an old Suburban jumps the curb, stopping next to me with a screech. "Thought I might see you here," Auntie cackles, rolling down the window. My heart is beating so hard it might explode out of my chest.

"What are you doing?" I yell. "You nearly killed me!"

"Stop being so damn dramatic," Auntie says with a dismissive wave. "What's your problem now?"

"I didn't sign up for this," I snarl, hoisting my backpack higher on my shoulder. "It was only supposed to be one year."

"Well, you were wrong," Auntie replies, unruffled. "So you have to deal with it. That's part of growing up."

"What do you know?" I sling back. "I grew up a long damn time ago when my mom walked out on me. Maybe before that, even. So don't give me this bullshit."

"You live under my roof, so I'll give you whatever shit I want," Auntie says unflinchingly.

"Maybe I can fix that," I snarl.

"Fine, you little brat. Go back out on the streets. Steal what you want. Run away whenever things get too hard. But don't pretend like that's a good life. Don't pretend what you're giving up here isn't better than that."

"I was *free*. I could go where I wanted, when I wanted. I didn't have to answer to anyone." I point a finger at her like she's the one I don't want to answer to the most. I am furious, and I finally have someone to take it out on. It feels good.

"You were alone, Trix. You were a little girl alone in a big world." She reaches out and snatches my hand. She opens it up with fingers that are surprisingly strong for such an old woman. "Do you see this?" she hisses, examining my palm. Her yellowed nail scrapes across my skin, tracing my lifelines. "It says you're a rose, Trix. And you have to decide if you'll bloom or if you'll wither. Put down roots or you'll die."

"That doesn't even make any sense," I spit out, jerking my hand away. "And I didn't say you could read my fortune."

"Honey, I could read your fortune just by looking at you."

"I didn't want any of this." And I don't know if I mean Rocksaw or the McCabes or my mom or my gift. I just know that I didn't ask for any of it.

"Well, you don't always get what you want. Sometimes you just get what you get. Now go on back to school, or leave town. You choose. You can bloom, or you can wither." And then the crazy old woman peels out, leaving me standing alone on the sidewalk.

My heart is drumming in my chest, and my face feels hot. I keep walking until I hit Main Street, and I follow it all the way to the McCabe Bakery & Tea Shoppe. I want to see it one more time.

The Suburban is already parked in front, and when I look in the windows of the tea shop, I see that they're doing brisk business. Auntie stands at the front counter putting scones in a pink paper box like she hadn't nearly run me over and given me an ultimatum with her weird fortune-telling abilities twenty minutes ago, and Mia comes out of the kitchen balancing a tray with teacups and muffins on it, totally oblivious to how close I am to running again.

I pull up the sleeve of my sweater, look at the scars.

They're not scars. They're a map. Where will they lead you?

I don't know where I'm going. I don't know why I wanted one last look at the stupid tea shop. Everything is muddled, and I'm angry, and deep down below that I realize that I'm hurting, and that part scares me the most because I didn't know it was there. It's more than a phantom pain, it's real, that aching absence of my mom and the Starlite Motel and everything I'd left behind in the city. I yank my sleeve back down again.

"Is everything okay, Trix?" I look up, and Mia is leaning out the front door of the shop. She must have seen me through the windows. "Oh, honey, are you hurt?" She hurries over to me and puts her hands on my face. She smells of lemon and chai, and something motherly that I haven't smelled since the Good Year.

"No," I mutter, pulling away.

"Trix," she says. "I want you to know that what I was trying to say last night, it wasn't that you should be ashamed of what you did. I wanted to tell you that I was grateful." She pauses, strokes my hair. "Grateful that being a McCabe helped you get by."

Being a McCabe has never been a gift to me. I am a survivor, nothing more, nothing less. And I should be on my way again. I should give up on this stupid idea that I can finish school and stay here with these women who think they understand me because we might share some DNA.

I catch a glimpse of Auntie again through the window. This time she's reading someone's palm since Mia's not there to shut her down. I recall the fortune she told for me. *Put down roots or you'll die.* I remember the closed-in walls of Shane's prison. The empty motel rooms. Isn't what I have here better than that?

I don't know if I can keep myself from running again. But I'm going to try. I promise myself. I'm going to try.

Moments pass between us, and Mia is silent, as if she knows something is happening, something that neither of us can force.

Finally, I speak. "I should probably go. I'm late. For school."

"Do you need a ride? I can take you in the Suburban." Mia doesn't say *so I know you're not running away*, but I can see it on her face anyway. Of course she knows what I was about to do. There's no other reason for me to show up here when I'm supposed to be at school.

"No," I tell her. "I can walk."

"Are you sure everything's okay?" Mia asks again.

I nod, hoisting my backpack up higher on my shoulder.

I want that aching emptiness to go away. I can do this. I can put down roots.

EIGHT

I CHECK MY CLASS SCHEDULE again when I make it back to school. It's already time for lunch. Thankfully Mia packed me food, which is in a tin Star Wars lunch box that I'm pretty sure is from the original franchise. I take it to the gym, which apparently serves as the cafeteria from noon to one. The room is filled with folding tables and long benches, and students are seated in strategically clustered groups. A few students sit in the bleachers, either on their phones or working on homework away from the noise and gossip of the lunch tables. The closest tables to the entryway look like they're full of anxious freshmen. I keep walking toward the tables that look most likely to be juniors or seniors.

I remind myself that I'm a junior now. No need to say anything stupid if someone asks me my year. Disappointment sits low in my gut, but I tell myself what Shane always said: *It is what it is.* And then he'd shrug. There's no use fighting what can't be changed.

I don't see Ember at any of the tables, so I sit down at the end of an empty one and start unpacking my food. Truthfully, I'm not sure if she'd want me to sit next to her or not.

I don't have to worry about being alone for long, because someone sits down across from me, setting down their lunch tray with a clatter. "Hey there." I look up to see Jasper Ruiz. Right away, I think of his brother, Jesse, who is forever immortalized in the trophy case near the front door of the school. "I wondered if you were going to grace us with your presence today," he says.

"Well, here I am," I reply, taking out a ham sandwich wrapped in wax paper, a plastic baggie of potato chips, a brownie the size of my palm, and an apple. Underneath the sandwich, in the bottom of the lunch box is a handwritten note that reads *Have a great first day! XOXO*.

It must be from Mia, because I can't see Auntie bothering to leave a pink Post-it in the bottom of my lunch box. Oddly enough, it makes my eyes feel hot.

"Everything okay?" Jasper asks.

"I'm fine," I tell him. "It's these gluten-free muffins that Mia makes. They make my eyes water." There's no muffins around, but Jasper doesn't comment on it.

"Hey, Jasper, what are you doing over here? Don't we usually sit at *that* table, or did I get hit harder than I remember at practice yesterday?" a guy asks, sliding his tray next to Jasper and sitting down. He's tall and broad-shouldered with black dreads nearly to his shoulders. He wears a letter jacket in the school colors, orange and black, for the Rocksaw Tigers. His gaze slides over to me. "Oh, *that's* why. New girl, huh?" He smiles and says to me, "Hi.

I'm Lincoln, but everybody calls me Linc. I'm a junior."

"Trix," I reply. "I'm a junior, too." *Two more years*, I remind myself. I can do this.

"I can't believe they chose fairy tales as the theme for the homecoming dance," a pale blond girl complains, sitting down next to Linc. Without saying a word, they trade food: her sloppy joe for his french fries.

Another girl follows her. "It's dumb, but next year we get to pick, and we'll choose something good." She uses one hand to toss her long, shiny black hair over her shoulder as she sits down next to the blond girl.

Both girls notice my presence as another boy slides onto the bench next to me. The blond girl's eyes widen, and the dark-haired girl's mouth falls open a little. Apparently new blood is something of a shocker here.

My benchmate, however, is oblivious to their surprise. "Hey, guys," he says, juggling a guitar case in one hand and a tray of what looks like half a dozen sloppy joes in the other. "Why are we sitting over here?" He does a double take when he sees me, like I was invisible before. He has longish red hair and dozens of freckles. He sets his guitar down carefully, but his sloppy joes not so much, and they nearly slide into my lunch box. "Sorry, um, is it okay if I sit here?" he asks me.

It's good to know that I've still got that air about me that suggests you should ask for permission to sit next to me. "I guess so," I reply, taking a bite of my sandwich.

The girls next to Linc exchange glances, as if subliminally communicating about the presence of a new girl at the table. "This is Trix," Linc announces to the latecomers. He points at the blond girl. "That's Adalyn." He gestures toward the girl with long, dark hair—"Ramani"—and then over to the red-haired boy—"Grayson."

"You must be the niece from the city that Mia was gushing about last week. My mom and I dropped in to the tea shop to ask about the concession-stand donations, and you were all she could talk about," Adalyn says.

"That's me," I say, able to keep a straight face even though I'm inwardly cringing, wondering what Mia told them about me.

"Are you one of *the* McCabes?" Ramani asks, taking a sip of her chocolate milk as if to fortify herself for the answer. "They're legendary."

"Yeah." I open my chips like I'm not waiting for them to ask about my gift.

"That's great!" Grayson raves, like we're some kind of national treasure gracing the Rocksaw people. "So, can you—?" Grayson asks before ending his question with another bite of sloppy joe.

"Eat lunch with you?" I finish for him, shoving a handful of chips in my mouth. "Yeah."

Adalyn and Ramani shoot each other a look of uncertainty.

"Trix helped me with pie deliveries on Saturday," Jasper offers. Clearly his opinion of me carries weight because they all visibly relax. The girls start eating and discussing homecoming again, and Linc asks Jasper if he's ready for the game on Friday.

I watch them while I eat, and it's clear that while they're a tight little group, Jasper is their hub. They look to him for his opinion about everything from the homecoming theme to what will be on the chemistry quiz next week. He laughs and jokes, and it's obvious that everyone adores him and he adores everyone. Jasper the golden boy.

"Are you going to go?" Adalyn asks, pulling me out of my observations.

"What?"

"Are you going to go? To homecoming?"

"Why, is that a big deal?" I fold the small pink note from Mia into triangles.

"Is it a *big deal*?" Adalyn gasps, putting her hand over her heart.

"Some of us feel more strongly about it than others. But it's almost two months away." Ramani laughs. "Not everybody has an inspiration board of dresses yet, Adalyn."

"Well, I was only asking," Adalyn huffs. "I'm trying to get to know her."

"Probably not," I reply, stuffing my empty food wrappers back into my lunch box and closing it with a snap.

"Do you have other plans?" Adalyn persists. "It's the last weekend in October."

"No," I reply without added explanation. It's best to cut these kinds of conversations off.

"Is Ember going?" Grayson asks around the guitar pick he's holding with his teeth. He's taken his guitar out of its case and is tuning it while he listens to the conversation. "You're cousins, right?"

"Yeah, we're cousins. I don't know if she's going. She

hasn't said anything about it to me."

"I don't think she says anything to *anyone*," Adalyn says.

I spear Adalyn with a glare. "Ember talks fine. Maybe she just doesn't want to talk to *you*." I get up and leave the lunch table. I wander around until I find my locker again, and by the time I get there I hear footsteps behind me, and I turn to see Jasper jogging to catch up.

"Jeez, you're elusive," he says, grinning at me. "I looked all over for you."

I look both ways down the hall. It's mostly empty because everyone else is still at lunch. "Yeah, it's a real big place. Hard to find me in this crowd."

"Well, I started in the library because that's where Ember usually eats lunch."

"So that's where she was," I say, opening my locker. It makes sense. Ember doesn't seem to like being around other people.

"You made quite an impression on my friends."

"Great."

"Are you always this prickly?" he asks. "I mean, *we're* bound forever by law of pie delivery, but not everyone has that kind of special relationship with you early on. You might scare off the less bold." He actually winks at me.

"I'm not here to make new friends," I reply. "I'm just here to graduate."

"So you must prefer *old* friends. Let me guess. The ones who can't call you because you don't have a phone signal?"

"Those would be the ones."

He nods, like he's considering something. "Well, if you give me a couple minutes after school, I can take you to Cedar Mountain before practice so you can check your messages. Maybe send a few texts or even make a call if the stars align."

"Would you?" I ask, embarrassed by the desperation in my voice. Usually I wouldn't look to anyone else for what I need, but I feel like if I could talk to Charly, somebody from my old world, maybe I could figure out this tangled mess.

"Anything for a fellow pie-delivery veteran." He starts walking away backward, the heels of his cowboy boots clicking against the linoleum. "I'll meet you by the front doors at three o'clock," he says. "Don't be late."

The only bright spot between lunch and my potential phone call with Charly is an art elective. I marvel at the array of materials in the small, sunny room. There's a supply closet with rows of charcoal pencils, colored pencils, pastels, watercolors, acrylics, and oil paints. I've never painted, but I've always wanted to try.

While the teacher is walking around checking on student projects, I creep into the supply closet, my hands whisper-soft as I touch the charcoal pencils. I slide two up one voluminous sweater sleeve and a slim carton of pastels in the other.

When I leave the closet, I see the teacher. "Well, hello!" she says cheerfully. She's got blond hair and glasses and looks faintly familiar. "I'm Miss Riggs. You must be Trixie."

"Trix," I correct her. "Trix McCabe."

"That's right," she says. "It was you, in McCabe's Bakery."

Then I realize that she's Ella, the woman who ordered the Bracing Blueberry pie on Saturday. Not only is she wearing glasses, she looks considerably better now that she's not bawling and honking her nose into tissues.

"How'd the blueberry work out for you?" I ask.

"Good. It was the perfect cure." She blushes a little as she motions for me to sit down at the end of a long table. I guess that's the thing about small towns. You never know when somebody you met bawling at a café is going to turn out to be your art teacher. "But enough about that, right? You're a junior, so we let you pick your projects; we only ask that you try a different medium every quarter. Do you have any experience working with clay?"

"No," I reply.

"Would you like to try it out?" she asks. "We got a grant for a kiln last year. Grayson could show you how to use the pottery wheel."

I look over and see him putting on some kind of messy apron. He smiles and gives me a small, encouraging wave. His is the only face I recognize other than Ella's—I mean, Miss Riggs's. "I want to paint," I reply.

"Sure, that's great. Why don't I get you some paper, and you can start working on some preliminary design ideas. Are you thinking oils? Acrylics? Watercolors?"

While Miss Riggs is digging around in the storeroom, I slide my pilfered charcoal pencils and pastels into my backpack.

"You can use this for today," Miss Riggs says when she returns. She hands me an ancient sketchbook nearly filled with mediocre work, and some nub-length pencils and charcoal. I find a couple of clean sheets of paper near the back, but they're wrinkled, and the whole thing is dusty. "I know," Miss Riggs says, sighing. "It's not the nicest paper. Let me get you a copy of the supply list for class. We have block scheduling, you know, so you won't be back until Wednesday. Make sure you have what you need by then."

The supply list is a lot longer than I expected. And judging by the Dollar Tree school supplies Mia sent with me today, the McCabes aren't exactly flush with cash to buy all these fancy materials. "What about all the stuff in the supply closet?" I ask.

Miss Riggs makes a face, like this part is uncomfortable for her. "Since it's an elective, and art's on a tight budget, students have to bring their own supplies. What's in the closet is what students have already contributed. Once you bring your share, you'll add them to the supply closet. Except for your sketchpad and canvas. Those are only for you."

I think of my sketchbook in my backpack. There's plenty of room in it, but I'd never pull it out and use it here. The thought of other people seeing pictures of Mom or Shane or Wendy makes me uncomfortable. They're mine. Just mine.

Even though part of me wants to turn inward, to focus on those pictures in my sketchbook, I'm drawn to the possibility of working with the charcoal, which I haven't used in months. It doesn't take long for inspiration to strike, and soon I'm lost to the world around me. As I begin sketching the preliminary work, I realize this is what I'd wanted to draw from the first time I laid eyes on it. My charcoal stick is sure, fluid strokes as I make out the front peak of the big, rambling farmhouse. The sun will drench the house in warm light, but there will still be shadows in the dense roses, night-dark between the thorny stems and leaves. I use the softest charcoals to deepen the shadows, my fingers to blend the shades, a chunky white eraser to highlight where the sun will hit the house.

Soon, my hands are black with charcoal, my ideas smeared across the fresh white paper. I've got the sketch finished by the end of class. There's not a lot of detail on it, but it's enough to frame the picture in my mind, open up the possibilities of what would be light and what would be shadow.

"That's really lovely," Miss Riggs says, stopping to stand behind me. "Such a mastery of shading. You have a lot of talent. How long have you been drawing?"

"Since I was a kid," I reply, putting down my charcoal stick. I feel myself blushing, which embarrasses me more than the attention she's giving me.

"Did you take a lot of art classes at your old school?" she asks.

"No. I only sketch on my own." I briefly recall scratching out a picture of a flower in the blank pages in the back of a bible in a motel-room end table when I was five. Mom said it was beautiful, but we shouldn't draw in that book. So we scrounged enough change to get a tiny spiral notebook from the QuikMart down the street. I stole a glittery, pink pencil with a panda-shaped eraser on top on the way out the door, Mom and I still not quite aware of how quick my hands really were. Or what they would mean to us in the future.

"Really? I'd love to see some of your other work." Miss Riggs's words bring me back to the present.

"I don't usually show anyone." I feel a twinge of unease. I don't like people prying into my past.

"What a shame. You're a very talented artist."

"It's not real art. It's just something I like to do on my own."

"It's still art, even if no one can see it." Miss Riggs gives me a small smile, as if she could possibly understand what drawing means to me. "I hope you'll reconsider someday. Maybe when you feel a little more at home here."

I shrug, thinking of the pages in my sketchbook in my backpack. I wasn't lying when I said they weren't art. They aren't. They are memories. The most precious ones I have.

When three o'clock rolls around, I hurry from Family and Consumer Science class to the front of the school. I wait impatiently next to the trophy case, scanning the crowds of students for Jasper. It feels weird to wait in front of his dead brother's memorial. Eventually the students disperse, and I'm left standing alone in front of the trophy case like some kind of loser. To look busy, I examine the trophies. I check the time on my phone. It's a quarter after three. The photo of Jasper's brother catches my eye again. I lean down to look at it more closely. They could be twins, except that Jesse doesn't have a scar like Jasper.

"Handsome guy, huh?" Jasper asks from behind me.

I jump, banging my head into the trophy case, which triggers a string of curse words that would have made Auntie proud.

Jasper gives me the smile that doesn't reach his scar. "I didn't make you for being skittish," he says.

"I'm not," I reply, rubbing my head.

"Checking out my brother?" he asks, that smile still in place.

"I was reading what it said on his picture," I reply.

"All-around perfect student. Amazing athlete. Great brother."

I don't know what to say to that.

"Hunting accident," Jasper says. "That's how he died. He was alone in the woods. He forgot to put the safety on his gun."

I'm transfixed by Jasper's mouth, the way he speaks slowly and clearly, like he's recounting a story that's begun to grow old to him. I suppose talking about a dead brother might be awkward for anyone.

My silence makes Jasper uncomfortable, and he shifts under my gaze. I'm sure he's tired of the questions about his brother, so I only reply, "Nice outfit."

"Thanks," he says, relief visible on his face. Jasper's changed into shorts, cleats, a T-shirt with the sleeves cut off, and a pair of shoulder pads for football. He carries a Tigers helmet in one hand.

"It must get you a lot of ladies around here," I add. "Do you play pitcher or what?"

"Running back." He grins, his scar tugging on his eye.

"I don't follow sports things."

"I figured. So you still want me to take you to Cedar Mountain?"

I cross my arms. "I will go to your make-believe mountain if it means I can get a phone signal. Hell, I'll go anywhere. Point the way."

We both laugh, Jasper's face losing that tight, controlled look from before. It's nice to laugh again, like I used to with Shane and Charly. Even though we don't know much about each other, Jasper makes me feel like myself again, who I was before I was always running.

I follow him around the back of the school and realize he's

not lying about Cedar Mountain because suddenly I spot it—there's a huge hill behind the football field. As we walk past the field, the rest of the football team is arriving in their practice gear, some stretching out and others standing in small groups drinking from water bottles and shooting the shit.

Nearly every one of them stops and nods at Jasper as we pass, some shouting hello, others asking who his new girlfriend is, and a few warning him to get back before Coach Mason arrives. He waves them all off, and we climb the hill together. It's covered in tall grass and short cedars, but there's a dirt path worn in the front supporting Jasper's story that it's used as a conditioning tool for the football team.

"Everybody likes you," I say as we climb. The path is narrow enough that as we walk, Jasper's shoulder pads bump against me now and then.

"Not *everybody*," he protests.

"Yes, everybody."

He shrugs. "It's a small town. It's not like there's anybody here who doesn't know me."

"Yeah, but just because they *know* you doesn't mean they have to *like* you."

He shrugs again.

"I'm not making fun of you," I add, thinking of how he'd called me prickly earlier. "I'm only making an observation."

"People might like you, too, if you didn't shut them down so quickly."

It's my turn to shrug. "I'm not used to all this small-town

interest. In the city, people pass by each other every day, and they don't ever say hi, exchange names, life stories. Doesn't it make you feel claustrophobic?"

"Sometimes," Jasper admits.

We reach the top of the hill. Someone left two folding lawn chairs and an empty six-pack of beer, the empties replaced neatly in the cardboard carton. "Nice," I say. There's a ring of stones with a burned area that looks like it's been used as a campfire.

"It's a hangout spot when it's not being used as a tool for torture."

"Ah," I say. "So, is it okay for me to sit here and make a call, or is your football team going to start running up and down this hill at any moment?"

"It's Monday, so we're running lines on the practice field. You're safe for today."

"Good to know."

"Good luck with your call," he says, nudging the tip of his cleat in the red-brown dust of the worn path.

"Thanks. And thanks for telling me about this place."

"Hey, so you know, I'll be at that same table tomorrow for lunch."

"Got it."

"You should come back. I'll hold Adalyn at bay if she gets too nosy."

"Isn't nosiness a part of your small-town charm here in Nowheresville, USA?"

"It is," he agrees. "But I'll defend you from it. Pie-delivery veterans stick together." With that, he turns and jogs back down the hill.

"My knight in shining armor!" I yell down the slope.

I can hear his laughter, even from here.

NINE

I HOLD MY BREATH AS I dial Charly's number, as if the two bars of signal might disappear if I do so much as exhale. The phone rings once.

"Trix!" she answers. "I can't believe it's you. Are you okay? I've tried calling a couple of times, but I got sent to voice mail." Charly's voice is like sunshine, like too much vodka, like a whole Never-Lonely Lemon pie.

"Yeah, I'm fine. I'm with my aunt." I can't believe it, but I'm smiling when I say it.

"Where?"

"A couple hours north of the city."

"Jesus, you're not even in the *city* anymore?"

"No. I'm in Rocksaw. It's pretty tiny."

"Rocksaw? I've never even heard of it. I've been so worried about you. I'm sorry about the cops. Mel tipped them off. Don't worry, I gave him an earful for you."

"Mel?" I ask, stunned.

"Yeah. Apparently once he knew you were signed on for another week, he called the cops. I guess they'd been around, asking about you. I grilled him about it and he said he thought you'd be better off with social services since your mom never came back."

That deep well of anger opens up, the one that I've spent a year trying to fill in. "He didn't have any right to do that," I choke out. "I was fine on my own."

"Oh, Trix," Charly sighs. "I know. And I'm sure Mel pocketed your rent money, too. But you'll find a way out. You always do."

I don't tell her that I made a plea deal, that I'm required to stay here for at least two more years. I don't say that today an old woman read my fortune and now, beyond all logical reason given my history, I'm doing my damned best to make sure I bloom and don't wither. I am trying to stay in one place.

Charly interprets my silence as agreement, and continues. "I have to tell you something. Shane called. He wants you to be here when he gets out."

"What?" I ask, my throat tightening up to the point where I can no longer breathe.

"He's up for early parole for all his good behavior. He finally finished his GED—did I tell you that?"

I can't make my mouth move, form words. Shane is coming home.

"He wants to see you, Trix."

"No. He doesn't."

* * *

104

"Trix?" Shane's voice is only a murmur in the big, cement-block-lined room. "How'd you get in here?"

"I stole Charly's ID so I could get in for family visitation day." We look alike enough that it worked.

He shakes his head, and I don't know if he's angry or worried.

"Shane," I choke out. "I am so sorry about what happened. And so sorry it took me this long to get to you. Things have been—"

"Stop," he whispers. The other men near him shift in their seats, leaning over to talk quietly to wives, mothers. "It's done. We're over."

"What do you mean?" I ask, starting to reach for his hand, needing some human connection in a world that has left me suddenly alone.

"Miss," a guard warns. "No touching. Hands to yourself, please."

I pull my hands back toward my side, the metal of the table cold beneath my skin, terrified that I've almost done something to get me separated from Shane so quickly. Mom left a month ago. Social services tried to take me into custody again when someone at school tipped them off. I'd barely escaped out room 7's bathroom window with my sketchpad, leaving a dent in the drywall right below the sill.

"Shane," I whisper. "Please."

"Charly was supposed to tell you. It's over between us. We can't do this, Trix." He leans back and rubs one hand over his shaved head.

"Charly's not at the Starlite," I tell him, clasping my hands together. Maybe I want to pray to a god who's never seen me before. Maybe I'm just trying to hold myself together. "She and Vince went somewhere."

"Damn it!" Shane swears, fisting his hands. "I told her not to trust that guy. He's trash. He'll screw her over and leave her. Tell her to come home."

"Shane, I'm not there anymore either. At the Starlite, I mean. I'm hiding. The police are looking for me. Mom disappeared. She just left." *I don't yet know how to describe that phantom pain that her leaving has given me. I am still reeling, still looking for something solid to grasp.* Let it be Shane. Please, Shane. Let it be you.

Shane leans forward and slides his hands across the table, puts them over mine. He knows we can't touch. I want to pull away, to keep the guard from seeing what he's done, but Shane won't let go. "Keep running. And stay away from the Starlite or they'll find you." *His thumb strokes the tops of my knuckles, as soft as a goodbye kiss.*

The guard comes to break us apart, the forbidden grip of Shane's fingers the last connection to someone who loved me, who cared what happened to me. Visiting time is over if you break the rules.

"Get out of here," *Shane tells me, his face contorted as if the words are made of broken glass. The guard hauls him to his feet. Shane is pushing me away, as strong as a two-handed shove, though we're not even touching anymore. Shane is abandoning me like everyone else has done.*

"Please, Shane." *I sound like I'm begging, but I never beg, so it has to be someone else saying his name like that as I stand up, tipping over my chair in my haste.*

"Don't come back." *He looks at me over his shoulder, distorting the tattoo of three feathers on his neck as the guard herds him out of the room. The other inmates and their families stare at me as I stand there alone.*

So I ran. I was always good at running. I'd been picked up twice, and put back in the care of the state thanks to the vigilance of Ms. Troy, who figured out my haunts long before anyone else did. And each time I ran again. I had every intention of running forever. And I had every intention of never seeing Shane again, too.

"Shane asked about you, Trix. He wanted to know if you were okay."

"My last visit was nearly a year ago, Charly. He had a lot of time to think about whether or not I was okay." Months after we'd parted, I recognized that Shane probably thought that dumping me so callously, so I would not come back to him, was doing what was best for me. Keeping me from waiting around for him, from staying in my old haunts, familiar, but dangerous for someone alone. He had sacrificed our love for my safety. It was a gift to me, but I'd been too hurt to see it. And I'd thrown it away anyway, returning to the Starlite.

"He's changed. He's grown up. He wants to see you again."

"Well, I've grown up, too. I'm with my family now," I say, even though the words are strange. "I don't know if seeing Shane is a good idea." Even as I say the last words, I'm looking at the scars on my arm and wondering how I can ever stay away from Shane if he wants to find me. He was my first love, my best friend. For a year, he'd been my safe place, a harbor in the storm. He'd been his own Good Year, even when everything else in my life was shit.

"Think about it," Charly says. "We can still have everything we talked about. A little house somewhere. The three of us, like it used to be."

"That was just a dream."

"Yeah, but it was ours. Don't let it go."

"What about you?" I ask, changing the subject. "Are you

okay?" My voice is hollow, tinny. Charly has always been kind of flaky, but she's the only friend I've got. I want to know that she's all right, that the police coming to the Starlite didn't cause trouble for her or anyone else.

"I'm fine. It was a shock when they hauled you off. A lot of people ran when they heard the cops were there. But I'm okay. So's Mom. I'm going to watch the twins tonight."

I nod, my throat tight. "I miss you, Charly."

"I miss you, too, Trix."

"I better go."

"Yeah, I get it. But Trix." She pauses a moment, and I can hear a door opening and closing, as if Janie is dropping off the twins. "We're friends. No matter what. So think about what I said. About Shane. I know he dumped you when he got in. But he really loved you. And you loved him, right? That's got to count for something."

"Goodbye, Charly," I whisper into the phone. My eyes are hot and wet, and I hate this stupid hill and my stupid phone provider.

"Goodbye, Trix."

When I hang up, I'm some strange, new Trix sitting alone in a lawn chair on top of Cedar Mountain. The thing about running is you don't have to have a destination in mind. But for once in my life, I'm already somewhere, and I have to figure out what to do now that the running part is over.

"There you are!" exclaims Mia when I come in the front door of the McCabe Bakery & Tea Shoppe, the brass bell ringing in welcome.

She's standing at the register, giving a woman her change. "We were starting to get worried about you."

It's barely five o'clock. The first thing I notice about the weekday-afternoon crowd is that there's a lot more teenage girls, and they are all gathered around Auntie, who's holding court in one of the back booths, telling fortunes.

"Are you okay?" Mia asks when the woman leaves with a pie. I can tell from the way Mia holds herself, every muscle tense, that she's warring between scolding me for being later than she expected and thanking me for not running away. One of the teenage girls with Auntie gasps with excitement and starts to dig in her jeans pocket, and Mia bellows out over the dining room, "No charging for fortunes, Auntie! You know the rule!" She mutters under her breath, "I've told her that a million times. I don't want to be giving out refunds for bad fortunes."

"I'm fine," I snap, ignoring her comments about Auntie. The phone call left me feeling raw, and I hate it.

Mia looks hurt. "All right," she says, her voice soft. "How about some pie?"

"I don't need any pie," I snarl, pushing past her and into the kitchen. I need to get to work. Anything to clear my head after that phone call with Charly.

I take a few moments alone in the kitchen to try to calm myself down, concentrating on breathing evenly, keeping myself in this moment and not the thousands of other moments that have come before it. I find my apron on the hook on the wall and put it on. The swinging door opens behind me.

Auntie gives me a hard look as she tucks a five-dollar bill

into her bra. I don't ask if she got it from the teenage girls, and she doesn't tell me, either.

"*What?*" I grumble.

"Bloom or wither," Auntie reminds me. "But know that you're rotting right now."

I grimace. I can see what Mia means about the bad fortunes. I'd like a refund on mine too.

Ember pops out of the walk-in cooler, sees my face, and goes right back in.

"Ember!" I call. Damn it. I follow her in, tugging down the sleeves on my sweater. Her back is to me again, and she's stacking cartons of eggs, pulling the oldest ones to the front. "Crap, it's cold in here. Aren't you cold?" I ask, rubbing my arms.

Ember doesn't answer.

"I'm sorry," I tell her. "I wasn't growling at you. It was Auntie. She really knows how to piss a person off, you know?"

Ember turns to me, her mouth pursed. "Auntie can be a little rude," she agrees. "But she's not mean."

"I'm not either," I tell her.

"I heard you yell at Mama when I was wiping down the kitchen a minute ago."

"I didn't yell at her."

"You weren't nice either."

"I'm sorry. I was thinking about something else. I took it out on her."

"She was worried when you didn't walk to the shop with me. She was afraid . . . maybe you ran away again." Ember sounds almost sad, like I've disappointed her with my behavior.

Strangely, it makes me feel guilty, a heavy feeling like the quilts on my bed in the attic that settle around me at night, as if darkness had weight. Ember hasn't asked anything of me, or acted put out by the attention her mom has given me or the clothes she bought for me. Ember is nothing like I expected her to be. But me, I'm exactly what everyone expected me to be. Angry, bitter, threatening to lash out or run at every turn.

"Why do you eat lunch in the library?" I ask, changing the subject.

Ember blushes, one hand finding her necklace and holding on to the tiny owl. She ignores the question. "I saw Jasper. He was looking for you. He said you'd bailed early on lunch with him and Grayson and the others." Her voice catches a little on Grayson's name.

"Jasper found me later."

"Jasper's nice," she says. "Not like some of the other kids at school. He never acts afraid, even when I accidentally touched him at the shop one day."

"You touched him?" I ask, my curiosity piqued. "So what's his greatest desire? His darkest secret?"

Ember shakes her head. "I shouldn't tell you."

"Because it's bad?" I ask. "It must be. Like his greatest desire is to chop people up into little bits."

No response.

"So then it *is* something weird. Like he wants to be one of those people with the fetishes on reality TV."

Ember shakes her head, her mouth twisting into a smile. "He just wants to be happy," she says.

"How can he not be happy? Everyone in town seems to love him. He's always smiling."

"Do you like him?" Ember asks, still holding her owl.

"Yeah, he's okay." I think of Shane again, and that heavy feeling. Then it hits me. "Why, do *you* like him?"

Ember shakes her head. "As a friend," she says. "I'm pretty sure the only guy I like at school doesn't know I'm alive. So I'm saving myself for Ren Rogers."

"Does Ren Rogers go to Rocksaw?"

Ember laughs. "No. He's a singer from Texas. You really haven't heard of Ren Rogers from the band Ren and Reckless? I saw them once when they played at the state fair a couple of years ago. Ren Rogers has the most beautiful voice," she says, and for once that reserve is gone, and her face lights up. "The band has this song, 'Your Touch,' and it's the most beautiful thing in the world. Here, let me play it for you." She starts to pull her phone out of her pocket.

"Can you show me out in the kitchen?" I ask her. "It's freezing in here."

"Oh!" she says, surprised, as if she'd forgotten where we're standing. "Okay. Yeah." She follows me out into the kitchen, which is empty now.

"Damn it," she says. "My phone's dead. I'll have to play it for you when we get home."

It's funny to hear her say *when we get home*.

Mom and I always referred to the Starlite and every motel before that simply by its name. *The Happy Host. The Budget Bunk. The Westport.* Even when we had the apartment, we'd called it the

Jasmine Dragon because it sat on top of the restaurant, and the two places had seemed like one.

I have a home now. It feels different. But everything in Rocksaw is different.

The tea shop closes at six, so there's only an hour left for me to wait tables. At a quarter till, I'm wiping tables and putting chairs up so that Ember can come out and sweep up when everyone is gone.

At closing time, Mia locks the front door and turns on a little radio at the front counter. She turns it all the way up on a local country station, and Ember sweeps while Mia follows her with a mop.

I put away my apron in the kitchen, where Auntie is counting the cash from the till.

"So you decided to stay after all," Auntie says, not looking up from the bills she's counting.

"I guess so," I answer.

"Good." She stuffs the money in a small zippered deposit bag. "This needs to be dropped off at the bank."

I keep staring at her because no one in their right mind would hand me a deposit bag full of cash. I didn't think I'd be tested so hard and so soon after I decided to stop running. I think of Mom at the Jasmine Dragon, and I suppress a shiver in the hot kitchen.

"Well?" Auntie says, ignoring the way I've hugged my arms to myself. "Can you run it over? The bank is right across the street. There's a deposit bin next to the front door. The slip's already in there. Just drop it in."

"Is this a test?" I ask her, reaching out and taking the bag.

She can't know, I remind myself.

"It's your job. Now do it."

I take the bag, tucking it under one arm.

Auntie grins to herself. "Connor used to stop by and take the bag for me. He said a gorgeous broad like me couldn't be wearing herself out running errands."

I don't reply. I don't know what to say. I file this information along with everything else I know about Connor so far and go out the back door of the kitchen. In the dim light of the alley, I feel the weight of the money in the bag. There's enough in there that I could put myself up somewhere nice for a while. Maybe a Holiday Inn.

I tuck the bag back under my arm and leave the alley.

Main Street is dead quiet; there is no one to even notice me.

I cross to the bank, a squatty brick building with a crooked Closed sign hanging in the front window. Coins jingle in the bottom of the bag as I walk, a happy tune that sounds like a death march to me.

It would be so easy to run.

My chest feels tight. The coins continue to jingle.

I rub a fist over my breastbone, as if I could loosen this awful feeling that makes it hard to breathe.

When I reach the entrance of the bank, I open the deposit bin beside the front door. I hold the deposit bag in front of me, the weight of it making my arm ache after carrying trays all afternoon.

It would be so easy. A piece of cake. Hell, a piece of pie.

My fingers surprise me as they release the bag. It falls into the dark deposit bin with a *clunk* when it hits the bottom, far from my reach.

It's like a hundred pounds are lifted off my shoulders. Relief courses through me.

One thing I know for sure. I wouldn't have thrown away the Good Year like Mom did.

TEN

AT FIVE O'CLOCK THE NEXT day, Ember points in the direction of Jensen's Office Supply. "He closes up shop at six, so run down there now if you need something. Did you ask Mama for money? She'll give you some if you need something for school."

I shake my head. "I don't need any." Mia had bought me basic school supplies before I arrived and clothes on Sunday. I didn't want to ask her for anything else. The McCabe women aren't dirt poor and hungry, but they aren't rolling in cash, either. After the chance they gave me, I don't feel like I should ask for anything more.

Besides, I've got a five-finger discount that's never let me down. The stationery place will never even miss what I take.

Ember pulls off her long, bohemian-looking scarf and dangles it out to me. The dress she wears today is a rusty orange with tiny butterflies scattered over the fabric and a pair of well-worn boots and bright-yellow tights. I saw her working on a design for a dress while Mia was cooking dinner last night, before I darted up the stairs claiming I wasn't hungry again because I felt the walls pressing in, everyone's voices too loud in my ears from the car ride back to the farmhouse. I think Ember makes a lot of her own clothes, not because she has to, but because it's her form of art. "Here," she says, surprising me with her kindness. "It's getting chilly."

I take the scarf, and note that the way she holds it, like everything else, is an artful dance of making sure she doesn't accidentally touch anyone skin-to-skin with her hands. "Thanks," I tell her. I feel sometimes like we're two kids on the first day of elementary school, awkward and unsure of what to say to each other.

"I'll tell Mama you've gone out to run an errand."

She doesn't add *so she doesn't think you're running away again*, but it's implied. I don't blame her. I haven't exactly been a model of good behavior so far.

Across the street, I spot Grayson and Linc coming out of Lee's General Store, each of them holding a Gatorade in one hand and a set of shoulder pads in the other, their hair wet and glinting from showering after practice. Ember stares at Grayson, her cheeks flushing. "I've got to go," she says quickly, darting back into the tea shop.

"Bye," I call to thin air. Across the street, I catch sight of Grayson watching the door close, as if he'd spotted Ember's flight as well. He looks almost disappointed.

Maybe Mia is rubbing off on me.

I hunch my shoulders against the chill, walking up the street to Jensen's. A stretch of trees grows in the middle of Main Street, separating the two redbrick lanes. The leaves are blazing orange and gold. It's idyllic, the kind of town that should be in movies or TV shows about happy families that overcome some minor adversity and open a llama ranch. Ember's scarf smells like coconut, and I try to remember the last time someone, other than the McCabes, who gave me something just because they could. Maybe it was Shane with his Coke-and-cherry slushes.

The little shops along the way are all busy. At each storefront, people pass in and out of heavy wooden doors with old brass handles and jingling bells that herald each arrival and exit. Everyone nods to me and says hello as I pass. I don't know most of them, but I give them sort of a nod in reply anyway. I guess that's what I'm supposed to do in a small town.

Rocksaw is nothing like the city. In the city, you keep your head down and pass by thousands of strangers, never looking at their faces or wondering who they are. In the city, your story is your own. But in Rocksaw, your story belongs to everyone else, too. Adalyn asked me today at lunch why I was staying with my aunt in Rocksaw, as if she had a right to know. And Grayson said he knew my dad before the bull ride that killed him, making that the third different way that I've heard of how Connor McCabe died. And in another twist of their lunchtime conversation, Ramani reminisced about how she had so much fun going to homecoming last year with her boyfriend, Jesse, and a quick glance at the recognition on Jasper's face confirmed that Ramani's Jesse was Jasper's mysterious dead brother. Jasper tried to smile at her, the kind of smile that moved his mouth but didn't go up to his eyes or tug on that thin white scar. But for the rest of the day, he was quiet, his golden-brown eyes looking for something past the faces of his friends, past the hallways of the school. Everyone here knows everyone else's story, played some part in it.

I don't think I want any part of my story to belong to someone else, too.

Jensen's Office Supply smells like licorice when I step inside. It's smaller than I expected, nothing like the chain stores I'm familiar with. There's a young woman at the counter ringing up a mother with two squawking kids who are fighting about which one gets to hand over the money. The aisles of the store are narrow and jammed full of merchandise. I skip two rows before I find the art supplies, slipping what I've been asked to bring to art class tomorrow into my backpack. A box of pencils, a set of oil paints, a jar of turpentine, another carton of pastels, a sketchbook.

I slip back outside to the sidewalk, letting the door's bell tinkle behind me.

While I'm distracted by the autumn foliage, I nearly walk straight into an old man heading into Jensen's.

"Excuse me, miss. Are you all right?" he asks. His back is hunched with the weight of what must be ninety years.

"Sorry. Yeah, I'm fine."

"Didn't find what you wanted?" he asks. "If you let me know, I can order it for you." He smiles at me and points to the Jensen's Office Supply sign. "I'm Jensen," he says. "And it looks like you're leaving empty-handed, so I must have disappointed you."

"I'm fine, thanks," I tell him, starting to move past him.

"You look like a McCabe."

I don't quite know what to say to that because not only do I look like my mom, the McCabe women don't look alike at all. The McCabe women are as different as shades of the rainbow, each one reflecting light and color in her own way. But I ignore that and answer him. "I'm Trix McCabe," I reply, stopping again and turning to face him.

The old man nods, holding out his trembling hand for me to shake. His skin is like dry paper when I take his hand. "Tobias Jensen," he says. "Nice to meet you." He smiles. "You know, you look a lot like Connor, actually."

"I look like my mom," I tell Tobias, pulling my hand away. Someone in this town should know the truth, and it might as well be this old man.

"It was too bad about that shark attack. Such a bright young man. Used to come in here all the time. He liked to draw, you know. Was always needing a new sketchbook or a box of pencils. He favored the vine charcoal, I believe. Extra soft, for the darkest color. Said you can't be afraid to draw the shadows."

Of all the different stories I've heard about Connor McCabe and his mysterious life and death, this one about the drawing hits the hardest, the closest to the most vulnerable parts of me. "Did you ever see any of them?" I ask. "Was he any good?"

"He was. Really had a knack for portraits. Capturing the essence of a person on the page. I asked once why he didn't paint instead. He said portraits were better in black and white because in real life everybody's just shades of gray."

I smile hesitantly. "Nothing's really black and white, is it?"

Tobias smiles back, his teeth yellow from tobacco. "Sure isn't. Come back again. I'll see if I can still get those charcoals in.

Grumbacher made them, I think . . ."

I nod once goodbye and carry on down the sidewalk, wrapping Ember's scarf more tightly around me, still thinking of what my dead father once said. *You can't be afraid to draw the shadows.* I wonder if he would look at me now and see all shadow or all light. But in the end, it doesn't matter what he would see. I'm blank space. I never existed for him. And until a few days ago, he never really existed for me, either. But coming here, listening to people's stories makes him seem more real than he's ever been.

The wind is stronger now, and the sunset a brilliant orange and pink that reminds me of sherbet that they used to sell at the little bodega around the corner from the Happy Host, a motel I stayed at off and on over the summer. My mind drifts back there, away from this little town, and I let the wind blow my hair back from my face, wishing I could fist my hands into the pockets of my familiar black hoodie.

I wish I hadn't decided to stop running. I can't put my finger on why, but now feels like a damn good time to hit the road.

But I promised myself that I was done with running. There's another feeling creeping up, too. That strange, new, heavy feeling that I think might actually be guilt. I feel guilty for stealing from that old man who tried to tell me about Connor McCabe. My father. The artist. The realization stings like a slap. I've never felt guilty about stealing in my life. Why should I? Wasn't I given this gift to use it?

"Hey!" I can barely hear someone yell over the cranking of an engine. It snaps me back to reality. "Need a ride?"

I look over and it's Jasper, puttering along beside me in his old black truck until it grinds to a halt. Given the way he was so quiet and withdrawn this afternoon at school, I'm surprised that he's stopped.

"It's only a few blocks back to the tea shop," I tell him.

"Yeah, but it's getting kind of cold. Cleo's got a good heater. Replaced the heater core myself a couple weeks ago," he says through his open window.

"Cleo? That's right. You named your truck." I let a smile twist my mouth.

"I told you, everybody names their truck. It's un-American *not* to name your truck." He taps the outside of the door, a hollow thump on the rusty metal. "And what kind of a guy would I be if I didn't offer you a ride when I see you outside walking?"

"The kind who wants me to enjoy fresh air and exercise?" I prompt.

"Okay," he says, his face shuttering again, like it did this afternoon. "I can take a hint. See you later." He moves to put the truck in gear, and I think about my promise not to run away anymore. It would be a lot easier if I actually tried to get to know people, maybe make some friends. Something about the way Jasper's face closed off again tugs at me, maybe because it reminds me of myself.

"Wait," I shout. "I'll take a ride."

"Pull up and out," Jasper reminds me as he starts rolling up his window.

I jump down from the sidewalk and hurry around the back of the truck, coughing as I wade through the exhaust fumes. It takes two tries for me to get the correct combination of up and out to get the passenger door open.

"Look at that!" he says, his voice a little strange. Forced brightness. "You got it open on the second try. That must be some kind of record. Award-worthy, even."

"Let me know if you need help spelling my name for the trophy," I say, climbing in and slamming the door shut.

"At an angle," he reminds me when I attempt to fasten my seat belt. "I won't help this time. You're obviously an expert."

"So true," I agree, getting it clicked in on the third try. "What are you up to?" I ask in an attempt to make conversation as he puts the truck in first gear. The class ring hanging on a necklace from the rearview mirror swings wildly as the truck lurches into motion.

"Going to deliver some pies for your aunts. Mia texted to let me know she had a few tonight and could use the extra hand."

"Ah," I reply. "Not needed on the farm tonight?"

"There's always work to be done on a farm. But Mia pays cash, and my dad pays in pats on the back. Something about pride in my family's work and all that."

"Cash is good," I agree. "Hard to spend pride."

"Yeah, but I still love it. Working on the farm."

"So, is that what you're going to do after you graduate?" I ask. "Run your family's farm?" I don't think a lot about the future. I guess I always thought I'd be drifting, sort of like my mom.

"Well, that's the plan now."

"Now?" I prompt as he pulls into a parking spot in front of the shop.

"It was supposed to be Jesse's future. Not mine. He was the oldest, so he was going to inherit the farm. Which is sort of ironic," he says, tapping the steering wheel absently as the engine of the truck rumbles, "because he never wanted the farm. I did."

"So now you get what you wanted."

"I do." His voice is dark. "Lucky me."

"I'm sorry," I say. "I didn't mean it like that."

"So you know all about me. What about you?" he asks, shutting off the engine. "Why did you come here, to Rocksaw, to live with your aunts? You blew off Adalyn when she asked today, and I get that—you two aren't super close. But you won't even tell me? Fellow pie-delivery veteran?"

He's right. I ask hard questions, but I rarely answer them. "My mom's gone."

"Like, she died? Was she sick, or in an accident or something?"

"No. Like, one day she got up and said she was going to get a pack of cigarettes, and she never came back. She didn't call. Nothing. She just left."

There's a strained silence. It feels good to say it out loud, though. To finally tell someone what happened without making it an awkward joke, like I did with Mia in the kitchen Sunday night. I feel like Jasper might understand. I don't know if others would. Ember has never pried. Truthfully, I don't know if I could ever tell Ember. Ember with her adoring mother. How could someone like Ember ever understand what it means to be abandoned?

Two women leave the shop, their arms full of pink carryout boxes. We watch them, neither of us hazarding a guess on whether they've got Bracing Blueberry or Cherish Cherry.

"Why do people do that?" he asks, his hands sliding from

the wheel. I know he's not talking about the women with their pies. "Why do they leave?"

I shrug. "Maybe she planned it. Or maybe she got into her crappy car and just kept driving because she felt like it." I put my hand on my arm, over where my scars are hidden beneath the sleeve of my sweater. "The police checked the morgues. Hospitals. They checked everywhere after social services brought me in. But they never found her."

Another long pause.

"I'm sorry," Jasper says finally. "I just wondered if you knew."

"It doesn't matter, does it? She left. All that matters is that she left, and I'm still here."

Jasper nods and unfastens his seat belt, his face somehow haunted again. "Hold on. Remember, you'll have to slide out this way or I can come around and open your door from the outside."

"I can slide out," I say, grateful for the change in subject. Jasper grabs his backpack and gets out first, and I slide across the bench seat and follow him out his door.

The inside of the McCabe Bakery & Tea Shoppe is warm and bright, the brass chandeliers casting a golden glow over the crowded tables. It smells of rosehip tea and blueberry today. Mia is standing at the register. "Did you get what you needed?" she asks me, her voice too cheerful. Even though Ember told her I was running an errand, she was still afraid.

I nod. I don't know how long it will take to convince her and Auntie that I'm not going to run again. I can scarcely believe it myself. But I can do this. I can survive two years here. Even though I'd willingly accepted the ride from Jasper, I feel a small sliver of regret that I told him about Mom leaving. Maybe that was a mistake. And something about his face tells me that my story touched something in him that hurts, too.

"And you brought Jasper back with you!" Mia exclaims, noticing him behind me. "How lovely! I've got more deliveries than I can handle. Two Ardent Apples to the principal again. Apparently, Auntie made some sort of deal with him. And a Bracing Blueberry to Maria Sanchez, and a chocolate cake to Mrs. Jindal. Six pumpkin pies to Lottie Peretti to take to bingo. I can't tell you how much of a relief it is to have you tonight. I've got a special order for Mitzi's sixty-fifth birthday cake, and the Silvermans are having a bat mitzvah, and I'm up to my eyeballs in pink cupcakes with strawberry cream filling."

"I'm here to help," Jasper says, giving her that familiar charming grin. I'm beginning to realize that it's only real about half the time. That's when it pulls at the scar. The other times, when it's only his mouth moving, those smiles are fake, some show he's putting on for all the people in this town who adore him. "Let me load up the truck and I'll hit the road."

"You're a treasure, Jasper."

She hurries to the kitchen to get the deliveries, and Auntie comes out to the dining room. "It's almost six o'clock. Go see if anyone needs anything to go." She makes a waving motion to send me back out to check the tables. "Tell Mrs. Gunderson I'll be out in a minute to give her another reading, though I can tell you for damn sure that nothing's changed since yesterday."

I look over at Jasper, who shrugs, indicating that no one

would think to disagree with Auntie. I guess I was sort of hoping to go on his delivery run with him, which tells me that I like him a little more than I thought.

"Boys later," Auntie says. "Go on. Get to work. I don't pay you to flirt."

There are a lot of smart-ass remarks I'd like to sling back at her, but instead I swallow them and grab my apron from where I left it on the table and put it on, pulling my notepad and pen from the pocket.

Half an hour later, Mia and Ember have finished mopping, and Auntie is nearly done counting the register drawer in the kitchen. I've wiped down the counter and am waiting for Auntie to give me the deposit to run over to the bank when I notice a black backpack sitting near the front counter. It's crumpled into itself, obviously mostly empty. I pick it up, looking it over to see if there's a name anywhere. There's nothing, and when I open the largest pocket, there are no books inside. So I pry open one of the smaller pockets and dig around until I find something. When my hand closes around it, I pull it out.

It's an orange pill bottle with a handful of small green pills, the orange plastic making them look almost brown in the bottle. I check the label.

Ruiz, Jasper.

I recognize the name of the prescription immediately from television commercials I watched in the Starlite. These are anti-depressants.

I'm so surprised that the container drops from my hand and rolls across the floor to the front window. I think about what Ember said of his deepest, darkest secrets. *He only wants to be happy.*

I drag the backpack along, chasing the prescription bottle. When I lean forward to pick it up again, the tiny hairs on the back of my neck stand up. I look up, suddenly sure that someone is watching me.

And I'm right.

Jasper is standing outside the shop, staring in the window at me. His arm is extended, about to pull on the door to come in, but it's been locked since we closed thirty minutes ago.

My stomach drops, and I shove the pills back inside his bag, knowing that there's no way he could have missed seeing me holding them up, reading the label like I had any right to pry into his personal life.

I stride over to the door, click open the lock, and step outside with his bag.

It's twilight now, and Jasper's hands are shoved in his pockets, his arms tight to his body, like he's cold.

"I found your bag," I say. "I wasn't sure whose it was. I didn't mean to—"

Jasper grabs the bag from me. "I've got to go," he says. "I'll see you later."

For the first time since I've met him, he doesn't even try to fake one of his charming grins.

He just takes his bag, gets into Cleo, and drives away.

ELEVEN

Back at the farmhouse, I help Ember unload empty muffin and scone trays. Mia is cheerful, but somehow strained, and it makes me uneasy.

"Girls?" Mia says when we dump the trays in the kitchen for her to wash. Her voice is strangely high, and I wonder why she's nervous. "Has either of you seen my wedding ring? I can't seem to find it."

Ember frowns, her green eyes meeting her mom's in a way that is strangely confrontational. "What do you mean, your wedding ring? You don't wear it anymore, do you?" The exchange speaks volumes to me. Ember's parents must be divorced.

Auntie makes a *harrumph* sound in the back of her throat, and mutters something about worthless ex-husbands.

Mia says softly, "Sometimes I do."

My chest tightens, my heart beating faster. Mia's going to ask me if I took her ring. There's no other way for this to end.

"I haven't seen it," Ember replies sharply.

Mia looks down at the worn kitchen island, her fingers sweeping along the grain of the wood.

I wait for her to ask.

Moments pass.

I touch my scars over my sweater again. I wish I'd never stolen the ring.

My face feels hot, and my chest hurts because my heart is beating fast, too fast. Maybe I should tell her that I took it. Maybe I shouldn't say anything. Maybe I should deny ever seeing the ring.

"Isn't it Ember's turn for dinner?" Auntie asks, breaking the silence. "I'm starving."

"I'm trying a new recipe," Ember says.

Mia replies cheerfully, "I can't wait."

I flee, taking my homework upstairs to my room to work at the little desk under the eave. Hands still shaking faintly, I set it all up, stacking the history book, the biology book, and the spiral notebook so that they make a neat little pile arranged by size. I pick up a plain yellow pencil and open the first book. Chapter review questions for American history. I open the book to page thirty-two, looking at the set of five questions. This should be easy. I pull the notebook off the pile next, opening it up and writing my name in the corner of the page. I read the first question, about European colonies in the United States. The words start to swim a little, the black ink blurring against the white paper. I used to be a decent student. But it's like my brain has gone rusty during the time I took off from school. Or maybe I'm just distracted by this bizarre feeling of guilt.

I look at the second question, about the mystery of Roanoke. Everybody who lived in Roanoke disappeared. Kind of like I used to disappear. Now I'm here, though, putting down roots, or whatever, like Auntie said. *Put down roots, or you'll die.*

I draw a small rosebud in the margin of the paper. Then a whole cluster of them, vining between the margin and the metal spine of the notebook. I shade them dark, think about what that old man, Jensen, told me about Connor. *You can't be afraid to draw the shadows.*

My thoughts flit back to finding that bottle of pills in Jasper's backpack. It wouldn't have been so bad if Jasper hadn't caught me. I think what made it more awful was that he didn't even tell me off. He just took the bag back and left, like he was more hurt than angry.

And then I cringe thinking about Mia's wedding ring. I hadn't known that she would miss it so quickly. I should have put it back when I decided I was going to stay. I can't put it back in her room now, or it will be too obvious that I took it, then felt guilty. I have to find a way to make it look like Mia misplaced it herself. The worst part is that I've done everything Ms. Troy cautioned Mia about.

I slam the history book shut, hoping I'll be more focused later. I feel too guilty to sketch with my stolen supplies right now. I tap my fingers on the textbook. I guess I could go downstairs and see what the McCabe women are up to. Maybe Mia will have forgotten about the stolen ring.

I'm at the top of the stairs on the second floor when I smell it. That bright, spicy smell of fresh ginger. With the weight of the last few days hanging on me, I feel that phantom ache now more than ever.

I slide down to sit on the top step and lean my head against the stair railing.

"This place is really nice, Mom," I tell her hesitantly. I am twelve years old. The air in this building smells like ginger, and the windows in the stairwell are foggy from the steam of the kitchens below. We are climbing the steps to our new apartment. Mom looks different, almost like they replaced my old mom with this new one when she was in rehab. Her face is fuller, smoother, and her dark hair thick and shiny. She looks back over her shoulder and smiles at me, fidgeting with her hands like she's nervous.

Finally we stand in the tiny apartment. It sits above the Jasmine Dragon in Little Chinatown, a small section of the city, home to a popular open-air market with freshly plucked ducks hanging by their smooth pink necks and ropes of long beans nearly the length of my arm; some small shops; at least a dozen restaurants; and a theater called the Imperial Palace that only charges two dollars to see movies that have left the regular theaters a month or so earlier. The apartment is papered in the same wallpaper as the restaurant dining room below, pale green with the faintest lines sketching out bamboo in the background.

"Do you like it?" Mom asks. "Ms. Troy helped me get the job and the apartment. I'm waitressing downstairs. A few day shifts, but mostly evenings, when they're the busiest. But don't worry, Mr. Yang says you can come downstairs and sit with his kids if you want while I'm working. He says there's a booth in the back where they do their homework together."

The night of Mom's first shift, I sit across from Wendy and Jack Yang, nervous, watching my mother wander between tables like she doesn't really know what she's doing. Wendy is twelve like me, and her little brother, Jack, is ten. They both have straight, thick black hair and study me carefully with serious expressions when I climb into the booth with them.

They are already a team, a unit, a family, and when they exchange a look as I get out my crinkled school papers and a yellow pencil that needs sharpening, they communicate more than I could say with a dozen words. My hands are sweating, and I wipe them off on my jeans, feeling my face burn with embarrassment under their gaze.

But then Wendy smiles at me, and it's a beautiful sunshine smile. I don't ask for anything, but she offers to share her ice-cream-cone-shaped pencil sharpener, and it makes me feel warm inside. My most recent foster home was with the deeply religious woman and her husband with the leather belt, and each meal and ride to school was a reminder that my presence was somehow an affliction that must be dutifully borne.

As the days go on, I do my best to move in the shadows, to never be a burden here. To never peel back the layers of my new, beautiful mother to see if the old one is underneath. I ask permission to sit in the booth with Wendy and Jack each night, to get a glass of water from the kitchens, to use the restroom off the dining room. They laugh after a few weeks and tell me that I don't need to ask, and their father, Mr. Yang, tells me to stop scurrying like a little mouse.

Even as my mother stays tightly folded in a bud of fresh beginnings, the Yang family expands and blooms before me. Mrs. Yang met Mr. Yang when he moved to the United States from China to work for his uncle in the Jasmine Dragon. Mrs. Yang was studying art history in the city, and she came into the Jasmine Dragon looking for dinner and left with the phone number of a clumsy waiter. They fell in love and took over the Jasmine Dragon when Mr. Yang's uncle passed away. Mr. Yang smiles when Wendy and Jack come down into the dining room in their school clothes each morning, their faces bright and freshly washed. They do not ask for our story, but let us start over here, a crisp, blank first page.

A month passes. Wendy and I stand outside the music shop where she takes piano lessons on the edge of Little Chinatown, and she points at the electric guitar in the window and tells me she wants to be a rock star with pink hair. She asks me if I will be in her band someday, and I tell her I will. We pinky promise because we are best friends now.

Mom learns how to be a good waitress, and Mr. Yang is pleased with her work. He gives her a raise, promises to help her learn book-keeping if she wants. Mrs. Yang says I am too skinny, and she tells me to eat from the buffet during dinnertime. When business is slow, Mrs. Yang sits at the booth with us and plays games. She teaches us to bluff in Texas Hold'em, and we ante up with peppermints from the dish by the front register. Then she admires my sketches when I get brave enough to show them to her, and finally I shyly offer her one of Wendy and Jack side by side in the back booth. She says she will frame it, and I am happy, but too nervous to show her the sketch I made of Wendy and me side by side in the back booth, as if we were sisters, as if I was a part of their family.

After each game of poker, I put my peppermints back in the dish by the front register, still in their wrappers.

I don't steal anything here.

I say please and thank you, and I never swear because Mrs. Yang declares it isn't polite, especially in front of the customers. The Jasmine Dragon is a perfect world, like a snow globe, and I don't want to do anything to break it.

But even though I am happier and safer than I have ever been, sometimes I am reminded that Mom and I had a life before this one. One night it is too warm in the dining room, and I push up my sleeves. The scars on my arm are still young and stand out bright pink against my skin.

"Ew!" Jack says, wrinkling his nose. "What happened to your arm?"

"Hush!" Mrs. Yang says, holding a tray with a small pot of steaming jasmine tea for the elderly couple who always comes on Wednesdays. She has stopped to check on Wendy's book report and is witness to my embarrassment. "Trix's scars are her own. She doesn't have to tell you anything."

I pull my sleeve back down, my cheeks burning. I don't want the scars to be my own. I wish they were someone else's. I wish my arm was as smooth and perfect as Wendy's, who elbows Jack before smiling at me sympathetically and sliding her pink eraser across the table to me like she did with the ice-cream-shaped pencil sharpener on the first night I met her.

The scars faded a little, but they never went away.

I breathe deeply of the ginger again at the top of the stairs. I can hear the McCabe women talking and plates and glasses clinking as someone sets the table. I pull myself up and turn around, going back down the hall to the attic entry. I close the door to the steps once I'm inside the stairwell, blocking out the smell of ginger. I climb the stairs, my footsteps heavy and slow. I make a nest out of the pillows and quilts and wait for sleep to take me back to the Jasmine Dragon and the Good Year.

I wake. When I check the time, I see that it's almost midnight. The room is stifling, small. Every muscle in my body is tensed, screaming *run, run, run*. Away from the fading smells of ginger, of the Good Year, of these women I stole from, even as they welcomed me with open arms. I don't belong here. I roll off the bed, crouch down on my hands and knees next to the banana crate. I pull it forward and the wads of stolen money and Mia's ring spill out. I grab the ring, because it's the one thing I have to return before I run away again. I open the door to the downstairs carefully, not surprised when I hear the door bump against a dish on the floor. It's pie.

I reach down and pick up the small plate. I take a sniff. Lemon. Never-Lonely Lemon. I wonder if it was Ember or Mia who left it there. I take the pie downstairs to the kitchen. Auntie is sleeping on the couch while the television drones on.

I should drop Mia's ring on the dining room table and leave.

Instead, I go out the front door, sit down on the front steps with my pie. I take a bite, letting the tang of the lemon burst on my taste buds, almost as bright and beautiful as the stars. The wind rustles the leaves of the roses. Their scent is sweet and heady, something altogether different from the spicy, bright ginger I smelled earlier. The McCabes and the Yangs. Who knew I would be thinking of them both out here in the middle of nowhere. Two families, one cobbled together and one the perfect unit that was once everything I ever wanted.

I eat the pie, trying to find all the constellations I can recognize. The Big Dipper. The Little Dipper. Orion. Ursa Major. I know there are more, but I don't know all their names, or where they might be. I guess there's probably a book about them in the library, or maybe something I could look up online.

When I get to the flaky, golden crust of the pie that's dented in little half-moons in the shape of Mia's thumb, it reminds me of the pleats in Mrs. Yang's dumplings. I feel something within myself shifting, like a dulling of all the sharp things inside me.

"Mrrooowww," Bacon croons behind me, sliding up against my arms, which are propped up on the step behind me.

"Go away, cat," I tell him.

Bacon doesn't listen, twining around my limbs with his fat tail, flicking it in my face when I don't reach down to pet him. "You're not a Persian, you know," I tell him, rubbing my nose to get the cat hair out. "That's what I wished for." Bacon yowls again, nudging me with his head. I stroke him along his back, and he purrs, the sound like an engine running.

I go back inside, carrying the pie plate with me. I leave it in the sink, then open the fridge to see what they made. It still smells faintly of ginger in here, but the aromas of baked goods are slowly taking back over. I find a plate on the middle shelf that's covered in plastic wrap, what Mia must have saved for me. It's some kind of chicken with broccoli in a brown sauce dumped over a pile of white rice.

I rummage around until I find the silverware drawer, and on

the inside edge of the drawer are a few sets of mismatched chopsticks. I take out two of them and sit down at the work table where Mia rolls out her dough, remembering the booth where Wendy, Jack, and I used to sit and do our homework. I eat the cold food.

I roll Mia's ring between my fingers, wondering why trying to change is so damn hard.

This tastes nothing like the food I used to eat at the Jasmine Dragon. But then again, I'm nothing like the girl who used to live there.

I wish I could be her again, though. Because that girl would stay. She'd go back up to bed, crawl under the covers, and wait for sleep to bring her a new day, fresh with possibilities. Just like the Jasmine Dragon had been once. A new start for her, and for Mom.

I rinse my plate in the sink.

I leave Mia's ring behind the flour jar on the counter, as if she'd casually taken it off to knead dough.

And then I climb the attic stairs to my very own bedroom to wait for a morning that is fresh with possibilities.

TWELVE

THE NEXT MORNING, I GET dressed in a hurry and head downstairs, hoping that I'm going to hear Mia announce that she found her ring while she was up baking. I find myself oddly nervous, my normally cool, steady hands warm and damp.

"We missed you at dinner last night," Mia says when I enter the kitchen. There's no edge to her voice. No accusation. Only the tiniest hint of disappointment. I wonder if it's about the ring, or the dinner.

"But we won't miss her tonight," Auntie says, looking at me but continuing to talk to Mia like I'm not here. "She *and* Ember have kitchen duty. Trix's going to start pulling her weight around here. No more hiding up in her room."

"I'm not hiding," I mumble as I grab a sausage-and-cheese scone from one of the trays. Sometimes I just need space. But last night was different. I was going to come downstairs. I was really going to try.

I don't know how to explain what the smell of ginger did to me, how it sent me back in time to some other place, some other girl. All I know is that it's the good memories that cut the deepest, because those are the ones where you remember what you've lost.

"Well, you're doing a great job at the tea shop," Mia says, giving me an encouraging smile, and twisting another knot of guilt in my gut. "Customers keep telling me what a great waitress you are. It's been such a weight off my shoulders to have an extra set of hands around the business."

I flick a glance at Ember, sitting at the table in the dining room, who always avoids the customers. She's pretending she can't hear us as she peruses her homework with her earbuds in, but I know that she keeps the volume low enough that she can always hear what's going on in the kitchen. She doesn't make eye contact with me at all. Today she's wearing a deep-maroon dress with small blue rosebuds, blue tights, and suede boots. There's a tiny maroon bow at the end of her crown-braid. She's got her own sense of style, and I admire that about her. I only feel at ease in the loose, swingy sweaters Ember and Mia selected from Rory's Treasures. Something about them makes me feel safe like I do in my black hoodie, and I think Ember knew that when she picked them out.

I take my scone to the dining room table next to Ember, but after I take a bite, I realize I can barely swallow. The scone is good, but my mouth is dry, and I feel almost nauseous with worry over whether or not Mia will find her ring this morning. So I set the pastry down and organize my backpack instead, sure to wedge my sketchbook in with the books I brought home. Looking at the history book, I remember that I didn't finish my homework, and I grimace a little.

Mia drops off our lunch boxes on the table, sliding the Star Wars one toward me. I look for any sense of resentment in her body language, but there is none, no extra shove of my lunch box, no angry sniff. She just turns and heads back to the kitchen as she rattles off a list of things to do today to Auntie. I wonder if Mia put another pink Post-it note inside my lunch box today.

"Are you eating lunch with Jasper and Grayson and all them today?" Ember asks. There's something almost wistful in her voice.

"I don't know. Probably." I suddenly recall the unfortunate incident with Jasper's backpack and his antidepressants last night. Jasper might not be all that happy to see me at his usual table.

Ember's brow furrows and she opens her mouth like she's thinking about saying something, but Mia interrupts.

"Look!" Mia calls from the kitchen. "My ring!" She holds it up, a small gold band that glints in the morning light pouring through the kitchen windows.

Relief floods through me. I thought I was going to have to hide it in a more obvious place.

Ember, rather than looking relieved or pleased, makes a face like something tastes bad, either her mom being careless with the ring, or the fact that her mom still wears it even though she's divorced.

Auntie is less subtle. "Too bad," she says. "I thought you were finally free of it." She gives me a pointed look, and I dodge her glance, pretending to still be rearranging things in my backpack.

The feeling of relief is like a warm breeze moving through me, thawing out that heavy frost of guilt.

On the ride to school, no one mentions the ring, or supplies any theories as to how it ended up behind the flour jar.

But they don't say they knew I didn't take it either.

When we get to school, Ember is still quiet, not that that's unusual for her. I wish I hadn't taken the stupid ring. Because as we enter the front door of the high school, I realize that out of all the students who crowd the halls, Ember might be the only person who understands what it's like to have a gift that makes people distrustful of you. Even if you're sometimes worthy of that suspicion.

"Hey," I say before we part ways in the main hall. I know I might get totally shot down, but I'm going to try anyway. "Would it be weird if we ate lunch together today? In the gym?"

"*What?*" she asks, as if I'd said something inappropriate instead of asking her to lunch.

"Let's sit with the other juniors. You know, Adalyn and Ramani. Grayson." I tack that last name on there, remembering how her face lit up when I mentioned him this morning.

"I don't eat lunch there," she says, grabbing her owl necklace. "It makes everyone uncomfortable."

"Who cares if other people are uncomfortable?" I ask. "If they don't like it, they can leave."

"Why does it matter to you where I eat lunch?" she asks.

"I don't know. I thought it would be easier if we didn't have to act like we're strangers at school." I shrug, unable to say, *because I've been lonely for the last year.* And I think Ember's been lonely most of her life. "We work together. We live together. We're in the same class . . ." I let my voice drift off because all my reasons sound stupid, even to me.

"Fine," Ember says. "I'll think about it. But if I come, then tonight you help me with dinner and you do your homework downstairs with me. I know you didn't do any of it. I saw your empty notebook this morning when you were packing your bag. I know the terms of you staying here. You have to graduate, or you could go to jail."

"Why do *you* care?" I ask her, because I'd think me getting sent off to jail would be no skin off her nose.

"It makes Mama sad when you won't come down. And she'd be devastated if you got sent away. Every time your social worker calls to check on you, Mama looks like she's going to jump right out of her skin."

I make some sort of half shrug.

Then she's quiet for a moment, studying me. "I knew you didn't take it."

I don't reply. I just feel my heart explode in my chest, her words ringing in my ears.

"The ring. I knew when Mama said it was missing that she'd misplaced it. I never thought you took it. I know you must have worried that we did."

I press my lips together, my eyes feeling a little hot. I wish I was worthy of her trust.

Ember gives me a small smile as she turns to go to her locker. I see Linc and Ramani and others in a small cluster by mine, but as I approach, they leave, and Jasper is the only one who remains, standing in front of his locker. His backpack sits on the floor by his feet, still looking mostly empty, except probably for the bottle of pills I found in it yesterday.

Jasper looks up and sees me watching him. His golden eyes are unreadable. Then he turns away from my gaze and slams his locker shut. Shouldering his backpack, he walks away without so much as a wave.

I can't say that I blame him.

I have two classes with Jasper this morning, and in both he manages to avoid me. He's flanked by Grayson and Linc most of the time. Grayson and Linc both say hi, and Ramani comes to sit next to me in American History, offering to share her notes with me when it's obvious in our group discussion that I didn't do the assignment the night before. She's probably only spending time with me because Adalyn isn't in this class, but I'm grateful to her anyway. I try to show it by giving Ramani what I'm sure is a rusty smile and flipping the bird to some guy in the back row who keeps asking her for her phone number and ignoring the polite brush-off she gives him.

And then there's lunch.

I get my lunch box out of my locker. I look both ways for Ember, but I don't see her in the hall. I wonder if she's going to blow me off. We are not friends, not really.

But when I get to the gym, there she is. Ember, standing near the doorway and bouncing on the balls of her feet, her arms hugged close to her, one hand clutching the handle of her lunch box against her side. Her earbuds are in, and her lips move to some song that only she can hear.

"There you are," she gasps out when she sees me, as if she's been holding her breath. She tugs the earbuds out of her ears.

"I told you I'd be here," I say evenly, though I'm surprised as hell that she's here.

"I know. It's just awkward standing here by myself."

"Haven't you lived in Rocksaw forever?" I ask her.

"Only since the end of sixth grade. Mom and I lived with my dad in Buffalo Hills before that."

"That's still, like, five years. You're not a new kid anymore."

"I know that," Ember replies, sounding hurt. "But once they found out what I could do, well . . . most people seemed uncomfortable with me."

"Again, I give no shits about whether or not other people feel comfortable. They can get over it or get out."

I lead the way to the table where I've been sitting with Jasper and his crew since I arrived. I guess I want to prove to her that I'm as good a person as she thinks I am.

"Does that mean you're not running anymore either?" Ember prompts softly behind me.

"Yeah, it does," I say with more conviction than I feel.

I sit down in my usual spot, and Ember slides in next to me at the very end of the table so that she doesn't have to be next to anyone else. Ramani and Adalyn approach, their eyes widening when they see Ember.

"Hi," Grayson says enthusiastically as he sits down.

Ember gives him an almost-smile. She begins to unwrap a ham sandwich, her movements graceful and efficient.

Ramani and Adalyn exchange glances as they sit down across from us.

"How's your homecoming prep going?" I ask loudly, knowing that it's a topic that Adalyn will latch on to immediately.

Adalyn's eyes shift from Ember to me. "Oh, um. Good. Thanks for asking. Did you want to help out after school next week? We still need some volunteers to help design the junior float."

This has backfired terribly. "Can't," I tell her after I swallow a bite of my sandwich. "We have to help at the shop."

"Of course," Ramani interjects, clearly attempting to keep the friendly conversation going. "Maybe there'll be something else you can do if you want to be involved."

Linc sits down next to Ramani, flashing Ember and me a smile. "More ladies at the table. I love this."

"Yeah, as if it's *you* they're coming for," Ramani teases.

"What?" Linc asks, splaying a hand across his chest, like he's been injured. "Are you saying it's not?"

Finally, Jasper approaches the table with his lunch tray, but he visibly slows when he sees me sitting here already.

"Look, statistics don't lie," Linc continues. "Two more girls started sitting here in the last week. It's got to be me. Who else? Ginger over here?"

Grayson retorts, "Girls like gingers. Way more than overgrown linebackers who write poetry."

Ember is blushing furiously now, and I think my prediction about her feelings for Grayson was correct.

Linc scowls. "I write *fan fiction*. You happened to see part of it that was written in verse. Get it straight." He looks over his shoulder at Jasper. "Are you going to sit down, or what?"

"Yeah," Jasper says, pasting on that grin that pleases every-one but doesn't reach his eyes. "I'm coming." He sits down on Linc's other side, making a big production of opening his carton of milk like it's the most important thing in the world.

"So are *you* going to homecoming?" Adalyn asks Ember, undeterred by Jasper's arrival.

Ember shifts under all the sudden attention.

"Yeah," I reply, throwing myself under the Adalyn-inquisition bus. "We're probably going."

Adalyn beams at me. "Have you bought a dress yet?"

Ember surprises me. "I'm making my own," she offers into the conversation.

"Really?" Ramani asks. "That is so cool. Do you make a lot of your own dresses? I always wanted to ask you where you get them. I don't see anything like them in the stores." She looks admiringly at the dress Ember is wearing now.

Ember nods. "I like to repurpose vintage stuff. Freshen it up. Give it life again."

I look over at Ember's dress again with renewed interest. That explains her and Mia's love of Sunday thrift-store shopping.

"This fabric was actually from a bridesmaid dress, but I cut it off at knee length and used the extra fabric to make long sleeves," she explains, plucking at one.

"That is so awesome," Ramani says.

"It is," Adalyn agrees. Then she changes the subject. "Trix, are you going to bring someone from the city to homecoming?" She's talking to me, but she hazards a glance over at Jasper when she says it.

Jasper focuses on the cafeteria's meat loaf, still not making any eye contact with me.

"No," I answer, taking a bite of ham sandwich rather than elaborating. Underneath the sandwich is another pink Post-it note. This one has a small, poorly sketched tiger who says in a lopsided speech bubble, *You look grrrreat today! XOXO.*

Adalyn starts in on a detailed description of her date: a beautiful, talented volleyball star named Maya who goes to our archrival school, Buffalo Hills High School (a crime against Rocksaw High that could only be forgiven for true love), who Adalyn happened to meet at a sample sale in the city when they both picked up the same dress from opposite sides of the clothing rack. Then Adalyn verbally illustrates her designer dress that will not exactly match her date, Maya, because they're going for a look that's complementary, not matchy-matchy, and the Corvette she's borrowing from her uncle to drive them to the dance. In the middle of her monologue, Grayson blurts out at Ember, "How's your sandwich?"

Ember freezes. A solid five seconds pass. "Um, good."

Everyone looks from Grayson to Ember, even Jasper.

Grayson's cheeks are nearly as red as his hair now that he's got everyone's attention. He swallows once, licks his lips, as if he's building courage to get out his next words. He falters twice before sound comes out. "So do you have a date to the homecoming dance?"

Ember acts like she didn't hear him at all and shuts her lunch box. She gets up from the table, pops in her earbuds, and walks away.

Ramani's and Adalyn's mouths are hanging open as they

watch Ember disappear from the gym.

"So was that a no?" Linc asks the table as a whole.

Grayson busies himself with his meat loaf, the translucent tips of his ears glowing.

"It's a no," I reply. "For both of us."

Adalyn bites her lip, looking at Grayson. She clears her throat. "So Maya's coming to visit this weekend, Grayson, and she's bringing a friend."

Grayson mumbles something unintelligible around a mouthful of meat loaf.

"I'm going to go find Ember," I say, latching my lunch box.

I find her in the farthest corner of the library, curled up on a beanbag chair in a reading nook with her earbuds in. She jerks them out immediately when she sees me. "Why did you make me do that?" she asks, a frown creasing the skin between her dark brows.

"Do what? Bail on Grayson when he was actually talking to you?"

"Why did you make me go eat in there with all those people? I *knew* something terrible would happen."

"You thought they wouldn't like you because you can read their secrets if you touched them. But they were actually really nice. You were the one who stormed off."

Ember puts her earbuds back in.

"I think he was maybe working his way up to asking you to the dance," I murmur loud enough that I know she'll be able to make out what I'm saying. "I saw you nab that homecoming flyer on my first day here. Kind of seemed like you wanted to go."

Ember pretends like she can't hear me.

"I didn't know you were making a homecoming dress. You don't make a dress if you don't actually want to *go* to the dance. Only Cinderella's mice do that, right?"

Ember purses her lips, like she's trying not to laugh. "I wasn't going to actually *go*. I've never even been to a school dance before."

"That makes two of us."

Ember looks at me. "Really?"

"Really." Homecoming is about celebrating home, and that's not something I tend to do. The idea of parades and parties and games and a dance to applaud Rocksaw High's and the town's shared history doesn't sound all that appealing to me. I'm still trying to figure out what home means.

"I just wanted to wear the pretty dress and have Mama do my hair and take my picture. Maybe send one to my dad, so he knows what he's missing." She says that last part with an edge to her voice.

"You could even actually *go* to the dance. As in, there could be a picture of you physically *at* the dance. With a boy," I tease her.

"It's not funny," she says, biting her lip. "I didn't know what to say. I was so embarrassed. What was he thinking? Everyone knows who I am. What I can do."

Something inside me softens for this girl who knows what it feels like to be betrayed by her own hands, whether she uses them or not. "Maybe he doesn't care. Maybe his deepest, darkest secret is that he has a crush on some girl who makes her own dresses and works in the kitchen at a tea shop," I murmur.

I leave Ember to mull that one over alone in the reading nook.

I can't believe I gave a pep talk to someone about attending a school activity. It's like I'm becoming some alternate version of Trix. Never in my life have I worried about homecoming dances or dresses. But there's nothing here about survival, and that's what my whole life has been about. It feels wrong. How can I keep a straight face when Adalyn obsesses over crepe paper and chicken wire floats when there are girls our age working in motel rooms to pay the rent, to get a hit, or to feed a hungry baby?

Girls like my mom used to be.

Things like homecoming are inconsequential. And I can feel it again, that deep pit of anger inside me. And beneath it, a sad sort of jealousy. How does it feel to only ever have worried about dances and pretty dresses?

And I definitely never wondered whether some boy was looking at me or his meat loaf. Jasper, having the nerve to ignore me all through lunch, even after we'd delivered pies and he'd taken me up to Cedar Mountain. Even after what I told him about my mom. And what he shared with me about his brother.

With Shane, everything had been straightforward. The first night, there were Coke-and-cherry slushes at midnight. The next night he beat the crap out of some big, creepy john who tried to back me into a dark corner when I was on my way to the Starlite's main office to pay the weekly rent.

And then Shane and I made out in an empty motel room, his bruised and bloodied hands gentle as they wove themselves in my hair.

Crystal clear.

***

Right after the McCabe Bakery & Tea Shoppe closes, I hurry down to Jensen's Office Supply while Mia and Ember are mopping up and Auntie counts the till. It's warm, Auntie says the warmest autumn she can remember, and I don't even need a jacket as I make my way down the sidewalks, nodding hello to the locals who pass and recognize me as one of the many McCabe women. Jensen's is closed, too, but there's a mail slot in the door. I pull all my waitressing tip money out of my apron pocket and stuff it in through the mail slot.

I've thought about this all afternoon during my waitressing shift, that feeling of relief I experienced when I returned Mia's ring. I've always stolen to get by. To survive. But I don't need to do it anymore. Maybe Mia was right, and it was a gift. It definitely kept me alive. But now it's time to say goodbye to stealing.

It's time to be a newer, better Trix. You can't steal from people if you don't intend to drift away again. And I mean to really put down roots here.

Then I jog back to the tea shop because Auntie should be done balancing the register and filling out paperwork, and I know this time I'll be able to drop that bag of cash into the bank deposit drawer without hesitating.

THIRTEEN

"I TALKED TO GRAYSON AFTER school today," Ember says that evening as we're chopping vegetables for dinner. Her phone blares her favorite Ren and Reckless song, "Your Touch." Its melody made up of crooning minor chords plays through the kitchen loud enough so that Mia and Auntie in the living room can't hear what she's saying.

"Oh, yeah?" I ask. We've barely spoken to each other for the last twenty minutes, and while I'm used to long silences by myself, I can sense Ember is growing uncomfortable with it.

"Did you know he plays the guitar?"

"Something about the case he's always lugging around gave it away."

Ember rolls her eyes and gives a small huff of laughter. "I think he's going to ask me to go with him. To homecoming."

Mia sweeps into the kitchen, beaming at us. "Look at you two, working together, getting to know each other. I love this."

She pinches Ember's cheek and makes a silly face. "What are you talking about?"

"Homecoming," Ember says, carefully not mentioning the boy who wanted to ask her to go with him.

"Are you going to the dance?" Mia asks, her eyes lighting up. "You didn't tell me. That must be why you bought that lavender gown last weekend. I wondered how you were going to turn that into a sundress. But now I see you had *secret plans*."

"I didn't know then for sure if I was going," Ember replies. She clears her throat before she announces, "But I've decided that I am."

"Are you sure you'll be okay?" Mia asks, shifting back into her normal protective mode. "You're not worried about your gift?"

"She'll be fine," I interject, because I'm beginning to see that Mia sometimes feeds Ember's fear about her gift, about how people might treat her because of it. "She doesn't have to hide away because of it."

Mia looks over at me, her pale face coloring. "Of course not. Oh, Ember, I'm sorry if that's what you think I meant. I just don't want you to get hurt."

"I'll be fine," Ember says, sticking out her chin a little. "I'm not scared. Grayson knows what I can do, and he doesn't care."

"Grayson O'Hare?" Mia squeals. "You've got a date and everything?"

Auntie comes into the kitchen to glower at the salad we're making, poking at a green leaf. "What's all this about a date?" she asks.

"Ember has a date to homecoming." Mia sighs, her hand over her heart.

"We're only talking. He hasn't actually asked me." Ember looks uncomfortable with all the attention. "You can go with or without a date, you know."

"About time you started dating," Auntie grunts. "When's the food going to be ready? I'm starving. It better not be all rabbit food either." She glares at the salad again.

"The pasta should be done soon, Auntie," Ember replies, smiling.

"We have to start thinking about who Trix can go with," Mia says, jumping to sit on the kitchen counter next to the salad. "There's Jasper, of course. I see real chemistry there. And then there's his friend Linc. He's a handsome guy. Who else? Roger Umberger's son, what's his name? Todd? He's a senior, I think, and he has the most beautiful blue eyes. He was in the shop this morning picking up a muffin before school."

"Todd Umberger is a tool," Auntie says, standing on her tip-toes to look in the spaghetti pot.

"I don't need a date," I tell her. "I'm not going."

"Of course you're going. Don't be silly. We'll look for a dress for you this weekend. Buffalo Hills has the best vintage dresses. But I think the best place for shoes would probably be Rory's Treasures on the main drag," Mia says, steamrolling on.

"I think I've already got a dress that would work for Trix," Ember says. "The burgundy one I picked up last month, remember? I was saving it for something special, and this is it. It's got awful puffed sleeves, but the color will be perfect for Trix, and I think I can make it into something she would really like." She looks at me. "I mean, if you want it. If you'd rather go with someone else's design, I understand."

Mia and Ember both look expectantly at me now.

"The spaghetti is turning to mush," Auntie interrupts. "We won't even have to chew it at this rate."

Mia sighs, pulling a strand of pasta out with a fork and testing it with a pinch. "Honestly, Auntie, it's barely al dente."

"I don't like it mushy," Auntie says. She looks over at me. "*Roots*, Trix," she says pointedly, reminding me of my fortune. "You're starting to wither."

"Fine," I growl, crossing my arms. "I'll go to the stupid dance if you stop talking about my stupid fortune."

"I can't wait," Mia coos. "I am going to find you the perfect date. And then I'm going to take a million pictures of you two. Maybe we can have one blown up to put on the mantel. Like a ten-by-twelve or something. Maybe bigger. Poster-size."

"Rein it in, Mia. It's a dance," Auntie says. "When one of them wins a Nobel Prize, you can think about putting *another* photo on the mantel."

"You tell me who you want to go with," Mia goes on, ignoring Auntie, "and I'll make him an Ardent Apple pie. You can deliver it. Ardent Apple *always* works."

"She doesn't need pie, Mama," Ember says, getting out the colander to drain the pasta.

"Of course she doesn't *need* a pie," Mia says. "But I want Trix to know that she can use pie if she wants to."

"Maybe *you* should send a pie or two," Auntie says to Mia. "I heard that Emmett Sorensen is single again. And I know very well he stopped to see you the last time he was in town, because I spied on you two from the kitchen. He was looking at *your baked goods*, if you know what I mean."

"Be careful you don't burn yourself," Mia says to Ember, ignoring Auntie.

Auntie, in turn, ignores Mia, talking to Ember. "You don't care if your mama dates, do you? She needs a new man."

Ember shrugs.

"Enough, Auntie," Mia says sharply.

"You're not getting any younger. Let me read your fortune. I bet it says you'll die miserable and alone if you don't ask Emmett out for yourself."

"*Enough*, Auntie," Mia says again, looking flustered now. "You ask Emmett out if you think he's so great."

"Maybe I will," Auntie replies. "He's a piping hot muffin, and I've got the butter," Auntie crows over her shoulder as she goes into the dining room.

"Oh my God," Ember says, rolling her eyes.

Auntie kicks Bacon off the dining room table and shifts the piles of magazines and books and puzzle pieces to one end. "Aren't you going to set the table?" she calls to me.

"Sure," I say vaguely, looking around the kitchen at all the dishes in the cabinets. I pick out a set of four mismatched plates and a handful of silverware from a drawer.

157

I put everything on the table, almost tripping over Bacon as he yowls and winds around my legs, hoping to be picked up or stroked.

Mia brings glasses of water. Auntie trails behind, bearing the salad bowl she retrieved from the kitchen. She looks down at it disdainfully the whole time.

Ember follows with a heavy, chipped crockery bowl of spaghetti and meatballs, setting it on the edge of the table and sliding it to the middle. I sit down next to Ember. Auntie takes the head, and Mia places herself across from me and Ember.

Mia looks admiringly at the spread of food. "We should've gotten wine, Auntie. This looks like we're at some fancy Italian place."

"I've got some moonshine behind the cereal in the cupboard," Auntie offers.

"Not quite what I had in mind." Mia beams at me. "Connor loved pasta. He used to make his own, homemade. It was so much better than what you can get out of a box."

Auntie sighs, as if she, too, is thinking of Connor's wonderful pasta. "Well," she continues in a doleful voice, "aren't you going to say grace before we eat, Trix?"

I open my mouth, trying to remember what that one deeply religious foster mom used to say before dinner, but no sound comes out. I'm just gaping like a fish.

"Fine, I'll do it." She clears her throat loudly before she begins. "Dear bounteous Lord, thank you for hot men like Emmett Sorensen, even if my niece is too stupid to ask him out." Auntie

158

throws her head back and cackles, and I realize this is another one of her jokes.

"Auntie," Mia grumbles, trying not to laugh.

"Amen," Ember says solemnly with her eyes closed.

"So yesterday I met the guy who runs the office supply store," I say, changing the subject.

"Mr. Jensen?" Mia asks, passing the salad to Ember after taking some.

"He was a fine piece of ass back in his day," Auntie says, dishing out spaghetti. "Almost as hot as my second husband."

Ember snorts as she serves herself.

And then maybe it's because we're sitting at the table like a family and it reminds me of the Yangs and when I used to wish that I'd someday have a perfect family, too, but I finally ask about what happened to my father. "Mr. Jensen said Connor was attacked by a shark. And the principal said he was hit by a train. And you told Ms. Troy that he crashed a fighter jet," I say, though it's more of a question than a statement. I'm waiting for someone to tell me the truth. For someone to give me more than a face that looks something like mine, a forgotten baseball glove, a love of drawing, and a mysterious death.

Mia looks like she's about to cry, her eyes tearing up. She's obviously been waiting for me to ask her about it. She presses her lips together and takes a deep breath through her nose before she repeats what everyone keeps telling me: "You look like him, you know." She looks at Ember. "Show Trix that one of Connor and your dad."

159

Ember gets up and brings a picture over from the mantel. I missed this one in my searches, probably because it was lost in the sea of Ember photos.

"That's Uncle Connor on the right. My dad's the one on the left."

Ember's dad is the man I notice first. He's strikingly handsome. He has short black hair, brown skin a few shades darker than Ember's, and a happy grin that makes dimples in each of his cheeks. His hand is on Connor's shoulder, the gesture casual, like they've known each other a long time. Then my eyes fall on Connor. He's average looking, a little shorter than Ember's dad. He's pale like Mia, with gray-green eyes and dark hair, a smile that's almost timid, as if he's not sure that he wants to share it.

I thought there'd be some sign, like a beam of light falling on me, when I finally saw him. But there's nothing. He's just a man, still only a small collection of facts.

"Were our dads friends?" I ask Ember. I don't know anything about her dad. Obviously he's not here. Something about him simmers between Ember and Mia, but I don't know why.

"They were best friends," Mia says wistfully. "Since they were kids."

I hazard a glance over at Ember again, and she's stopped eating, her face unreadable.

"Ember's dad will be here for Thanksgiving," Mia says, watching Ember, now, too.

Ember only shrugs.

"It would be fine with me if Jordan would stay in the city," Auntie huffs.

Mia shoots Auntie a glare. "I'd prefer he come here. Then we can enjoy the holiday together. Would you rather I send Ember to him? Then it would be the two of us staring at each other over a dead turkey?" She spears a chunk of cucumber in her salad with excessive force.

Ember's face is still tight, her green eyes beginning to look a little watery.

"Technically there'd be three of us this year," I joke, wanting to defuse the situation for Ember's sake. Truthfully, it's strange to think about being anywhere for Thanksgiving other than the motel room I was in last year. I don't think I've ever had a normal Thanksgiving, the kind with a big family around a table. Mom and I never celebrated it. Thanksgiving break was only a week in whatever motel or car we were living in when I didn't get free school lunches, and I had to go out and scrounge for something to eat midday. For the Yangs at the Jasmine Dragon, Thanksgiving was a great day to make extra money on all the families who accidentally burned their turkeys or didn't get them out early enough to thaw.

All three women lock eyes on me, pulling me out of my memory.

Mia smiles. "Of course. And Jordan will be able to tell you amazing stories about Connor."

"But back to the town gossip, *how did he really die?*" I insist.

Mia laughs, and shoots a look at Auntie. "Cancer," she says.

"What's so funny about cancer?" I ask.

"Cancer isn't funny," Mia says, more soberly this time. "It's just the obituary was. Connor had this really particular sense of humor. And even when he was sick, he was joking about how cancer was too boring a way to go. He said he wanted to go out with a bang. Some amazing story so that people around here would never forget him. In his last days, he told me that he'd taken care of everything. The funeral arrangements, the obituary. He said he wanted us to party when he was gone, not spend all our time planning services and crying. So the day after he died, all the local papers printed his obituary. *The Rocksaw Gazette. The Buffalo Hills Herald. The Evanston Eagle. The Smokestack. The Cottonwood Hollow Monthly.* Every one of them had an obituary for Connor McCabe."

"And?"

"And every one of them had a different story about how he died. Bull riding in Amarillo. Crashing a plane in the Sahara. Getting hit by a train in China. A shark attack in the Pacific. A volcanic explosion on Fiji."

"So he *lied*? And everybody believed him?"

Mia shrugs. "I'm sure there were a lot of people out there who knew it wasn't true. But everybody still talks about him like all those stories were real. It's nice, really. A way of honoring him the way he was, before he got sick."

"A guy who lied about shark attacks?"

"A guy who wanted to make people happy."

Lying about shark attacks seems like a weird way to make people happy, but I guess I get it. He wanted people to laugh with him, not pity him. I feel like every detail about Connor is just one stroke of the pencil, and someday there'll be enough strokes for me to truly see him. To make out his face, imagine his laugh.

"Wasn't there one about getting eaten by a tiger at a circus?" Auntie asks, twirling pasta on her fork.

I take the photo of Jordan and Connor back to the mantel and look through the other photos there, this time finally knowing which face I'm looking for. Behind a picture of Auntie and one of her husbands, I find another dusty shot of Connor. He's younger, maybe eighteen or so, wearing a very ugly suit with a girl who is obviously not my mother. Maybe a prom photo. Or homecoming, since that seems to be a big deal around here. I slip the photo out of the frame with whisper-quick hands. I tuck it into my back pants pocket, beneath my loose sweater.

It's not really stealing because he was supposed to belong to me.

After dinner and dishes, we go up to Ember's room. It's painted a pale peach, the doorways and windows framed with green vines.

"Did you paint those?" I ask her when I see the vines.

"With stencils," Ember replies. "Mama and Auntie don't care how I decorate. I'm sure we could paint your room if you don't like the color." She leads me to one corner of the room, where a dressmaker's dummy waits with a lavender gown on it. "This is it. My homecoming dress. I made it strapless. And then I cut it off above the knee and hemmed it. See the tulle underneath? I'm going to take it all out, then put one layer on top of the gown. It'll be like mist over the lavender satin. And I'll take in the waist a little and take off the stupid bow in the back."

"That sounds like a lot of work."

"It's a labor of love."

"You could just wear one of your regular dresses. They're nice."

"*You* would probably wear a hoodie," she says matter-of-factly, and it tugs a half smile from me, because I realize she's teasing me. And she knows me a little better than I thought. Ember continues, "But, let me show you the dress I'm thinking of for you." She opens her closet door and digs around in a mass of clothing until she's completely lost, just a disembodied voice in a tiny room of tulle, velvet, satin, and lace. "Wait . . . hold on . . . a second and I can reach it—"

"Do you need some kind of rescue team?" I ask.

"Got it!" she crows as she extricates herself from the closet. Her left hand drags out a burgundy-colored dress in a sateen finish. It's huge and frothy and incredibly ugly. She hangs it on the back of the closet door. "It's not anything now, but close your eyes and imagine what it could be. I'd take off the poufy sleeves, remove about half of the black tulle underneath, and then I'd hem it at the knee and split it up here on the side so a little bit of the black tulle would peek out. Kind of edgy, a little badass. Like you. And I think there'd be plenty from the bottom half of the skirt I take off to put on a long sleeve if you want it. Or we could do elbow-length gloves." She digs out a spiral notebook from the Dollar Tree and sketches it out with a pencil to show me as she gushes.

"I have a hard time imagining how you're going to turn this monstrosity into *that*. So I'm just going to trust you on this."

"You won't regret it!" she squeaks, more excited than I've ever seen her. "I've always wanted to make over a dress for someone else. I want to go to fashion school someday, and this—"

"Ember!" Mia calls, poking her head in the door. "You won't guess what happened! Your dad's on the phone, and when I told him you were going to homecoming, he said he was coming, too! He can't miss his baby girl's first dance!"

Ember's face falls from dressmaking exultation to shock.

"That's great, isn't it?" Mia asks, still beaming, as if she can't see the way Ember's expression has changed. She holds out her phone, her hand cupped over the receiver. "Do you want to talk to him?"

"No, Mama. Not now. Trix and I are busy. I've got to take her measurements." Her movements are stiff as she crosses the room to grab a yellowed measuring tape.

"Sure," Mia says, still covering the receiver. "I'll tell him you're busy. I can't wait for him to meet you, Trix. I'm going to keep it a surprise for when he visits," she whispers, a huge grin on her face.

I only nod, not knowing what else to do.

The door snicks shut.

Ember's face is sullen, her dusting of freckles a dark pattern across her cheeks.

"What's the matter?" I ask. "You don't want your dad to come?"

"It's not as simple as it sounds," she says, brandishing the measuring tape. "The whole thing is a mess."

I wait to see if she's going to explain why, but she returns to measuring, the moment of warmth and excitement cooling between us. She's careful not to touch my skin with her hands. She's going to let me keep my secrets because she has some too.

Later that night, I sit on my bed with all the lights on in my attic bedroom, and I slide the old photo of Connor out of my sketch-book. I open to a fresh page and begin to sketch.

An hour passes, and I pause only to ball my hair up on top of my head so that it doesn't get in my way. My hands are black with charcoal and I smudge it with an intensity I can't quite put into words, remembering what he'd told Tobias Jensen. *In real life, everybody's just shades of gray.*

When I finish, I set the sketchbook open to my latest picture upright next to the small mirror over the dresser. I study Connor's face, the planes and ridges, the wideness of his mouth, the crooked bump on his nose. And then I study my face in the mirror, search-ing for something to tell me that I'm wrong. Something to tell me that I am not all Allison Fiorello who abandoned me. Something to tell me that I am part Connor McCabe, that there is something of him in me that is light instead of shadows.

The only thing we have that's the same is the color of our eyes. But you can't see that in black and white.

FOURTEEN

ONE OF THE MANY JOYS of living in a small town is that when you
don't want to see someone, you start to run into them everywhere.

After more than a week of Jasper avoiding me at school, I
run into him at Lee's General Store while picking up sandwiches
for lunch on Saturday. We lock eyes between the aisles of the tiny
grocery store, me holding sandwiches for Auntie, Mia, Ember, and
myself, and Jasper gripping a box of Pop-Tarts. I open my mouth
to say something, but he turns on one heel of his stupid cowboy
boots and hustles down another aisle. It feels miserable to be blown
off while clutching an armful of lunch meat, and I want to tell him
that I didn't mean to find his prescription, but I'll be damned if I'm
going to chase after him like some kind of lovesick cow.

And that does it for me. I'm beyond feeling bad about looking through his bag. Now I'm just pissed.

So after lunch, when Jasper calls and tells Mia he can't make
any pie deliveries that afternoon because his dad needs his help

on the farm, I'm not surprised. Instead I get stuck riding shotgun with Auntie in the old Suburban for deliveries, listening to her tell me about her first husband, who died of a heart attack while they were having sex. "What a way to go!" She chortles, clipping yet another curb.

By evening, I'm pretty sure I've got whiplash from Auntie's driving, and my feet hurt from waitressing all day. All I want to do is go home, eat something, crawl into bed, and not think about Jasper at all. But on the way home, Mia says the car is almost out of gas, so she stops at Mitch's Gas Emporium to fill up.

And who's there, leaning up against the brick wall of the station, sipping a soda and laughing with Grayson and a couple of other guys from the football team?

Jasper *fucking* Ruiz.

Unaware of my angst, Mia reaches back from the driver's seat and hands me forty bucks. "Can you run in and prepay, hon?" she asks. "It'll take me a minute to get the stupid gas cap off. It *always* sticks. I've got to get it fixed."

"I've been telling you that for years, but you never do it," Auntie grumbles. "Bring me a beef stick," she tells me. "One of the hot ones." She notices the boys standing outside the gas station. "Oooh." She snickers. "Look at those beef *cakes*."

Mia ignores that last part. "You don't need any jerky," she says to Auntie. "We're going home to eat right now. I have leftover shepherd's pie in the fridge."

Ember sits forward when she sees who Auntie is talking about. "I'll go, too," Ember says, pulling out her phone to check her appearance in its reflection. "I'll find that spicy beef stick you like, Auntie. I know where they are."

Mia looks surprised. Ember never offers to run errands because that usually means she'll have to interact with other people. "Okay," Mia says hesitantly, handing Ember a couple bucks for Auntie's request, even though she'd told Auntie no snacks. She looks at me. "Tell them pump two, okay?"

"Or Ember could pay for the gas while she's hunting beef sticks," I say.

"Come on," Ember murmurs, tilting her head at the boys. Her eyes widen, imploring me. "I can't go alone."

"Ugh. You owe me," I whisper back.

Ember opens the door and descends from the Suburban gracefully, and I follow, nearly tumbling out behind her when I accidentally get my boot caught beneath the seat trying to step over an empty baking tray. I barely manage to remain upright when my feet hit the concrete.

The guys stop talking when they see us.

Jasper's eyes lock on me immediately.

Twenty-four hours ago, I still wanted to tell him I was sorry. But now, after a week and a half of him pretending that I'm invisible, I'm furious right back at him. I've been invisible for months at a time while I was drifting, and I'll be damned if I'm going to let someone make me feel that way on purpose.

Grayson waves us over as we approach the building, clearly thrilled to see Ember. He barely notices me. "Hey," he calls to her. "What's up?"

Ember smiles. "We just closed up the tea shop. So we're on our way home."

Grayson nods enthusiastically, like Ember's told him she's going to build a rocket out of Mia's gluten-free muffins and fly to the moon next week.

The other two guys say hi, but when another car pulls up, this one full of what look like senior girls, they peel off from our little group, leaving only the four of us. Jasper shoves his hands in the pockets of his jeans while Ember and Grayson talk, looking at anything but me now—the price of gas, the dumpster that's over-filled, the rust along the wheel wells of Mia's Suburban. I notice that Cleo isn't here, so he must be riding along with Grayson.

I clear my throat, unable to stand this awkwardness any longer. I tell Ember, "I'm going to go pay for the gas. You want me to get Auntie's jerky?"

"Sure," Ember says, handing over the cash carefully, so that we don't touch.

If Grayson notices, he doesn't mention it.

Inside the gas station, I find Auntie's beef stick and prepay for the gas. I take a long time folding Mia's receipt and tucking it into my pocket, and then double-checking the expiration date on Auntie's jerky, which looks a little dusty, to be honest. I ask the clerk if I can switch it for another one. He shrugs and continues watching football on the tiny TV next to the register.

When there's nothing left for me to do and I think Mia's probably filled the tank, I leave the gas station again.

Pump Two is empty. The Suburban is gone.

They left me.

Everything feels tight. I can hear my heart beating in my ears, pounding like the bass on a souped-up car. It's hard to breathe, like suddenly my sweater is too tight, or too heavy. I tug at the neck of my shirt to make it easier to get oxygen into my lungs. Against my will, my eyes are pricking with tears, like I'm some five-year-old who's been forgotten at the grocery store. I'm alone. And I don't know why it's so damn scary, because I've been alone a hundred times. A thousand times. But somehow it's different now.

"Hey!" Ember's voice calls, and I scan the parking lot frantically until I lock eyes on her. She's standing next to Grayson's Jeep, smiling, as if nothing at all was amiss. Relief courses through me when I see her face. "Grayson said he'd give us a ride home. Mama said it was okay."

I am still trying to process the raw, gut-wrenching fear that's ebbing from my veins. I look up, trying to will away the shimmer at the edges of my vision.

"Trix?" Ember calls again, her face revealing concern in the bunching of her eyebrows.

I realize I'm just standing there by the gas station door, holding Auntie's beef stick like I didn't hear a word Ember said.

I clear my throat before I yell back, "Yeah, I'm coming."

But then I notice Jasper's there, next to Grayson and Ember, and I curse my timing instead. Jasper looks like he's doing the same.

"Do you want to take a walk first?" Grayson asks Ember. "It's a nice night." I can tell he's looking for any excuse to spend more time with her, and she's not looking for a reason to leave town yet.

Ember looks over at me, her eyes pleading again.

My feet hurt, Jasper hates my guts, I'm starving, and I have to go play wingwoman.

"Sure. Fine," I say, unwrapping the beef stick and taking a bite.

Somehow we end up at the city park. It's dark, and Ember and Grayson stop and talk by the picnic tables. She perches on one end of the table, and Grayson stands before her, his head tilted forward as he listens intently to whatever she's saying. Jasper is texting someone on his phone while he leans against a set of monkey bars. I wander over to the swings that are situated in an island of play sand, some small part of me remembering a motel where Mom and I lived for a while when I was very young that had a playground out back. I plop down in the swing, the metal chains cold against my hands.

"Higher!" I squeal with laughter, the sunset bathing us both in pink-and-gold light.

Mom pushes me again, her hands warm on the small of my back.

I swing so high that I can see over the top of the motel, past the cars parked there, past the way Mom looked tonight when we had to split a package of ramen noodles for dinner. "Tomorrow will be better. I get paid tonight," she told me as she carefully divided the food.

But I'm not hungry when Mom is here. I drink her in, the way she smiles at me. I eat her laughter. I don't feel empty at all.

"We have to go in soon. Mommy has to go to work."

I know this because the sun is sinking, and she always goes to work at night.

But this time is ours, and I don't want it to end yet. I want to play just a little longer. "Not yet. Let's go higher," *I plead.*

Mom smiles when she says, "Oh, my Trixie"—I know even though I don't turn around because I can hear it in her voice. I save this moment, drawing it in my mind, memorizing every detail. Her hands, warm and firm on my back as she propels me higher, the smell of the metal chains on the swing, the way the motel falls away below me again.

"A teensy-tiny bit higher. But don't fly away on me, little bird," Mom calls, laughing now.

"Hey," Jasper says, startling me. His boots crunch in the sand as he comes to sit in the swing next to me. The light from the streetlamp casts the scarred side of his face completely in shadow, as if that part of him doesn't exist. The part I like the most.

"So you can see me now?" I reply, my voice tight. I take my hands from the cold chains of the swing, pushing away that memory of Mom and the swing set.

"Yeah, I've been kind of an asshole. I'm sorry about that." He runs a hand through his curls. "You didn't say anything to them. About the pills," he adds quietly, so his voice doesn't carry over to Grayson and Ember twenty feet away.

"Is that a question?"

"No."

"So then why say it?" I ask. Unable to keep an edge out of my voice, I realize that I am mostly angry that he thinks he can't trust me. Even after the secrets we've shared, the things I've told him that no one else knows.

"I was just surprised." His voice is soft, thoughtful.

"Why? You think that telling a bunch of your friends something they may or may not already know is the kind of thing that I would do?"

Jasper remains quiet.

"Well, news flash: I don't give a shit about your prescriptions."

"They don't know. About any of it."

"Any of what? You taking antidepressants? It's none of their business."

"Yeah. I guess not."

"Not unless you want it to be." I add that because I want him to know that there's nothing to be ashamed of. That there's nothing to hide. My anger is fading, retreating into the darkness as I rock gently in the swing.

"I don't."

"Okay."

"Okay." He's still sitting there, staring at me like he wants to say something, his boots looking ridiculous in the play sand.

"What is it?" I ask.

"You know about Jesse. My brother."

I wait for him to finish, grabbing the chains of the swing and leaning back to look at the stars.

"It just messed me up really bad when he died."

"You don't have to justify yourself to me." I don't want to be one of those other people in Jasper's life. The kind of person that he can't talk to, that he's afraid to confide in. I want to be his pie-delivery buddy. The person who knows how to open Cleo's door on the first try.

"I want to. I want you to know. I was worse. It was like being at the bottom of a hole and knowing there was no way I could ever climb out of it. But it's getting better now. I mean, I still have good days and bad days, but I feel like I'm getting better. The medicine helps a lot."

"That's good." I kick at the sand. "That's what medicine is for. It's to help you. There's nothing wrong with getting help." All I can think of now is Mom after rehab, Mom in the Good Year, her face full and shining.

"You don't think I should've just gutted it out, been a man and gotten over it?"

"I don't think I've ever told someone to gut it out. But I'll remember the phrase for the future. Could come in handy. Is that something you hear a lot?"

"Yeah, maybe."

"There's some things that gutting it out can't fix. Believe me, I know. If it was possible, I wouldn't be here."

"Where would you be?" Jasper asks, angling his swing closer to mine, until we bump together.

"I'd be with my mom," I say, my voice quavering a little. But the idea moves me in a way I had not expected, it pushes me to imagine the Good Year not as a collection of happy months, but as of Good *Years*. I let that image fill my mind, and I close my eyes. "I'd be living above a Chinese restaurant in a tiny apartment. I'd have a Persian cat. I'd be in a rock band. I would probably have pink hair." I chuckle when I say that last part because I remember how much Wendy had wanted us to dye our hair pink.

Jasper laughs, too, and when I open my eyes, he is closer

than before. I catch the scent of cinnamon on his breath. There's a twinge of urgency deep in my gut, and I finally admit to myself that I want to be more than Jasper's pie-delivery buddy. God forbid, I want him like I wanted Shane, and we all know how that ended. I want to feel Jasper's lips on mine, his callused hands on my skin the way they'd been when he tried to help me with the seat belt of his crappy truck.

He leans nearer, one curl falling over his eye, and I can feel the heat from his body, the smell of cinnamon and the leather from his jacket enveloping us. "I think I'd like to see you in a rock band," he murmurs, his breath tickling my ear, and for one brief moment I think he's going to kiss me, and I want it more than anything.

"Trix!" Ember's voice calls, interrupting the moment. "It's almost nine. Grayson's going to take us home now."

Jasper winces, like cold water's been thrown over the both of us.

The ride back home is quiet. Ember sits shotgun in Grayson's Jeep, and they're talking about music that I've never heard of. Meanwhile, in the back seat, Jasper's boots are planted wide, the fabric of his jeans rubbing up against my knee, and every once in a while he leans forward to add something to the conversation with Grayson and Ember, and his knuckles graze the top of my thigh, and we both know it's on purpose.

At the farmhouse, all the lights are on, blazing a welcome return. I can only imagine that Mia is peering out between a set of calico curtains right about now, nearly dying inside with excitement.

In the dark interior, Jasper's hand grabs mine, and it's warm and rough like I remembered it. "Sorry," he says, "wrong buckle." But he's smiling that grin that pulls the corner of his eye down, and I know that I'm not the only one who wanted that kiss on the swings.

Ember and I get out, and Jasper climbs into the empty passenger seat. We wave goodbye to them from the front porch steps. The scent of the roses surrounds us, and for a few moments, as Grayson's Jeep crunches down the gravel drive, we are silent.

Finally, Ember turns to me. "Thanks," she says. "That was really cool of you."

"Sure," I say, my voice much cooler than the rest of me. "No big deal."

She smiles.

"What is it?" I ask.

"Grayson asked me to go to the homecoming dance with him."

I grin back. "Well, the good news is I know someone who can make you a dress."

When we enter the house, the spicy scent of ginger hits me immediately. Auntie is brewing a pot of tea. "Come here," she calls from the kitchen. "I'm trying this new ginger-jasmine tea. I think we could offer it at the shop."

"No," I say immediately, taking a step back.

Mia sees my reaction, and she frowns. She gets up from the couch, folding a magazine and tucking it beneath the crook of her arm. "Is everything okay?"

All I can think of is Mrs. Yang at the Jasmine Dragon, carrying a fresh pot of ginger-jasmine tea to the elderly couple who came every Wednesday to their restaurant. The what-ifs with Jasper make me imagine myself there again, a seventeen-year-old Trix who might've been in a rock band, who almost had a mother who never left her. I tell Mia, "I think I'm going to go to bed."

"Aren't you hungry?" Mia asks, coming closer. She holds up one hand, as if she wants to check me for a fever.

"No," I croak out. "I just want to go to bed. Please just let me go." My voice quavers, and I am ashamed.

Ember frowns a little, and I know that she's disappointed in me.

I flee upstairs anyway, and I wait until I'm safe in my room before I go back to the Jasmine Dragon.

The Yangs invite us to celebrate the lunar New Year with them in late January. Jack says it's better than Christmas because all the children get the best gifts: red packets, beautiful red-and-gold embossed paper envelopes with money inside them.

When the evening of the lunar New Year arrives, I'm nervous because I know that it's a special holiday, a family event that Mom and I have been invited to join, one night for us to be part of the Yangs' beautiful family. Mrs. Yang teaches me to make dumplings, her hands over mine as she shows me how to make tiny pleats in the dough so they stay shut after we've put pork filling inside. I can't seal them as well as she does. Wendy, Jack, and I fill the metal trays with rows and rows of dumplings, more than I think we will ever be able to eat. The restaurant is closed tonight, and Mrs. Yang plays contemporary music instead of the instrumental kind that usually plays softly in the background of the dining room.

Mom helps Mrs. Yang steam the dumplings in the kitchen, and Wendy, Jack, and I play Scrabble with Mr. Yang. We have special rules so that we can play slang words, too, and we use a battered dictionary to solve our arguments. Mr. Yang only listens to American music on the small radio in the kitchen while he cooks, and if he hears a word or a phrase he doesn't know, he writes it down and looks it up in the dictionary after the restaurant closes. Sometimes the list is only one word, other times three or four slang words or idioms splashed with smoky sesame oil. He nearly trounces us in Scrabble, but when I get up for a drink of water, I notice that he holds back at the end and doesn't play aspire for two rounds so that Jack can play ago on a triple word score tile and win the game.

When the food is prepared, we all sit down at the big guest table in the middle of the restaurant. Mrs. Yang made all my favorites because she says I still look too skinny, but there are new foods, too: a whole roasted fish with its eye staring up at me; brown, wrinkled duck eggs; a shredded-cabbage salad with fermented tofu. We eat with chopsticks, family style, all of us sharing the same dishes. Mrs. Yang smiles at me when I use my chopsticks faultlessly after practicing every night for two weeks with Wendy. Not too high, not too low. And never spear them into the rice like a grave marker. Jack says a bad word when he pulls a fish bone from his mouth, and Mr. Yang taps him lightly on the back of the head, admonishing him with a smile. They are a family, and they are perfect, and for this one night, Mom and I get to be a part of that.

I think that maybe someday Mom and I will be a family like the Yangs. Maybe someday I will have a father, too, and a little brother like Jack, and we will sit around the table and share a meal like this.

I bite down on something hard in my dumpling. Confused, I reach up and pull a shiny penny out of my mouth.

Wendy notices. "Look!" she says. "Trix got the coin!"

"Look at that!" Mrs. Yang says. "You will have good luck this year, Trix. Money will come to you."

I can't imagine being any luckier than I am right now. Mom squeezes my hand, and she smiles at me. She looks exquisite in the golden glow of the restaurant chandeliers, and I can forgive her anything.

I put my new lucky penny in my pocket and vow to keep it forever, like this warm, happy feeling that radiates through me, lighting me up until I feel like even my scars are glowing and beautiful.

At the end of dinner, Mr. Yang gives us our red packets. Mom gets teary and says I can't accept it, but Mr. Yang tells her all children get a gift tonight. Mom lets me keep it, and I tell myself that I will save it all so that next year I can buy a gift for him.

A week later, Mom slips and falls in the kitchen and hurts her back. One of the cooks broke a bottle of oil on the floor and didn't clean it up well. Mom goes to the doctor, and he gives her some pain pills. I go with her to the pharmacy to get them, my lucky penny in my pocket. A month later, her back still hurts, and she goes back for more. She starts going out at night, after her shift, leaving me upstairs alone. Sometimes she comes back smelling like smoke and beer. Other times she smells only of ginger. I lie in bed alone waiting for her, rubbing my lucky penny between my fingers.

I am afraid that things will go back to the way they were before. I pretend to have stomachaches, lots of them, so that Mom will stay home with me after her shift. I hold my penny as she reads to me, her voice *detailing the many exploits of Harry Potter. I don't know if she leaves after I fall asleep.*

Six months later, the cabinet above the sink in the bathroom is filled with little orange prescription bottles. I watch from our apartment window as a strange man meets Mom behind the Jasmine Dragon. He gives her pills in a small plastic baggie. I ask her about them, angry that she is using again. She rubs her hand over my hair, tells me it will be all right. The pills are just for her back.

Mrs. Yang frowns when Mom's eyes start to get that glazed look. She's tired, I tell Mrs. Yang. I don't know if Mrs. Yang believes me, but she tells Mom to take the afternoon off to rest.

While Mom takes a nap, I rub my lucky penny, waiting for it to work, to change our luck, which seems like it is running downhill again.

My fingers, damp with sweat, slip on the copper coin, and it falls to the floor. My breath catches in my throat, and I am on my knees, crawling after the penny as it rolls along a groove in the wood floor, straight to the air-conditioning vent by the wall.

I reach out and slap my hand down, stopping the penny just in time, before it plummets.

I stare down the air-conditioning vent, a deep, dark hole that seems to descend into nowhere.

Inspiration strikes.

I dump all the pills down the toilet and flush them away. I rub my lucky penny between my fingers, sure that I have fixed things this time, and our luck will return.

When Mom wakes up, I tell her what I've done. At first I think she will be angry, but she's not. She starts to cry and says she's sorry.

She takes me in her arms and holds me, and we rock together in the tangle of sheets in the middle of the bed, her tears wet against my hair.

I am too scared to tell Mrs. Yang what happened, afraid they will kick us out if they knew how close we'd come to losing everything again. So that night I lie and say Mom has the flu and can't come down for the dinner shift. Mrs. Yang makes a sympathetic sound in the back of her throat and sends me back upstairs with some soup.

Mom seems better again. She goes to work; she smiles like before. Mr. and Mrs. Yang smile, too, and the tightness in my chest eases. I have my lucky penny to thank for all of it.

More time passes. The lunar New Year is coming soon. I am excited. I have a new shirt that I will wear, and I have saved some of my red packet money from last year to buy Mr. Yang a new dictionary of American slang and idioms because Jack accidentally spilled a glass of Coke on his when we were playing Scrabble together in the back booth. Everything is going to be perfect.

But it's not.

In the space of a moment, I know the Good Year is over.

Mom wakes me up. It is dark. Sleep makes me slow. She doesn't smell of ginger, but of something stale, like dishrags that need washing. "Get up," she says. "We have to go."

I search desperately in the sheets for my lucky penny.

"Damn it, Trix, come on." She's got something in her hands. It's the deposit bag that Mr. Yang takes to the bank every night after close. Sometimes he asks Mom to take it if he's had a long day, like when one of the cooks calls in sick. I keep frantically digging through the sheets. If I have my lucky penny, I can stop this, like I did when I dumped the pills. Mom won't leave the Jasmine Dragon. We will be a family like

the Yangs, and everything will be like a beautiful snow globe.

Mom yanks me out of the bed, pulling hard on my arm until her fingernails dig into my skin, making tiny crescent moons beneath my pink scars. "I said get up, Trix!" I stumble out of bed, and she grabs my sneakers from under the bed and tosses them at me. "Get your shoes on. Hurry."

"Where are we going?" I ask, pulling on my shoes.

"Don't worry about it. Get your damn shoes on." In the light from the bedside lamp, I see them. The fresh track marks on her arm. I've seen them before, back before she went to rehab. There's a deep, sinking feeling in my stomach.

"No," I tell her. "I don't want to leave."

"You're coming with me, Trix. Now shut up and get your coat."

"Let me stay here," I beg.

I want to stay here forever in the Jasmine Dragon with the Yangs. I want to find my lucky penny. I want to show Mrs. Yang the perfect pleats I can make in the dough of the dumplings. I want to give Mr. Yang the new dictionary that I bought for him. I want Wendy to be my sister, to be my best friend forever.

Mom yanks my arm again, and she drags me along with her while tears prick my eyes, hot and wet. I follow her down the staircase, past the steamy windows, and out into the dark night.

FIFTEEN

MY OLD LIFE WAS HAUNTING me, so I find myself on Cedar Mountain. It's Friday afternoon, and I'm sitting in the abandoned lawn chair on the crest of the hill, checking my phone messages with the one bar of signal I can reach. One text message from Charly. *Big surprise soon. Wait for it!*

After our last phone conversation, I have a feeling that the surprise is Shane coming home. I wonder if I will be able to resist him if he calls, the sound of his voice deep and smooth like the softest, darkest charcoal. He was my safe place. My shelter. Maybe I loved him because he was the first person to ever love me back. Or maybe it was because he was the only person who ever shared his dreams with me. Dreams that were far beyond the Starlite, far beyond the cramped rooms and cardboard-thin walls and the smell of sweat that clung to the sheets and the glint of needles that littered the parking lot.

I remember what Auntie said when she read my palm. I

thought Shane was going to be my roots once, him and me in the little house he dreamed about. But that feels like forever ago. I've moved on. There's a space and distance between us now that can't be bridged.

"Hey," a voice calls from the slope of Cedar Mountain below, pulling me from my thoughts. I see a dark head appear, then a set of shoulder pads. Jasper. "I wanted to give you fair warning before practice starts. We're doing hill climbs for conditioning today. There's about to be forty guys running up and down this hill." He's wearing a short red practice jersey that covers his shoulder pads and chest but still reveals his tan stomach, and the barest hint of a V-cut above his hip bones reawakens the ache I'd felt with his knuckles brushing against my leg in the back seat of Grayson's Jeep.

"Thanks," I tell him. Pulling my gaze up from his midriff, I put my phone away. "I don't think I want to be here for that."

"I didn't figure you would. Even though it will be a majestic pack of men, none of them will be as impressive as what you're seeing here." He tilts his head forward so a dark curl tumbles down over his forehead. There's been tension between us all week after the almost-kiss at the park, but neither of us has been able to act with so many of his friends around.

I laugh. "Wow. I'm overwhelmed right now."

"I thought you might be." When he smiles, it reaches his scar, so I know it's real. I wonder if some part of him is lighter because he's not alone with his secret. I hope so. I know that one person can't fix another. But if me sharing some of his secrets, some of his pain, can help him a little, then it's something I'm glad to do.

"I'll try not to faint or anything on my way down the hill."

"I'll walk with you in case you do." He holds out his Tigers helmet as if to show me the way.

"Such chivalry."

"So, are you adjusting to life in Rocksaw?" he asks as we climb down the steep hill together.

"It took a little while, but I think I'm getting the hang of it."

"The key is to always say please and thank you and watch out for fugitive cows on the road by your house. Oh, and never turn down food when it's offered to you," he says.

My footing slips a little on the steep path, and Jasper snakes out an arm around my waist to steady me. It's warm and firm, and lingers a little too long. I wish he'd leave it there. "Thanks." There's a beat of silence before he removes his arm and I reply to his earlier statement. "There's a lot of food in my life now. Mostly pie."

"I bet there is. Mia's pie is famous. And so are the McCabe women. All of them have gifts, or so the story goes. Even the ones who marry in. 'Like calls to like,' or so they say." He raises an eyebrow and looks at me.

"That's what I hear, too."

"So are you going to tell me what you can do?" He neatly avoids the root of a cedar jutting up from the dirt, his cleats sure after years of running up and down the path.

"Maybe I'm the exception that proves the rule."

"I definitely believe you're exceptional."

We both laugh. "Wow, you're really laying on the charm today. Let's just say I can take what I want when I want it," I tell him.

We've reached the bottom of Cedar Mountain, and I glance back up at the top, wishing we were there instead of here, in plain view of the entire football team warming up for practice. We stand there anyway, neither of us wanting to leave the other.

"Really? Anything?"

"Anything."

"That's awesome. Do me a favor and take some of my homework sometime."

I laugh. "No thanks. My five-finger-discount days are done." I hike my backpack up a little higher on my shoulder.

"You know, there's an old story that back when they founded Rocksaw, the McCabes were one of the first families here. And their daughters were so beautiful and so strangely gifted that people in Buffalo Hills thought they were witches and wanted to run them out of the area." He nods west, as if I am to understand the location of all the neighboring towns by now.

"So they came at them with pitchforks and torches?"

"They did. The road to town crossed through the two largest homesteads in the area, and they were about to have a bumper crop of wheat. But the owners set fire to it all to block the road to keep the mob out."

"They set fire to their farms to keep the Buffalo Hills people from getting the McCabe women?"

"They did. And the mob turned around because they thought if the McCabe women were so powerful that they'd make the Rocksaw farmers burn their own crops, maybe they shouldn't be messing with them."

"So are these Rocksaw families still around?"

Jasper tucks his helmet under one arm like he's pondering the question. "Well, the Ruizes are, but the Smithfields eventually moved on. Florida, I'm pretty sure."

"Of course the Ruizes would have been involved," I reply.

"We're in all the good stories." He gives me an exaggerated wink. "I've got an uncle who's a sheriff's deputy in Cottonwood Hollow. You wouldn't believe what he's seen over there."

"I think maybe we need a little fact-checking on this one." The wind picks up, blowing my hair and tumbling his dark curls.

"And that's only one of the great Rocksaw stories. There are hundreds. But the McCabes are legendary." He reaches out and tucks an errant strand of hair behind my ear, the act small and gentle, but setting every nerve ending in my body on fire. I really wish the entire football team wasn't fifty yards away, grunting and guzzling Gatorade.

Jasper clears his throat before saying, "I'd better get to practice."

"Yeah," I agree, falling in beside him as we walk toward the practice field. "I've got to get to work, anyway."

"So are you coming to the football game next week?" he asks.

"Well, the McCabe Bakery and Tea Shoppe is manning the concession stand to help fund-raise for the big homecoming festivities. Mia says we're to be there under penalty of death. Or extreme disappointment, anyway. So, the answer to that is yes. I'll be there."

We've reached the practice field, where large clusters of boys wearing shoulder pads and helmets are gathered. Someone whistles and calls, "Woo-hoo, go, Jasper! Get you some, son!"

"Shut it!" Jasper yells back. He looks at me. "Sorry. Cedar Mountain is also kind of a hookup spot. They might have gotten the wrong idea."

His words hang between us, as if the wrong idea didn't seem so damn right.

"I didn't realize Cedar Mountain was such a cultural landmark in this town," I reply, staying focused in front of our audience.

"We're full of surprises like that." He grins at me again, his scar pulling down in a way that makes my stomach do a backflip. "Mia texted me and said she needs pie delivery tonight. Any chance you could come along?" He pauses, reading my face, and as if to sweeten the deal he adds in a mockingly husky voice, "Maybe I could take you for a ride on my tractor later." He's barely able to keep a straight face.

"Oh, definitely. Can't wait for that." I shoulder my backpack.

"Then I'll see you at six."

I jog downtown to the tea shop, a stupid grin plastered on my face thanks to Jasper and his tractor joke and the possibility of seeing him alone again tonight.

My backpack bangs loosely against my back because it's only got my sketchpad in it, the one with all my most prized sketches in it. Between classes I was working on one of Mia in the kitchen at the tea shop. I wanted her there amid the chaos of tea kettles and baking sheets, her red hair pinned up in a fiery mass. I wanted to capture her there, where she is her most vibrant, her most creative. And I want one of Ember, too, but she should be sitting on the front steps of the farmhouse in one of her beautiful dress creations.

And one of Auntie on the couch, asleep to the background noise of her latest television show, her silvery gray hair spilling across a cross-stitched pillow.

Suddenly I have all these ideas, and my fingers ache to sketch them out, color them in pastels or ink. I'm in love with the oil paints in art class, the piney smell of the turpentine, the way the colors can be worked and reworked on the canvas I stretched myself, changing, deepening into something beautiful and complex. Some days I think I'm like those oil paints, deepening, changing every day, and one day I'll be able to change the planes of my face, the shape of my nose until I look more like Connor, until I can believe everyone when they tell me I'm like him.

Mia jumps when I scoot in the door of the tea shop.

"Sorry I'm late!" I gasp, sliding my backpack off my shoulder.

"I was kind of freaking out," Mia squeaks, clutching her apron. "I mean, I'm glad you're okay. But you were later than usual, and Ember didn't see you after school. So I was worried. Could you call next time? Something to let me know that you're okay?"

"I'm sorry," I say, following her behind the counter and back into the kitchen, her anxiety dampening my mood. I don't know how long it will take for her to believe that I'm not going to disappear. I don't know what I can do to prove that I've changed. Maybe she'll never really believe that I'm here for good. The thought eats at me. I have changed. There are parts of me that are the same Trix from when I got here, but there's more that isn't. The old Trix wouldn't have a job. The old Trix wouldn't have said *sorry* when Mia asked me to call.

The old Trix would have been long gone weeks ago.

I grab my apron off the hook on the wall. "I was up on Cedar Mountain."

"What?" Mia and Auntie exclaim at the same time. Auntie nearly drops the kettle she was filling at the sink.

"With a *boy*?" Mia asks, clutching her apron again, this time in anticipation.

"No. Well, *yes*, but that was later. I only went up there to check my messages. I have NorthStar, and that's the only place my phone gets a signal. I needed to see if my friend called me. It had been a couple days since I checked."

Mia's face nearly crumples. "Oh, sweetie, I'm so sorry. I had no idea. How awful for you to have no way to talk to the friends you left behind."

"Jesus, Mia. She's all right," Auntie says, setting the kettle on the stove. "It's a phone, not an oxygen tube."

Mia shoots a glare at Auntie. "She has a right to talk to her old friends, Auntie."

"It's okay," I tell Mia, feeling guilty for being frustrated with her earlier. "There was only one text message. She's busy now, I guess." I don't say that Charly has probably forgotten about me. It's been weeks since we've seen each other. She's undoubtedly found new friends now. Maybe a new boyfriend. She's probably waiting for Shane's return, until the moment that she has him to take care of her again. He always promised that he would take care of us, and I'm sure nothing has changed as far as he and his little sister are concerned. It's only me who's out of the picture now.

"I'll get it taken care of," Mia says. "We'll get you a phone on my plan, and then you'll have a signal since it's a local provider." She reaches out and pats my hand. "And then you can call me if you're going to be late."

"It's not a big deal," I tell her. "I'm fine."

Mia gives me a tight smile, like no matter what I say, nothing will mitigate the guilt of keeping me away from my city friends, even if it wars with her constant fear of me returning to my old habits and running away. She's not alone. Guilt churns in my gut, too, over the promise of a new phone that works anywhere in Rocksaw. Mia doesn't know that the only thing Charly would do with easier access to me is try to get me to come back to the city.

"Oh," Mia adds, her face still looking unusually strained. "Ms. Troy called. She has to push back her home visit. She's not feeling well. But we'll see her at the end of the month."

I shrug. "It's not a big deal. I've done lots of them."

Mia looks like she wants to say more, but she holds her tongue for once.

About fifteen minutes after we close, Jasper pulls up outside the McCabe Bakery & Tea Shoppe in his old black truck, Cleo.

"Oh, good!" Mia exclaims from where she's been mopping the dining room floor. "Jasper is here. I swear, I don't know what I'd do without him." She looks at me. "Can you help me get these boxes out to his truck?"

I nod, taking a deep breath before I say, "Jasper asked if I could go on deliveries with him tonight. Is that okay?" I've never asked anything, least of all permission to go somewhere with a boy. *See?* I want to say to Mia. *I'm different. I'm changed.*

Mia beams. "Of course you can. I can run the deposit over

to the bank." She strokes a hand over my hair, the gesture stirring some long-ago happy memory. "I'm so glad you're making friends here."

Behind her, Ember makes an *ooooh* face that looks like she wants to ask a million questions. I feel like we're finally more than strangers who live in the same house. I feel like we're becoming friends.

I pull off my apron. My tip money is jammed in the front pocket, so I fold it up and stuff it into the pocket of my jeans along with the principal's stolen fountain pen, which I keep on me at all times so that if I get an idea, I can sketch it out.

Okay, so there's a *tiny* bit of old Trix still around. I'm not returning the pen.

Mia and I go outside with the delivery boxes as Jasper is getting out of the truck. "Hello, Ms. McCabe," he calls when he sees us. "Sorry I'm running a little late. I got held up."

"Tractor problems?" I ask.

Jasper fights a smile as Mia hands him a stack of pink bakery boxes.

"Oh, you're perfect, Jasper, as usual. Auntie just boxed up the last of the pies." She hands him a note with the names and addresses of the orders when he's secured the deliveries in the wooden crate. "Now don't keep our Trix out too late." She winks at me.

"Got it, Ms. McCabe," Jasper says, giving her a salute.

"Curfew is ten," she says, trying to look serious when I can tell that she's secretly giddy.

I get Cleo's passenger door open on the second try. The seat belt buckled on the first.

"Nice," Jasper says. He holds up the list, checking it in the glow of the dome light. The light gleams on the gold class ring hanging from his rearview mirror.

"Is this yours?" I ask him, gently picking up the ring. One side has drama masks and the other has a football. But the graduation year is wrong.

"Jesse's. This was our truck. Before. We were supposed to share it."

"Oh," I say, letting the ring drop softly back on its chain. "He liked acting and football, huh?"

He smiles faintly. "Yeah, he used to drive my dad crazy saying he was going to move to LA and try to make it as an actor. Dad, of course, wanted him to stay on the farm."

"Seems like it would have been easier to let you inherit the farm if you wanted it, so that Jesse could've gone to LA or do whatever he wanted to do."

I can tell today is better than the day in the lunchroom when Ramani spoke about Jesse at last year's homecoming. Then, Jasper had become more closed off, distant. Tonight, when Jasper talks about his brother, his face is alive, expressive, not shuttered. "A lot of things could be easier with my dad. It's just who he is. Everything is about tradition. The oldest son inherits the farm, like he did and his father before him. And every few years he buys a few more acres, another field or two to plant, building this empire for his family." Jasper touches the class ring where it hangs. "And with my mom, everything is about appearance. My parents are Catholic, and they belong to a small church. Mom is always on every fund-raiser and charity-event board. So she wants us to be a model family so we don't embarrass her." He lifts the ring to let the ruby stone catch the light.

"So is that why Jesse was president of everything and in all the clubs?" I ask. "His plaque in the high school makes him look like he was Superman."

"Pretty much. And it got to him. He used to be this happy-go-lucky kid, and then he wanted to be an actor, and there was all this crazy pressure from our parents to do the responsible thing, to do the thing that *looked* good."

"And then a hunting accident," I say, finishing the story. I'm sorry I said it as soon as the words leave my mouth.

"And then a hunting accident," Jasper echoes, letting the ring drop back on its chain again.

There's a brief moment of silence, and in that space, I remember what Jasper asked me before, about why some people choose to leave us. And I wonder if everything about his brother's story happened the way he told it to me. "I'm sorry. That must have been really awful," I say quietly.

"It was." He starts the truck, puts his hand along the back of the seat while he backs out of the parking spot. He moves it back down to shift the truck into first gear, brushing against my shoulder. "But I don't imagine having your mom walk out on you was stellar fun, either."

Now I know he's thinking of our last conversation, too. He's opened up to me, so I feel like I should reciprocate. "I used to wish that my mom would just get better. That she would love me enough to stop using, and then we could be a real family. We could be like this really nice family that we lived with for a little while in the city."

"What changed?"

I shrug. I don't say Mom could never forgive me, or herself, and that maybe we never had a chance of being happy together. And maybe that's why she left.

We're at the first stop, and I tell Jasper I'll wait in the truck for this one. I sit in the dark cab, watching him walk up to the brick ranch-style house, his back straight, his arms full of pink bakery boxes.

I wonder if I'll ever see Mom again. Or if I will go through the rest of my life trying to piece together all the good moments we had together to block out the bad ones. I wonder if she thinks of me, too. I wonder if she misses me. I wonder if she recalls how she used to push me high on the swing. How she used to lay me down in the bathtub and tell me not to unlock the door. I close my eyes, as if I could block all of it out.

Jasper changes the subject when he gets back in the truck, like we subconsciously agreed that we'd had enough deep introspection for the night. "So are you going to homecoming with anyone?" he asks.

"Where have you been?" I tease, trying to fill myself with light, to remind myself of that wanting I feel with Jasper, a feeling that can drown everything else out if I let it. "Adalyn's been leading the inquisition for two weeks now. I've either got a mysterious date from the city that I won't tell her about, or I'm going stag because I'm such a badass rebel."

"Yeah, but once she starts talking about homecoming these days, I kind of tune her out. There are only so many times I can debate whether or not fifty yards of streamers will be enough to wrap the lampposts down Main Street, or if we should let the seniors pick out the party favors. I'm no saint."

"Well, the answer to the my-date mystery is the badass option. I'm going solo. Ember invited me to go with her and Grayson, but I think that might be kind of awkward."

"It wouldn't be awkward if we doubled," he replies, pulling up in front of Mitzi's Love Shack. "Last delivery," he announces, as if he didn't just sort of ask me out.

"You and me? Go with Grayson and Ember?" I manage to say it like he hasn't been on Mia's Top-Three Potential Dates for Trix list that she runs through every night at dinner.

"Don't sound so shocked. There are lots of girls who think I'm a real catch. I mean, I drive Cleo. I have great hair. I deliver pie." He makes a sweeping gesture with his hand over the dashboard that suggests I could have all of this by going with him.

"Pretty hard to turn down after you consider the great hair."

"It is, unless you'd really rather go stag to homecoming. Or you're planning on asking someone else, either hipster city guy or Rocksaw redneck."

"I didn't have plans to ask anyone. And I barely know anyone here outside of your crew."

"*Our* crew," he corrects. "You were accepted into the fold when you started taking on your share of the homecoming conversation with Adalyn."

"I am so honored. Is there a matching tattoo or something I can get?"

"I'll get you a business card for our local tattoo parlor." He opens the door and this time I slide out after him. "So is that a yes

197

to homecoming, or are you changing the subject to politely avoid rejecting me?"

"It's a yes."

He grins, and it tugs on his scar again. I realize that that's one of the things I like about him. He could pull those tumbled curls down to cover that scar, but he doesn't. He always flips his hair to the other side, like he's damn proud of that scar.

I wish I could be that brave.

"I have to come with you for this one," I tell him, leaning against the bed of the truck. "In case there's another naked guy who chases you."

"I'll never forget that day. It's burned into my long-term memory." He laughs, reaching into the bed and getting out the Cherish Cherry and Ardent Apple.

"Mine, too. Especially the way he was all red from the hot tub. Like a giant lobster."

Jasper makes a face and shakes his head vigorously to get rid of the image, messing up his black curls.

When we get to the cottage door, I reach under the mat for the key, opening the door slowly for Jasper as he waits next to me. Empty.

The cottage is dark, so I flick on a light. The hot tub is covered, and there's a gift basket on the table that's been opened, some of the cheeses and nuts scattered across the table. Jasper sets the pies down and picks up a note.

"Look at this," he announces. "It says, 'Thanks, Mitzi, but we had to go back to the city for a family emergency. The Grangers.'"

"So I guess they won't need the pie, then." I notice the bottle of champagne that's still in the gift basket, unopened. "I guess they won't need this, either," I say, picking up the bottle, a grin stealing across my face.

"Are you thinking what I'm thinking?" He laughs back at me.

"I hope so."

"We save the tractor ride for date number two."

Jasper and I sit on top of Cedar Mountain in the abandoned lawn chairs, passing the opened bottle of champagne between us. It's cheap and pink and it sparkles and burns all the way down, like swallowing stars.

"Best view in town," Jasper says, taking the bottle from me when I pass it back to him.

"Look at all the shops down there," I say, pointing at the sprinkling of lights way down along Main Street.

"There's the McCabe Bakery and Tea Shoppe," he says, leaning over and pointing out the shop. He maneuvers his arm over along the back of my lawn chair like he did in the bench seat of the truck earlier. His breath is hot against my skin, his lips barely grazing against my ear. It's cold outside, and our breath is beginning to come out in soft clouds, but the alcohol makes everything feel warm and fuzzy.

"Is it okay for you to drink with the medicine you're taking?" I ask, suddenly remembering that he's mixing champagne and antidepressants.

"It's fine," he says. "I'm okay." There are a few silent moments, just a deep breath in and out from both of us before he speaks again, his voice softer. "I just want to be Jasper with you.

Not Jasper with the dead brother, okay?"

"Okay."

He leans his forehead against my hair, his breath even and warm against my cheek.

I want him to laugh again. "Do you see Auntie down there?" I ask. "I bet she sees us."

"Auntie sees everything," he says with a chuckle as he starts to lean back, as if Auntie really could spot us. "She read my palm once and told me that I had a special touch. I could only make things grow, no matter what else I wanted. And that's when I admitted to myself that all I ever wanted was to farm, even if it was supposed to be Jesse's life and not mine." He holds his hand out, looking at his palm, and I surprise us both by turning to face him and placing my own hand over his, as if I could wipe away both our fortunes and start new.

We stay that way for a few moments, and then my fingers weave between his, and our hands are clasped together. "Well," I say, clearing the silence between us, "I hope Auntie doesn't see this."

I release his hand, fist my own in his soft, faded plaid jacket. And then I kiss him.

His mouth is soft and warm and the faint stubble on his chin a little rough against my skin, like I knew it would be. Every electric moment of waiting to be alone for the last week ignites, and I forget everything else. There's only me and Jasper now. He reaches up and cradles his hand against my cheek, deepening the kiss, and his mouth tastes of cheap champagne. One of his curls falls against my forehead.

"I hope she doesn't see this, either," Jasper whispers in my ear, pulling me over from my chair to his so that I'm sitting in his lap. My foot tips over the bottle of champagne, but neither of us cares as the rest of the pink liquid runs frothy rivers between Jasper's boots into the dirt.

His hands are warm, the calluses from farm work scraping gently across the skin where my sweater has ridden up on my waist. I feel warm and supple inside and out, like his hands and his kisses are thawing me after years of being stiff and cold and alone. I unfist my hands from the front of his jacket, sliding them inside his coat and against his white T-shirt, slipping them around his sides until I can splay them against the planes of his back, holding him like he's holding me. All I can think is that I want to stay here with him forever: wanted, wanting.

Two minutes before ten o'clock, Jasper drops me off at the McCabe farmhouse, barely idling his truck up along the lane that's flanked by deep-red roses. "We made it," he whispers, as if Auntie could hear us all the way out here. "Ten o'clock exactly." He touches my cheek with the backs of his fingers, leans in for one more kiss. It's softer, quieter than the others. A good-night kiss rather than a goodbye.

"Good night, Jasper."

"Good night, Trix."

SIXTEEN

THINGS BEGIN TO SHIFT EVER SO slightly. Ember takes out her earbuds when I come downstairs in the mornings. She waits for me after school, and we walk down to the McCabe Bakery & Tea Shoppe together. Sometimes we talk about school, or boys, or a new song on the radio. And sometimes we don't. But even when we are silent, there's a feeling of comfort between us now. A sense of loneliness lifting a little for both of us.

When Ember and I get to the tea shop after school today, it's doing brisk business, or at least it would be, if anyone was manning the empty counter. Neither Mia nor Auntie is anywhere to be seen, which is strange because we have a rule that there always has to be at least one McCabe at the counter at all times. When Ember and I enter the front door, there are two women and a farmer in coveralls waiting near the pie display for take-out bakery orders. They murmur to each other, but clearly nobody dared to do anything like bellow for Auntie, who would undoubtedly somehow curse them with a bad fortune. The tables have more customers who are sipping their tea and chatting, so Mia and Auntie must not have disappeared that long ago.

Ember notices the oddity immediately, her dark brows quirking in concern as she glances over at me.

"I've got it," I murmur, nodding at the front counter.

"I'll head to the kitchen and put on the kettle," she replies, slipping past me and into the back.

I toss my backpack behind the glass display and start taking orders, my fingers used to the cranky register by now. When I've taken orders and handed out several pies and a dozen cupcakes in pink bakery boxes, I head back to the kitchen to see what's going on.

In the back, Ember's got the walk-in cooler open barely a crack, but it's enough for the raised voices to carry out.

"This is what I'm talking about!" Mia's voice is shrill. "This is the kind of thing you always do."

"All I did was give Emmett Sorensen your phone number," Auntie huffs.

"You told him I would go out with him! You practically offered me up with a muffin!"

I peer in through the crack next to Ember, shocked to see Mia and Auntie facing off in the cooler, their breath fogging between them.

"You should be grateful I did it! God knows you'd never do it on your own. You're too busy fixing everyone else up so you don't have to think about your own sorry state." Auntie waves a finger at Mia.

"Just stay out of my life!" Mia cries, throwing up her hands.

"I'll stay out of your life when you start living it! Stop mooning over your asshole of an ex-husband! Move on! For both you *and* Ember."

"Leave Ember out of this," Mia warns, her voice tight. I wait to see if she's going to grab a stick of butter and hurl it, but instead she whirls around to exit, and nearly bowls over Ember and me as she stomps out.

Ember and I dart out of the way, but there's no hiding.

"Girls!" Mia cries, her hand over her heart. "What are you doing?"

"Trying to fill orders," I say, as if we didn't hear anything. "Need some creamer, three refills on chamomile, a chai, two poppy-seed muffins for Mrs. Jindal and Gladys Gunderson. Lots of customers out there."

Mia smooths her red hair. "Right, of course. Auntie and I were having a meeting." She snatches the order ticket out of my hand and stomps out of the kitchen. Auntie follows soon after, grumbling. She clanks the big kettles on the stove, making as much noise as she possibly can, as if she knows it will annoy Mia.

Ember's face is tight, her green eyes watery. Without a word, she dashes out the back door into the alley.

I hazard a glance over at Auntie. "Seriously, is no one ever going to tell me what is up with Ember's dad?" I ask. "Why all the weirdness? They're split up. It sucks, but it happens."

Auntie puts her hands on her hips. "You'll have to ask Ember," she says. "It's not my story to tell." She hooks a thumb toward the door. "Why don't you go out there and see if she needs anything?"

"You don't need me?" I ask, surprised.

"No, go check on Ember. Maybe you'll be the one to knock some sense into her. Or better yet, *Mia*." She rattles one of the big kettles with vigor.

In the alley, Ember is sitting on a stack of wooden pallets, leaning up against the brick wall of the building, her eyes wet. "Hey," I say, sitting down next to her. "Everything okay?"

Ember shrugs, swiping at her eyes.

"I'm sorry," I say, even though I still don't know what's going on.

Ember sniffs. "I'm the one who messed up."

"What?" I ask. "You just got here. That's not even possible."

"No, I mean with my parents. It was my fault, what happened."

I wait a beat, giving her the space and time she needs to tell her story.

Or to not tell it at all.

Finally, she speaks. "You know my gift. Well, one day, about four years ago, I gave my dad a hug, and all of a sudden I knew that he didn't love my mom anymore. He was in love with someone else. A woman he worked with." She looks down at her hands where they're folded in the lap of her dress.

"So what happened?"

"I tried to keep it a secret as long as I could. I begged Mama to make him pies. Ardent Apple. Cherish Cherry. But she always refused to make pies for Dad. She said she wanted him to love her just because. But he didn't. And I knew why." She sniffs again, wiping her nose with the back of her hand.

"So what did you do?" I try to keep my voice steady. I knew what it was like to have your gift betray you. It had nearly cost me everything to refuse to use it.

"I didn't say anything. And every day he hugged me and told me he loved me, and Mama thought we were the perfect family." She sits up, moving so that her legs are tucked underneath her. She hugs her arms to her chest because it's starting to get cold. "You know what Mama's deepest, darkest secret is? It's that she'll lose the people she loves. Like she lost her parents, and then Uncle Connor. So how could I tell her that she might lose my dad, too?" Her voice breaks at the end.

Ember's pain is my own, aching in my chest. What a terrible decision to be given to a twelve-year-old. And I know all about that.

Voices carry down the alley as a pack of high schoolers in letter jackets go by on the sidewalk, passing us where we sit in the shadowed alley. Ember stiffens, but they don't notice us. They are laughing and teasing, one boy crying foul when a girl steals his baseball cap.

Ember waits to be sure they're gone before she continues her story. "And then one day Dad told her he was leaving. And I begged Mama to give him pie. All of it."

"Did she?" I ask, even though I know she must have refused or he would be here now.

"No. She said she didn't want to win him that way. She

didn't want to have to win him at all."

"I'm sorry."

"That's not the worst part. He hugged me after they loaded up the moving truck with all his stuff, and suddenly Mama looked at me, and she *knew*. Every time I touched him, I had read his secret. His deepest, darkest, worst secret. And I kept it from her."

I let the weight of her words settle around me. She had betrayed Mia. Betrayed her like I had betrayed Mom.

"She barely spoke to me for weeks. Almost a month. She didn't bake. She wouldn't touch any of her Bracing Blueberry. And we moved in with Auntie because we couldn't make it on our own, and Auntie saw what was happening. She woke Mama back up, demanding pies and scones and cookies and everything else under the sun to sell at the tea shop instead of only the boring muffins she made. And then Mama was happy again. She loved me again."

Her words send me back to Mom, and the Good Year. I lean my head back against the cold brick wall. I'd believed everything had been fixed while she was in rehab. All the bad things would go away, and the scars on my arm would fade into obscurity because I had a new, beautiful, vibrant mother who loved me and wanted to take care of me. Everything seems possible when someone loves you. Even forgiveness. But when I look at Mia and Ember together, I don't believe that Mia ever stopped loving her daughter, even in whatever fog of grief she'd been mired in.

I wish I could say the same about my own mother. I wish I could say that I know she loved me, that she forgave both me and herself. The thing is, I'll probably never get to ask her either.

I don't think the old Trix, the one who had been dumped

here, angry and scared, could have forgiven her mother.

But I think this new Trix could. I hold on to that thought, letting it keep me warm as a chilled gust cuts through the alley.

"Do you want some pie?" I ask Ember, breaking the silence.

"No." She bites her lip and looks over at me. "Can we sit out here a few more minutes?"

"Sure," I say. "We can stay as long as you want."

We lean against the brick wall of the tea shop, both of us content with saying nothing at all.

SEVENTEEN

THE NIGHT OF THE FOOTBALL game against Buffalo Hills, Mia directs Ember and me as we unload the back of the Suburban that she's parked behind the concession stand. The building is painted a garish orange with two wide waist-high openings in the front equipped with small counters for serving food. The football stands are still empty, but the first bus from Buffalo Hills pulled into the high school parking lot ten minutes ago.

When I remember the story Jasper told me about the Buffalo Hills mob coming for the McCabe women, I understand the rivalry between the two towns a little better. The pep rally at the end of the school day was wildly well attended, townspeople and high schoolers alike cheering along a cacophony of slightly off-key brass instruments, and badly painted banners depicting the Tigers eating the Buffaloes.

As we carry trays of brownies, cookies, and pies, Mia tells me about Connor playing in the game against Buffalo Hills his senior year. He'd scored the winning touchdown. His teammates had dragged him up onto Cedar Mountain to party late into the night, and Connor had his first hangover the next morning.

I wonder if Connor and I stood in the same spot on Cedar Mountain the last time each of us was there.

"Okay," Mia says, not knowing she is interrupting my thoughts of Connor. "We push the baked goods and the hot cocoa for our side. The pies are already cut, and we'll sell them by the slice for three dollars each. The brownies, cupcakes, and cookies are all a dollar fifty. A couple girls from the homecoming committee and their moms will be tselling hot dogs and popcorn from that window," she says, pointing to the other side of the small building.

"What does it matter which window we sell out of?" Auntie asks. "We're all in the same stand. There's no wall or anything." Auntie waves an arm out on the other side of the concession stand to make her point. "All the money goes into the same till."

She and Mia had a cold war after their fight in the walk-in cooler that lasted for about twenty-four hours. But then someone left chocolate in someone else's room, and soon after, regular conversation resumed while watching an old romantic comedy and drinking wine on the dilapidated couch in the living room.

"Mrs. Stuart made sure I was aware that we were to stay on our side of the concession stand," Mia says, her voice clipped, as if the idea annoyed her.

Auntie wrinkles her nose. "Seems like Mrs. Stuart needs the stick pulled out of her ass. We're donating all our profits to the stupid homecoming committee. You'd think they'd be a little more grateful."

"Gemma Stuart has never been grateful for anything in her life," Mia replies. She hazards a glance at me and Ember. "Forget I said that," she says.

"Said what?" Ember asks, holding back a smile.

From what I've learned over the last couple of weeks of planning this concession stand fund-raiser, Mrs. Stuart is Adalyn's mom, she was once Rocksaw's homecoming queen, and something vicious happened between her and Mia when they were in high school.

Sure enough, Mrs. Stuart, Adalyn, Ramani, another girl named Vera I recognize from my history class, and a woman who must be Vera's mother soon arrive, looking like they're ready to do battle. They're all wearing sets of black cat ears, and their faces are painted like tigers, with stripes on their cheeks and black tips on their noses and a set of drawn-on whiskers each.

"Please tell me we don't have to wear cat ears to work in here," I whisper to Mia as they fuss around with boxes of food they've brought with them.

Mia purses her lips, suppressing a smile. "No, Trix."

I let out a sigh of relief. It's bad enough that I'm crammed in this concession stand hawking cupcakes; painted-on whiskers might have done me in.

Not to mention the fact that I'm really hoping to see Jasper, and I don't want the indignity of cat ears if I do. I smile to myself. And if we had any time alone, he'd *definitely* smudge my drawn-on whiskers.

Mrs. Stuart says something about a cash box and hurries back out of the concession stand.

As soon as Vera's mom sees Auntie, she jets to Auntie's side, holding out her hand and asking questions about her last reading. I manage to catch the words *inheritance* and *estranged*. They have a hushed conversation that ends with Auntie patting Vera's mom on the shoulder and telling her to come by the shop tomorrow for some tea.

"Mia!" Mrs. Stuart coos when she returns with the cash box. "You *did* make it. I'm so glad. Mrs. Jindal couldn't make it tonight. Poor thing has the stomach flu."

"Gemma, so lovely to see you," Mia says, pasting a smile on her face. She self-consciously fluffs her red hair.

But Auntie is unable to ignore the barb in Mrs. Stuart's words, and she grumbles, "We *said* we'd be here, so we're here." She arranges cookies nearly twice the size of a grown man's palm that we spent hours wrapping in clear plastic wrap and tying with orange and black ribbons last night.

Mrs. Stuart's cat ears seem to prick up when she overhears Auntie, and she gushes, "Well, I know things can get so busy for women like yourself."

Auntie shoots Mrs. Stuart a look that could melt her whiskers right off.

"Entrepreneurs," Mrs. Stuart clarifies at the look. "Women like Mia don't have as much time as stay-at-home moms."

Mia flushes as she arranges brownies with orange sprinkles on a tray. This is the first time anyone has seemed to dislike the McCabes, and I'm really starting to wonder what happened between Mrs. Stuart and Mia in high school.

"But she *does* have a business that can donate two hundred

dollars' worth of baked goods," Ember retorts.

I raise my eyebrows at Ember. This isn't the Ember from a few weeks ago who hid in the library with her earbuds in. This Ember takes shit from no one.

Adalyn is completely unaware of the entire conversation, focusing on hanging orange and black tulle around their order window, but Ramani looks uncomfortable, toying restlessly with her cat ears.

"It's lovely that local businesses give back to the community," Vera's mother says, trying to make peace. "Especially one as well-loved as the McCabe Bakery and Tea Shoppe." Vera nods in agreement as she loads the hot-dog roller on the back counter using a set of metal tongs.

Mrs. Stuart opens her mouth to say something again, but Ramani interrupts the awkward moment with exuberant cheer. "Hi, Ms. McCabe. So nice to see you again. My mom said to say she's so sorry she couldn't make it. My brother offered to cover for her, but Mrs. Stuart said we'd be okay without him."

"Your brother is the guidance counselor, right? Is he single?" Mia asks, wasting no time getting down to business.

Ramani winces. "Definitely. The breakup was ugly too. He was all set to propose, and his college girlfriend dumped him. And now I can't get away from him. Seven years of college and grad school, and he comes back home to haunt me in high school, of all places." She rolls her eyes, and it makes Mia laugh.

"You know," Mia says. "Ella, the art teacher, is single, too. And right around your brother's age. She came by the shop the other day asking me about available guys that I knew of in town."

"I'll pass the word," Ramani says, grinning.

"You tell him to come to me," Auntie says. "I'll tell his fortune. Strapping young man like that, I bet he's got more love lines than he does fingers and toes."

Ramani laughs. "Ew. I don't even want to think about that."

Vera's mom titters.

Annoyed by the interest in the McCabes, Mrs. Stuart holds up the cash box. "Here's this," she says. "Let's put it on this table in the back by the hot-dog roller so that it's safe."

"Of course it's got to be on *your* side of the stand," Auntie mumbles under her breath, opening a stack of disposable plates.

Mrs. Stuart clears her throat and raises her eyebrows, and Vera's mom looks slightly uncomfortable.

Thirty minutes of subtle gripes later, the stands around the football field are filled with families dressed in either orange and black or brown and white, and there's a line nearly thirty people deep at our concession-stand window. It's cold and windy, and the gusts wail through tiny cracks in the stand, threatening to snatch away napkins and plastic cutlery when I hand them out. The pies are selling fast, and I take handfuls of cash from the Rocksaw residents as well as visitors from Buffalo Hills who have heard of Mia's bakery.

The Buffalo Hills fans seem friendly, and if anything, excited to try food from the McCabe Bakery & Tea Shoppe. I wonder again if the story Jasper told me about the Buffalo Hills mob coming for the McCabe women is true. I wonder if those Buffalo Hills people would be rolling over in their graves knowing that their descendants were lining up to eat Mia McCabe's pie.

We keep a tally sheet to mark how much money we've made, and I run back and forth from the cash box making change, lifting up the top tray of the cash box to stuff the big bills, twenties and fifties, into the bin underneath.

A little voice in my head says that it would only take one slip of my hand to pocket a couple of twenties and fudge the numbers on the tally sheet to cover it up. That would buy two big, fancy sketchbooks at Jensen's Office Supply. Or order pizza, breadsticks, and drinks from the Italian restaurant three doors down from the tea shop.

My hand hovers briefly over the cash box.

No.

I'm not that girl anymore. I have a paycheck from the shop, even if it's not a lot. I earn my money now. I don't steal it. You don't steal from a town where you mean to put down roots.

I look over my shoulder and catch Mrs. Stuart looking at me with narrowed eyes.

I snatch two quarters out of the change slot and hand the customer their change and cookie.

Let her stare. I know I didn't do anything wrong.

The crowd in front of our window keeps us busy, and I can't see much past them. All I get of the football game are the glaring lights in the sky that block out the stars, and the cheers and sighs of the crowd to indicate how the game is going.

Ember actually helps with the customers instead of staying in the back of the concession stand. Her face is a little grim, as if she's determined to do her part, but not sure she likes it.

Mia opens her mouth once or twice to say something to her

like, *Oh, honey, why don't you stay in the back if you're uncomfortable?* But each time Ember brushes past her, still working, still making herself participate rather than hiding away. I think after joining the lunch table and getting invited to homecoming by Grayson, she's realizing that hiding away might have been safe, but it wasn't living. Not really.

I do my best to manage as many of the customers as I can, but I'm proud of the way that Ember is holding her own. I hope that when she looks at me, she sees that I'm trying to change, too.

At one point, there's a discernable gasp from the football stands, as if the entire audience sucked in their breath at once. Then, a few moments later, the announcer says something about hoping it's not as bad as it looks, and asks the crowd to move so the EMTs can get on the field.

"What is it?" I ask Ramani, who's salting a bag of popcorn for a customer. My thoughts immediately turn to Jasper, and I wonder if he's okay. I've seen enough of their practices to know that football can be a brutal sport.

Ramani asks the Buffalo Hills man ordering the popcorn if he can tell us what happened, and the man stands on his tiptoes to look out onto the field over the concession-stand crowds. "Looks like someone got hurt," he says. "One of the Tigers."

Jasper, is all I can think.

The announcer says something, but through the ringing in my ears, all I catch is "number fifty-two."

"Who is that?" I ask, my heart hammering in my chest.

"It's Linc!" Ramani cries. She puts a hand over her mouth,

her class ring flashing in the fluorescent lights.

Her gesture frightens me because I have seen it before.

Charly stands in the doorway of room 7, her dark hair damp and clinging. It's raining outside behind her, the soft kind that mists until everything glitters. Her eyeliner is smeared, and her mascara is beginning to drip in dark lines down her cheeks.

"Charly, are you okay?" I move aside so she can come in.

But she stands rooted, immovable. Instead, Charly lifts her hand to her mouth, her gold rings glinting on her fingers, like she could push the words back in, make the truth stop being real.

"It's Shane," she whispers finally, removing her hand.

"Where is he?" I ask, pushing past her into the dark, wet parking lot, searching for him, for that crooked grin and the wide shoulders beneath his leather jacket. The neon sign flashes NO VACANCY, reflecting in puddles and mist to cast an eerie red glow.

Red like blood.

I whirl on Charly. "What happened?"

"He got shot," Charly cries, throwing her arms around me and sobbing into my neck. "You told him not to go alone, but he went anyway."

"Trix!" Ramani yells over the roaring applause of the crowd, bringing me back to this moment. "The announcer says he hurt his shoulder, but he's up on his feet now. I'm going to go out and see if someone can tell me what happened." She tugs off her cat ears and runs out the back door of the concession stand, letting in a huge gust of wind as she goes.

I am frozen in place near the cheerfully decorated cookies, goose bumps rising on my arms as if I am still standing out in the rain.

"I hope Linc's okay," Ember says, coming to stand next to me. She is real, and warm, and smells of coconut. She reminds me that I'm in Rocksaw, not the Starlite. "But at least Ramani ought to make him happy."

"What do you mean?" I ask, attempting to look like everything is normal. I shuffle cookies around on the tray like I'm organizing them.

Ember bites her lip. She looks around, and when she decides that the stand is too loud and busy for anyone to pay us any notice, she continues, "Linc accidentally high-fived me in PE last week when I spiked the volleyball into Nancy Miller's face—not on purpose—and I saw that he's got a thing for Ramani, but he's afraid to ask her out because Jesse *was* his friend and Jasper *is* his friend, and he doesn't want to make things weird."

To me, this is yet another moment illustrating how everyone's stories in Rocksaw intertwine, sometimes so closely it seems like they're chapters in the same book. "I guess that might be awkward. But why doesn't he just talk to them?"

"And say *what*? Jasper, I want to date your dead brother's girlfriend?" Ember asks.

"Yeah, exactly that. And anyway, it's Ramani's business if she wants to date him." I look out the front window of the concession stand and catch a glimpse of Ramani waiting for Linc as he comes off the field. An assistant coach is carrying Linc's helmet, and Linc is walking, but cradling his left arm, his face tight.

"I picked up something about a bro code." Ember continues, "That part was a little fuzzy. His high five was pretty fast."

"Do you think we should say something to Ramani about it?" I ask. "She must care about him a little bit if she went out there to check on him."

Ember shrugs. "I've never had close girlfriends. I don't know the protocol. Also, I think it might be spying, since *technically* Linc didn't tell me on purpose." She sighs. "I probably shouldn't have told you, either. But it's one of those problems that you wish you could fix for them."

I nod. Ember's got to figure out her own set of rules for her gift, the same as I have.

"Maybe we could convince Linc and Ramani to go on a *triple* date with us to homecoming?" Ember says hopefully.

I tease her, "You sound more and more like your mom. The next thing we know, you'll be matchmaking full time and baking pie."

Ember pulls a face at me.

"Girls!" Mia chides. "Stop playing around and help me out. I need six chocolate-chip cookies, two slices of Lucky Lime, and eight cups of hot chocolate, three with marshmallows and five without."

"Yes, Mama," Ember says, hurrying to get the cups.

Ramani returns to the concession stand, breathless and pink-cheeked. "Linc's okay," she says. "It looks like a dislocated shoulder, but nothing broken. His mom and dad are taking him to the emergency room."

"Did you get to talk to him?" Ember probes.

"Yeah," Ramani says. "He says he'll be back in fighting shape by homecoming."

"Well, yeah, *priorities*, am I right?" I manage to say with a straight face.

Ramani rolls her eyes. "Says the girl selling tiger muffins."

"They're *cupcakes*," I correct her airily.

Ramani and Ember laugh, and even though I'm in a tiny concession stand with women wearing cat ears, I feel pretty damn happy now.

With five minutes left to go in the game, the Tigers are only one point ahead, and Mrs. Stuart decides it's time to shut down the concession stand and count the cash box. We've sold out of nearly everything we brought; only a half-dozen white-chocolate-macadamia-nut cookies are left on the back table. There are still at least three dozen hot dogs and bags of chips on the other side of the concession stand, as well as a thick layer of burned popcorn on the bottom of the popcorn machine from when Vera forgot to put in the oil.

"Let's load up the trays in the Suburban," Mia says to Ember and me.

"What do you want me to do about the cookies?" Ember asks. "There are only a few left."

"We'll see if Mrs. Stuart and the girls want them," Mia answers. "As a thank-you gesture for including us in the fund-raising."

I want to say that they ought to be thanking *us* for donating all the baked goods in the first place, but I hold my tongue. How Mia wants to navigate these waters is up to her.

Mrs. Stuart is hunched over the cash box with a calculator, furiously hitting the keys with her orange-and-black fingernails.

When we've loaded up the Suburban with our trays and the remaining disposable plates and cups, Ember and I stand outside the concession stand for a few minutes and watch the game. "See that?" Ember says, pointing to the Tigers player with a seven on his jersey. "That's Jasper." She finds the player with the number nineteen. "That's Grayson."

"How do you know that?" I ask.

"I picked up a program," she says, handing me the folded piece of orange paper she's pulled from her pocket.

"I thought maybe you'd been studying without me."

Ember smirks and shakes her head. "We should probably go see if Mama needs any more help. Plus, I'd like to rub it in Mrs. Stuart's face that we pulled in more money than she did."

I laugh because I really like this Ember that stands up to jerks.

Back inside the concession stand, everyone but Mrs. Stuart is gone, probably taking out the trash to the dumpsters or running things back to their vehicles. She stands in the middle of the room that still smells of burned popcorn and hot dogs, her hands on her hips, her face red beneath her whiskers. "All right," she says to me. "Where is it?"

"Where's what?" I ask, immediately on edge.

Ember pauses next to me, her whole body tensing visibly at

221

the tinge of accusation in Mrs. Stuart's voice.

"The money," she hisses. "There's exactly forty dollars missing from the cash box."

I let out a little laugh before I can stop myself. Wouldn't you know it? I stopped myself from stealing anything, and someone else did it for me.

"I can assure you," I reply, offended—after all, *I have a gift*, damn it—"if I had stolen money, I wouldn't have been stupid enough to get caught."

"So you're bragging about it?"

"No, I'm saying I *didn't* steal it."

"Empty your pockets," Mrs. Stuart says.

"No."

"Empty them right now, young lady."

"Why do you think Trix took the money?" Ember asks.

"I saw her standing over here a little too long earlier in the evening. She looked awfully suspicious."

"I can look how I want. I didn't take anything."

"We know you were in some kind of trouble," Mrs. Stuart says. "That's why you were dumped on Mia. Teenage girls don't just show up out of the blue like that without a reason."

"You don't know shit," I reply, my temper flaring. "So you can back the hell off."

"Excuse me? You steal from the homecoming committee and then you have the audacity to speak to me that way?"

"I can speak to you however I want if you talk to me like that."

"What's going on here?" Mia asks, coming back inside.

Auntie and Vera's mother follow behind her, surveying the scene.

"We're exactly forty dollars short, and I saw your niece over here messing around earlier," Mrs. Stuart huffs. "And now she was *very* rude to me."

"*You* were very rude *to me*," I retort. Every muscle in my body is screaming *run* because it would be so much easier to leave this situation than to face it. But I have to be brave like Ember, facing down the things that I'm afraid of. If she can touch the hands of dozens of strangers in two hours, then I have to try to hold my own against Mrs. Stuart.

Mia looks at me, and I realize as I watch her face, the furrowed brow, the pursed lips, that she's trying to decide who to believe before she speaks again. Trix: abandoned, thief, drifter. Or Mrs. Stuart: PTO mom, former homecoming queen, and longtime acquaintance.

I guess things don't look so good for me right now.

Mia touches her left hand, the empty finger where she sometimes still wears her wedding ring.

Of course, the wedding ring.

I close my eyes, hold my scars, and will my skin to turn to steel. There was another time that I didn't steal, even when someone begged me to. It was a moment that set Mom and me down a path we could never come back from.

One breath, two, three.

"If Trix says she didn't take the money, then she didn't take it," Mia says.

Her words snatch my breath away, and I open my eyes to make sure that what I heard is real.

"Besides," Auntie adds practically, "if she *did* take it, you wouldn't know."

"Well, we know that no one else took it," Mrs. Stuart says. "So where could it be?"

"Excuse me?" Mia says, putting her hands on her hips so that she mirrors Mrs. Stuart. "What is that supposed to mean?" Mia's fighting for me. Finally, someone is fighting for me.

"It means that we all know that none of the other girls took it. Come on, Mia. Be reasonable. Trix is clearly running from some sort of colorful past. She must have done *something* to get kicked out of her parents' house."

"Colorful past?" Mia says. "She's a seventeen-year-old kid from out of town, Gemma. Not a seasoned convict. And if she says she didn't take the money, then she didn't take it."

"Well, I'd like to know where that money is, then."

"Did you look around? Under all the equipment? On the floor? Did you do a second count to make sure your totals are right before you accused her of stealing?"

"I counted twice, Mia. I'm not an idiot."

Mia turns to Auntie. "Tally the money again. We all know math wasn't Gemma's best class in school." She looks at Vera's mom. "Help me look around the concession stand. We're going to figure this out." Then Mia points at me and Ember. "You two, go wait in the car." Ember opens her mouth to disagree, but Mia merely adds, *"Now."*

Outside the concession stand, while the crowds are filtering back to the parking lot to head home, I realize that I'm sweating and my hands are shaking. I feel like I could puke. "Are you okay?" Ember asks, looking worried.

"I'm fine," I tell her. Everything in me wants to shut down, turn inward. I hold my arm, my fingers squeezed over my constellation of scars. I didn't do this. I didn't take the money. But the way she looked at me, the way Mrs. Stuart pointed her finger at me cracked something inside that I thought I'd sealed shut a thousand times over.

This won't be like the other times. I fight to make myself stay here, in this moment. Not like the other times before, with the ginger. The glinting rings. *Don't think about it, Trix*, I tell myself.

"Come on," Ember says, her voice keeping me grounded. "Let's go to the Suburban. Mama will make this right."

Mine couldn't, I want to say. But I don't.

Twenty minutes later, Mia comes back to us, her face pale and tight. Auntie follows her, still getting into the passenger side door when Mia cranks the engine. Mia peels out as soon as Auntie shuts her door, making me think that maybe crazy drivers run in this family after all.

No one speaks. Anger fills the car.

"What happened?" Ember asks after a beat.

My hands are still sweating, and I put them under my thighs, my chest tight and heaving. Maybe I was wrong about Mia fighting for me. She's furious. She's going to ask me to leave. She covered for me in the concession stand to save face, but now it's all over. She's thinks I stole that money, like I stole her wedding ring. She's never going to trust me after this.

Auntie cackles, breaking the silence. "It was too good. I wish I had a camera."

"We shouldn't gloat, Auntie," Mia chides, her voice softer than I expected. "Even if it feels damn good."

Something loosens a little in my chest.

"We found the forty dollars under the hot-dog roller. The wind must've blown it under there, or it got stuck on the bottom of the change tray and then fell out when someone lifted it," Auntie crows. "You should've seen Gemma's face."

Mia lets out a chuckle. "I thought her whiskers were going to fall off." Then just as quickly, she frowns again. "But you know she only accused Trix because she still hates me because she thinks I stole Jordan from her in the tenth grade."

"Well, it serves the old biddy right. Accusing our Trix of stealing," Auntie harrumphs.

Our Trix.

I let out a breath of relief.

I think I could get used to that.

EIGHTEEN

THE DAYS BEGIN TO FALL into a pattern. Ember and I go to school. Jasper and I steal moments alone between football practice and work. And then there are his pie deliveries, which tend to double in time when I ride along. I work my shifts at the tea shop, where the regulars know me by name. And then every evening I park myself at the dining room table with its worn, scarred top perpetually covered in stacks of books, half-empty teacups with chipped saucers, and a napping Bacon.

Because the table is where everything really happens. If the house is an atom, the dining room table is the nucleus. After work, Ember and I do our homework there while Mia and Auntie squabble back and forth in the kitchen if it's not our turn to cook. I'm finally able to focus on my schoolwork with my new routine, my grades getting back to what they used to be before I quit last year. Then we eat dinner at the table, and I learn that while Mia is an excellent baker, none of the women in this house is a particularly good cook. The sauces are always too bland, the meat a little charred, the vegetables limp. The only food we're really good at making is pancakes, so we eat breakfast for dinner at least twice a week.

At the table each night, Mia continues to list every high-school-age boy she saw that day who could possibly take me to homecoming. Auntie categorizes the boys as she complains about dinner: tool, turd, a hot muffin she would butter.

I haven't said anything about going to homecoming with Jasper yet. I guess I'm afraid once I tell them, they'll never let me live it down. Mia will be planning our wedding, coming up with seating charts and possible names for our future children. Ember's noticed how Jasper's moved across the lunch table to sit next to me, how he waits around by my locker between classes, and that I never miss a chance to help him deliver pies, but she wisely says nothing in front of our audience at home.

After dinner, Ember brings down one of our dresses and works on it at the table with a sewing machine that looks like it was made before the Civil War. Mia thumbs through fashion magazines that customers leave in the shop and tells random stories about Connor. Each anecdote I catalog away in my brain, imagining every story a stroke detailing some small crevice or shadow on his portrait, making him clearer, stronger. And Auntie yells commentary from the couch in the living room, letting us know when her favorite show about Hollywood psychic pets comes on. It's the only thing that will make her switch from the made-for-TV movie network.

But tonight is different. Tonight, as we're sitting down to eat pancakes for the second time this week, Mia slides a phone across the table to me. "Here it is, Trix. This one's on our local network, so you'll have a signal everywhere." She smiles at me. "I got them to put your old number on it and transfer all your contacts."

"Thank you," I tell her, picking up the phone.

"Don't see why kids need phones on them all the time," Auntie grumbles.

"She needs to be able to contact her friends. Besides, what if there was an emergency? Like the house was on fire?"

"Well, she wouldn't know it because she'd be fiddling around on her phone."

Ember chokes back a laugh, nearly spitting out her mouthful of banana-nut pancake.

"Go ahead," Mia tells me, ignoring Auntie. "It's rung three times since I activated it. Somebody named Charly? Is that a boy from the city?" I can tell from her tone that she's dying to know.

"Charly's a girl."

"Oh," Mia says sadly, taking a delicate bite of blackened bacon. I can tell she wants more, some detail or tidbit that will shine more light onto my murky past. "Maybe you'd like to invite her to come stay with us for a weekend."

"Yeah, maybe sometime," I reply noncommittally.

"Go on," Mia says. "Call her back. I'll clean up the kitchen."

I go outside and sit on the front porch. It hasn't been cold enough to kill off the roses, so I settle on the first step, stroking the delicate, velvety petals of a low-hanging bloom. Bacon follows me, yowling while he twines himself between my boots. I look at the phone again. Three missed calls from Charly today. What can that mean? Deep in the pit of my stomach, I know.

I call Charly back, my heart beating frantically in my chest: half dread, half anticipation.

It rings only once before he answers.

"Trix? Trix, is that you?"

Shane.

"It's me."

"Where are you? Do you need me to come get you? Are you all right? Charly said they took you."

My chest hurts. Maybe my heart cracked my ribs while it was beating so fast. "I'm okay, Shane."

"Tell me where you are. I'll come get you. I don't care how far it is."

"I don't need you to come get me."

"Why? Is there a bus you can take back? Are you on the bus?"

His faith that I will always find my way back to him, to the Starlite and those Coke-and-cherry slushes, nearly makes me lose my conviction. I know what I have to say, even if each word is a struggle to get out. Because I know it will hurt him, even if there are months and miles between us now, even if it is the right thing to do. "No, Shane. I'm with my family now."

"Trix. You don't mean that. I'm your family. Me and Charly, *we're* your family. I know I was a jerk when I broke up with you. I was an asshole. I hurt you. I know that. But I didn't want you to wait around for me those two years. It wasn't fair to you." He takes a breath like maybe his chest hurts, too. There is something vulnerable in his voice when he adds, "But Charly said you waited anyway."

Silence on the line again, like he's expecting me to assure him that I did. Like he knows, deep down, that I'm going to tell him that I've always loved him because he's the only person who ever loved me back. To tell him that I want everything to go back to the way it was. To tell him I need him to save me like he always wanted to save me. A year ago, I thought that was possible. But now I know it's not. I'm changing. I'm *changed*. And it's not Jasper or Ember or Mia or Auntie who changed me. I changed myself. I put down roots.

"Shane," I murmur, but I can't get anything else out because it aches too much.

"I've got plans for us, Trix. It'll be just like it used to be. We'll get that little place we talked about. I've got connections with a guy—"

I say the hardest five words, my hands trembling so much that the phone quakes against my cheek. "I'm not coming back, Shane."

I end the call.

My eyes are blurring already, and then all at once I'm sobbing on the front porch of the big, rambling farmhouse full of McCabe women, the only witnesses a fat, orange cat named Bacon and the jungle of roses around me.

I pull up my sleeve, looking at the scars that haunt me the way Shane has, the way my mom always will, cursing at the way they make me wander the Starlite Motel and the Jasmine Dragon when I close my eyes.

I tug out the fountain pen from my pocket. On top of the first scar a few inches from the crook of my elbow, I draw a blooming rose, its petals black-tipped with ink. And then another, and another, until my arm is covered, and instead of a constellation of scars, I have a constellation of roses.

I'm still outside when the stars appear, even though it's too cold now to be sitting out here without a jacket. My body eventually stops shaking, apart from the occasional shudder, and the tears have finally dried when Ember joins me. She's in her pajamas, wearing an old yellow-and-white afghan like a shawl, holding a blue afghan in the crook of her arm. She stops above me on the top step and lowers the blue afghan over my shoulders. Then she sits down next to me.

"Nice night for looking at the stars," she says quietly.

"Yeah." I surreptitiously wipe at my nose.

Ember lifts a hand like she wants to squeeze mine, but stops. She won't take secrets I don't offer.

"I'm here if you want to talk," she says, putting her hand back in her lap.

Long, quiet moments pass. It's only the sound of the wind rustling the leaves and blooms of the roses. Beneath the sweet scent of the flowers is the crisp burst of fall leaves, the tang of a frost that promises to arrive soon. A purr in the back of Bacon's throat. The creak of the wooden stairs as Ember leans back on her elbows to look at the stars. The sigh of her breathing; quiet, patient, someone who will wait for me to find the words I need. The patience of a friend, the patience of family.

I look down at the constellation of roses on my arm.

"I used to love him."

Ember shifts slightly, waits for me to continue.

"But that was a long time ago. I'm not that girl anymore."

Ember sits up, adjusts her yellow afghan-shawl over her shoulders. "I'll get the blueberry pie."

NINETEEN

THE SEVENTEENTH OF OCTOBER. SOMETHING about that date niggles in the back of my brain when I check the calendar before we leave for school. The only thing Mia has written on the date is *pay car insurance*. Nothing important.

When we get to school, Jasper's not leaning against my locker, waiting with that grin that tugs on his scar. He's not at the morning classes we share, his desk scrunched close to mine. And when noon rolls around, Jasper's not at the lunch table, either. Adalyn is, though. She apologized to me profusely after her mother's behavior in the concession stand, and things are good between us. Now she has notebooks spread across the table with schedules for homecoming activities that still need volunteers, lists of community donors for the dance, spreadsheets with columns and rows indicating the location and amounts of chicken wire and tissue paper stashed around the town of Rocksaw that will go to decorating.

"Where's Jasper?" I ask anyone else who can hear me over Adalyn's frantic planning.

Linc, still recovering from his football injury with his arm in a sling, looks up at me from his cheeseburger. "I haven't seen him all day. Maybe he's got that flu bug that's going around. I heard someone threw up all over in the locker room last night. Super nasty."

Grayson nods, making a face.

"No, you jerks," Ramani says, and when I look over at her for the first time, I realize her eyes are red. Dry, but red. Like she'd been crying earlier.

"What?" Linc asks defensively. "It *was* nasty."

"It's October seventeenth," she replies.

"I know, I know! Twelve days until homecoming!" Adalyn exclaims, only halfway in the conversation.

Ember's eyes widen at Adalyn's outburst. Ember's been at this table almost as long as me now, but Adalyn's intensity still alarms her. One day, Adalyn will storm boardrooms and presidential elections, command a fleet of ships or an army of business executives. But sometimes she still misses the little things.

The date finally comes back to me when Ramani says it, and I remember where I've seen it written before. In the trophy case by the principal's office, beneath the photograph of Jesse. My stomach sinks.

"It's the anniversary of Jesse's death." Ramani's voice quavers. I nearly forgot that she went with Jesse to homecoming last year, that they'd been dating. She mourns him perhaps nearly as much as Jasper does.

Adalyn shifts at Ramani's tone, finally involved in the conversation, and she drops her pen and reaches over to hold Ramani's hand, giving it a squeeze.

"Oh, crap," Linc mutters, reminded not only of Jasper's pain, but maybe also a little of his own romantic angst. "I should call him. Maybe we should ditch and go find him." He looks at Grayson for confirmation.

"We've got a chemistry test after lunch," Grayson reminds him. "It's worth twenty-five percent of our grade. Skip that and you'll be benched for the season. Not to mention your parents will kill you and ban you from your fan-fiction sites for the rest of your life."

Linc grimaces. "Well, when you put it like that . . ."

"I don't have chemistry," I offer. "I'll go look for him." I'll have to miss class, which Mia won't like, but I have to know that Jasper is okay.

Ramani looks relieved. "I don't think I can do it," she admits, wiping at her eye.

"It's fine," I tell her. "I'll find him. Good luck on your chemistry test, guys."

Adalyn sends me a grateful look across the table, and she nudges Ramani. "Come on," she says. "Let's go get something chocolate from the vending machine and sit outside for a few minutes. Some fresh air sounds good."

"Check the cemetery first," Grayson tells me as I leave. "If he's not there, he's probably at home."

"I'll tell Mama you might be late when I get to the shop today," Ember offers with a small, encouraging smile.

Outside the school, I call Jasper's phone. It rings three times and then goes to voice mail. The fact that he doesn't answer worries me even more. I think back to the last time I saw him, yesterday afternoon, replaying our conversation in my head. Had he seemed distant? Was there something that I should have noticed, some sign that would have prevented him ghosting me?

It's a thirty-minute walk to the cemetery near the edge of town. I hug my jacket close to me, wishing I had a car. There was public transportation in the city, so I never learned how to drive. But out here it seems like a necessity.

The cemetery is a sprawling, hilly maze flanked on every side by tall, ominous-looking evergreens. I open the rusty gate and let myself in. There are all kinds of gravestones. Massive monuments, among them an angel standing six feet tall, staring down at me like I'm an intruder; tiny stones barely visible beneath the fallen leaves; new mounds of dirt with only a white cross to mark them until something more permanent arrives. A windmill creaks in the distance with every shift of the wind, the sound echoing and ghostly.

Around one hill, I find the McCabe family plot. A lot of them are so old that I can barely read the names, but there's one new enough to decipher. *Connor McCabe. Beloved brother and son.* He lived thirty years. He died when I was only eight. Of course it doesn't say *beloved father.* He had never been a father. I wonder if he would have been a good parent. If he would have taught me how to ride a bike like that picture of Ember and her dad on the mantel at home. I wonder if he would be showing up to watch me get picked up by my date at homecoming too.

One story that no one has ever bothered to tell me is why my father was never in my life. Not Mom, before she left. Not Mia, nor Auntie. Nobody. But the fact that no one has offered that tale, when there are so many they are willing to share, makes me wonder if my entire life has been wrapped in secrets. The only question is whether it was Mom keeping me secret from Connor, or Connor was not so perfect, and he kept my existence from the McCabes.

It's easy for the McCabes to put it all on Mom. After all, she'd abandoned me. How could their perfect Connor have neglected his own child?

With every little bit of Connor that I am given from others in Rocksaw, I get a clearer picture of him, but the truth is, I'll never know him. I'll only ever have shadows of him, bits of anecdotes, gray-green eyes, and our mutual love of drawing. We didn't share any of our years. Any of our chapters.

I lean into the wind and keep walking. The Ruiz family plot is near the back of the cemetery, almost all the way to the evergreens. There's no Jasper here, but there are several bouquets: sunflowers, a sheaf of wheat, a handful of yellow roses, and a pot of dark-red chrysanthemums on the elaborate stone that is clearly the newest of the plots. The gravestone is black granite with gray writing: *Jesse Eduardo Ruiz. We'll keep you in our hearts, unchanged, perfect forever.*

I stand there for a few moments, imagining what Jasper must have felt as he stood here. Wondering which of the flowers are from him. "He really loved you," I tell Jesse, even though he can't hear me. "I'm sure he'll take good care of Cleo for you." I pause another moment. "I think Ramani misses you, too. But she might not be ready to visit yet. Don't take it the wrong way."

The Ruiz family farm is five miles from town, so before I hike all that way, I do a quick search on my phone for Jasper's home number. I find it and bolster my courage because I might have to talk to one of his parents if they answer, knowing that they are probably struggling with this day as much as Jasper.

It rings three times before someone picks up. Crap. His mother. "Hello?" she says.

"Hi, um, I'm sorry. Is, uh, Jasper there? Could I talk to him?"

"Jasper? No, he's at school. Can I take a message?"

"No. Thank you." I end the call. Maybe Grayson and Linc don't know Jasper as well as they think they do.

By the time I walk back to school, it'll be over for the day, so I decide to walk back to the tea shop instead. Mia looks up when the bell on the front door jingles. "Wow," she says from behind the glass display counter, where she's been adding in her afternoon's baking of Lucky Lime. With the homecoming game coming up, there's been a big run on it. Girlfriends of football players have been buying it for delivery to their boyfriends. Hell, even the mayor was here buying some, but I heard that's because he's got a fair bit of money on the game. Auntie's been reading the fortunes of quarterbacks and linebackers and tight ends to see if any of them can reveal any tidbit about the upcoming game. They're great customers because they can each order half a dozen muffins and eat them in one sitting.

"You're here early today." Mia straightens up. "You must've flown."

"Something like that," I mumble, not wanting to tell her I ditched school. I have a feeling Mia might think that's a more serious offense than I do. Of course, I ditched about six months of school last year, so I guess one afternoon doesn't feel like that big a deal to me. All I care about right now is where Jasper might be.

"So that's all?" she prompts.

I flick a glance over at her, and I can see that her mouth is tight.

"That's all."

She gives a small sigh but lets the subject drop. "Ms. Troy is coming for her home visit tomorrow," she reminds me. Ms. Troy was supposed to come earlier, but she'd been sick with some mysterious illness and had to placate herself with another phone interview about my activities, behavior, and general progress.

"I know," I tell Mia. "It's not a big deal. She'll just want to see that you keep your meds and sharp objects locked up." I throw out the last part as a joke to try to ease the tension, but Mia doesn't laugh.

When Ember finally appears, she tells me Jasper never showed up at school after I left, either, and he hadn't answered when Grayson called him after the chemistry test.

I spend the rest of the afternoon thinking about Jasper, worrying about where he might be and if he's okay. He's never said it outright, but I think there's a lot more to his story and Jesse's than what he's shared with me. I get that. I do. There are parts of my story that I don't want anyone to know, sketches that I don't want anyone else to see. My darkest chapters belong only to me.

And that's when I remember what he said when we were up on Cedar Mountain. It was the best view in town. He liked it up there, looking at all the tiny lights of Rocksaw below. I glance out the window. It's starting to get dark.

"Mia?" I call into the kitchen. "I'm going out." I snatch my backpack because I know I won't be back before we close.

"What? Where are you going?" she calls back, but I'm already out the front door.

I jog all the way back to the school. Football practice is over, so the field is empty. The sun is setting, and Cedar Mountain is silhouetted against the bright oranges and pinks streaking the sky. I climb the hill with way less speed than the football team, careful to keep to the packed dirt of their well-worn path.

Sure enough, there's Jasper at the top of the giant hill, sitting in one of the empty lawn chairs. He doesn't look surprised to see me. He leans back in the chair, his hands cupped gently over the ends of the armrests like he's completely relaxed, just some guy watching a sunset on the top of Cedar Mountain, not a boy on the first anniversary of the death of his big brother. There's a bottle of cheap watermelon wine next to him.

I drop my backpack and sit down in the chair beside him. Picking up the bottle to see how much is left, I give it a sniff. "This smells gross," I say by way of greeting, handing the bottle back to him.

Jasper nods. "It is. I stopped sipping on it about an hour ago. It was all my parents left out of the locked liquor cabinet. Obviously they left it out because they *hoped* it would get stolen."

I nod sympathetically.

"So what are you doing here?" he asks, setting the bottle down and leaning back in his lawn chair. He crosses his boots at the ankle.

"Just hanging out."

"You come up here a lot to hang out?"

"I do when you're here."

His mouth twitches, but it's not a smile, not a frown. It's not anything.

We sit in silence for nearly an hour, watching the sky grow purplish and then black. Far below in the small town of Rocksaw, lights begin to appear, like tiny stars in the twilight.

Jasper shifts, and his lawn chair squeaks in protest. "Jesse and I used to come up here and get roaring drunk." He pauses, like he's remembering. Like he's going somewhere else, like I do sometimes. He rubs a finger over his lips before he continues, looking away from me, into the distance. "We'd bring our sleeping bags and stay out all night. And Grayson and Linc would come, and a couple of older guys from Jesse's class. We'd light a bonfire, and Grayson would bring his guitar and pretend he was Ren Rogers from Ren and Reckless." He smiles to himself. "Jesse would tell him to play rock music or shut the hell up."

"Sounds like a good time."

"It was."

Another pause, and I reach over and put my hand on top of his.

"He didn't have a hunting accident, you know," Jasper murmurs.

I take a breath before I give a small nod, waiting for him to tell me how all those little pieces of Jesse's story fit together.

Another pause. "He was unhappy. So unhappy. He stopped going to school, going to football practice. I had to drag him to homecoming because Ramani would have been devastated if he didn't show. She knew something was up, too. We both did. My dad kept saying, 'Man up. Shake it off. There's nothing wrong with you.' And then one night he didn't come home. I looked all over town for him. Mom and Dad called the cops. They thought maybe he'd run away to LA to become an actor like he talked about before he became depressed. I don't think they ever suspected, not even a little, how badly he wanted out of the life they had planned for him." Jasper's voice breaks. He takes a few ragged breaths, like he's trying not to cry.

I hold his hand tighter.

"So when I felt like I was sinking, like everything was getting darker and it was hard to breathe, hard to get out of bed in the morning, I kept thinking, this is what happened to Jesse. Next it's going to be me they find out in the woods. And there'll be some story about my hunting accident, about what a tragedy it was to lose someone so young."

"But it's not," I tell him. "It's not you. You're not Jesse."

"Because I went and got some pills. That's why. Otherwise that could have been me, too. He wasn't broken; he *needed help*. I needed help. My dad doesn't even know about the antidepressants, or that I went to talk to a doctor about how I felt. Mom took me once to see our family doctor, and she signed some forms and told me never to say anything to my dad. If he knew, he'd say the same thing to me that he said to Jesse. Man up. Gut it out. Shake it off."

"You don't know that. Maybe your dad changed after Jesse."

"You don't know him. He hasn't," Jasper says fiercely.

"So then tell him to fuck off," I say, furious that his father would treat him that way.

"I can't just tell him off. He has the keys to the kingdom. I've always wanted that farm, even when Jesse thought it was the end of the world. Even when it *was* the end of the world, for him." His eyes are haunted, like he feels guilty for wanting something that his brother hated so much.

"Jasper, this is serious. You can't hide this from your dad forever. You need help right now. That's okay. Maybe someday you won't. But what are you going to do if your dad finds out? Stop taking the antidepressants before your doctor says it's okay?" All my thoughts are reeling, and deep in the back of my darkest corners, I realize that I was scared when Jasper went missing because I didn't know if he had hurt himself. If he had gone off the meds or taken a turn for the worse without me seeing it. Just like with my mom in the Good Year. It hurts to think of him putting himself in danger to make his dad happy. "Are you willing to risk everything for that stupid farm?"

"It's not any of your business, is it?" he shoots back angrily. "You've been here, what, two months, and now you think you know better than anyone else?" He stands up. "We needed to keep it all a secret. Jesse's suicide would have ripped this town apart. *He* was the golden boy. Everybody loved him. Class president, team captain. Could you imagine looking at Ramani and telling her that her perfect boyfriend killed himself? Could you tell my dad?" He almost laughs, a strange, choked sound, and it's the saddest thing

I've heard in a long time. "Yeah, that's the best part. He doesn't even know. My mom didn't tell him. She let him believe that it was an accident because she knew the truth would kill him. Suicide is a sin, you know. So she threw away the goodbye letter in Jesse's room before he could find it. But not before I could."

"I'm sorry, Jasper," I say softly, trying to imagine how much that must have built inside him in the year since Jesse's death, secrets weighing him down until he could barely move.

"You should go," he says, sitting back down.

"All right," I tell him, standing up and grabbing my bag. I didn't know how much it would hurt to be pushed away again, to be reminded that my chapters in Rocksaw have barely begun, to be told that I am still an outsider. To not be able to help the people I've started to care for.

I walk all the way back to the farmhouse with only the cows along the road to keep me company. Inside, I toss my backpack carelessly on the dining table. I don't give a crap about my homework tonight. Mia is in the kitchen, and she calls to me, but I ignore her. The thing about being pushed away is that it feels a little bit better when you get to do it to someone else, too. That way you're not hurting alone.

TWENTY

THE NEXT MORNING, I REMEMBER that Ms. Troy is coming for a home visit. I get to miss the first two periods of school. At least I can avoid seeing Jasper for a little longer.

I come downstairs and find Mia standing at the table, looking down at something, transfixed. I know I should apologize for blowing her off last night, but something inside me is still hurt, still raw. And it wants to stay that way a while longer.

Mia turns a page of what she's looking at, a long curl of her red hair falling against her cheek.

I stop at the edge of the dining room when I see what's on the table. My backpack is open, my pens and papers and books spread everywhere. There's a roll of paper towels at the edge of the table, an overturned teacup. I recall that I threw my bag on the table last night without thinking of anything but my homework inside. I didn't remember what else was in there.

Mia isn't checking my homework. She's looking at my

sketchbook. My secret one, the one that has my whole life inside it.

"What are you doing?" It comes out more like an accusation than a question.

Mia jumps. "I'm so sorry, Trix. I spilled my cup of tea on your backpack. I took everything out to dry it off, and I saw this . . . and I . . ." Her face is pale, her eyes moist. "Connor loved to draw. Did you know that?"

"Is it ruined?" I ask, my voice shaky, hurrying around the table to look at it. Everything is in that book. It's the inside of my heart, as if I'd ripped it out of my chest and smeared it on each page.

Mia shakes her head no, takes a small step aside so that I can look more closely at the sketchpad.

Mia holds the corner of a picture of Mom. Vines of cigarette smoke curl up around her face as she sits outside our room at the Starlite in one of the rusty wrought-iron chairs. "Is this your mother?" Mia asks.

"Yes." The word almost chokes me. Because that is also my face. That is the face I see every day in the mirror and wonder if I am her. Or if I am only seeing her because I can never forgive her and she can never forgive me for what I did.

"And this is where you lived?" She points at the Starlite sign that hangs over the parking lot. I don't respond.

She flips to another page. Wendy and me sitting in a booth at the Jasmine Dragon.

The outside of the Jasmine Dragon, its sign lit up in yellow colored pencil.

An empty motel room.

A woman with two small children holding a Golden Corral menu.

Charly with the twins, red plastic cup in hand.

The Eastside Mall.

Shane, leaning on the door of room 7.

Two hands clasped together on the bus.

Ember sitting on the front steps in one of her dresses, Bacon perched on the step above her.

"There are a lot of places in this book. A lot of people."

"You didn't have any right to go through it," I tell her. "It's private. That's my life. Not yours."

"Everything about you is *private*, Trix." There's an acidity in her tone that I feel like I've been waiting for all this time.

Finally, I am a burden. Finally, I am just what I expected I would be here. Not a McCabe, just Trix. Abandoned. Thief. Drifter.

"How come we never knew about you? How come your mom never called us and asked for help if things were that bad? We were here the whole damn time. Your father should have met you before he died. He had a right, damn it. Connor had a right, and so did I. You shouldn't be a stranger to us. You shouldn't be some puzzle that I have to solve." By the end of her rant she's nearly yelling.

"*You?*" I yell back. "*You* are mad at *me?* You just went through all my shit without asking, like I'm some kind of criminal. Like I'm some kind of *thief* because that's what I am, aren't I?"

"It was an accident, Trix. But looking at these pictures kills me. I keep waiting for you to tell me what happened. I tried to tell you everything I knew about Connor so that you'd understand that he would have wanted you, that *we* want you. And now you're skipping school and running off and not telling me where you're going. I had no idea where you were almost all day yesterday. The principal called to tell me you skipped your afternoon classes. I'm supposed to be in charge of you. Ms. Troy is coming for a home visit any minute now, and what am I going to tell her?"

"What exactly do you mean, *what happened to me*? All those years, what happened to me? Or just the last six months? I was alone. I was fucking alone. Where were *you*? Why weren't you looking for me?"

"We didn't even know you existed. Suddenly Ms. Troy shows up at my door saying, 'Oh, hey, there's this kid out there and you're her only family, but we can't find her right now.' Can you imagine how that felt? You think I don't lose sleep wondering how many nights I was in a warm bed and you were out on the streets somewhere? But you won't even *tell* me."

"Well, it's not like I had any control over when they figured out *you* existed. You're so quick to throw my mom under the bus, but did you ever think maybe Connor knew all along and he just never told *you*? But she used to sell herself for money sometimes, so maybe he was one of *those* guys." I don't really think he was a john, but it feels so good to see the shocked look on Mia's face. Oh, no, her brother wasn't perfect. No one perfect could make someone like me. "Do you want to talk about all of that, drag it all up? I can tell you everything, all the dirty details if it makes *you* feel better."

There's a knock at the door.

"Pull yourselves together," Auntie commands. She must have come down the back stairs and been listening to our fight. "We're not throwing all this away over one stupid cup of spilled tea." She looks at me. "Answer the door. And try not to be an asshole."

I cross through the living room and open the door, my chest still heaving with anger. Ms. Troy is waiting outside on the front porch, the scent of roses in the early morning surrounding her. Her face is rounder, softer, than it was when I last saw her.

"Trix," she says, coming in and giving me a hug, not noticing the hurt and rage that are rolling off me in waves. "You look amazing. So good." She looks around the farmhouse. "It smells wonderful in here, doesn't it? Like walking into a giant muffin." She laughs nervously.

"Ms. Troy," Mia says, coming in from the kitchen. Her face is flushed, but her eyes are dry. She smooths her cardigan and gives a big smile. "Come in, please. Have a seat in the living room."

"I think I hear the kettle," Auntie says, darting a glance between Mia and me again. "I'll go check."

"Yes, some tea would be nice. Thank you," Ms. Troy says, sitting down on the couch. She keeps looking around the room, like something is wrong. Maybe she heard our fight.

I sit down next to her, my hands clasped tightly between my knees.

Ms. Troy opens and closes my file in her lap. She looks at me again, then at Mia, who comes to perch in the armchair diagonally across from us.

She clears her throat. "I've talked to you several times on the phone, of course," Ms. Troy says quietly. "And I'm so happy to hear that things are going well for you. Your school counselor reports that your grades are up. You've been working a part-time job. You seem to be making a real place for yourself here."

I nod.

"I wanted to make sure you know that I'm so happy that things are going well this time, Trix." She pauses again, adjusts the file on her lap, as if she is trying to find the words to say something uncomfortable. Finally, she says, "But I'm afraid I have some news." She puts her hand on my shoulder. I know that touch. The Bad News Touch. "It's about your mom."

My eyes feel hot. "My mom? Did you find her? Is she okay?"

"No, Trix." Ms. Troy purses her lips, pauses. "Your mother passed away."

Time slows down.

There's light and shadow, the rise and fall of my chest as I breathe.

I hear Mia's sharp gasp, the sound of Auntie murmuring a swear word from the kitchen. Then I feel Mia's arms around me, she's crossed the space between us, and she's holding me, the scents of lemon and chai enveloping us both.

"How?" I ask, my mouth moving without my brain. I untangle myself from Mia. I need to know.

Ms. Troy looks at Mia, as if she's not sure if she should say what happened.

"Tell me."

Mia nods to her.

Ms. Troy speaks. "She overdosed, Trix. Someone found her in a motel on Gage and Tenth."

"The Happy Host." I know it. I've stayed there. Yellow wallpaper. Orange carpet. A little bodega just around the corner that sells sherbet the color of sunsets.

"Yes. That's the one."

"Was she alone?" *Please let her not have been alone*, I beg some unknown deity.

"Yes. A maid found her."

Her words sink in. This would be the last chapter in my mother's story. A cold, unforgiving end, alone in some cheap motel room. No one to cry over her. No one to say that they were sorry, or that they still loved her despite everything. Somehow when I look away from Ms. Troy again, the roses are still blooming outside the front windows. The wind rustles through their leaves, setting the flowers to nodding again. Everything else is still beautiful.

"I'm going to my room now," I announce, getting up from the couch.

"Trix," Ms. Troy says. "We need to talk about a few things—"

"Trix," Mia calls after me as I reach the staircase.

"Let her go," Auntie says, entering the living room with a tray of tea. "Give her a little time alone if that's what she needs."

I climb all the way to the attic. My room is the same as I left it less than an hour ago. But I am not the same. I crawl into the bed, digging myself under a mound of quilts until I'm only a bump on the bed.

There, in the darkness of my quilt cocoon, I wait for tears to come.

But they don't. I don't feel anything. In fact, I'm so empty that it rings in my ears. A silence that is somehow loud. I pull the blankets tighter, but they can't help me. The feeling of numbness stays, settling in like a hard frost, killing off everything it touches.

TWENTY-ONE

414 Main Street. Rocksaw, KS. 66554.

Send.

A message dings instantly in return.

I climb down the back staircase. I hear Auntie and Mia murmuring in the living room. Ember should be in school.

They won't miss me till I'm long gone.

I wait around the corner of Jensen's Office Supply, in the alley, my arms crossed to ward off the chill. A yellow Camaro with black racing stripes prowls down the main drag slowly, as if looking for someone.

I step out from the alleyway.

The Camaro stops.

The window rolls down.

"There's my girl." Shane grins at me. "I knew you'd change your mind."

Seeing Shane is like finding a piece of myself that's been missing, like going back in time before Ms. Troy arrived at the

McCabes' door with her Bad News Touch. My new world is crumbling, but my old one is there to bring me back to who I've always been. Trix. Abandoned. Thief. Drifter. All the dark, shadowy parts of me are fitting back together, making perfect sense in the way that they always have.

"You made good time," I say, getting in the passenger side of his car. It's all black leather upholstery and smells faintly of cigarette smoke.

"Anything to bring you home," Shane replies. He leans over as if he's going to kiss me, his breath smelling of mint. I take him in, a face that was once so familiar I could have drawn it in the pitch dark. His time in prison has made him older, harder. There were only traces of a boy when I knew him before, but they are completely gone now.

I put a hand up to stop him from getting any closer because as much as I love seeing him again, it aches, too. "Hey, hold on. We're not together. You dumped me, remember?"

He laughs, opens his eyes, and reaches over to tug up the sleeve of my sweater, kissing my scars instead. The touch is familiar, intimate. "I'm sorry," he says against my skin. His lips twist into a smile even as he says it. He's happy. Happy to see me. Happy to kiss me, even the darkest, most shameful parts of me.

I take a moment, breathe deep. "I am, too. But we're still just friends."

"Friends." Shane groans as if he's been wounded.

"Charly says you did really well while you were in. You got your GED."

"Yeah, I was a real model of good behavior." He cracks a

grin at me. "Except for the whole getting locked up in the first place part."

He could always make me laugh, even when things were hard.

"Where'd you get the car?" I ask, pulling my hand away to gesture at the Camaro.

"Borrowed it from a friend."

"You've made some new friends since we last saw each other. All your old ones were shitty and broke."

"Mmmm, but the old ones are the best," he says, reaching over and taking my hand again. "I missed you."

"I missed you, too, Shane."

Shane fills the drive back to the city with funny stories: guys he met in prison, how excited Charly was when he showed up at her door, the other men in the halfway house where he's been living. Everything about him is easy. And that's what I need right now. I don't tell him about Mom. I don't tell him about the McCabes, or Jasper, or the group of friends I made in Rocksaw. No, let them wait. This moment is just for us, for what we used to be together.

When we get to the Starlite, I have this strange butterfly feeling in my stomach. Even after nearly two months away, after the news Ms. Troy brought to the farmhouse door, I half expect to see Mom sitting outside room 7 in one of those rusty wrought-iron chairs, smoking those cigarettes she stepped out to buy.

But she's not. She's dead in some morgue. She'll never sit here again.

There's a churning nausea in my gut that follows the butterflies. I push away another image, this one of her on a motel-room floor, alone. Her dark hair unfurled over the cheap, threadbare carpet around her. No, no. I can't think of that now. I force myself to smile at Charly where she stands in the parking lot waving at us.

Shane squeezes my hand. "It feels like stepping back in time, doesn't it?" he says. "But things are going to be better than they were before, Trix." Shane's promises are familiar, comforting. I lean into them.

I get out of the car as Charly throws her arms open wide, running to meet me. "Trix!" she exclaims. "I've missed you so much."

I hug her back. "I missed you too, Charly."

"Come inside!" she says, herding me to a familiar room. "We have to catch up. I got your old place, room seven."

Shane closes the door behind us and shuts the blinds. He locks the door and turns on the radiator heater, which rattles and moans. I look around. Room 7 is the same as I left it. The worn coverlet on the bed. The hot plate. I wonder if my secret jar of cash is still in the toilet tank.

"Shane tell you about his big plan?" Charly asks, flopping into the only armchair.

Shane shakes his head, sitting on the edge of the bed. "I haven't said anything yet."

I look back at Shane. "What plan?" I ask.

He shrugs. "I'm still thinking about it. I met this guy while I was doing time. He can get me into that upscale mall on the East Side after closing. There's a jewelry store. I'd be in and out in a few minutes. Split it fifty-fifty with the guy. But it would be more than enough to get us out of here if you still wanted to come."

My heart seizes in my chest. I am silent for a moment, trying to find the right words. But this is Shane, and they don't have to be perfect. They just have to be real. So I let it all out. "Are you fucking serious? You just got out of jail. What are you doing? Trying to get back in?"

Sure, I've stolen more wallets than I can count. Pocketed candy bars and phone chargers. Gift cards and chewing gum. But this is different. This is even bigger than the house he got shot trying to rob. And there is someone else involved. If life has taught me anything, it's that you can't trust just anyone. Especially when there's money involved.

Shane's eyes narrow, and I know I've struck something in him. "I'm a nineteen-year-old with a prison record. Who do you think is going to hire me?" he scoffs. "And it's just an idea. I don't need you to approve. I can do it on my own." He is shutting me out, like he did the day when I tried to visit him in prison and he told me to run away and never come back.

I close my eyes briefly, remembering the robbery he attempted alone, the one where he nearly died. How I spent a year blaming myself because my gift could have hidden him, could have saved him. When I open my eyes again, Shane's gaze is burning into me. And though the rest of him has aged, his features harsher than before, these are still the same dark eyes of a boy who used to bring me Coke-and-cherry slushes from the QuikMart late at night when I was alone. And lonely.

"You can't go by yourself, Shane." And as I say it, I know it's wrong. It's everything I've been trying to change about myself for the last two months. But look how that's ended for me. Shane.

Shane is home. Shane needs me. It feels good to be needed some-times.

"Sure I can. I'm a big boy." He shows me the biceps he's been working on in the training yard.

Charly rolls her eyes.

"Come on," he says. "We'll talk about it later. Are you hun-gry? Let's order a pizza from Sal's. Ham and pineapple. And then we can catch up."

The time passes quickly. Hours seem like minutes going by in flashes of my old life. There are stories that I can finish word for word before Shane tells them: the morning when the buses were running late so he hot-wired a car to get me to my Spanish test on time; the summer afternoon when Charly and I nearly got arrested for hocking pickpocketed wallets; the night when we slit the tires of that john who tried to back me into a dark corner before Shane rescued me. I recall, my voice sounding strange and distant, as if it belongs to someone else, the time the three of us snuck into the West Side City Pavilion long after midnight and skated on the freshly smoothed ice, the air crisp and cold and perfect in a world that was so deeply scarred.

Later, I'm drunk on vodka. Charly started making drinks around five o'clock, pouring them with her typical heavy-handedness. Everything is better than I remember it. We laugh louder, longer, with more abandon. We're happy again. Just the three of us, like the old days, lounging and watching mindless TV to forget everything bad that's happening around us.

Shane is shirtless sitting next to me on the bed, and Charly lounges in the chair by the door, her legs thrown over one cheaply upholstered arm and her red cup pressed to her lips. When I think Shane's watching the television and not me, I stare at all the small white scars from the birdshot he took in the gut two years ago when he broke into that house without me. That guilt, buried deep, emerges again, and I wish that I could have been there to protect him with my gift, to keep him from harm. How differently my life might have turned out.

But I stare too long, and Shane sees me looking. He smiles at me, putting his arm over my shoulders and leaning his cheek against the top of my head. "See if you can find something good in all of those. Maybe the Little Dipper or that guy with the bow and arrow. What was his name?"

"Orion. The hunter."

"Definitely. Look for him. Sounds manly."

The vodka hums through my fingertips as I trace his scars like he used to follow mine. "I don't see Orion. I think at best you've got Ursa Major."

"Bears are good. *Very* macho." He chuckles deeply, and it vibrates through both of us. "Maybe I should get the outline tattooed so it connects them. Been a long time since I got one done. Remember when you drew the feathers? One for you, one for me, and one for Charly?" he asks, touching the three feathers on his neck.

"I sketched them out on that napkin in Golden Corral and you swore that you were going to get them tattooed on you. I couldn't believe when you actually did it."

"I always do what I say I'm going to do."

His words echo in my head. I told Ember that I was going to stop running away. But I'm here. I'm a liar.

While the laugh track on the TV sitcom plays, I wonder what Ember is doing right now.

Shadows move along the wall as the seconds pass. But maybe it's hours. It's dark outside.

"I wish I had some pajamas. Something to change into."

Shane laughs. "I prefer to sleep naked, myself."

"Let's go get some pajamas." I have a sudden desire to put my gift to work, to prove to myself that I still have what it takes to survive on my own.

"Sure," he says, pulling himself up from the bed. "Give me a minute and I'll get us a ride."

When he returns, he leads me out to an older Mustang that smells like patchouli oil when I climb inside.

"What happened to the Camaro?" I ask him when he gets in the driver's seat.

Shane grins as we whip out of the parking lot of the Starlite, the world spinning beyond us. "My friend needed it back. So I borrowed this one instead."

And then we're at a Target, weaving through the aisles. I can't believe Shane managed to drive us here. He seems sober, like Charly wasn't pouring his drinks nearly as strong as she was pouring mine. The floor tiles seem a little wavy, and Shane laughs when I tell him. I wander into the pajama section, picking up a nice pair of loose, comfy pants and a T-shirt. But then I spy a scarf down the aisle. It's printed with blue-and-purple feathers on a silvery gray background, and it reminds me of Ember. She would like it. I pick that up, too.

My mouth still tastes like ham and pineapple pizza, so we make a detour to get a toothbrush and toothpaste. On the way, I see a T-shirt that would look great on Shane. I pick that up, too. It's like my hands have magnets in them. I keep picking things up, and damn, it feels so good.

Finally, I am the old Trix again. There's no guilt, no worry. Only the rush of getting exactly what I want. And I walk outside Target with all of it in my arms. No one stops us, because I have a gift, you see.

In the parking lot, I slip my arm through Shane's to steady my walk. Everything is like it used to be. There's no one judging. No one testing me. There's just the boy who loved me unconditionally. No matter if I was a shade of gray or deepest shadow. "Shane," I say, my breath coming out in small puffs of white. "Don't do that job alone."

Shane lets out a small sigh. "I shouldn't have mentioned it. Charly wanted me to. But it was stupid. I can do it by myself." He pauses, rubs my arm with the back of his knuckles. "I need enough to get a new start somewhere else."

"I'll come with you this time," I say, wanting this feeling to stay forever. Wanting to turn back time, to when we were us, and Mom was only a thin motel wall away, forgiveness still conceivable.

Back to when another Good Year was still possible.

I lick my lips, as if I could taste the promise on them. "My gift will make sure we don't get caught. And it will be a new start for both of us."

Shane looks down at me. His breath ghosts between us in the cold night air. "Are you sure?" he murmurs, his voice deep and dark. "We can't go back on our word once I call this guy."

"I'm sure," I say.

Shane helps me get into the car and shuts the door. When we start driving, I close my eyes because it feels like the car is moving too fast, golden streaks of light against my eyelids. "Are those the stars? I thought you couldn't see them in the city," I ask Shane, my eyes still closed.

He reaches over and takes my hand. "They're stars, Trix. Every constellation you could dream of."

TWENTY-TWO

My head is throbbing.

The light pouring in through the motel blinds tells me it's long past noon. Shane steps through the motel-room door with coffee and a heavy plastic bag from the QuikMart.

"Ugh," I groan, sitting up. There are flashes of memories: pizza, vodka, promises, starlight. "Why did you let me drink that much?"

"I tried to stop you after your third, but you told me to stop being a boring old man."

I sort of remember that. "Did we go to Target last night?"

"Yeah, you wiped out half the store." He gestures toward the pile of stuff in the corner of the motel room.

"That's what I thought." I find myself grinning, that high of taking what I wanted with no regrets coming back to me.

"You were amazing. No one noticed you. You breezed

through there, picking up whatever you wanted and then walked out the door. The alarms at the exit didn't even go off. Not even for that pair of sunglasses you picked up."

"Sunglasses?"

Shane points to the pile again. "You were busy last night."

"Shit. I am good." We both laugh.

"Here, I brought coffee if you want it. Or Gatorade and some ibuprofen if you don't. I even found the donuts with cinnamon and sugar that you like."

Actually, I'm dying for one of Mia's muffins and some Earl Grey, and the sudden thought of the McCabes makes me uneasy. "No tea?"

"I don't know if they have tea at the QuikMart. I can go back and check if you want." He's always wanted to take care of me, and it shows.

"Coffee's fine. I'm going to take a shower."

I grab a sack of clothes on my way into the bathroom. We're still in room 7. I know, because I recognize the small gouge mark I made by the tiny window in the bathroom. I know if I looked behind that bland beach artwork on the wall next to the bed, I'd see the picture I sketched at thirteen, one of me and Mom, to remind me that it would only ever be the two of us, scarred and broken. No mantel lined with family photos for us.

I get in the shower, letting the warm water sluice over my face. I turn it hotter still, waiting to see if it's going to wake me from this strange dream. I'm back in the Starlite. Shane is here. I've got a bag full of stolen clothing sitting on the sink. We are going to pull a job that will give us a fresh start. We'll get out of the city. We'll go somewhere new.

Somewhere where my mom isn't dead. Somewhere where the smell of lemon doesn't make me feel homesick. I wonder what Mia is doing now. If she's worried about where I am, or if she's relieved that it's all over. Auntie will mutter about my fortune. And Ember. She will hate me for breaking my promise to not run away. But eventually she will put away the homecoming dress she was making for me, and I will become a distant memory, the scent of my skin each time I tried the dress on for her fading from the fabric until it is gone completely.

When I get out of the shower and towel myself off, I grab the clothes I picked out last night. A big hoodie. A baggy pair of jeans. Yes, I am the old Trix again.

When I emerge from the bathroom dressed in my stolen clothing, there's a strange man in our room.

"Who are you?" I ask, glancing at Shane, who is closing the front blinds.

"This is the guy I was telling you about. Don. I let him know we're in."

"This is about the jewelry store," I say, looking at Don again. He's older, with slicked-back hair and a scruffy day-old beard. He smells like sour beer.

"It'll just be you against a bunch of security cameras and maybe a couple of guards if they're on that side of the mall," Shane says. "You proved last night that alarms don't pick you up. Don has everything else we need."

"Where are we going to fence all this high-dollar crap?" I ask. I've stolen things before, but never anything that required this much work. It was always easy stuff, pickpocketing and shoplifting. Survival stuff.

"Don has connections."

Don leers at me, playing with a chain around his neck. He makes me uneasy, not just about our safety in this room, but the whole deal. "Don't worry about it. I'll make sure you get your cut," he says.

"Just give us what we need and get out," I reply, my voice hard.

Don looks to Shane, who nods. He tosses a set of keys to Shane. "Meet me in the parking garage at Eighth and Tannen when you're done tonight."

He leaves, but the sense of apprehension is still with me. Don reminds me of too many dealers, too many johns who hung around Mom when she was alive.

No, no. I can't think of that now. I can't think about Mom or anything that came before today.

This will be a new start.

Every intersection we drive through in the dark of night tells a story. I've stood at every crosswalk, losing myself in the crowd, my hands stealthy as I snatched a wallet or a watch. I've waited at every bus stop, my shoulders hunched against shadows and cold, wondering which motel I should stay in for the night. My hands tremble as I remember those days, the sheer vulnerability of them, and I slide them under my legs, the material of my new jeans scratchy against my skin.

Shane parks this latest car he borrowed, a bland but new Chevy sedan, on a side street behind the mall, next to an assortment of high-class condos. He shuts it off, but as he reaches for his seat belt, the alarm goes off. The lights flash and the car alarm shrieks, echoing through the city streets.

"Shit!" Shane swears, kicking beneath the steering column. He leans beneath it, reaching up with one long arm to tug at the wires under the dash. I look frantically around for the police, but it's only annoyed passersby, their arms loaded with bags from the upscale department stores in the mall. To them, we're only a couple of stupid rich kids who don't know how to shut off their car alarm.

Finally, the alarm stops. I can still feel my blood pounding in my ears, looking around to make sure that no one has suspected anything's amiss. Shane sits back up, visibly sweating.

"So you borrowed this car from your friend, huh?" I ask breathlessly.

"Yeah. Nice guy."

"I bet." We both laugh nervously, but I can't help but wonder if this is a sign that we shouldn't go through with our plan.

"It'll be over before you know it." He smiles at me, but it does nothing to lift the heavy weight that settles over my shoulders.

I follow him to the mall, remembering all the small details I'd collected about the place, the ebb and flow of shoppers, the best times to work through the crowd. The security guards are in their usual spots by Nordstrom and Saks. It's nearly nine o'clock at night, so the crowd is beginning to thin out. People are going home, leaving to get ready to go out on the town in their newly purchased clothing. Everyone is distracted, peering through shop windows to see if they've overlooked any good sales, or looking down at their phones.

I pick out at least five easy marks as we wind through the crowds. I mentally calculate how much cash they'd likely have on them. Enough to put me up in a cheap motel for at least a week.

We pass the jewelry store, Markus. It's a little boutique, not a chain. I remember the old man who runs it, that he likes to go to the hot-dog cart on his twenty-minute lunch break. He's been here even longer than I've been using this place as a means of easy money. But he's in the shop now, wearing a green sweater-vest and talking to a young couple who look like they're probably shopping for engagement rings. I consider the long hours, the struggle that goes into owning your own business. How it would feel if someone walked into the McCabe Bakery & Tea Shoppe and took everything that they could grab. Or if someone had gutted the bank deposit bag from the Jasmine Dragon after a busy night. Another quiver of unease winds through me.

Next to Markus is an empty shop. Another store, Celebrations, has put up a few mannequins in the empty front window to advertise their wares while the space is available for lease. They wear short, poufy dresses—the kind of thing you might wear to a homecoming dance. I think of Jasper, and I wonder who he will go with now that I'm gone. And then I wonder if Ember will finish my dress, sure that I'll come home soon.

Not home.

I don't have a home.

Shane peers into the empty storefront. "This is it," he says. Behind the mannequins, the rest of the store is black, in darkness until someone moves in.

"This is what?" I ask.

"Where we'll hide out until the mall closes." He takes my hand and leads me down a service hallway a few feet away. We follow the hallway for at least thirty feet before we take a left turn, and I know we're behind the shops now. Shane listens quietly for anyone else who might be lurking in the dimly lit hall, but there's nothing, only the sound of the two of us breathing as we stand behind a door marked *136*. Shane pulls out a set of keys from his pocket, finds one that fits, and opens the lock.

Inside, the storeroom is dark and dusty. Shane pulls a small flashlight from his pocket. There are boxes everywhere, some of them open, as if someone left in the middle of packing up their business.

"Come on," Shane says. "Let's have a seat. We've got a while to wait."

We move a few boxes around until we've cleared a space on the back wall to lean against. There's a small sliver of light coming in from the door opposite us. It must lead to the shop out front, where the dresses are displayed.

"So what's the plan now?" I ask Shane as we settle in next to each other.

"In a few hours, we go back out to the service hall and in through the stockroom door of Markus."

"We're just going to waltz in there?" I ask. "Won't the

jewelry be all locked up?"

Shane pulls the keys back out of his pocket and jingles them. "All the good stuff is kept in cages in the back office. They're welded into the floor and wall, perfectly secure against anyone who doesn't have the keys. But we have what we need." He shows me a small key with a *1* written on it in permanent marker. "Don swiped the spare set and made copies when he was doing maintenance there for a busted pipe."

"Don's a busy guy." I lean forward to adjust a shoelace on my sneakers.

"No shit. But he needed someone to go in. He's got a bum leg. Couldn't be fast if his life depended on it. Even if he could have figured out a way to cut the alarms on the exit, the security camera and the patrol would have done him in."

"And you thought you could do it alone?"

"I was hoping you might come along this time."

I sigh, sinking back against the wall.

Shane reaches over to hold my hand again.

I pull away. "You're not my boyfriend, you know. You're my accomplice."

Shane gives a low laugh in the back of his throat. "I remember when you moved into the Starlite. All quiet and mousy. I barely noticed you. Then I go away for a year in juvie and you're some badass in a hoodie, flipping me the bird when I see you and Charly talking in the parking lot."

I vaguely remember the moment he's describing. I was thirteen when Mom and I moved into the Starlite, and Shane and I never interacted. He was just Charly's older brother who was always in trouble. But he got sent to juvie for a year not long after that. I was a lot harder when Shane came home compared to when I'd first moved in. My time at the Starlite had made me that way.

I wonder what young Trix, before she grew tough and wary, would think of me now. Back when her scars were still fresh, and she played poker for peppermints.

How ashamed she would be.

Or perhaps she wouldn't even recognize me at all.

"By the time you got out of juvie, you'd grown a foot and shaved your head. I thought you were some stupid john hanging around. I didn't know you were Charly's brother," I tell him.

"Well, after you flipped me off, I *knew* I had to get to know you."

"I thought my TV was on too loud."

"It wasn't. I just wanted an excuse to see you."

"That was a dumb excuse."

"Well, it worked, didn't it?"

"Only because you brought Coke-and-cherry slushes the next time you showed up at my door. If they'd been blue raspberry, I wouldn't have even bothered letting you in."

Shane cracks a grin. "See how easy it is with us? We just fit, Trix. You and me."

He's right. Everything is easy with Shane. Easy because it's habit. Because we both already know all the dark crevices, the unspoken wounds, of the other. But as I sit there in the dark with Shane, I start thinking maybe some of my old wounds have begun to heal over. Stealing used to feel like I was getting even with the world for the shitty life I'd been handed. But now, after the time I'd spent with the McCabe women in the bakery, I feel uneasy about robbing this old man who probably worked his whole life to have this little shop in this fancy mall. More than that, I feel uneasy putting our fate in the hands of a man like Don, who gives me the creeps.

I feel like this is a mistake.

"And after this?" I ask, my voice tight.

"Whatever you want. Wherever you want. Just name it. We can hit the road and see where it takes us," Shane tells me, tapping his knees with the tips of his fingers.

I like that image, but when I picture us, we're not the two people sitting here in this dark storeroom. We're me at fifteen. Him at seventeen. It's Trix and Shane before everything else happened. The years in prison. The two months in Rocksaw with the McCabe women.

"And what happens when we run out of money?" I ask him.

"We do it again."

"And again? And again?"

Shane frowns. "What's the matter?" he asks.

I look at my hands, wonder at this strange gift that I've been given. I refused to use it once before. That destroyed us, Mom and me.

My voice strains when I finally tell him. "My mom is dead."

"What?" Shane is incredulous.

"She's dead. She overdosed in a room over at the Happy Host. Alone."

He lets out a long sigh. "Fuck it, Trix, I'm sorry." Shane's arms close around me, safe and strong.

"I don't want to end up like her. Dead in some motel room. Alone." I murmur the words into Shane's shoulder.

"You won't, Trix. You won't. It's going to be okay. I'll take care of you. I *want* to take care of you."

I pull away and look him in the eyes, needing him to understand how devastated I am that Mom and I could never find forgiveness. That we would never have another Good Year. I hadn't realized how much her death had shaken me. Not until I stood on the brink of letting go of everything good I've built in the last two months. "She never got out of that shitty life. And you know what? This job won't get us out. It won't matter how far we run, or where we go."

"This will work, Trix."

"No. Nothing's going to change. She's still dead, and you and I are just digging ourselves in deeper until we get caught, or we cross the wrong person and then we end up like her. Dead in some motel room."

I feel him pulling away, not just physically, but totally, completely.

I will either sever us completely or save us from ourselves.

"We can't do this, Shane."

"Are you serious?" Shane hisses, getting up. I stand up, too, so that we're facing each other. His brow is furrowed; he's angry. No, he's disappointed. Abandoned.

"I can't do this." No, that's wrong. And in this moment, I have to choose my words carefully, be completely honest with him or I'll never be able to live with myself afterward. "I *won't* do this."

"Fine," Shane grinds out. "I'll do it myself. I've got the keys."

I grab his hand this time, like he's done hundreds of times for me. "Don't, Shane. Leave with me. Just walk away."

"Walk away? With Don waiting for us? Jesus, he'll have guys after me in a fucking heartbeat if I don't hold up my end of the deal."

"Come with me. Come back to Rocksaw. We'll figure it out. I can find you a place to stay."

"And do what? You know how many people are just so fucking eager to hire some nineteen-year-old with a prison record?" He tries to pull his hand away, but I hold on tight, as if I could make him change his mind with only the power of my touch.

"*Try*, Shane. Just try. For me."

"For you? Why should I do shit for you? You're going to walk out and leave me after everything? I stole a fucking car to come get you when you needed me."

"Do it because we're friends. Because we've always looked out for each other. You and me and Charly."

"Only, you're not looking out for me. You're just looking out for you now."

I let go of his hand.

Something inside Shane is unleashed when I let go, and he punches the wall behind us with a strangled sound of anger, busting a hole in the drywall. Then he slides back down onto the floor, tugging up his black hood so I can't see how much I've hurt him.

"Please, Shane." I sound like that girl who visited him in

prison thirteen months ago, my voice some stranger's, begging him not to let go.

"Go home, Trix. Just go home."

And I do.

I leave through the service-entrance door in the back of the mall. I know there are alarms, but they don't go off when I pass through. The employee parking lot is empty but for a few cars, probably the night-shift security guards, the patrols Don had been worried about.

I walk all the way to the bus stop without looking back, my hands fisted into the front pockets of my hoodie, leaning into the bitter October wind. The songs of the city welcome me back even as they make me feel more alone than ever. I try to shut down the rest of my senses, focus solely on the scuff of my sneakers over the pavement, the distant echoes of sirens and car horns, the shout of someone hailing a taxi.

When Ms. Troy told me Mom was dead, I couldn't feel anything. Only numbness. But I feel everything now. And holy shit, does it hurt.

When I reach the bus stop, I stand there alone, my hood pulled up to shadow my face. I clench my jaw until it hurts, forcing myself not to cry. Staying is Shane's choice. I have to make mine now. The city bus is driving toward me; I can hear it almost a block away, engine whirring and groaning as it shudders with every gear shift.

I catch the sound of footsteps hitting the damp pavement at a quick clip, and a burst of adrenaline surges through my veins, preparing me to fight if need be. I turn around before I'm blindsided, thinking that it must be Don or one of the guys Shane was talking about coming at me from behind. Retribution will be swift after all.

But it's not. It's Shane. He's breathing hard, and the street-light glints against his shaved head where his hood has fallen back. He stops next to me, turning to face the bus that's pulling up to the stop, like he's just some other passenger waiting next to me.

I reach out my hand. He takes it and we get on the bus together.

We sit in the back of the almost empty vehicle. Our hands are still clasped between us, his knuckles scraped and swollen from where he punched through the wall. "Thanks," Shane whispers without looking at me, his voice raw.

I don't answer, I just hold on, wishing that I could reverse time, the last two years between us. And at the same time, wishing that everything had happened just the same.

We get off at the last stop, walking back in the dark to the Starlite. It's cold, and I stuff my hands into the front pocket of my hoodie. Shane walks close to me, our shoulders bumping against each other.

"I guess I can't give you a ride home since I left the car. But you can use my phone to call your aunt," Shane says.

"What are you going to do now?" I ask.

We stop at the edge of the parking lot of the Starlite. The NO VACANCY glares in the dark as we stand facing each other, savoring these last moments of what we used to be.

Shane answers, "I've got a little stash. Think I'll take a Grey-hound bus out of town for a while. Start over somewhere new and let this shit with Don simmer down. Charly can come if she wants."

I nod.

"You can always come with us too," he says hopefully.

I press my lips together before telling him, "I think I'm going to go home."

Shane nods, a faint, sad smile on his face. "I thought so. If you ever change your mind, you've got my number."

"You could come with me," I offer, my voice breaking, even though I know he will say no.

"Thanks," Shane says, his voice still soft. "I don't think I'm cut out for Rocksaw." He raises one hand and rubs the back of his scraped knuckles against my cheek. "But I think you might be."

I look away, afraid that I might start to cry. This is really goodbye between us. Among the rusting sedans and sports cars, I recognize an old, beat-up, blue Suburban parked by the front office.

It's oddly comforting, that battered SUV. And despite how much this goodbye hurts, I find myself beginning to smile. "Actually, I don't think I'll need that phone call after all." I remember Charly, who must still think we're at the mall. "Will you tell your sister goodbye for me? Tell her I'll call her soon."

"I will." Then Shane notices the Suburban, too, and the out-of-county stickers on the plates. "I'll see you around, Trix." He touches his lips to the top of my head and fades back into the darkness, leaving only the faint scent of mint and cigarette smoke that I remember from our first kiss.

TWENTY-THREE

THE DOOR TO ROOM 7 of the Starlite is wide open, spilling a swath of light out into the dark parking lot. I hear Mia roaring before I see her. She's cussing someone out like nothing I've ever heard.

". . . Renting a room to a minor? Are you serious? Do you know how much trouble you could get in? I ought to call the goddamn cops right now! *Where is she?*"

I enter the room soundlessly to see Mel holding his hands up like Mia's going to hit him. She looks like a wild thing, her vibrant hair tied up in a messy bun and her face red and blotchy. I've never seen her so angry, not even when she yelled at me. She's clutching my sketchbook, and I can see it's open to the picture of the Starlite's neon sign.

"Mia."

She freezes mid-rant, her shoulders moving once, as if she's taking a deep breath. She turns to look at me as I approach her.

Mel sees an opportunity to escape, and he hurtles out the

door as fast as he can, brushing against me as he goes.

"Trix." Mia takes two swift steps and seizes me in a hug that smells of lemon and chai.

Her embrace is the only thing that gives me the courage to say what I want, mostly because I know that I'm putting everything on the line. After running away, Mia may not want me to come back with her. I may have ruined everything, just like I have so many times before. But I say it anyway. "I want to come home."

And then she's laughing between sobs, and I'm crying, and neither one of us is letting the other go.

In the parking lot, Mia accidentally kicks a discarded needle on the pavement and pointedly ignores catcalls from some men leaning against an old Cutlass. Once we're inside the Suburban with the doors locked, she says it's too late to drive all the way back to Rocksaw, and she takes us across town to a Holiday Inn and gets us a room. She makes a phone call outside in the hall while I get undressed and crawl into my own full-size bed. I fall asleep before she comes back inside, taking comfort in the muffled rise and fall of her voice on the other side of the door.

The next morning Mia keeps the conversation light, telling me that we can go downstairs and get something quick to eat from the breakfast buffet before we leave. Surprisingly, she grabs one of their muffins. I guess eating someone else's baked goods must feel a little bit like a vacation for her.

I keep waiting for the other shoe to drop, for Mia to yell at me like she did at Mel last night. I ran away. I did exactly what Ms. Troy warned her I'd do the day she dropped me off at the farmhouse. I haven't changed. I haven't put down roots. I am a failure, a thief, a drifter. The pile of stolen items in my motel room proves it.

But there's nothing. Only a placid smile as Mia checks out at the front desk. We get into the Suburban, and Mia backs it out of the parking space. We turn out onto Charles Avenue, but we don't immediately head toward Rocksaw. It's unnerving, and so is her silence.

Finally, I can't bear it anymore and ask, "Are you going to yell at me now?"

Mia purses her lips, like she's determined. Her eyes are unreadable.

We're near Little Chinatown. I recognize the city blocks as we pass them.

Finally, she speaks. "I love you, Trix. I need you to know that no matter how many times you run, no matter how far you go, I'll keep looking for you."

I've got that heavy feeling of guilt again. And something more, something warm underneath that heaviness that makes my eyes feel hot.

"I'm sorry I yelled at you. It's been hard for me to stand back and let you decide what you are and aren't willing to share with me. It's different. With Ember, I was there for everything. But with you, it's like I'm stepping in at the end of the game, the last inning. And I don't even know how to play." Then she slows the car. I realize we're pulling up in front of the Jasmine Dragon.

"What are we doing here?" I ask. Everything comes back to me in a rush. The Good Year. The wallpapered apartment. The back booth. Mom's face, full and pretty. The dictionary. The spicy scent of ginger.

The Yangs will not want to see me. The last time I was here, Mom robbed them of their bank deposit. Oh no, this is a bad idea.

Mia pulls my sketchbook out of her purse and hands it to me. "When you ran away, I went through this whole book, looking for every place you drew. The Westside High School. The Jasmine Dragon. The bus stop on Fifth and Yates. The Eastside Mall. All three Golden Corrals *near* the Eastside Mall. The Starlite Motel." She points to the Jasmine Dragon outside the Suburban. "I met Mrs. Yang here. I showed her the picture that you drew of yourself in the booth." She holds the sketch out to me. It's me sitting next to Wendy, something I'd drawn when I was lonely and wishing that I had a sister, a friend.

"She knew right away who you were."

"What did she say?" I ask, unable to look Mia in the eye.

"She said you were a sweet girl, and she always wished that your mom had taken the deposit but left you behind."

I'm tearing up again, and there's no gluten-free muffins to blame it on.

"We talked for a little while."

"And she told you everything?"

"She told me a few things. I understand that I'm never going to know everything, Trix. You don't owe me that. You don't owe me anything. But maybe someday you'll tell me more."

I nod. Because I'm not ready to tell her everything. Some things are best left in the past. But other things. Maybe I could let them go if I told someone else. Maybe those wounds would heal over a little faster.

I touch my sweater over my constellation of scars before I pull up my sleeve so that she can see them. "I never told anyone." Not even Shane, who so lovingly traced the marks with his fingers, his lips.

Mia shuts off the Suburban, but the radio continues to play that song that Ember loves so much, "Your Touch." She looks at me with all her focus, waiting for me to tell her.

"I was ten years old." I feel the moment taking over, pulling me back. Every word now is a struggle, like I have to pull it from some dark place inside of me, syllable by syllable. "Mom knew what I could do. It was a part of how we'd always gotten by. But one night she was really messed up, and she owed her dealer money. She wanted me to sneak into the motel room next to us and steal some cash. The girl who stayed there had just gotten a lot of cash from her dad. I guess she was a runaway. Only fifteen. And she told Mom about it all because she was scared and relieved and afraid that her dad would never love her after everything she'd done. He wanted her to come home, and he'd wired her the money to get there."

I press my lips together, hoping it will keep me from crying. "But I told Mom no. I wouldn't steal from that girl. She just wanted to go *home*." I can't stop my voice from breaking because I know what it feels like to want to go home. I know that now. "And Mom was so mad, and so fucking high that she did this to me. I had to be punished for refusing to steal from that girl."

Mia's eyes are wet. "Oh, Trix, I'm—"

"That's not all of it." I have to get this all out now before I lose my nerve. "After that I turned her in. I went to my teacher at school and I told her my mom was an addict, and that we were lying about where we lived. And they took me away from her. Mom checked herself into rehab. And I went into foster care for the first time.

"And then I realized what I'd done. I was angry, and hurt, and I'd betrayed her. My mother. My only family. I thought maybe she would never come back for me. I ran away three times trying to find her. I was sorry. I just wanted to go home, like that girl in the room next to ours. And Mom *was* home. I loved her." I swipe at the tears again.

"But even years after everything, I don't think she could ever forgive either of us for what we did. And that's why she left."

"Trix, you can't think that. You can't put her leaving on you."

"Why else would she have left?"

"I don't know. There could be a million reasons. But you can't keep taking responsibility for her and what she did. She was the adult. You were the kid."

My voice breaks again. "But she can never come back now. How can I tell her that I forgive her?"

"I don't know, Trix. I don't know. But you have to believe that no matter what, she loved you, okay? There's no one in the world who wouldn't love you."

"After she got out of rehab, she got a job here and a little apartment up there." I point at the small window on the east side of the building. "I thought we were finally going to be a perfect family."

Mia hands me a tissue from her purse. After I've wiped my eyes and nose, and taken a few deep breaths, she reaches over and squeezes my hand. "Let's go see Mrs. Yang. I promised her I would bring you by when I found you."

The front door is locked because the restaurant doesn't open for another two hours, but when Mia taps quietly at the door, someone answers it.

The girl who opens it is my age. She has shoulder-length black hair, with some brightly dyed pink strands hanging on either side of her face. She wears a short apron around her waist and a pen tucked behind her left ear. It's Wendy. "We open at eleven," she says at first. Then her mouth forms a perfect O in recognition. "Mama!" she yells over her shoulder. "Come out here! You won't believe who it is! It's Trix!" Wendy smashes me into an enthusiastic hug before herding me into the dining room with one arm locked around my shoulders. I admire her pink hair again and wonder if she got a guitar and started a rock band like she wanted when we were twelve.

Jack is wrapping silverware in paper napkins at the familiar back booth. He stands up when he sees me. I can't believe how big he's gotten. He blushes, his voice cracking a little. "Hi, Trix. Long time no see."

Mr. and Mrs. Yang come in from the kitchen. For a moment they stand there, and I wonder if they are comparing me to the little girl who used to live here, who used to play poker for peppermints and never swore.

They look the same as I remember, as if I've stepped back in time. I glance briefly at the stairs that lead to the upstairs apartments, as if Mom might be on her way down for the lunch shift.

Mrs. Yang pulls me back to this moment. "Trix! It's you! I can't believe it! We've wanted to see you again for so long." Her face would be happy if it weren't for her wet eyes, like mine now. She hurries to me, folding me into her soft arms. She runs a hand over my hair when she pulls back again to look at me, and suddenly I remember her doing that in the Good Year, the gesture casual and yet devastatingly kind to me when I was twelve. "It's so good to see you, Trix. I've always worried about you, wondering where you were. If you were okay. Mia says you're living in the country now? With your cousin and another aunt?"

I nod, still trying to find the words to tell her everything I wished I could have before Mom and I left.

"Trixie," Mr. Yang says, joining his wife. He lets out a sigh of relief. "I've waited a long time to tell you thank you." He hugs me, too.

"Thank you?" I ask, confused.

Mr. Yang pulls a battered pocket-size copy of *American English Idioms and Slang* out of his back pocket. "When Mia stopped by yesterday, it reminded me of this. I found it when I was cleaning out the little apartment a few weeks after you left. It had my name on it, so I thought you wouldn't mind if I unwrapped it." He smiles at me. "It has been well-loved, as you can see. Many Scrabble feuds were settled."

"I still say slang words shouldn't be allowed in Scrabble," Jack pipes up, earning a sharp elbow from Wendy.

Part of me is twelve again, watching them with awe and

desperation in my gut. Wishing I could be a part of the magic that they had so easily. The same magic that's in the McCabe farmhouse. "I'm sorry," I tell them before I lose my nerve. "About what my mom did. I always wondered why you never called the cops."

Mrs. Yang makes a small sound in the back of her throat. "Your mother was a troubled woman," she says. "We didn't want to make things worse for you. But we didn't know you had other family. She always said you two were alone. Perhaps we would have done things differently."

"There's no reason for you to apologize," Mr. Yang adds. "You didn't take the money. We knew that."

"We're so happy that you're okay," Mrs. Yang says. "And we want you to know that the door here is always open for you. We expect you to visit. Let us know how things are going. You and Wendy will be starting university next year. We could always use another waitress, and there's an apartment upstairs, you know."

I nod, my throat tight. There are so many things to tell them. I am no longer the little girl who put the peppermints back in the bowl after she won them in poker. It will be two more years before I can even consider college. But I have time. These things can wait.

"Oh, wait!" Mrs. Yang says, looking at Mia. "I have what you asked for." She goes back to the register at the counter and digs around underneath it.

While she's occupied, Wendy grins and hands me her phone. "Put your number in it!" she says. "We have to catch up. I have a million things to tell you. And I want to hear everything. Do you come to the city a lot? Maybe we could meet up."

"Not a lot," I say.

"But we could come more often," Mia adds. "If Trix wanted to visit."

Wendy nods enthusiastically.

Mrs. Yang returns with a small manila envelope and hands it to Mia.

"Thank you," Mia says. "I really appreciate you finding these for me."

"Of course." Something passes between them, a smile that is almost sad.

Mrs. Yang hugs me again. "Come back anytime," she tells me.

Wendy waves as we leave, and Mia's arm is over my shoulders as we step outside onto the curb.

In the Suburban, Mia hands me the envelope before she starts the engine. "I thought you might like something to put on the mantel," she says.

I take the envelope from her and open it, sliding the contents out into my hands.

Photographs. There are only a few of them. One of Wendy and Jack playing Texas Hold'em with me, our peppermint betting chips in the middle of the table. Wendy is grinning goofily and Jack is frowning at his cards. I'm smiling primly and my cheeks are pink, like I'm blushing with excitement and pride that I'm included in the shot.

There are two more of me studying with Wendy and Jack. They're wearing their school uniforms, and I'm in jeans and a pale-blue polo that Mrs. Yang gave me for my birthday. I was so happy to have that shirt that I wore it even though it was short-sleeved and showed my scars. Wendy had one in the same color, and we used to wear them on the same day so we could be twins.

The final two are from when we celebrated the lunar New Year with a big dinner. The moment I got my lucky penny. One is of me making dumplings with Wendy and Jack. The last is of me sitting at the table with Mom. Her arm rests casually on the back of my chair, almost a hug as she leans toward me. Her face is still full, her eyes bright. Her dark hair is styled in curls that cascade over her shoulders. She was beautiful, my mom in the Good Year.

I don't want to think of her dead in some motel room. I want to pretend she's still here, in the Good Year.

"This one?" I ask, holding it out. "Could we put this one up?"

Mia touches the corner of the photograph lightly. "This is your mom?"

I nod.

"We'll get a frame and put it up when we get home. And maybe one of you and your friends, too? It sounds like you were very close with Wendy."

"If you think there's enough room," I say, looking over the pictures again. I can't quite say what it means to have these. I've looked at Ember's pictures on the mantel, wishing myself into the frames.

"We'll make room, Trix," Mia says.

TWENTY-FOUR

WHEN MIA AND I WALK through the front door of the farmhouse, the normal smells of freshly baked pies are gone. Instead it's a cacophony of cheese and ham and tomato sauce and garlic drowning out faint strains of lemon. The dining room table is laden with foil-covered dishes. I don't know why it looks like we're about to host a buffet for thirty people, but I'm starving and thrilled to see it all. But I need to go to my room first.

Upstairs, I change back into the clothes I left behind. My phone is on my bed along with my backpack. I pick it up and see about a million missed messages from Jasper, Ember, Ramani, and the rest of the crew from school. I scroll through a few before deciding that it's best to leave them for another time. The first few are frantic texts about where I've gone, and the glimpses I catch of the rest all have the word *mom*. I'm not ready to read them yet, so I return downstairs.

I find Mia in the kitchen.

"Perfect timing," she says when she sees me. Evening light wanes through the kitchen windows. "I warmed up the blueberry pie for you in the oven. Getting ready to make up a few new ones while I'm at it."

"Blueberry for breakups," I say quietly, my voice a little creaky.

"Heartbreak is heartbreak." She cuts a slice of the blueberry pie on the cooling rack and puts it on a chipped yellow plate. Without looking, she reaches into a drawer and pulls out a fork. She hands them both to me. "Eat up."

"What's with all the food in the dining room?" I ask through a mouthful of warm, sweet blueberries. I chew and swallow before Mia answers, relishing that feeling of comfort.

"The neighbors brought it when they heard about your mom."

"We don't have neighbors. We have cows."

"Well, the town, then. That's what people do when someone passes away. They bring food. Everyone's been asking to see you. Auntie said the phone's been ringing off the hook."

"How does everyone know already?"

"Auntie called the *Rocksaw Gazette* before it went out yesterday. Judging by when the casseroles started showing up, I think most people found out about the service before the paper even came out. Everyone knows Orla, the copy editor, can't keep her mouth shut."

"What service?"

"The funeral service for your mom."

I hadn't even thought about a funeral. Funerals are for people with big families, lots of friends. Mom had me, and whatever dealer she was hooked up with at the time of her demise. "No one's going to come to a funeral service. And anyway, who would put one on?"

"We're putting one on. She'll be buried in the McCabe family plot."

I nearly drop what's left of my pie, remembering the sprawling, hilly cemetery where Connor McCabe and Jesse Ruiz are buried. "You can't mean that. She wasn't a McCabe. She doesn't belong there."

"She'll be buried there. The same as Connor. And someday me and Auntie and you and Ember."

"Wow, that's something to look forward to." I try to crack a joke, anything to make this feel normal.

Mia smiles, nudging the pie plate I'm holding.

I take another bite. The pain in my chest eases a little more with the sweet, heavy taste of blueberry.

"I'm sorry," I tell her because I don't think I actually said it before. "For running away. And for yelling at you. It's hard for me to talk about things that happened before I came here."

Mia shakes her head. "We both said things we shouldn't have. It's water under the bridge."

"But I was wondering," I say after I take another bite of pie, "when you and your husband divorced, Ember said you were real torn up about it, but you wouldn't make any pies. Why didn't you eat any Bracing Blueberry?"

Mia shrugs one shoulder. "Heartache's not all bad. It reminds you that what you felt was real."

I stop chewing. "So maybe I should let myself hurt for a while?"

"I think you've had enough hurt. Eat the pie. Tomorrow it will hurt again."

"Will it ever go away?"

"A little bit each day."

I put the pie down. "It would be easier if we had ever been able to forgive each other. But everything between us was always so complicated."

Mia nods. "You're not ever going to have all the answers, Trix. Neither am I. But try to remember the good parts. Your mother is really beautiful in that photo from the Yangs. I think we should use that one in the service program. So everyone could see her when she was doing well."

"That was the Good Year," I say, surprising myself by sharing so much. I imagine that detail filling out, taking shape with the things Mrs. Yang and I have told her. Maybe this will be a new chapter. "That's what I always called it. I really thought we were going to make it."

Mia begins rolling out more pie dough. "You did make it, Trix."

"But she didn't."

"I didn't know her." She pauses rolling out the dough. "But I think any parent would be happy to know that her child is safe and loved. Even if they aren't the ones loving and keeping them safe."

I nod.

Mia starts rolling out the dough again.

"Where's Ember?" I ask.

"She and Auntie got back while you were upstairs. I think Ember's out on the front porch. There's going to be a hard freeze tonight. She's saying goodbye to the roses." She picks up her circle of dough and puts it in a pie tin. "She was pretty upset when you ran away. Just so you know."

I nod, because it's no surprise to me. Scrounging around the kitchen counters, I locate a Never-Lonely Lemon. "Is it okay if I take this outside?" I ask.

Mia reaches down to the silverware drawer and pulls out two forks in reply. "Grab your jacket. It's cold outside."

I shift the pie and two forks to one hand and snag the blue afghan off the couch in the living room on my way out. The yellow afghan is missing, and I know where it is.

It's twilight outside, and Ember's sitting rigidly on the middle step, wrapped in the sunny-hued afghan. She's watching the stars come out and doesn't bother to look back at me when I begin to climb down the steps. I guess she knows it's me. And she's definitely still angry with me for breaking my promise to her about running away.

I settle myself next to her, setting the pie down on the step between us and stabbing the two forks down through the crown of meringue and into the crust so that they stand up on their own.

"Hey," I say carefully.

"Hey yourself." She doesn't even look at me. Her hands are knotted in her afghan-shawl, and anger shimmers in the air between us.

"I'm sorry," I murmur.

"For what?" Her voice is still sharp.

293

"For running away when I promised you I wouldn't."

And then Ember lets go, tossing off her blanket because she's got more than enough rage keeping her warm. "I don't get it, Trix. You can't run away when you get mad. Or hurt. You've got to stay and fight for what you want." She turns to face me. "Remember when we were in the concession stand and Mrs. Stuart accused you of stealing? You stayed and fought. And I stayed with you. Because we're friends. No, we're *family*.

"I worked in the dining room of the tea shop by myself last night, did you know that? While Mama was bawling her eyes out and driving all over the city looking for your sorry ass, I stayed and I fought. Even though it was scary and hard. I can't stop my gift. I can't give it up like you can. I can only try to be brave and fight."

"You are brave, Ember."

"You're damn right I am."

"I'm sorry. I wish I could take it back—"

"We made a deal. I'd stop eating in the library by myself. I'd make an effort to get out there and make friends and live my life. You'd stop running away."

"I came back," I offer lamely.

"So that's supposed to erase it all? Mama and Auntie came and pulled me out of school to see if I knew where you'd gone. Mama was bawling, and Auntie yelled at her for yelling at you, and then I yelled at Auntie for yelling at Mama." She sniffs. "Ramani called me at lunch to say that when she was on her way to the dentist's office, she saw you get into a strange car. That's the only way we knew you weren't even in Rocksaw anymore. Can you imagine what that felt like, to hear Ramani tell us that you could be anywhere? Did you even *think* about us?"

My shoulders tense beneath the afghan.

"Who was it? Who picked you up?"

"Shane."

"The boy you used to date? I thought you said it was over." She grabs a fork and digs out a mouthful of pie. "I'm pretty sure we sat right here and ate blueberry pie and you cried about how he broke your heart a long time ago."

"It is over. We're just friends."

"Jasper was really worried. He ditched school to look for you when I texted him that you'd run off."

I get defensive when Jasper's name is brought up. "Well, I did that for him the other day, so I guess we're even."

"*We're* not even, though."

I pick up my fork and stab absently at the pie. A few quiet moments pass. Just the scrape of our forks against the pie tin. I don't know what to say. I don't know how to make things right again. "What can I do?" I ask finally.

"Do you care?"

"Of course I care. I'm here, sitting on the front steps in the dark eating pie with you. I don't know how else to say I care." I gesture with a hand at the tin.

Ember sighs. "I know. I'm sorry that I was so angry. I know you're hurting, too." She waits a beat, picking up her blanket and pulling it around herself. "I'm real sorry about your mom." She sits back down next to me.

That ache in my chest returns, and I pull my own afghan

closer. "What about me and you?"

"We're okay, I guess, since you brought me pie." She gives me a small smile before picking up her fork and taking another bite. "I'm not really lonely anymore. I guess all the lemon worked."

I nod. "Me, neither."

"So do you want to talk about your mom?"

I shake my head. "Not right now."

"I called Grayson to tell him you were okay. I told him to tell Jasper and everybody. I hope that's all right. Jasper was really worried. We all were."

I know she's changed because she includes herself in Jasper's crew, it's not a *them* and *us* thing anymore. "Your mom says the roses will die tonight."

"Yeah," Ember says. "It always makes me sad. Even though I know they'll come back."

"This may sound stupid," I begin awkwardly. "But I want to put some on my mom's grave. When I visited the cemetery, I saw that a bunch of people had put flowers on Jesse Ruiz's grave. And if I was going to put flowers on my mom's grave, I'd like them to be our roses." I wait to see if Ember is going to say it's impossible, or ask why I'd want to put flowers on the grave of a mother who abandoned me.

But she doesn't.

Instead, she stands up, letting her yellow afghan fall again to the worn wooden steps behind her. "Come on," she says. "We'll go get Auntie's garden shears and clip the buds. With any luck we can put them in water and they'll bloom in time for the service."

Her hands are loose at her sides, and I realize that I want to do something I've been afraid of since I met her.

"I'd like to share with you," I tell her. "If you want."

I reach out slowly to show her I'm serious.

Ember begins to pull away, as if she's sure I'm not remembering what she can do with a touch of her hand against mine.

I wait for her decision.

Ember gives me a small smile. "All right," she says. "I'd like that."

Her palm is cold against mine from sitting outside for so long. Ember's eyes widen as my deepest secrets and fears roll through her.

Somehow, sharing with her makes me feel a little lighter.

"Don't worry," she says when she lets go. The scent of roses hangs around us, sweet in the tang of the coming frost. "This will always be home if you want it to be."

TWENTY-FIVE

On the morning of my mother's funeral service, the day dawns bright and clear and cold. A hard frost hit two days ago, killing off the roses, as we thought it would. At the cemetery, I hold the bouquet Ember helped me pick, thankful the blooms opened in time for me to put them on Mom's freshly mounded grave. There's going to be a reception at the McCabe Bakery & Tea Shoppe, but Mia promised me that if it was too much, I didn't have to go. She'd navigate the crowds and casseroles and condolences for me. I appreciate the offer, but I know that no matter how hard it is, I wouldn't miss it.

I'm not an idiot. I know that funerals cost thousands of dollars, and that Auntie and Mia paid for this one not because they had any regard for my mother, but for me. This is a gift to me. After everything I've put them through, they're still trying to show me that they love me.

I think I'm still trying to figure out what love is, although I have a patchwork collection of answers.

Love is wishing with your eyes closed. Love is American slang dictionaries for Scrabble. Love is Coke-and-cherry slushes at midnight. Love is watching the lights come on in town from lawn chairs on Cedar Mountain. Love is lemon-meringue pie on the porch steps. Love is stopping at the end of the driveway and turning back around when all you want to do is run away.

As we stand over my mother's grave, listening to the Rocksaw Community Church's pastor give a sermon for a woman he never knew, it's hard to explain how I feel. Mom and I never had a perfect relationship. Even in the Good Year, we'd been two people trying to play a part. Me, the good, sweet, obedient daughter. Her, the repentant, loving mother trying to make a new life. Maybe we both failed. Even with all the blueberry pie I've eaten in the last few days, the pain is sharp and fierce when I stand here in front of her grave. I know she's dead. And even though I want to wish it so, she's not in the Good Year. She's not going to show up again, her face full and her hair thick and shiny as she shows me around her new apartment.

And yet there's also a sense of release. A release from waiting for her to get better. A release from waiting for her to come back for me. A release from wondering if I'd done something differently, or been better somehow, if she could have forgiven me. It's slippery, that feeling of release, because it also comes with a haze of gut-sickening shame for feeling it.

Mia puts a hand on my shoulder, interrupting my thoughts, as the pastor finishes his sermon. Afterward, we stand in a row: Mia, me, Ember, and Auntie, receiving the condolences of what must be the entire town of Rocksaw. I don't know why they all showed up. Maybe it's because the McCabe Bakery & Tea Shoppe has been closed for the last two days and they're all dying for a pastry fix at the reception.

The townspeople come in a long line, one after the other, hands that squeeze mine, arms that hold me as they murmur words that get lost in the noise of the crowd. Only the bravest citizens hug Ember or take her hand, but she turns no one away, as if trying to show me that we're in this grief together. I shake my head at her, *no*, but she only reaches over and quickly squeezes my hand twice in hers, as if to say, *it's my choice*.

My teachers are here, and the principal who agreed to take Ardent Apple pies in exchange for my school fees. Tobias Jensen from the office supply store. The knitting club that sits in the back booth every day after school at the shop. Grayson and Linc. Ramani and Adalyn. Mrs. Stuart and Vera's mother and other people I suppose are probably parents.

The Yangs, Mrs. Yang's eyes red and wet, the familiar feeling of her hand stroking over my hair, the quick squeeze from Wendy, who brings me a small gift that she presses into my hand. Mr. Yang, who solemnly pats my shoulder and tells me he is proud of me for being strong. Jack's bashful hug.

I open my hand to see what Wendy pushed into my palm. It's a Scrabble tile, a *T*, strung on a silver chain. And I remember the Good Year again, with Mom and the Yangs. The most perfect year of my life.

Maybe, someday, I will have another Good Year.

Ms. Troy. She embraces me, sniffling, her nose red. She looks heavier. I guess I didn't notice when she appeared a few days ago with the news. I'd been too shocked, too hollow to really notice not just the roundness of her face, but the thickness of her waist. "I'm so sorry, Trix. You know I always hoped for the best for you and your mom."

I nod, because I don't know what to say, how to form the words to properly express the tangle of emotions this day brings to me. Ms. Troy hugs Ember and Mia next, but when she gets to Auntie, the hug she throws around her nearly knocks the old woman over. Auntie grunts.

"You were right. Thank you so much." Ms. Troy reaches down and puts a hand on her stomach. "I'll be twenty weeks tomorrow. I was so worried that I would miscarry again."

"Of course I was right," Auntie says, looking almost offended. "I have a gift, you know. I'm a McCabe woman."

And then there is Jasper. His face is sober, no smile, real or fake, tugging on his scar. He takes both my hands in his, and they're a little rough, just like I remember them from the first night we spent on Cedar Mountain. I wonder if it was hard for him to come here barely a year after he buried his brother. I wonder if he will visit Jesse's grave on his way out of the cemetery. I wonder if anything has changed since he confessed those things to me on Cedar Mountain, his breath reeking of watermelon wine and hurt.

I remember when we first met, and I thought he was a golden boy. He's still golden, but there are darker parts to him, too. We both have our own dark chapters. And it's that same small-town phenomenon, how everyone here shares little bits of your story, but never the whole thing. The pastor spoke of my mother as a woman who was taken too soon, who had so much left to give. Jasper knows the part of her story when she walked out to get a pack of cigarettes and never came back. Mia knows the scars on my arm are from Mom and that she could never forgive herself afterward. I feel a little lighter knowing I don't carry all those dark pages by myself.

I look over at Ember as Jasper releases my hands and moves on to clasp hers. Yes, I have gotten what I always wanted. My deepest secrets. Not a perfect family, after all. But a constellation of women, connected by pie and fortunes and roses. And love.

Later, the four of us sit around the table eating Bracing Blueberry together. It was a difficult day for everyone. Auntie's eyebrows shoot up suddenly when I reach up to brush the hair out of my face, and she swallows a mouthful of pie. "Give me your hand," she says to me.

"What?" I ask, putting down my fork.

"Has something changed?" Ember asks, her interest piqued.

Auntie nods and reaches for my hand. I give it to her, and she uncurls my fingers, traces her knotted ones over my palm. "Look at that," she says. *"Look at that."*

The rest of us hold our breath, waiting for her to continue.

"Your life line's changed. Look at those new shoots coming up. Your roots aren't all about survival, anymore, Trix. You've got new gifts unfurling, tiny leaves waiting for sunlight to let them grow."

"What does that mean?" I ask, wondering if I'm losing my quick, quiet hands.

"Just wait," Auntie says. "Wait and see what blooms for you. Everything evolves, Trix. Even DNA."

TWENTY-SIX

I'M SITTING ON TOP OF Cedar Mountain, my boots crossed at my ankles as I watch the sun set. Mia gave me the rest of the week off. I'm supposed to be at home, catching up on homework I missed and somehow sewing shut the gaping hole in my heart left by my mother's death. But it's not really like a gaping hole can be filled. I don't know how to explain this to the new counselor Mia makes me go see, how to put it into words, what exactly my mother is to me now that she's really gone.

Mia is the beaming sun that the McCabe household orbits around.

My mother was not the sun. She was a storm, thunder and lightning that swelled and ebbed, destructive and beautiful. She is a gentle ache of promise, and of what might have been, that comes and goes. She is the smell of cigarette smoke, the spicy tang of ginger. She is the Good Year and the Starlite and the dark shadows among the roses that I sketch in the margins of my notebook paper.

And I am Trix McCabe. One of the Rocksaw McCabes. Once abandoned. Former drifter, thief. Presently high school junior and waitress.

The quickness in my hands seems to be fading, and I wonder if Auntie is right, that I am changing, and there are new things on the horizon for me.

In my sketchbook, I draw the small town below, the angles and planes of the tiny shops and broad streets testing my skill in perspective. My sketchbook is almost full. Time to take my paycheck down to Jensen's Office Supply and get a new book to fill. My mind buzzes with other images I want to capture in the blank pages of my new book. Auntie making tea. The knitting club in one of the back booths at the shop. Mia kneading dough. The way Linc looks at Ramani, like her smile is full of stars, even though she's still dreaming of another. Moments in time that make up Rocksaw.

I hear his boots in the dirt before I see him.

Jasper climbs up the well-worn path, his black curls damp and shining from a shower after football practice. He smiles when he sees me, the movement tugging on his scar.

"Hey," he says, standing almost awkwardly in front of me. "Is it okay if I sit down?"

I gesture at the lawn chair next to me. We haven't actually spoken since the last time we were here. He'd dropped by the farmhouse twice since the funeral, and both times I told Mia to tell him I was out. I'm not angry with him. I'm not even hurt anymore.

But reaching out again only means that I could get pushed away, and I have to decide that I'm okay with that. "It's a free country," I say blandly.

He sits down in the lawn chair, tilting his head so that his curls fall back. "Nice night," Jasper says, making small talk that reveals his discomfort. "Warm for the end of October."

I nod, still sketching. "I guess so."

"Your drawing is nice."

"Thanks."

"We've missed you at school."

"I come back next week."

"After homecoming?"

Our entire conversation is stilted, and I don't care. These aren't any of the things that we need to say. So I shrug. "I guess so."

"It's good if you wait till you're ready. Don't rush it."

"Yep."

"I only took a couple days after Jesse died. I went back to school too soon. I was a mess."

There's a twinge in my chest. "That's too bad."

A few quiet moments pass before Jasper speaks again. "We talked. My parents and me."

I continue sketching, waiting for him to finish his story.

"After I told you to leave, that last time up here? I thought about what you said. I was angry, and stupid. But you were right. So I told my dad about my depression, and the medicine I'm taking for it." He taps his hands on the arms of the lawn chair. "He was angry and shouted a lot, and then Mom told him to shut the hell

up, that she wasn't going to lose another boy like she lost Jesse."
He pauses, swallows. "Dad was devastated. I think he suspected
that Jesse had taken his own life, but to hear her say it out loud . . ."
Jasper's voice trails off.

I stop sketching.

"I just wanted you to know. That even though I was angry
that night, I listened. And I'm sorry. I'm sorry I yelled at you.
Sorry I told you to leave. I was scared that I couldn't do what you
said. I couldn't stand up to my dad, tell him that I was doing what I
wanted even if it meant losing the farm." He pauses, and there are
a few even breaths between us in the silence. "He's not speaking
to me. Or to my mom. But I'll give him time. Maybe he'll come
around."

I take his hand.

He squeezes my fingers, and we watch the sun sink down
until Rocksaw is bathed in darkness, stars flickering into existence
above us.

Ember's father's arrival on the evening of homecoming is preceded
by a flurry of cleaning. Mia dusts the entire farmhouse, sending
Bacon yowling to the top of the kitchen cabinets to escape her
feather duster. Since Mia is always baking, the kitchen is still spotless, and the only room in the house she hasn't been scrubbing for
the last forty-eight hours.

"I don't know why you're cleaning for Jordan," Auntie
grumbles. "He walked out on you, not the other way around. His
ass can sit on a dusty chair for all I care."

Mia continues to dust the mantel, adjusting the newly framed pictures of me and Mom, and the other of Wendy, Jack, and me playing poker.

"You don't need to repeat history to me. I know. I was there, remember?"

"Well, I won't be bending over backward for him, so don't get any funny ideas about that."

"I won't, Auntie."

Ember comes downstairs after putting her backpack away. She watches them both warily, her eyes darting every so often to the windows. The football game starts in an hour, and she's wearing a long-sleeved shirt under Grayson's white visiting jersey, which is far too big on her, so she's knotted it artistically to one side and paired it with bright-orange leggings and little suede boots.

"Nice shirt," I tease her from the couch, where I watch the proceedings from an afghan cocoon. I have no intention of going to the homecoming game or the dance following. I could hear the band from the parade on Main Street all the way here, and I saw a plane fly over town at some poignant moment, trailing a banner that said, "Go Tigers." That was enough for me. "You should pair it with cat ears for the full effect, though."

Ember was a little disappointed when I reassured her again last night that I wanted to stay home. "I'm not ready to go and pretend that I'm happy yet," I told her. "Next week. Next week I can get through all the sympathy hugs and the 'I'm-so-sorrys.'"

So instead she got out the blueberry pie and we ate it sitting on the floor of her room next to her dressmaker's dummy, admiring the dress she'd made for me that I wasn't going to wear.

Now, looking down the football jersey, Ember blushes. "Grayson gave it to me to wear at the game tonight. I didn't want to be rude."

"It's cute. You look very sporty."

Auntie snorts. "She looks like she could wear it as a nightgown."

Mia sighs. "I wore Jordan's jersey to the homecoming games, you know."

Auntie rolls her eyes. "And we all know how that turned out."

Mia's green eyes shoot daggers at Auntie.

There's a rumble of a truck coming up the drive. "It's Daddy," Ember hisses at her mom and Auntie, as if it will make them play nice over him for once.

Auntie sighs dramatically and flops down next to me on the couch.

There's a knock on the front door, and Ember lets her father in. Mia stands next to the fireplace, crossing and uncrossing her arms like she's not quite sure how to pose for her ex-husband's arrival.

"Hello, darling girl," Jordan says, scooping Ember into a big hug and spinning her around like she's still a child.

Despite how nervous she's looked about his visit, Ember beams in his arms. "Hi, Daddy," she says when he sets her down.

"Look at you," he says, standing back and holding her at arm's length. "You get prettier every time I see you." He looks over at Mia. "Just like your mama, huh?"

Mia smiles, and he holds out a bouquet of red roses for her. "I knew yours would be done out here, so I brought you these."

"Thank you," Mia says, blushing. "That was thoughtful of you. I'll go put these—"

"I'll do it," I interrupt, pulling myself out of my afghan cocoon. Mia had wanted me to meet Jordan as a big surprise since Connor was his best friend, but somehow watching them all together makes me feel awkward and intrusive. I'm happy for Ember, but I don't feel like I belong in this scene. Taking care of the flowers gives me an easy out.

Instead of letting me flee, Mia seizes me around the shoulders. "Jordan, this is Trix. My niece."

"Nice to meet you," Jordan says, giving me a nod and a smile, even though he's clearly confused.

"Do you see the resemblance?" Mia asks, nearly bursting.

"To who?" Jordan asks.

Mia waits a few moments, but it's clear that Jordan has no idea who I am. So she nearly shouts in excitement, "To *Connor*. Trix is Connor's *daughter*." Mia uses her hand to sweep the hair back from my face, as if that's going to bring my dead father to life before his eyes.

Jordan tilts his head at her, frowning, as if this is some joke that he's not quite falling for. "Connor didn't have any kids."

"He did. With Allison Fiorello. Trix's mom."

"Allison Fiorello?" Jordan says, looking over at me uncomfortably. "Maybe we should talk about this outside."

He doesn't say it outright, but I know from his tone that he thinks my mom was a big, fat liar. Mia darts a glance back at me before following Jordan out onto the porch.

Maybe there's a reason Mom never looked for my dad, never

told him I existed. Maybe she just put his name on my birth certificate so that I'd have one on it. Maybe he was just a name on a line and not my father at all. Maybe I'm not even a McCabe. Maybe I've spent all this time trying to become a member of this family just to have it stolen away from me at the last moment.

I look around the farmhouse, wondering if I'm an imposter here.

"Come on," Auntie says sharply, jerking me out of my head. "We can listen from the kitchen."

Ember and I follow her to the kitchen, where she cracks open the window so that we can hear their voices carrying from the porch.

"Look, I just think you might have been taken in, Mia. You've always been looking for ways to connect to Connor, even though he's gone. And I get that. He was a great guy. My best friend."

"Social services contacted me. Connor McCabe is listed as the father on Trix's birth certificate." I can't see Mia, but I can hear the hurt in her voice. She wanted to surprise him, believing that finding the daughter of his long-lost best friend and her beloved brother would have been some kind of wonderful gift for them to share.

"You didn't *know* Allison. I did. She and Connor were together *very* briefly back when he was in college. They weren't even exclusive."

"I don't care how brief it was, Jordan. Connor is her father. Just look at her. Look at her eyes. Those are Connor's eyes."

"And I'm going to tell you what I told Allison when she

showed up at our apartment while Connor was studying abroad—that baby could have been *anybody's*. Her parents disowned her after they found out she was pregnant. Even *they* knew she was bad news."

"Are you serious?" Mia sounds shocked.

I wish I could say I blamed her, but I can't. It all makes sense now why Connor was never in my life.

He wasn't my father.

I back away from the window, wishing that I hadn't eavesdropped after all.

Ember looks struck by the news as well, and she hurries out of the kitchen for the front porch, as if to avoid having Jordan come back in the house again.

I retreat upstairs, letting Bacon follow me.

My room seems stifling, and I wish that Jordan wasn't out on the front porch so that I could be sitting on the stoop right now, smelling the sweet, heavy scent of the roses. But then I remember that there's nothing out there but thorns and wilted leaves.

I recall the pastels in the desk drawer under the left eave that I stole from the supply cabinet in the art classroom on my first day of school. I dig around until I find them. I slide open the box. Slim sticks of dark ruby, violet, emerald, tangerine, gold, gray, black, and brown. I know exactly what to do with them.

The first dark-amethyst rose is nearly the size of my hand, and I stand on my bed while I draw it out on the sloped ceiling. And the next is smaller, the size of my palm in a bright ruby red. Another, larger in sapphire blue. Another in sunset pink. One more in autumn orange. The green vines come next, shadowed in inky-night-blue and black. They form the shape of the Big Dipper, pointing the way to true north, to the true Trix McCabe. Bacon winds himself between my legs as I draw, crooning cat songs to keep me company.

An hour later, the ceiling above my bed is nearly covered, and my hands and forearms are smeared with color, making even my scars seem beautiful.

TWENTY-SEVEN

THERE'S A KNOCK AT THE bedroom door at the bottom of the steps. "Come in," I call. It's been at least three hours since Jordan came and dropped his suspicions about my family history at Mia's feet. I've been waiting in the calm before the storm, wondering if Ms. Troy is on her way, coming to take me back to the city, to some group home where I can be corralled until I finish high school. Maybe I'm not blood at all, my fortune some ever-changing, ever-shifting thing that pushes me around like a fallen leaf in a storm. I'm just some girl. Some girl who might corrupt Mia and Jordan's daughter, steal their valuables, and run off in the dark of night.

I wonder if the farmhouse and the McCabe women are about to become just sketches in my book, like all the people and places that have come before them. But I won't run away. I'll wait to hear what Mia has to say. This time, I won't let go first.

Mia climbs the creaking attic stairs, looking a little sheepish. "Hi, honey," she says. "Are you doing okay?" She glances up at the ceiling, at my constellation of roses, and lets out a small gasp. "You've got such a talent, Trix. It really is amazing."

I shrug, feigning indifference until she drops the bomb.

"I guess you heard Jordan. I know Auntie and Ember did."

I wait, focusing my gaze on the roses above us.

"I'm so sorry, Trix," she says.

I take a deep shuddering breath, waiting for her to finish with, *but you have to go.*

"You should've had a chance to know your father. And Jordan is responsible for that. I had no idea what happened. He never told Connor about Allison being pregnant because he thought you couldn't be Connor's. And I understand if you don't want him at the house again. If Ember wants to see him, I'll drive her into the city."

"Wait, *what?*" I ask, sitting up. "You mean you don't believe him?"

"Believe what? That he sent your mom away, thinking he was protecting Connor? Sure, I believe it. If Connor had known about you, he would've stepped up. He would've been a father, even if he and your mom weren't together anymore. That's what I could never figure out after we found you—why we didn't know about you. Connor had his faults, but I know he would have wanted you. All this time I thought it was your mom who kept it from Connor. I'm so sorry."

"Yeah, but what about what Jordan said? About how I might not even be Connor's?"

Mia shrugs. "I don't care, Trix. You're my family. You're mine. That's all that matters."

315

"Even if he's right and I'm not your blood?"

"Even if he's right and you're not my blood."

I grab Mia and hold her, breathing in the chai and lemon. "Thank you."

Mia hugs me back. "I want you to know," she says into my dark hair, "I think Jordan is wrong. I do think you're a McCabe. You've got a gift, like the rest of us. You've got Connor's eyes. You've got his artistic talent." She lets me go, and we both look up at the roses. "Although to be fair, I don't think he was quite as good an artist as you. But I think Auntie's got some of his sketches in her bedroom. We'll have to go look. Maybe you'll want to hang some of them in here."

"Well, not if they're not any good," I say, trying to keep my voice steady.

Mia laughs. "Well, yeah. Understandable."

"But about Jordan. I don't want to keep Ember from her dad. Somebody did that to me, I guess. But I don't want to do it to her. That's not fair."

Mia sighs. "That's very big of you. But honestly, Ember's so mad right now I don't know if she wants to see him for a while. But I wanted you to know that you don't have to put up with him if you don't want to."

"She'll want to see him. Eventually."

"We'll see. It's up to her." Mia swipes at her nose. "I know I don't want to see him for a long, long time. I think this has cured me of Jordan permanently. No more mooning over what used to be."

"Auntie will be glad."

"Yeah. Auntie's not exactly who I imagined myself growing old with, though."

"I know a woman who makes an excellent Ardent Apple, and I have it on good authority that there are a fair number of eligible men in Rocksaw."

Mia laughs again. "Do you think you could talk to Ember, or are you done for the night?"

"What's wrong?" I ask. "Isn't she at the game?"

"God, no. She's in her room. Crying. Convinced you'll hate her forever for what Jordan did to Allison."

I sigh. "We need the Bracing Blueberry. Heartbreak is heartbreak."

"I'm on it."

I bring two plates of blueberry pie into Ember's room. She's sprawled out on her stomach across her bed, still in Grayson's football jersey, though she's taken off the leggings, and her long legs and feet are bare.

Auntie's right. The jersey *could* be a nightgown.

"Hey," I say, sitting down on the edge of the bed. "Brought you a snack."

"Why are you here? You must hate me."

"I don't hate you."

"You should. My dad is a dick. *My dad* is the reason you don't have *your dad*."

"Technically, I don't have my dad because he's dead."

Ember props herself up on her elbows to glare at me over her shoulder.

"Come on, sit up and take this pie. I'm tired of holding it. Blueberry pie is heavier than it looks."

Ember sits up and faces me, taking one plate. "Fine," she sighs. "I'll take the pie."

"Thanks."

We eat the pie without talking, with only the clinking of the forks to fill the silence. Truthfully, I don't even feel like I need pie. I feel pretty good after what Mia said. Even if I'm not blood, I'm still family. I'm still hers.

Finally, when only the crust is left, I ask her, "Do you feel better?"

"A little better. But I'm still mad."

"I'm not mad," I admit.

"Why?"

"I'm kind of relieved, actually. I mean now I know why Mom never talked about Connor. Why she never looked for him or mentioned him to Ms. Troy. She thought he didn't want me."

"I don't know why that makes you feel relieved."

"I never wondered about why I didn't know Connor until I came here, but by then it was too late to ask my mom. Now it's sort of like she answered me." The phantom pain lessens.

"I guess," Ember says, but she sounds doubtful.

"I used to wonder why she even had me. Why she kept me. She could have had an abortion or put me up for adoption. But now I know that at some point in her life, she was a mother who wanted me, even if she was the only person who did. She wanted me." So much of Mom's past is clearer now. She'd been young. Disowned by her family when she got pregnant with me. Of course she'd done whatever it took to take care of us. She was being a mother in the only way she could.

Ember leans her head on my shoulder. There's something so comforting about her touch, knowing that there's someone out there who has seen all my dark places and still loves me.

"You know," I say, changing the subject to something lighter. "Your dress is finished. You missed the game, but you don't have to miss the dance. You still have time to get ready."

"I don't think I feel like going," Ember admits.

"What do you mean? You spent weeks on your dress."

"And yours, and *you're* not going."

"I'm not going back to school until next week."

"That doesn't mean you can't go *anywhere*," she says, looking suddenly inspired as she grabs her phone.

"Where am I going to go in a dress like that?"

"Just put it on. And meet me downstairs."

"But I—"

"I put it in your closet this morning. Go."

It's dark by the time Grayson arrives to pick up Ember. I'm standing awkwardly in the dress Ember made, which I admit is gorgeous, even if it's not comfortingly protective like a hoodie. Ember worked her magic to turn that poufy monstrosity into something beautiful. She left off the sleeves after all, and I look down at my scars, wondering if it was a mistake to wash off all the color from my earlier drawing with pastels. But I'm going to be brave like the rest of the McCabe women. I'm going to look down at my scars and know that they point north, past all the things that hurt me, to a future that's beautiful.

Mia takes a photo of Grayson and Ember standing at the foot of the stairs. Grayson's ears are pink from all of Mia's attention.

"You next," Mia says to me. Stand there at the bottom of the steps so I can get one of you in your dress."

"Don't forget her date, Mama," Ember says.

I look up to say that I don't have one, but that's when I spot Jasper standing at the screened front door. I bite my lip trying not to smile when he looks so earnest, waiting there for me to notice him.

Mia looks over too, and her smile nearly lights up the room. "There you are, Jasper. Hurry over and stand next to Trix. I need more photos for the mantel."

Ember laughs. "You're going to need another mantel soon."

"Well, there's plenty of space on the walls, too. We could blow them up bigger for the walls, you know. Poster-size."

Jasper crosses the living room, holding a small box in his hands. He's dressed in black pants, a white button-down shirt with a couple buttons undone at the neck, and a black vest. His worn brown cowboy boots have been replaced with shiny black ones.

"I got this for you," he says, holding out the white cardboard box. He opens it for me so I see two dark, wine-colored roses on a hunter-green band.

"Just now?" I ask.

"Well, I got it this morning. On the off chance you changed your mind tonight."

"I'm glad you took that bet," I murmur.

"I am *dying* right now," Mia whispers loudly to Auntie.

Jasper laughs and takes the corsage out to put on my wrist like Grayson did with Ember earlier. I know he sees the scars, but he doesn't flinch, doesn't stare. He just slides his finger over the last one near my wrist as he helps me with the corsage. His touch is gentle, firm.

"Thank you," I whisper.

He grins at me, the kind that tugs on his scar.

"Okay, look at the camera," Auntie says. "One hand on her waist. Not too high. And not too low, either," Auntie warns. "Now Trix, put your hand on his shoulder so we can see the corsage."

We maneuver ourselves awkwardly until Auntie is happy, and Mia takes a million photos, and then more photos of all four of us together, and then a few more of only me and Ember. "In case you dump these two hot muffins for new ones next week," Auntie explains.

"Mama, can we go now?" Ember asks, her cheeks glowing with excitement. "It's getting kind of late."

"Oh! Yes. Of course," Mia says. "Just, um, remember to have fun. And be safe. And be home by ten."

Auntie groans.

"Okay, midnight."

Auntie groans again. "We'll leave the door unlocked. Come in sometime before sunrise. And don't be drunk *or* pregnant."

"Got it," Ember and I say in unison.

Mia sighs this time. "I love you, girls. Have fun."

"Come on," Auntie says, pulling her away. "We'll get out the tequila and make margaritas. And there's going to be a marathon on my movie channel tonight. Women who killed their husbands. Should be inspiring."

Grayson and Jasper exchange an uncomfortable look.

"Bye, Mama! Bye, Auntie!" Ember calls.

I could have gotten Cleo's door open on the first try I think, but Jasper opens it for me. "It's a date," he says with mock solemnity. "You have to let me open it for you on a date."

"Where exactly are we going?" I ask.

"Just wait and see."

"That sounds ominous."

"Trust me." He takes my hand, and his touch sends shivers of anticipation through my veins.

Grayson and Ember follow us in his Jeep, a blinding set of headlights behind us as we wind down the country road into town with an audience of cows along the way. The main drag of Rocksaw is quiet, all the little shops closed for the day. There are still streamers and ribbons hanging from streetlamp to streetlamp, puddles of confetti from the parade this afternoon. The trash cans are overflowing with paper cups and popcorn. A mostly destroyed piñata of the opposing team's mascot, the rhino, hangs from the streetlamp on the corner by the McCabe Bakery & Tea Shoppe.

"Looks like it was a big day," I comment.

"Oh, it was. But make no mistake, it's still going strong. Homecoming's a marathon, not a sprint." He squeezes my hand.

"I feel like I should've trained more. Maybe upped my cardio by jogging up and down Cedar Mountain a few hundred times."

We turn toward the high school. "Well, you might get

your chance tonight," Jasper says.

"We're not going to the dance, are we?" I ask as we drive through the packed high school parking lot. My chest feels suddenly tight thinking of trying to endure all the pitying looks, the sincere apologies that I'm not ready to accept without crumbling a little. I just want to be happy tonight. "Ember said we weren't."

"We're not. No huge crowds. Just friends."

We turn up toward the football field, which still has its lights on. The stands are empty, the concession stand closed up. At the edge, Jasper turns again toward the practice field, and I realize where he's going.

"Cedar Mountain?" I ask.

"Look," he says, pointing toward the top of the massive hill. I can make out a small flickering orange light.

"Is that a bonfire all the way up there?"

"And I have it on good authority there'll be hot dogs. And marshmallows. And terrible, terrible music."

I remember what Jasper said about partying there with his brother, the bonfires they would have with friends. And I know that he is giving me a little piece of that. A piece of him that is wounded and scarred. When he parks the truck, I wrap my arms around his neck, breathing in the scent of him, cinnamon gum and the faded pipe tobacco smell that lingers in the truck.

"Thank you," I whisper.

"Don't thank me until you sit through one of Grayson's songs," he whispers into my hair, his arms wrapping around my waist and pulling me closer.

I tip my face up and kiss him.

When we hear Grayson's Jeep pulling up behind us, Jasper takes my hand and helps me out of the truck. In the back he's got extra lawn chairs and blankets, and he pulls them out as Linc clambers down the hill with Ramani. Linc's shoulder is out of the sling, and when Ramani stumbles in her pretty shoes, he reaches out lightning quick and keeps her from tumbling down the hill. He doesn't let go until they reach the bottom of the hill.

"Oh, you made it," Ramani says, running up and seizing me in a hug. "Thank goodness. I was worried I was going to have to listen to Linc rehashing the game by myself all night." She and Linc are both in their homecoming finery, and I realize that they all gave up going to the dance tonight for me.

Linc helps Jasper carry the chairs and blankets, and Grayson and Ember emerge from his Jeep. Ember's face is suspiciously pleased. Grayson's hair is a little messy, and he's got his guitar, and Ember's holding some of the afghans from the farmhouse.

We climb up the hill, everyone carrying something. At the top, the bonfire is dancing columns of gold and red, and there's already a cooler with a few sticks leaned up against it for roasting marshmallows and hot dogs.

Jasper arranges our chairs around the fire, with Ember and Grayson sitting to one side of us and Linc and Ramani on the other. Two empty seats are across from us, so I assume Adalyn and her girlfriend, Maya, will be making an appearance later. For Adalyn to ditch the events she's been planning for months is pretty impressive.

Ramani starts roasting marshmallows and feeding them to Linc, who's burning five hot dogs on one stick. Ramani wrinkles her nose at them. "How can you eat them like that?"

"They're best when they've been completely charred," Linc says. "It adds texture. Trust me."

Grayson helps him eat them, and I decline everything but a couple of marshmallows. Something about hot dogs burned on a stick does not appeal to me. I guess I haven't acclimated to Rocksaw quite that much yet. Jasper pulls out a bottle from the cooler to pass around. Everyone partakes a little except for Ember, who takes one sniff and wrinkles her nose, passing the bottle along while the guys laugh at her reaction.

After a few swigs of bourbon, the fire shimmers and the stars above us seem to flicker, too. Everyone is laughing and recounting old memories, stories they've told a million times that are part of a shared history going back as long as they've known each other.

Ramani tells a story about when Jesse skipped school to go to a rock concert and, ironically enough, got caught there by one of Rocksaw's Catholic priests. Grayson recounts the tale of how he won his guitar in a bet with a guy from Buffalo Hills who thought there was no way he could drink a gallon of milk in under a minute. Jasper tells about the time we were chased by a naked man at Mitzi's Love Shack. And I know that someday this bonfire will be a story that we all share, a chapter that's the same in every book.

Grayson gets out his guitar and sings "Your Touch," and everyone sings along except Ember, who watches him like he's the greatest guy to ever set foot on Earth. After that, he sings an old rock song, and I know it's for Jesse, and I hold Jasper's hand so that he knows he's not alone with his memories tonight.

A few hours later, Adalyn and Maya appear, and the bourbon

and marshmallows are passed around again, and Grayson repeats his repertoire of five songs.

A little past one in the morning, everyone is starting to fall asleep in piles of quilts and afghans, the fire burning down to a quiet glow.

"I suppose we ought to be heading home," I whisper to Jasper.

"Soon," he says, tugging me toward him by my hand. I crawl out from under my afghans and curl up in his lap as he adjusts his own blanket to fit me under it. I tuck my head in the crook between his chin and shoulder. "Let's just watch the stars a little longer," he says.

"Which is your favorite constellation?" I ask, looking up at the sky.

I know he's smiling, the kind that tugs on his scar, even though I don't look up. "That's easy," Jasper says. "The Big Dipper. You'll never lose your way if you can find it."

"That's what I've heard."

ACKNOWLEDGMENTS

I HAVE TO START BY giving so much gratitude to my agent, Kristin Nelson, of Nelson Literary Agency, who made all this possible. Thank you for believing in me and my stories, and for being such a great source for advice and expertise. Another huge thank-you goes to Angie Hodapp in Literary Development at NLA, whose feedback and direction helped shape Trix's story as it was just beginning.

Thank you to the HarperTeen family, especially my marvelously clever editor, Alice Jerman, who warmed my heart when she said she found comfort in this story. Alice carved out Trix's tale with an expert touch, and it was so exciting to find what was hiding in that manuscript. Thank you to Emilia Rhodes, who first saw the potential in *A Constellation of Roses*, and who laughed along with Auntie like I hoped she might. More gratitude goes to Clare Vaughn, who makes sure I'm always on track, and who loves Jasper as much as I do. Alexandra Rakaczki and Maya Myers did a lovely job polishing all my words and helping me untangle what shall henceforth be named "The Shane Timeline." Thank you, ladies! I must've gotten an extra helping of Lucky Lime to have gotten to share the making of this book with all of you.

To my husband, who is a limitless well of support, thank you. I can spend my time daydreaming new stories and not watching where I'm going because I know I'll never get lost with you by my side. To my gorgeous, brilliant, and fierce daughters, I love you always. Thank you for being my biggest fans and my best supporters.

Thank you to Rhonda and Alexis, who read early drafts and helped me find the good stuff. More gratitude goes to my ever-brilliant critique partner and friend, Katie. You are awesome, and thank you for spending so much of your time thinking about pie with me. This is where I make a white wine joke, and nobody gets it but you.

Thanks to the Electrics, my IG Skulls and Debut Ladies, and the wonderful crew of YA and MG writers I've met since I started this publishing journey. I love sharing it with all of you!

Finally, thank you to those who will read this story and find little bits of themselves in the McCabe women, in Allison and Connor, Shane and Charly, Jasper and Jesse, and the rest of the Rocksaw crew.

May your darkest chapters be short, and your story long.

READ ON FOR AN EXCERPT FROM

THREE UNUSUAL FRIENDS. ONE INESCAPABLE BOND.

the
deepest
roots

MIRANDA ASEBEDO

ONE

THE THING ABOUT TORNADOES IS that they're a game of odds. Every die cast has to fall against you at the perfect moment. And when you live in the small, rural town of Cottonwood Hollow, Kansas, you think, *What are the odds it'll hit here out of all the places in the county?*

Well, my odds have been shit lately.

"Why aren't you at the shelter, Mom?" I yell as I slam the front door shut behind me. She's got all the windows of our old single-wide trailer open, and they seem to suck in and amplify the tornado siren. The sky outside is a greenish gold, the color of an old bruise that is faded but still tender to the touch.

Mom should have left twenty minutes ago, when we were first put under the tornado warning, the radio blaring an advisory to take immediate shelter. Red let me off my shift at the auto shop early so I could beat the storm home, but when I passed

Cottonwood Hollow's community tornado shelter and didn't see Mom's car, I knew something was wrong.

Mom's face when she sees me is one of surprise, quickly over-shadowed by a tightening of her mouth, that face she makes when she's afraid. "What are you doing here?" she shouts back, her voice accusatory, as if I'm the one who's done something wrong. "You should have stayed in Evanston. I texted you to stay put. You would've been safe in the shop." She holds Steven's halter with one hand. Steven is a giant, beastly mix of generations of mutts who's begun to howl in concert with the tornado siren.

"My phone's out of minutes! I came back to meet you in the shelter," I shout back. "What the hell are you still doing here?"

"Garrett told me no pets allowed in the tornado shelter after Missy Underwood's dog bit one of the Pelter kids." Garrett Remington is the mayor of Cottonwood Hollow, and also our landlord. He may or may not have been one of Mom's previous boyfriends, too. He brags around town that he's descended from *the* Remingtons, and I think that's probably the only reason a creep like him got elected mayor.

"Tell Garrett to screw off." I bellow over the sirens and Steven's howls.

This is the most communication we've had in days. Mom has been conveniently away when I've been home, or sleeping, which is a sure sign that things are going to shit. Mom faces problems like an ostrich, head in the sand.

"I thought you would stay at the shop!" she yells again, look-ing frustrated, as if I've spoiled her plans. "It's too dangerous to go back out now!" The wind outside picks up, careening through the open windows and knocking over a lamp near the couch.

"This isn't the safest place to be, either!" I retort.

Mom avoids answering me, instead shouting back, "We have to close the windows!"

Tornadoes make you realize your priorities, too. So as Mom and I are running around closing windows, she's dragging Steven with one hand, as if he might run off and be lost forever in the storm. With her other hand, she gathers her beloved, yellowed, dog-eared paperbacks and stows them away in drawers and cupboards like that will save them if the tornado sucks us up. I'm thinking of Lux and Mercy, and wondering if they're okay. I'm hoping neither of them does anything stupid when I don't show up in the tornado shelter, like coming to look for me and getting stuck in this deathtrap with me and Mom. And I'm still hoping that wherever this tornado touches down, it won't be here.

The screams of the siren subside, as if to make sure that we hear the first ball of hail like a bullet cracking against the shingles. A few vengeful shots follow, and then what sounds like all-out war.

I run to the window to look at my car, a 1972 Mach 1 Mustang parked in the front yard. I'd rescued it out of a barn and meticulously restored it. If we had a garage, or even a carport, it might survive this. All I can think about as I watch the chunks of ice pounding down is the force with which they collide into metal that I've spent years of my life Fixing. I feel the ache in my muscles, in my bones, of every hour spent under the hood of that car. Every dent, every chip from the crash of hail might as well be on my own body. That car and I are one and the same. Years of work, years of struggle. Damn the odds. Damn this day.

My attention is torn from the Mach because behind it, nearly a mile to the north near the old Remington homestead just outside of town, I see the dark funnel stretch toward the pasture like a hesitant finger. When it touches down, a shadowy cloud of debris builds around it. Maybe for once luck will be on our side and it'll suck up the curse along with the old Remington place.

A massive gust of wind hits the trailer like a slap, and it reels in response, rocking back against the tie-downs holding it in place. A punch of fear-soaked adrenaline bursts and spreads through my middle. Mom's breath catches, and she steadies us both with a hand on my shoulder.

"We should probably move away from the windows," I say, as the trailer rocks again.

I follow Mom into the hallway, the only part of the house without windows or furniture, a place we might survive if the tie-downs don't hold and the trailer rolls. Steven sits beside us, wagging his tail like we're all just hanging out together on a typical Sunday.

"What's going on?" I ask quietly, staring at the faded wallpaper, hands clenched around my knees. If we're going to die here, I want to know why.

Maybe it's because she thinks this might be the end, but for once Mom doesn't sidestep. "I didn't want to run into Garrett at the tornado shelter. We're late on the rent." She can't even look me in the eye when she says it. "This storm might buy us a couple more days if he's out checking damages on his other properties."

"I gave you my half!" I grind out.

"I didn't have mine." Her voice is barely a whisper over the roar of the wind and rain.

Mom shuts down again, her eyes closed, as if she's waiting for the end. She tries to hold my hand as the trailer rocks, the windows shaking.

But I pull away. "We'd better not die in this trailer."

Twenty minutes later, the storm has passed and there's a fist pounding on our front door.

"Jesus," Mom swears, opening her eyes. "If that's Garrett, don't answer it."

"Jesus isn't going to save us from Garrett." I pull myself up from where we've been hunched in silence, hoping the trailer didn't get thrown across Cottonwood Hollow.

The cheap, faux-gold doorknob turns as I approach it, and Lux pushes in, and then despite the tornado missing us, I know my odds are really going to shit today. When things are bad, I try to keep Lux and Mercy from stopping by. There's nothing worse than the way Lux's green eyes watch my mom laugh too loudly, or make too many jokes to cover up the fact that we're huddling around space heaters because we don't have the cash to fill the propane tank. And Mercy, well, she'll start to poke around in the kitchen, quietly note the empty cupboards, and then the dinner invitations will start.

"What the hell?" Lux says, brandishing her phone above the large, voluminous mass of strawberry-blond hair balled into a messy bun on the top of her head. Strands have fallen loose to

5

frame her heart-shaped face and dimpled chin. "You don't know how to use one of these anymore?" She shoves her phone nearly into my face.

Mercy follows Lux inside, squeezing me in a fierce hug that constricts painfully around my waist as she smashes her cheek against my chest. "Rome!" When she says my name, it's half reprimand, half exultation. "Why in the world did you stay in this *trai*—" She stops, casting an uncomfortable look at Lux and continuing her tirade of concern. "*House* when you know it's not safe? And why didn't you answer your phone?"

"I need to put more minutes on my phone," I mutter, irritated that she can't say *trailer* without thinking she'll offend me. And because somehow it does, a little. I give her a quick squeeze and then step away.

"Lame," Lux remarks with a roll of her eyes. "Next time let someone know what's up."

Mom got up from the floor of the hall while Lux and Mercy were talking, and now she sits down on the couch, pulling one of her books up from between the cushions like nothing is wrong.

"Did you see how close it got?" Mercy asks. She senses something is wrong, I can tell by the way she's inching toward the kitchen, trying to get a look around. "Dad stayed out on the front porch and watched while we were in the basement. He said it touched down about a mile north, not far from the Remington place."

I nod, heading off Mercy and pretending I'm really just putting the fallen lamp back on the end table rather than herding her. "Yeah, I watched it. Then we went to the hall." I gesture nonchalantly toward where we'd just been cowering, trying to divert Mercy's attention from the kitchen and its empty cupboards. "Really makes you evaluate your life goals, though, right? Of all the places to die, I don't want it to be in a trailer." I laugh too loudly.

Lux raises one eyebrow, like my forced humor isn't fooling her. Mercy purses her lips, like it's all she can do not to start lecturing me again about how dangerous it was for us to stay here.

"I've got to go check on the Mach," I announce suddenly, pushing past them both and putting my hand on the knob of the front door. It's better if I get Mercy and Lux out of here.

I look back over my shoulder at Mom, who's reading with Steven's head in her lap like nothing happened.

"See you later," Mom says, giving me a lazy wave. As if she's carefree, as if we aren't behind on the rent, as if we didn't just wonder if we were going to die together in this tin can.

"Lock the door," I tell her. "Don't answer it." Garrett is just dick enough to throw us out for being late. Holding that kind of power over his poor female tenants is something he savors.

As I open the door, Steven's ears prick up and he leaps off the couch, squeezing between me and the door and bounding down the rickety front steps.

"Steven!" I yell. "Stay!" Steven's not really one for commands, though, and he continues to trot out to the yard, sniffing at downed branches and licking stray bits of hail.

Outside, Mercy's little sister, Neveah, is stacking larger chunks of hail near the dirt road, making an impossible army of tiny snowmen at the beginning of May. Neveah is eight, and a miniature copy of Mercy. Thick black hair, tan skin, dark-brown eyes, and arched, expressive brows. She must have begged Mercy to tag along when they came out to check on me. Steven sticks his snout against the nape of Neveah's neck where she crouches with her snowman army, and she laughs and waves him off.

I make a beeline for the Mach, relieved when I see that there are far fewer dents and dings in the heavy metal of the car than I thought there would be.

"I guess we should be getting home," Mercy says. "It's almost eight. We just wanted to make sure you were okay."

Lux is still looking back at the trailer, probably wondering why I told Mom to lock the door and not answer it.

Fluffernut, the Ruizes' cat from a couple trailers down the road, slinks out from underneath the Mach, where she must have been riding out the storm. She yowls pitifully.

"Oh, little kitty, you poor thing!" Neveah croons, coming to pet her.

At the sound of Neveah's voice, Steven halts his investigation of a stray branch and heads back in her direction. He spots Fluffernut and lets out a sound that is half snort, half gleeful bark. Fluffernut puffs up and hisses, arching her back, but Steven doesn't recognize anything but a new friend and charges toward her anyway. Fluffernut shoots out of the yard and into the dirt road with Steven in pursuit, barking joyfully.

"Steven!" I call. "No! Stay!" But once again, Steven has his own plans.

"I'll get him!" Neveah shouts, and she races after him. The sight of Neveah chasing him spurs Steven on, and he abandons his hunt for Fluffernut and charges off toward the open pastures of

Remington land in the direction of where the tornado just touched down.

"Neveah, wait!" Mercy calls. She looks helplessly at me, and I shrug.

"She'll be fine," Lux says. "There's nothing out there but dirt and grass."

"There's snakes," Mercy retorts. "And who knows what the tornado sucked up and spit out over there."

Lux's full mouth twists in amusement, and her green eyes meet mine. "We'll go get her. Come on."

There's no sidewalks out here on the edge of Cottonwood Hollow, so we walk along the edge of the dirt road, kicking chunks of hail along the way. Cottonwoods line the road, their leaves quaking and sighing as if they're relieved that they survived the storm.

Before we reach the farthest edge of town, Rick Ruiz stops me outside of his double-wide. It's the nicest one out here, with real siding and little green shutters on the windows. He's fixing some of the white plastic skirting around the bottom, standing it back up where it's been blown in by the storm. I'd given up years ago trying to keep the cheap skirting on our old trailer nice and put up plywood around the bottom instead to keep out the possums and the stray cats. It's not pretty, but it's functional.

Rick is still in his sheriff's deputy uniform, which means he must have rushed home to make sure Marisol and Letty were okay. When he and Marisol moved here seven years ago, they'd known that the girls of Cottonwood Hollow were different, but two years later when they had their daughter, Letty, it was up to Mom and me to explain to them exactly why their daughter could name all the American presidents in order after reading a book from the library at the age of three. Letty was a Wit.

"Rome?" he asks me. "Everything okay? Marisol said she didn't see you or your mom and Steven at the tornado shelter. She and Letty were worried."

"Need a hand?" I ask, changing the subject as I gesture at the electrical box that's hanging off the side of their house by one bent screw. A cottonwood branch fell on the power line during the storm, and the force nearly yanked the box clean off. Wires tangle behind it, some exposed and partially severed, wet and glistening.

"Would you mind?" Relief softens his features.

"Of course not," I reply, wiping my hands on my jeans.

Rick hurries over to the small shed near his back deck to get his toolbox.

"We'll wait," Lux says, stopping and crossing her arms. Thanks to Rick, she's thinking again about why I wasn't in the tornado shelter, and I know she's waiting to see if I give anything up. But Mercy, eyebrows bunched, looks concerned about letting Neveah get too far away. I can see the top of Neveah's head out in the pasture, and fleeting glimpses of Steven loping through the tall grass.

"Go on," I tell Mercy with a jerk of my chin. One ruddy curl falls loose from my ponytail and bounces against my cheek. "We'll catch up."

Mercy nods gratefully and chases after her sister. From a distance, she's so tiny she looks much younger than seventeen. The

10

dark clouds have moved out, and the setting sun casts a lambent glow over the pasture where they're headed.

Rick brings me his toolbox. He's only a little taller than me and built as wide as a door, all of it muscle. My talent for Fixing has come in handy for both of us over the years since our mutual landlord isn't known for his prompt responses to things like maintenance requests.

Lux is careful not to smile at Rick, using what Mercy and I call her Stone Face. Rick knows what will happen if a Siren smiles at him, though, and doesn't take it personally. He gives her a hesitant wave.

I run my hands along the wires that go into the house behind the box, smoothing the thin metal hairs together with my fingers, twisting them back into firm, capable strands. I barely feel a rush of electricity beneath the pads of my fingertips. It licks with a swift, teasing tongue. Then I push the box back up to the house and take the power drill from Rick. He's already found the screws I need and holds them in his wide palm, waiting to hand them to me when I'm ready. Holding the box against the house with my forearm, I use the drill to reattach the box to the house.

I don't need a test to know when something is Fixed, but I tell Rick, "Give the lights inside a try."

Before he can run back around the double-wide to the front door to yell at Marisol to hit the lights, she comes out on their front stoop. "The power's back!" she shouts with a relieved wave. "Thank you, Rome!"

"How much do I owe you?" Rick asks.

I am surprised, because so few people offer money. The

currency in Cottonwood Hollow is usually food or favors between neighbors and friends.

"Nothing," I tell Rick, though we are behind on the rent. "Just being neighborly."

Marisol is undeterred, and she calls from the front door, "I've got the fixings for a casserole, so Letty and I will bring one by later."

"I'll do you one better," Rick promises. "The next time I catch you racing the Mach, I'll be sure to look the other way."

"What more could a girl ask for, Deputy Ruiz?" I ask with a grin as we leave. "See you later."

"I don't think you needed to Stone Face Rick," I tell Lux as I wipe my dirty hands on my jeans.

This immediately nettles her, and she tightens her arms across her chest. "Better safe than sorry," she huffs. "You should've heard what the man at the gas station promised me this morning."

"I hope it was free gas. The Mach needs a fill-up."

"It was pumping he offered," Lux says, "but not that kind."

"Gross," I reply, sticking out my tongue. "That dude is a meth head."

"Yeah. Well, my pretty face doesn't care. I was laughing at that text message you sent before your phone ran out. And he was just *there* in the crossfire." She frowns, her full mouth tightening. "I've gotten good at controlling it. I hate it when it happens out of the blue like that."

Lux is what we call a Siren, and flirting from her—devastating smiles, sparkling laughter, or what Mercy calls her "sexy voice"—leads men to profess their undying love. Or at least to do whatever she wants. When we were younger, we thought it was funny, letting Lux charm our math teacher into believing we'd turned in our algebra homework and that he'd just misplaced it. It was less funny when the forty-year-old teacher declared he was in love with her.

The irony is that Lux doesn't even like boys. She told Mercy and me last summer, as if we hadn't known for years already. The three of us have always been friends. Lux's and Mercy's faces are as familiar to me as my own, every expression a story written in a language that only we three can understand.

The more generous locals say the daughters of Cottonwood Hollow have unique talents. Fixers, Finders, Sirens, Enoughs, Strong Backs, Wits, Sights, Readers, and Healers. Some are talents that I've heard of but never seen. Ten years ago, when I was only seven, the townspeople thought maybe it had something to do with the water, and they had bake sales and softball tournaments and hot-dog-eating contests to raise the money to get it tested. But nothing in the water was out of the ordinary. Only the girls were.